BN TOLER

DESPERATELY SEEKING EPIC

DEDICATION

To my most epic adventures.
Jackson, Gracey, and Brey.
I love you.

CHAPTER ONE
Clara

reply   Posted: 4 days ago

◄ prev   ▲   next ►

⭐ **Desperately Seeking Epic**

You're my father.

I don't know much about you. I know your name is Paul James, you're a thrill seeker, and once upon a time you did stunts and people called you 'Epic.'

I've been told you don't know about me. That it's complicated.

But for me it's simple.

Here's the thing: I'm twelve years old . . . and I'm dying.

And as much as this could crush my mother, I have to meet you before I go.

In time, I'm sure she'll understand. She's still in love with you.

So, Epic, if you read this, please come back. You don't have to be my dad. You don't even have to tell me you love me or you're sorry. Just come see me.

Patiently waiting, but running out of time,

Neena

THE COFFEE MUG in my hand crashes to the ground, cracking in half, the brown liquid splashing my bare legs.

"She didn't," I gasp.

Ignoring the sting from the coffee droplets dripping down my legs, I hustle to the counter where the small television is and turn up the volume. My favorite morning show, This World, This Morning, is on. The blonde news anchor, Veronica Marsh, sits across from her co-anchor, Brett Adams, a large screen behind them depicting a Craigslist ad titled: Desperately Seeking Epic.

"This," Veronica swivels in her chair and motions to the screen, "just breaks my heart, Brett."

"Mine, too," Brett agrees. "This Craigslist ad was posted four days ago and has spread among social media like wildfire. This World, This Morning is working diligently to locate the author of this ad because we'd love nothing more than to help her find her father."

"That's right," Veronica chimes in. "So if any of you know this young girl or a Paul James that goes by the name 'Epic,' go to our website and email us. And, Neena . . ." Cringing, I listen as Veronica says my daughter's name, her tone full of intent, "If you're watching this, we'd love to have you on the show."

Hitting the power button, I spin around with the intention of bolting up to Neena's bedroom and giving her the verbal thrashing of her life, but I slip on the coffee I spilled two minutes prior, landing hard on my ass.

With a groan, I move slowly to my knees, attempting to pull myself up, but can't seem to complete the task. *I don't do happily ever after* echoes somewhere deep inside of me. Even the memory of those words is like a hard punch to the gut. From out of nowhere, a sob bubbles up and bursts free from my chest. How could she do this? And why wouldn't she have asked me first? My body shakes as I continue to cry, the images of Paul flickering through my mind like a TV channel with poor reception; quick, and not nearly long enough to really understand. Which is Paul down to a T. You only ever get a taste, and it's never enough.

I nearly jump out of my skin when someone lightly touches my shoulder. When I jerk my gaze up, Neena's red and swollen eyes meet mine as she flops to her knees on the floor near me.

"Don't," I sniffle. "The floor is sticky and you'll get your pajama pants wet. Please look out for pieces of my mug. I broke it." And I point to where the mug lay in front of us.

She ignores me and sidles closer. "I'm so sorry, Mama," she whimpers after a moment. I forget about the coffee and pull her in, hugging her tightly. I'm mad—mad as hell. But I can't watch her unravel, not now, not when there's so little time left. "I didn't know they'd put it on a television show."

"I know that, honey. But now it's out there. They'll find him."

Pulling away, she wipes at her nose with her forearm. "But that's a good thing."

I exhale slowly as I stand, then bend down and help her to her feet. I have no way to explain how *not* good it is if they find him. She's a hopeful child with this romanticized idea her biological father will meet her and fall in love. That's extremely unlikely, and the last thing she needs is to have her father reject her on national television.

I don't do babies and white picket fences.

I've only ever wanted to protect her. But maybe I can't protect her anymore. She's bright and loving, and extremely curious. And when it comes to Paul, it's better to keep most things in the dark.

"I know he may not want to meet me," she admits. "I know he may not love me."

I crush her to my chest for another hug. "It's impossible not to love you, sweetie."

We shuffle to stand in the kitchen and hug. "We'll try to find him. But please don't get your hopes up." I can't tell her I've already tried, repeatedly, to reach him. I can't tell her I've taken drastic measures in a last ditch effort to bring him back. It would only create false hope and break her heart if he doesn't show.

"I won't. Thank you, Mama."

CHAPTER TWO
3 Months Ago
Clara

I NEVER DRINK.

There have been less than a handful of times when life has handed me a bad day and I turned to a bottle to drown it away. Today is one of *those* days.

My office light flicks on and I wince, squinting my eyes as I spin around in my leather office chair, the amber liquid in my paper cup slushing about, landing on the test results on my desk.

"What are you doing?" Marcus asks as he stares at me from the doorway. He strides cautiously toward my desk, his expression one of uncertainty.

I chuckle as I gaze giddily at the paper cup. "I'm drinking."

I'm not looking up at him, but I can feel him deflate. All the hope he carries inside of him melts from his body, evaporating. "Fuck," he hisses, and punches the visitor's chair to his right. My glance flicks to him as he shakes his hand out, sitting in the very chair he just assaulted. He points at the bottle of Hennessy on my desk. "Pour me one."

I use the desk as leverage to push myself out of my chair and stumble over to the watercooler and grab another cup, swaying on my way back. Plopping back in my seat, I pour his drink and slide it across the desk. I raise my cup with an unceremonious grip and grumble, "Here's to life shitting all over everything."

Marcus reaches for the cup and clenches his eyes closed before nodding once and choking down his drink. When he's done, he crushes the cup in his small hand and tosses it in the wastebin. "How long do we have?"

The question reaches out to me, wrapping its cold and unforgiving fingers around my throat, choking me with emotion. I have to swallow hard more than once and blink a few times to keep myself from crying. "Six months. A year if we're lucky."

"How'd she take it?"

"Like she always does." Tentatively, I sip my lukewarm drink, then add, "Like a trooper."

He nods a few times, just as I have for the past hour, and I can tell he's trying to keep it together, too. "We need to get Paul to come back. Maybe he's a match. I know it's a long shot, but maybe—"

"You think I haven't tried to reach him by now?" I suddenly snap. "I've emailed, called . . . nothing. He won't respond. I even had Richard try, figuring he wasn't responding because it was me." My heart squeezes a little.

"Then there's only one other way to get Paul's attention, forcing him to return."

"Oh yeah," I snicker disdainfully. "What's that?"

"Money."

My facial features, once weighted with despair, perk up. The idea is brilliant, and I'm pissed at myself for not thinking of it sooner. "Can he sue me for that?"

"Do you really care? Any judge with half a heart would side with you anyway."

That's true. Looking at my watch, I note it's ten until five. Richard always answers his phone before five. Standing, I step around the desk unsteadily, the effects of my evening alcohol consumption catching up with me, and drop to my knees in front of Marcus so that we're at eye level.

"Oh, shit. Don't hug me," he grumbles.

Yanking him to me, I whisper, "Oh, shut it, and bring it in." I squeeze him tight, lifting him from the ground. Marcus is barely three feet tall, suffering from achondroplasia, a form of dwarfism that affects bone growth. What he lacks in height he certainly makes up for in personality. I've never met a more colorful person in all my life.

Leaning back and sitting on my heels, I wipe fresh tears from my face. "Do you think it will work? Do you think he'll come back?"

"Of course, he will," Marcus insists, grabbing a tissue from the box on my desk and handing it to me. "He needs money to fund his traveling."

"Don't tell Neena, okay? I couldn't bear for her to know he was here and didn't want to meet her. It would crush her."

"I know he doesn't have the best track record, Clara, but he's not all bad." I nod once, not because I agree; quite the contrary. I strongly disagree. Paul James is one of the most selfish men I have ever known. But Marcus and I, although we agree on many things, always seem to butt heads on this one subject. "Once upon a time you thought I was an asshole. Look at us now."

"I still think you're an asshole," I jest. "Just a loveable one." He snorts and I chuckle through my tears.

"If we can get him home, he'll help," he reiterates.

"I hope you're right," I admonish as I stand and brush my skirt off. "But please, not a word to Neena," I reiterate.

"Not a word," he promises. "I don't want you to get your hopes up though, Clara. He may not be a match."

I pull in a deep breath, swallowing around the lump in my throat. I know he's right. There's a very strong possibility Paul will not be a match for Neena and all of this would be in vain. But we have to try. We have to. A horn sounds off from outside.

"That's my cab. I'm heading home. I'll call Richard on the way."

"Kiss Neena for me." He waves. "I'll close up."

CHAPTER THREE

Paul

Account Balance: $1,425.00

I NARROW MY eyes, not sure I'm reading it right. Yep. Definitely reading it right. *What the fuck?* There should be thousands more in this account. Clicking on the *Deposits* tab, I see the last direct deposit was a little over three months ago. The quarterly deposit should have been made one week ago.

"Motherfucker," I growl. It's going to cost me a fortune, but I have no choice. I pull out my cell and dial my attorney, Richard Mateo.

It rings once and he picks up. "Paul," he states my name plainly.

"Richard," I drone. "Been expecting my call?" I've never been one for respectful greetings, especially over the phone, and I'm not starting now.

"As a matter of fact, I have," he admits.

"I just logged on to my bank account and found the quarterly deposit hasn't been made."

"Well, Paul, I've called you several times, but it always goes straight to voice mail. And your voice mail is full. I've also sent you emails." I clench my phone tighter. I never check my email, and I loathe voice mails.

"Where is my money?" I snap, my temper flaring. A tiny young woman glances at me, my tone having drawn her attention, but she quickly looks away when I give her a look that says, '*mind your own fucking business.*'

"The agreement calls for an annual meeting once a year. Ms. Bateman is withholding funds until the meeting is held."

"What?" I laugh because it's the most ridiculous thing I've ever heard of. "Why in the hell is that in the contract?"

"Because I wasn't aware it would be an issue. You gave me power of attorney and I made the decisions I thought would benefit you best."

"How is an annual meeting going to benefit me?"

"Because you should want to know how your business is doing," he answers making me feel like an idiot. I *should* be checking on the business. It is half mine. But checking on the business would mean seeing *her*. "She wants you to come home, Paul. She wants a meeting."

"We've never even had an annual meeting," I argue, clenching my fist.

"It's in your contract."

"It's been over twelve years since that contract was signed, Richard, and we've not had one annual meeting," I point out again. "Can she legally withhold my money?"

"Well . . . maybe not legally. But you can't fight her on it without coming home and taking her to court. Just have the meeting. She'll pay you. Then you can go back to gallivanting around the world."

I don't even bother to respond. Hitting *End* on the call, I power it down and jam it back in my pocket. This sounds just like Clara. Always playing her hand and seeking the power in our agreement. The bulldozer. If she can't get what she wants, she'll run you over. I can't imagine why in the hell she wants me to come home now after all these years. I thought for sure the first year I was gone she'd reach out to me, ask me to return, but I got nothing. Her life rolled on as if I never even existed in it.

Logging on to *Hotwire* to find the cheapest airfare I can, I curse the situation.

Home.

I have to go home.

Her.

I have to face her.

The two things I've been running from. If she thinks our reunion will be pleasant and professional, she's got another thing coming. I'm going to make sure she never asks for another fucking annual meeting ever again.

CHAPTER FOUR
Clara

"TURN IT OFF, Neena," I warn as I sift through a stack of papers on my desk.

"It's not on," she lies. Lifting my gaze, I find the lens of her camcorder five inches from my face.

"So you're just holding it in my face for no reason?"

"Uh-huh."

"Go film Marcus," I groan.

"He's prepping."

"Damn," I mumble. "What's today?"

Neena grins so wide I don't even have to look at her to see it; I can feel it. "The fifteenth."

Shoving the papers back in a folder and tossing it aside, I take Neena's face in my hands and press my lips to her forehead. Exhaling a sigh of relief through my nose because she has no fever, I murmur, "You look tired, baby."

"I am tired," she admits.

"Lie down for a bit . . . please. After the guys go for the first jump, I'll wake you and we'll go get some lunch."

"Fine," she huffs weakly, scratching her scalp, her purple scarf that covers her bald head moving back and forth as she does. She doesn't want to lie down, but this is our daily routine now, and she knows I'll nag if she doesn't. The corner of my office is decked out with a single bed covered in a plush, neon comforter and pillows. The walls surrounding it are covered with posters of Neena's favorite band; *Masters of the V*. Unfortunately, my job doesn't allow me the luxury of taking off to care for my ailing daughter. I have to work—something I feel horrendously guilty about. But Neena insists she'd rather be here at the office with me and Marcus and the guys than sitting at home in her room. Her diagnosis is dismal but I've promised myself two things. One: never give up. I will fight to save her until the bitter end. Two: try to make every single day as happy as I possibly can for her, just in case . . . in case we lose. After she lies down and turns on her iPad so she can watch a movie on Netflix, I kiss her once more, grab my travel coffee mug, and turn the office light off, quietly shutting the door. Passing by the storage room where we keep the jumpsuits, I see Marcus buttoning up his custom-made suit. I give him a pointed look and he shrugs, giving me a pointed look back. "Three times per month. That was the deal."

"You're going to get us sued one day, ya know?"

"Nah," he laughs. "It's all in good fun."

"Let me at least get their credit cards before you come out."

He lifts his sparkly blue eyes to meet my gaze, his stare filled with mirth, and winks. He lives for these three days a month when I allow him to be a prankster. The corner of his mouth lifts in a slight smirk. "Of course."

Heading out front, I flip the OPEN sign and unlock the front door. Sipping my coffee, I check to make sure the waiver forms are on the clipboards and plenty of pens are in the cup in the center of the table. The doorbell jingles and Larry and Bowman walk in, both laughing.

"Morning, boss," Larry calls.

"Morning, Clara," Bowman follows.

"Morning, guys. Heads-up, Marcus is in the back prepping, so you better make yourselves scarce or he'll get pissed."

"Oh, shit," Bowman chuckles. "It's the fifteenth."

Bowman and Larry are former military, both paratroopers during their time in service. They're my most reliable and highly trained jumpers. They're not cheap either, but aside from their experience they're both extremely attractive and my female clientele flock to them like flies on shit. Larry is your classic *Tom Cruise*, with dark hair and eyes, and Bowman is a blue-eyed stud with a knee weakening smile. Since word of mouth is my best advertisement, I pay their hefty commission and they flirt their asses off with anything with breasts.

"How many today?" Larry asks as they pass by me.

"Twenty-five."

"Yes," Bowman coos. "Perfect day for jumping, too."

Ten minutes later, our first two jumpers come in; a big guy and a tiny brunette. It's always a mystery on who Marcus will pick in these situations. I never know because there's really no rhyme or reason to his choosing.

"Bradley?" I question.

"That's me," the big guy responds.

I run through the formal greeting with them and hand them all their waivers to fill out and sign, basically stating they can't sue us if they get hurt, and their families can't sue us if anything happens to them. After I offer them coffee, Bradley hands me his credit card to pay for their jumps. As I turn to leave them to their paperwork while I run his card, the door jingles, causing me to turn back.

My heart drops to the floor and I suck in a deep breath as memories from what seem like a lifetime ago crash over me.

I don't do happily ever after.

He's here.

Paul has come home.

CHAPTER FIVE

13 Years Earlier

Clara

"I DON'T UNDERSTAND," I repeated for the thousandth time. "He's leaving me his business?"

Mr. Mateo leaned back as he removed his glasses and tossed them on the desk. "Half his business. The other half he's leaving to his nephew. Paul, Mr. Falco's nephew," he explained, "is interested in buying out your half."

"It's a skydiving business?" I questioned. He'd already told me this, repeatedly, but for some reason I couldn't quite wrap my head around it. The fact I was even sitting in this office was mind-boggling, let alone apparently inheriting a skydiving business. The anxiety was enough to choke me. My hands were knotted in my lap, my knuckles white from squeezing so hard.

"That's correct, Ms. Bateman. A prominent one in the area, at that. Mr. Falco was a great business man."

"How wonderful for him," I sneered, clenching my hands tighter. I hated myself for even being there. Did Dennis Falco really believe by leaving me half of his business he would somehow be absolved from the horrible thing he did? Did he think I would just forgive him?

Mr. Mateo sat up, his fancy leather desk chair squeaking as he shifted his weight, and opened the folder in front of him. After slipping his glasses back on, he grabbed an envelope and slid it across the desk to me. "He asked that you get this letter."

A letter? What could this man have to say to me? I'm sorry for what

I did? I'm sorry I ruined your life? I stared at the legal-sized envelope, debating whether or not I should leave it. Wouldn't that be the ultimate middle finger to Dennis Falco? Then Mr. Mateo grabbed what looked like a brochure and placed it beside the envelope. Hesitantly, I picked up the brochure and read over it.

Where ordinary becomes extraordinary!

The brochure was covered with pictures of what appeared to be clients on their jumps, with pictures taken while in the air. Opening it, in the center was a photo of a tan-complexioned man, Italian maybe, with big brown eyes and the most beautiful smile I'd ever seen. He looked like he had a thousand teeth all perfectly placed. He'd definitely had braces at some point in his life—teeth were a specialty of mine. And he had the cutest dimples—as if he wasn't already gorgeous enough.

Above his picture in bold lettering was: MEET EPIC, STUNTMAN EXTRODINAIRE.

"That's Paul James. He's your partner," Mr. Mateo volunteered.

"They call him 'Epic'?"

"He was a movie stuntman until he got injured. That was a few years ago. He's a bit of a draw for the business."

Moving my gaze back to the envelope, I continued debating whether

I should take it or not. "Does his nephew know about this? About him leaving *me* half?"

"He knows half of the business was left to someone, but not who."

"This is . . . surreal," I managed.

Mr. Mateo gave a sad smile. "The business is very hands-on. Mr. Falco jumped almost every day until he got too bad off to. His nephew, Paul, also jumps every day. While the business is successful and profitable, your half would only sell for forty or fifty thousand judging by the numbers I've been provided."

"How long do I have?"

"Thirty days. In thirty days if you have not taken possession it will be sold to Paul and you'll be paid the value of your half. I hate to cut this meeting short, but I have an appointment across town, but here's my card." He slid the tiny card beside the envelope and stood. "If you have any questions, please feel free to contact me."

Numbness blanketed me as I grabbed the envelope and card and slipped them in my purse. The man who killed my parents, robbed me of a beautiful childhood with my mother and father, left me half of his skydiving business. This is the kind of shit you just can't make up.

After I left Mr. Mateo's office I headed back to my hotel room, feeling completely deflated. I'd only arrived in Virginia the day before and I already hated it. It was eighty-five degrees when I landed and that day it was forty-two. My allergies were going nuts, and it felt like someone had dropkicked me in the face.

After shedding my dress pants and heels, I slid on my favorite sweats and lay on my bed. I looked at my cell and sighed. No new messages. Kurt must've had another hectic day, but I dialed him up anyway, knowing he'd probably be interested to hear what the lawyer had to tell me.

"Babe," Kurt answered.

"Hi," I squeaked, surprised he answered on the first ring.

"How'd it go today?"

"Well," I sighed. "Apparently I'm the proud half owner of a skydiving business."

Silence.

"Kurt? You there?"

"Skydiving?" he questioned.

I rolled to my side and let out a longer sigh. I seemed to be doing a lot of that lately. "Yes. He left me half of a skydiving business."

"Why?"

"I don't know," I admitted, letting my gaze flick to my purse. "I'm guessing it's his way of saying he's sorry." I paused as I glanced again at my purse, where the letter Mr. Mateo gave me remained. "He left me a letter."

"What does it say?"

"I haven't opened it yet. I'm not sure I want to."

"Babe," Kurt said his pet name for me, his underlined pity prevalent in his tone. "Are you okay?"

Licking my lips, I inhaled deeply and nodded yes a few times before answering. I know he couldn't see me, but I guess I was confirming it with myself first. *I am okay. I will be okay.*

"Yeah. It's just . . . hard, I guess."

"I'm sorry I couldn't be there. Things have been so hectic at work."

"I know," I assured him, even though I really wished he would've come with me. "I'm okay. I have to decide what to do within thirty days or they'll automatically sell my half and give me the money."

I finished telling Kurt what the attorney said. I also told him about this so-called man they called Epic, too. "What are you going to do?" he asked.

"Is it wrong I'd like to sell it and burn the money?"

He chuckled, the sound deep and comforting, warming my heart. "I think we could come up with a better use for that money. Even if you only donate it to charity or something."

I bit my lip, wondering if I should say what I'd really like to do with the money. The last time I brought it up Kurt seemed panicked at the thought. "We could use it to have a baby."

"Clara," he groaned. "We've discussed this a million times." I rolled my eyes with his words.

"It was just an idea," I piped back, my annoyance clearly obvious.

"Clara . . . I just can't go through that again right now. Now's just not the time."

"We only tried for a year. The doctor said seeing a fertility specialist would help."

"I can't go back to the robot sex. You were so single-minded and it literally became mandatory sex only when you were ovulating. There was no . . . passion. I can't take you living in depression every time your period comes. I'm sorry. I know I sound like a dick, but with the way things have been between us, I just think . . . maybe we need to wait. Or . . . maybe we're not meant to have a baby."

In that moment, my eyes burned with tears. My body failed me. It couldn't do the one thing that women are meant to do. And when it couldn't, I went nuts trying to make it happen, and nearly lost my marriage in the process. Sex wasn't about intimacy or being close—it was to get pregnant. I took my temperature every morning. I made him promise not to masturbate around my ovulation cycle. And I'd forced him to wear regular boxers instead of boxer briefs. Even the acupuncture was a fail. Finally, after a year with no success, when my doctor said we should see a specialist, Kurt lost it. In my obsession I had forgotten him—how to love him and make him feel wanted.

"I thought we were doing better," I added after a beat. When he came to me and told me he was miserable, that he loved me but couldn't take the stress of it anymore, I'd backed down. I begrudgingly put trying to have a baby aside to save my marriage. We went to counseling and we worked hard to rekindle our sex life together. I thought with time and a better mind-set—a healthier mind-set—maybe we could try again after some time. But he just wouldn't come to the table.

"We are," he concurred, "but I think we need more time."

"How much more time?" I asked.

"Clara," he said my name sternly. Like if I were a child. "I'm done talking about this. It's your money, do what you want with it, but don't spend it planning on a baby anytime soon because that's not *my* plan."

I frowned, my heart sinking deeper in my chest. "Fine," I mumbled. "I have to go."

"Don't hang up while angry with me."

"I'm not angry," I lied. "Just tired. I'll call you tomorrow."

"How long did Dr. Shelton give you off?"

"He said I could have off until Monday if I wanted."

"Are you at least going to go and check out the place before you tell them you'll sell your half?"

"I don't know. I guess I should. I'll fill you in tomorrow." I knew I was being short with him, but I couldn't help it.

"I love you," he murmured.

"Love you, too."

After hitting *End* on the call, I tossed my cell phone away from me to the end of the bed as if by doing so I in some way was hurting Kurt. Sitting up, I pulled my purse toward me and dug inside. I pulled the envelope and brochure out and placed the envelope on my nightstand. I wasn't ready to read it yet. Opening the brochure, I read over it once more, finding two typos. Apparently jumping out of airplanes doesn't require good grammar. How could they give these things out like this? It looked completely unprofessional. I tapped a finger on my leg as I stared at my cell. I couldn't deny I was curious. The reason for which I'd been left this business wasn't great, but it's not every day a girl inherits half a skydiving business. Maybe I should go and check it out. What could it hurt? I could overcome my fear of heights and jump. Probably. Maybe. I hoped. Closing the brochure, I found the number on the back and dialed it.

It rang four times and I pursed my lips. How in the hell did this place run? On the fifth ring a deep voice answered, "Sky High."

Furrowing my brows, I said, "Um . . . hello. I'd like to schedule a jump."

"When?" he asked simply. Judging by his deep and haughty voice, I imagined some giant of a man on the other end of the line. Then I wondered . . . *could this be Paul James?*

"Is there anything available tomorrow?"

"Yep. Nine a.m. I need your credit card info to charge the deposit. If you don't show, we keep the deposit."

After fumbling through my purse, I found my wallet and gave him my name and credit card number.

"Wear pants and comfortable shoes; tennis shoes are best. Be here twenty minutes early to fill out paperwork."

"Okay."

"See ya then." The line went dead and I tossed the phone back on the bed. I was less than impressed by whomever that was on the phone. How about a little more friendliness? Jackass. How the hell were they getting clients with people like that answering the phone? Maybe selling *was* my best bet.

Lying back on the bed, I stared up at the ceiling, a noticeable war of confliction battling inside of me. My life was nowhere near what I thought it would be. I thought I'd have a family by now. I thought I'd be *happily* married. I thought . . . so many things. Closing my eyes, I willed the worry away, telling myself that tomorrow was another day.

CHAPTER SIX

13 Years Ago

Paul

I WAS IN the back office when she walked in, all frail-looking, and with her blonde hair tied up in a bun. She was hot in a subtle way. I watched her over the video monitor as she held her jacket in front of her and scanned the pictures on the wall. *Why was she twisting her face when she looked at the photos of me?* I wanted to murder Marcus for scheduling her so early. If we'd had more than one client to take up, that would've been understandable, but to schedule one person for a dive at this hour was a waste of money and most importantly *my* time. But on the bright side, this was an ample opportunity to watch Marcus in action. I lived for this shit.

Sitting in my ratty office chair, I propped my feet up on the desk and watched.

Clara

NO ONE WAS up front when I walked in. I decided I'd wait a few minutes before calling to the back. At least their poor customer service allowed me an opportunity to check the place out a bit. Holding my jacket tightly to my abdomen to hide my shaky hands, I scanned the photographs on the wall. Most were crooked. Several were warped inside of the frame. The walls were off-white, with random stains here and there. The place was a shithole.

"Señora," a deep, accented voice called to me. When I turned, my brows rose in temporary shock, but I quickly schooled all my features. An elf, he's a freaking elf . . . *shit* . . . you're not supposed to call them that. A little person? I shook my head as I worked hard to look at him without staring. I didn't want to gawk . . . it's not like I thought less of him or something because he was little. I wanted to look at him with respect, yet not seem too . . . stare-y. Was that a word? His thick, dark mustache didn't quite match his blonde hair, which he wore slicked back. He wore what looked like a jumpsuit, like you'd see in a movie like *Top Gun,* only pint-sized.

"Um," I cleared my throat, "hi. I'm Clara." I reached down with my right hand and his smaller one accepted it before bending slightly to kiss it. Was he for real? He'd just kissed my hand . . . what the hell?

"My name is Marcello. I will be your instructor."

School your features. School your features. My instructor? As in this man, who was significantly smaller than me, would be the one I'm strapped to when I jumped out of the airplane? My heartbeat increased tenfold.

"Now, I tell you this," he continued, speaking in broken English in his thick accent, "I the best jumper you ever meet."

Oh my God. He's serious. I'm supposed to jump out of a plane with him? Shit.

My mouth opened to protest, but what were the right words? How could I get out of this without completely offending him? *Don't you think you're a little small for me?* didn't quite sound like it would go over well.

"Now, you come stand here." He pointed at the space in front of him where he now stood in the center of the room. Reluctantly, I obeyed as I racked my brain for a way out. Stomachache? Yeah, I could say the nerves got to me . . . that should work.

"Sir, I think maybe I'm not ready for this. I'm terrified of heights and I'm not feeling well all of a sudden. Maybe I'll come another day."

"Ohhhh," he uttered with a deep chuckle as he pried my coat from my hands and tossed it on the table behind him. "You be okay, I promise. Marcello never lose his jumper yet."

"But—"

"No buts." He wagged his stubby little finger at me. "Today, we live!" he exclaimed. "Now, put this on." He tossed something at me and after

I shook it out, I realized it was a jumpsuit for me. "Go on," Marcello insisted.

My brain was yelling, "*Flee*," yet my body kept going along with everything, unable to stop myself. I got one leg in over my shoe, then the other until I managed to put my arms in. "Here, let me help you," Marcello called out as he grabbed a bar stool from the corner and dragged it over, setting it in front of me. Awkwardly, he attempted to climb up, until finally, exasperated with the effort, he flopped down on the seat and looked at me.

"You mind giving me a hand, here, Señora?"

Without thought, I rushed to help him, wrapping my arm around his waist and hoisting him up. He was surprisingly heavy for his size. Once he was standing on the stool, he slicked his hair back with one hand and adjusted the collar of his suit with the other. "Gracias." He nodded.

"Now, to you." He began buttoning my suit as we stood eye to eye; me on the ground, him on the stool. "Okay," he took my shoulders and turned me so my back was to him. "When we are up there in the . . ." his wording drifted off, "the . . . what is that thing called?" he mumbled to himself.

"The plane?" I squeaked out, panic choking me.

"Aw, yes, the plane. I'm so stupid," he chuckled. "When we are up there, I will come behind you and begin hooking us together."

"We're not hooked together before we get on the plane?"

"Oh, no . . ." he laughed haughtily. "That would be awkward. You're a beautiful lady . . . it would make being a man . . . how you say . . . difficult."

My mouth popped open, but he continued on, loudly, stopping me from voicing my objection.

"Now, señora, I know you say you're nervous, but I do this many time."

"How many times?" I asked as I spun around to look at him.

"Oh, so many," he assured me with a bright smile. "At least twice."

"What?" I shrieked. That was it. I was done. I could no longer pretend for the sake of not possibly offending him. A bell from the back sounded loudly and Marcello shook his hands.

"You help me down, please?" he asked. "I turn alarm off."

He wrapped his short arms around my neck and I lifted him off the stool, placing him on his feet on the ground. "You wait here. I be right back." He scurried down the hall toward the back into a room and a few seconds later the alarm shut off. My chest constricted with anxiety. *It's going to be okay, Clara*, I inwardly told myself. I stared straight ahead, fists balled up at my sides, and told myself to just leave. So what if they took the deposit? There was no way I could jump out of a plane with that tiny man. *On the count of three. One, two . . .*

"I come back for you, señora," Marcello called as he came back down the hall. He lugged something heavy behind him, the weight so much that he stopped every few seconds to adjust his grip. *Ah, crap*. Finally, he got a good hold on the giant item and came toward me, the thing he was dragging bumping along behind him. When he reached me, he dropped the straps and put his hands on his hips, working hard to catch his breath.

"What is that?" I asked, pointing to the thing he dragged in.

Letting out a long breath, he turned, hands still on his hips, and in his deep accent replied, "That's the chute."

My eyes felt like they were about to bulge out of my sockets. I'd had enough. This was over. Frantically, I unzipped my suit and started jerking it off. I couldn't get it off fast enough. "What's wrong, señora?"

"I'm sorry, but I think I'll need to come back another day." I grunted as I fought to get the suit over my sneakers.

"Okay, Marcus," another voice called, causing me to jerk my head up. "I think you've gone far enough." And there he was. Paul James in the flesh. Looking more handsome in person than he did in his pictures.

"They never make it this long. She's a real gem," the man whose name was apparently Marcus chuckled in a very non-accented voice, and his small but manly looking face lit up with a grin. In fact, I recognized his voice. He was the guy that answered the phone the day before. I'd imagined a giant on the other end of the line, certainly not "Marcello," or Marcus, or whoever the hell he was.

I stared at them blankly, still trying to understand what was happening. I wasn't an idiot. It appeared the little man had played a joke on me, but that just couldn't be, right? This was a business, for God's sake. You don't do shit like that to your clientele.

Paul looked down at his clipboard and lifted a page, seemingly reading over something, but I could see from where I stood it was only a blank piece of printer paper. "You are . . ."

"Severely unamused," I answered snidely. "Do you think this is funny?" I asked, looking directly at Marcus.

His head reared back slightly. Was I the first person to confront him over his "jokes"? "Yeah," he snorted. "Actually, I do."

Stepping toward him, I looked down, my stare burning into his. "Tell me, little man, do you enjoy using your short stature as a crutch so people can empathize with you? Or has being vertically challenged always given you a free pass to behave like a huge assclown?"

He glared up at me. "Excuse me? Vertically challenged?"

"Oh," I snorted. "Please understand any empathy or politically correct standards I held myself to a minute ago are long gone. You're a petty little shit who thinks it's funny to prank unsuspecting customers who are probably already nervous as hell by making them think they are tandem skydiving with a man too small to do it. What the hell is a matter with you?"

Crossing his arms, he inhaled deeply. "I've had a lifetime of jokes played on me, lady. I think you run-of-the-mill folks can handle a few minutes of it."

"Well, whether those people were average, tall, or short, you're still an asshole," I stated bluntly. Looking up to Paul, I said, "And you're the owner, I presume?"

"That'd be me," he confirmed.

"You condone this?"

"Life's too short, lady. Lighten up. It was only a joke. I'll tell you what," he spoke softly. "You jump for free today."

I lowered my head, attempting to calm myself. This was the most poorly run business I had ever seen. They had employees playing pranks on customers, no phone etiquette whatsoever, no one to greet people as they entered, and now they were offering a free jump to pay me off for offending me?

"Sure," I agreed, my eyes wide, indicating my annoyance. "Let's get this going."

CHAPTER SEVEN
13 Years Before

Paul

S HE HADN'T SPOKEN a word since we'd left the office. We drove separately to the airfield. Every time I talked to her, she simply nodded to acknowledge me. Even when we climbed onto the plane and I introduced her to Sap, our pilot, she couldn't even muster up a greeting for him. Damn, she sure was wound up tight. I mean, she was a babe, for sure, but she had an air about her I didn't much care for. As if she was so much better than me. Whatever. Clearly she had a stick up her ass and lacked a sense of humor. She wasn't the first one to get pissed over Marcus's little joke, but usually we had them chuckling a little after they'd cooled down. But not this chick. Hell, no. I couldn't even get a smile out of her.

As we were ascending, I couldn't wait to get this shit over with, and send her on her way. When we'd reached 4,000 feet, I got on my knees and yelled over the engine for her to do the same. As I buckled us together, I could feel how tight and rigid her body was. She was scared shitless. Since the day was a bust and I doubted she'd give the business any glowing reviews or bring us any new business, I decided to enjoy myself . . . at her expense, of course.

Leaning over, I put my mouth near her ear so she could hear me. I paused a moment, not sure why I was so stunned by her scent. She smelled like clean linens; like when my grandmother used to hang my clothes out on the line on a hot summer' day. I have always loved that smell—so fresh and crisp. "You scared or something?" I managed to shout after a beat.

She shook her head no as her eyes squeezed shut. *Oh yeah, she was scared.*

"Well I am," I falsely confessed, hiding my smile behind a serious façade. She glanced back at me over her shoulder with a wide, questioning look.

"You never know what could happen," I continued when I knew I had her full attention. "I mean . . . the chute could fail to open. I could have a heart attack midair. We could land hard and break our legs. You just never know." I looked at her in the most thoughtful of ways.

She turned her head forward and I felt her inhale as her back pushed into my front. Smiling to myself, I checked the buckles one more time and slipped my helmet on. There's always risk involved when jumping, but I knew we were safe. I just wanted to mess with her one more time.

"Okay, I'm going to open the door and I want you to stick your feet out on that step right there, hands go here." Taking her hands, I placed them on her shoulder straps. "When I tell you to, you're going to push off the platform and keep your hands right here until I tell you to let go. Your legs need to stay between mine and—"

"I can't do it," she blurted out as she pushed back, away from the door. As she pushed, pain shot up my back as I fought not to let her topple us over.

"Calm down," I grunted. "Everything is okay." Drama queen.

"I can't do it," she insisted, panic laced in every word.

"I promise—"

"I'm not fucking jumping," she hissed, interrupting me. Throwing my hands up, I began unbuckling her.

"We're not jumping, Sap. Take us down," I shouted over the engine. Once she was free from me, she plopped down, pulling her knees to her chest and staring off into space. What a fucking waste of my day. The damn jump was free. Come on, lady.

When we landed, she climbed out of the plane, peeled off her suit, and left it crumpled on the ground. Apparently I was also a maid service. As she marched to her car, she didn't even bother to say bye or thanks or screw you. She just left.

"I hate to see her leave, but I love to watch her go," Sap murmured.

Cutting a look to him, I smirked. "You're a dirty old man, Sap."

He smirked back, the wrinkles around his eyes creasing. "I've been called worse."

As Clara slammed her car door and started the engine, I said, "She'd eat you alive."

"Nah," Sap argued. "A woman like that just needs a man that appreciates her spirit."

"Is "spirit" a code word for ass?"

He snorted a laugh. "Sometimes they like to hand over the reins."

"Sap." I chuckled. "What the hell are you talking about, old man?"

He slapped me on the back, hard, knocking the air out of me. "She needs to rule the world, boy, but needs a man that can rule her."

I snorted. How wrong he was. "She'd likely castrate any dude that tried to *rule* her."

Sap's mouth quirked to one side. "Paul, for all the women you've been with and all the places you've been, you sure don't know much about the opposite sex."

"I know enough," I argued as I unzipped my jumpsuit. "And I know she's a prude that needs to get laid." That chick was a complete killjoy.

"You see a prude. I see a woman waiting to be unleashed."

"Oh yeah?" I chuckled. "Saw all that in the fifteen minutes you were with her?"

"Yep."

"Okay, Sap. We'll be back in an hour, and I promise this time we're jumping."

CHAPTER EIGHT

Paul

I'D CERTAINLY TAKEN her off guard showing up unannounced. She looks like she's seeing a ghost.

"Where's the professional greeting?" I jest. I'm trying to piss her off as much as the announcement of her bullshit meeting did to me. Shit, I'm still pissed. And the Clara I remember would give me an eye-roll and tell me to fuck off. But she doesn't do that. She just stares at me, her mouth slightly open. Two people, clients, I assume, sit at the table in the corner filling out their paperwork as Clara and I remain eyelocked.

"Who ready to jump today?" a deep Spanish accent asks. One second later, Marcus rounds the corner, his hair slicked back, wearing a wicked thick, black mustache. His diving suit is covered in Mexican flags, and his front tooth is capped in gold. Grinning, I shake my head. I can see he's really upped his game since I've been gone. As soon as he turns his head toward me, his smile fades and he darts his gaze to Clara.

"Paul," he intones in his normal voice. "It's been a long time." He clears his throat and extends a hand to shake mine. I look at his hand and curl my lips.

"I don't want to shake your hand." I smack it away and his head rears back slightly, shock strewing across his face. "What the hell is that?" I grimace. Marcus is *my* best friend. We don't shake hands. "Come give me a hug, man." I grab him in a bear hug and lift him off the ground, squeezing him.

"My ribs," he groans as I squeeze harder. When I set him back on his feet, his face red as a ripe tomato as he gasps for air.

"You've gotten a little soft in the middle since I last saw you, old friend," I joke. "Guess that's what old age will do to ya."

"I'm two years younger than you," he replies morosely. "I'm also about three feet shorter than you and I still have a bigger dick."

"Marcus," Clara shrieks as I laugh.

Turning to the two customers at the table, he waves. "Sorry. But it is big."

"Oh my God," Clara sighs. "Let me get Bowman and Larry to finish up in here." Clara scurries off down the hall and Marcus and I move to the small couch by the entrance.

"She's still wound up tight," I comment as we sit.

"She has her reasons," Marcus argues and my brows furrow. Is he defending her? That's new. They hated one another when I left.

"Oh does she?" I ask sarcastically.

"Paul," Marcus says, his gaze fixed on the wall. "You've been gone a long time."

"And I'd still be gone if she hadn't cut off my money," I add.

Marcus snorts and shakes his head. "It was the only way to get you to come home."

"And why did I need to come home?"

He places his little hands on his face and rubs hard a few times. "Because—"

"Marcus," Clara calls, interrupting him as she gives him a pointed, wide-eyed look. "I think we need to get the van ready for our jump."

I haven't jumped in months and the idea of doing it again brings a small smile to my face. "Maybe I'll jump, too." I stand and begin to head toward the back, but just as I'm about to pass Clara she presses a firm hand to my chest, stopping me. *Here we go.* I knew as soon as I said I'd jump she'd throw a hissy about it.

"I'll get you a suit," she tells me. "You stay here."

I stare at her as she heads back down the hall, blinking a few times, wondering what's happening. She didn't even bat an eye about me jumping.

"Okay." I snort as I spin around back to Marcus. "What the hell is up with . . ." My sentence trails off when I realize Marcus is staring out the large front window into the parking lot where a couple of teenagers are pulling what looks like camera equipment out of a van. A pretty brunette in skinny jeans, a green shirt, and a black beanie motions her hand several times, indicating for the others to hurry up. Quickly, her two male friends gather everything and one slams the van door shut.

"Who is that?"

"I don't know," Marcus says, simply. Seconds later, the bubbly brunette breezes in, forgetting to hold the door for her friends.

She takes a slow look at the place, nodding to herself until her gaze lands on me. "Holy shit." She gasps. Looking back to her friends that have just walked in, she squeals, "That's him." She points a tiny finger at me. "That's Paul James."

Both of the guys dart their stares at me, their eyes going wide when they realize it's true. "No way," the taller one with shaggy hair says.

The brunette beams a huge smile at me and I take a step back. What the fuck is going on here? "Mr. James, I'm Ashley King. I go to Redford High." Then jabbing her thumb over her shoulder, pointing at her friends, she adds, "And this is Zane and Mills, my crew." I'm confused. Why are kids from the local high school here?

"Yeah, how about you turn that camera off," I tell the one she indicated as Zane, who is holding a camera on his shoulder, taping our conversation. Ashley looks to Zane and nods yes, telling him to do it. Zane rolls his eyes but drops the camera to his side.

"Turn it off," I order him. With a grunt of protest, he turns it off.

"That a boy, Zane." I applaud.

"Your name is really Zane?" Marcus questions, his hands on his hips as he gazes up at the trio, his expression stoic.

The one called Zane looks down, and his head rears back as if he's only now just noticed Marcus. "Holy shit," Zane exclaims. "You're a midget." Immediately, Ashley turns and smacks him on the back of his head. "Ouch," he whines. Kids.

"You don't call them that, Zane." Then looking at Marcus, she smiles brightly. "They prefer to be called little people," she adds.

"Or just people . . ." Marcus replies.

"I'm sorry about him," Ashley continues, ignoring Marcus and Zane. "He's not the sharpest tool in the shed."

"I'm sorry," I intervene. "Ashley, is it?"

"Yes, Mr. James, and might I say I am a huge fan." She steps toward me, reaching out a hand, but when I cross my arms she drops it. "We've watched every YouTube video of your stunts available. You are an amazing man."

"And that would probably mean something to me if you were legal, hon, but seeing as how you're not, let's skip your mediocre attempt to appeal to my vanity. What do you want?" It's been years since I've been recognized or interviewed. A large part of that probably has to do with the fact I've been living in other countries for the past twelve years, but that's not all of it. My glory days are long gone, my legacy having faded.

Ashley nods, understanding I'm not susceptible to flattery. "I'm here about *Desperately Seeking Epic*."

"What?" I ask, furrowing my brows in further confusion.

"The Craigslist ad." Without looking, she reaches a hand out and snaps her fingers. Mills immediately hops to and pulls a paper from his backpack, handing it to her. As I reach for it, Marcus snatches the paper from her hand and backs away.

"Look, kids, he's just gotten into town," Marcus interrupts. "Why don't you guys call tomorrow and maybe he'll have time to discuss this with you."

"Is Neena here?" Ashley asks, stretching her neck to look over my shoulder and down the hall.

"Neena?" I question. "Who the hell is that?"

Ashley's expression falls into a look of confusion as her gaze meets mine. Then she looks to Marcus. "He doesn't know about the ad or Neena yet?"

"You need to go. Now," Clara interjects as she charges in. "This is a place of business and if you're not here to skydive then you have no reason to be here."

"Freedom of the press, lady," Zane quips, but backs away when Clara steps toward him. The woman has a mean look that could cower a grizzly bear. I don't blame him.

"I imagine you're all skipping school right now, yes?"

The three look at each other, but Ashley, the boldest of the crew, shrugs nonchalantly. I want to smile a little because in some ways she reminds me of Clara. "Sometimes we have to make sacrifices to get the story," she replies. "Like Tom Brokaw in Baghdad."

"Well, kid, this ain't Baghdad and you sure as hell ain't Tom Brokaw," Marcus announces as he moves to herd them toward the door.

"And if we don't leave?" Zane asks, standing firmly.

"I may look small, kid, but I can kick your ass," Marcus threatens, jabbing his finger at Zane. "I'm the perfect height to headbutt you right in the balls."

"We're underage," Ashley argues. "You can't touch us."

Turning to Clara, Marcus gives her a look before he falls back, landing on his ass. He howls in pain as he grabs his gut and rolls to his side. "He just kicked me, Clara. Did you see that shit?"

Rushing to Marcus's side, Clara kneels and acts as if she's checking him over. Then she looks up to the trio. "How could you kick this poor innocent man?"

"We didn't do anything to him," Ashley cries as Marcus moans louder.

"Hate crime!" he shouts, jerking out a hand and pointing a finger at them, only to pull it back in to his stomach, feigning pain.

"How could you kick this tiny man?" Clara stands, her tone angry. "Get out. Now!"

All three of them have their mouths open in utter shock, but after a moment Ashley smirks a little and snorts, realizing they've been defeated. Jutting her chin, she motions for Zane and Mills to go. "We'll be back," she warns.

"Why?" Marcus yells dramatically, his face red and voice deep with emotion. "So you can finish me off? Haven't you tortured me enough?"

The bell on the door jingles as the three rush out. Marcus stands and watches them, and Clara remains on her knees beside him. When they finally look at one another, they smile widely and Marcus helps her to her feet.

"What in the hell was that?" I ask in disbelief. What were those kids talking about?

"That was phenomenal acting," Marcus answers as he takes a bow.

"You missed your calling," Clara compliments him.

"Yeah, well, the world of skydiving needed me more."

"Holy shit!" Someone gasps and we all turn to see the woman waiting to jump holding a piece of paper, looking from it to me and back again. Marcus must have dropped the paper Ashley was trying to hand to me and this woman picked it up. "You're her father."

The room goes silent until I chuckle. "I don't have a kid, lady."

The woman ignores me and looks at Clara. "Aren't you Neena's mother?"

I dart my gaze to Clara who is standing as still as a statue, blinking profusely. When Clara doesn't answer, the woman's boyfriend stands and takes the paper from her. "Babe . . . I don't think this is any of our business."

As he hands the paper to Marcus, the woman apologizes. "I'm so sorry. I shouldn't have . . . It's just with it being all over the Internet and on the news . . ."

"With what being on the internet and news? Will someone please tell me what in the hell is going on?" I say, my voice rising and my frustration skyrocketing. It's been like a goddamn zoo in here this morning and I'm tired of it. I just wanted to meet with Clara and piss her off to the point where she'd give me my money and never ask me for an annual meeting ever again. I didn't sign up for these theatrics.

"Mom," a small voice interrupts, and we all turn to the back hall where a tiny girl stands wearing black yoga pants and a sweater jacket. Her head is wrapped in a purple scarf. She's thin and pale, but her eyes . . . something about them has me fixated, and I can't stop looking.

"Neena," Clara sighs and rushes toward her. "You're supposed to be resting."

"It sounded like Marcus was hurt. I was worried," the girl responds as Clara tries to shoo her back down the hall.

"I'm okay, kiddo. Don't worry," Marcus assures her. "Go back to bed."

Even as Clara gently pushes Neena back, Neena and I remain with our eyes locked. Her eyes. *What is it about her eyes?* After a minute, Clara wins and manages to get Neena down the hall. The room is silent for a moment until Bowman and some other guy I haven't met before come out, suited up, ready to jump. Bowman gives me an awkward wave as he moves his gaze to Marcus. Marcus quickly shakes his head, indicating for Bowman not to say anything.

"We have to head to the airfield," Marcus tells me. "You should stick around. There's a lot you've missed since you've been gone." Then he hands me the paper and leaves.

I can't even read it yet. I'm still lost in thought. *What is it about her eyes?* I scratch my head, wondering why they look so familiar when suddenly it hits me.

They're *my* eyes.

She has my eyes.

But that's . . . impossible. I'm numb with shock. And fear. I look at the paper in my hand and begin to read it.

Desperately Seeking Epic ⊠

You're my father.

The words seem to blur together forcing me to stop reading. And before I realize it, I'm sitting on the couch with the paper clenched tightly in my hand. I can't will myself to read any more. It just can't be true. How could it? How could it be true? Because if it is true, it means I have a kid that's been fatherless for her entire life. It means Clara hid her from me. It simply can't be true. Surely she doesn't hate me that much that she'd omit the fact we have a child together. The longer I sit, the more horrendous my thoughts become.

"Paul," Clara says my name, her voice faint. Jerking my gaze to hers, she swallows and her eyes go wide. She can see how angry I am.

"Is it true?"

She drops her head, frowning a little. Her blonde hair cascades over her shoulders, and she hunches them ever so lightly. She doesn't speak, just nods yes.

I stand and grab fistfuls of my hair as I pace back and forth. "So she's what? Thirteen?"

"Twelve," Clara answers, her voice raspy. She still hasn't looked up.

I laugh with disdain. "Aw, fucking perfect, Clara. You hate me that much you'd hide our kid from me?"

Whipping her head up, she glares at me. "I tried contacting you for months after she was born. You didn't respond to one email."

"I don't check that shit. You know that."

"How else was I supposed to reach you? You didn't even get a cell phone until two years ago, and the only way I found out about that is because Richard told me."

"Well, cutting my money off worked. Why didn't you do that sooner?"

"Because I didn't think about it until now. And before she wasn't . . ." She pauses as if choking on her next word.

"She wasn't what, Clara?" I snap, sick of her theatrics.

"She wasn't dying," she growls at me through clenched teeth.

I stumble back a bit. Dying? This day has been a mind-fuck of emotions. First seeing Clara, which initially brought on the old feelings of want and lust, and oddly wanting to strangle her. Then hearing I have a kid I didn't know about. I'm still trying to digest that one. Now my kid is dying? That's a lot, even for a fuck-up like me.

"Of what?" I manage.

"Leukemia," Clara answers softly.

"What about chemo or—"

"She's been through two rounds." Clara cuts me off. "She needs a bone marrow transplant. Even with it, her odds are poor, but it's her last hope."

"Or what?" I ask stupidly.

Clara closes her eyes and inhales deeply, making me hold my breath. "Or she dies. A few months ago they said six months to a year. That's when I cut your money off. There's a very small chance you could be a match, and if you are . . . Paul . . ."

"Don't even say it." I hold my hand up, stopping her, and her face falls, transforming into despair. Did she think I'd say no? That I'm that big of a bastard? "I'll do whatever I can to help."

She swallows hard, her chest convulsing as she tries to keep her emotion at bay. "Thank you."

"I want to meet her, Clara," I say.

Inhaling a deep breath, Clara nods a few times. "Yeah, okay. Dinner? Tonight at my house?"

"Yeah, sure," I agree. "You still living in that shithole?" I jest, trying to lighten things a tad.

She snorts. "You mean my home with character?" she jokes back. "Why yes . . . yes I am."

I chuckle a little. "Should I bring anything?"

"Paul . . ." she replies, her tone serious. "She's a little girl. Don't . . . hurt her. Don't make her fall in love with you if you know you're just going to take off again."

I don't know what to say. A part of me wants to yell at her and tell her to stop busting my balls and acting like I'm some kind of asshole. Another part of me knows I kind of am an asshole. But not completely. I'm not a complete asshole by any means. Okay, maybe half of one. So I reply lamely with a simple, "Okay."

"Seven."

"See ya then."

CHAPTER NINE
Clara

OPENING THE OVEN, smoke wafts out, hitting me in the face, burning my eyes and making me choke. "Shit," I grumble as I close the oven door and turn it off. The smoke detector goes off, shrieking, and I quickly grab the broom and bang it until it crashes to the ground, spitting the battery out, which disappears under the fridge.

"Out of all nights, you pick this one to cook," Marcus murmurs before sipping his wine as he sits at my kitchen table. Leaving the smoke detector where it dropped on the floor, I ignore him and turn back to dicing cucumbers for the salad.

"We'll just order a pizza," I snap.

Marcus grins. "Neena will be pleased."

"Why didn't you bring Mei-ling?"

"She had to work," Marcus grumbles. Mei-ling, Marcus's barely-speaks-English Chinese girlfriend, works at a strip club, although he prefers to call it a gentlemen's club. I guess it makes him feel better about the situation. She's an incredibly sweet young (and by young, I mean *young*, but she's at least of legal drinking age) woman.

"You're nervous," he observes.

"No I'm not," I mumble.

"Yes, you are. I can tell."

"And how is that?"

"Your foundation isn't blended all the way. You're way too detail-oriented to let that happen."

Immediately, I drop the knife in my hand, rush to the hall bathroom, and look in the mirror. Damn. Did I put my makeup on in the dark or something? I curse as I rub at my jawline and neck, until it's blended. As I walk back in the kitchen, I roll my eyes as Marcus grins behind his wine glass. Jackass.

"You look beautiful, Clara," Marcus adds, and I smile faintly.

"It's not about . . . that. This is about Neena. Besides, Paul is a shit."

"Yet you put on makeup, attempted to cook a meal, and you're wearing a dress I haven't seen you in since Bowman got married."

Looking down at my sundress, I sigh. He's right. I'm ridiculous. "I'm going to go change," I say, but the doorbell rings.

"It's go time." Marcus lets out a deep breath.

"Thanks for being here tonight."

Marcus nods once and motions a hand toward the living room. "After you."

I walk quickly to the front door after the bell goes off again. "Neena," I call up the stairs as I pass by. "Come on down. He's here." When I open the door, Paul is turned, facing the front yard with both hands in his pockets. Turning, his gaze meets mine before trailing down my body and back up again. My right hand holds the door and my grip tightens as a familiar feeling from so long ago rushes through me. My cheeks heat and I smile slightly, trying my damnedest not to full-out grin. It's been a long time since a man looked at me that way—at least any I've noticed.

He steps to me, one step, then another, until he's right in front of me. Leaning in, he kisses my cheek. My head rears back slightly; I'm shocked by the greeting.

"Clara." His voice is deep, in all the right ways, making my belly clench.

"Paul," I reply in an even tone.

He looks to the left where my hand still holds the door, then his hand brushes against the wood of it. "Glad to see the door is still holding up," he quips.

I want to chuckle, and remember that moment of heat and passion when he pressed me against this door and kissed me like I'd never been kissed before in my life. But that little voice inside of me pipes up. *He left you, Clara.*

"Come in," I add, stepping back so he may enter.

"Marcus!" Paul beams.

"Where's my kiss on the cheek?" Marcus jests as they shake hands.

"Saving yours for later," Paul replies as they laugh. When he turns back to me, he wipes his palms on his shorts and lets out a long breath. He's nervous. I didn't realize that Paul James could get nervous. "She here?"

"Yeah. She's in her room. She'll be down in a minute."

"Does she know I'm coming?"

"Yes, she does," I tell him. "You ready?"

"I think so."

Shutting the door, I move to the bottom of the stairs. "Neena?" I call, louder this time.

"I'm right here," she groans, and we all whip our heads to the living room. She was hiding behind the recliner. Her camcorder is in her hand; red light on.

"Can we turn the camera off for a moment, Neena?" I beg.

"It's not on," she lies, like always. But I can't ever seem to be upset with her for more than a second.

"Neena," I warn lightly.

"Fine," she huffs and powers it down. She's wearing one of her favorite scarves around her head; it was mine once. It's green and has a soft flowery design made up of pink, white, and brown. She's traded her usual yoga pants and rock T-shirt for a frilly black skirt and pink tank top. She's a sight for sore eyes and I can't help grinning. At least I'm not the only one that dressed up.

"Will you come here, please?" I ask her, holding my hand out. Her eyes dart nervously between me and Paul before moving to Marcus. Marcus nods once, letting her know it's okay; she has nothing to be afraid of. Hesitantly, she moves from around the recliner and walks over to us. When I look at Paul, he seems transfixed; he can't stop staring at her. His expression is stoic, but it could mean anything. I can't tell if he wants to smile, puke, run away, or hug her. When Neena reaches me, she curls into my side and lowers her head, peeking up at Paul.

"Neena," I say, quietly. "Honey, this is Paul James. Your father."

Paul swallows hard and plasters on what I assume is his best smile, but it looks forced and incredibly uncomfortable. "Hi, Neena," he utters as he holds out his hand to shake hers. Neena lifts her head and gives him a whisper of a smile as she takes his hand.

"Nice to meet you," she replies.

"You have my eyes," Paul states as he moves his awed gaze to me. "She looks just like me."

"Yes," I murmur. "I know."

"But way better looking," Marcus cuts in.

"Agreed." Paul nods.

The room falls awkwardly silent, but Marcus breaks it when he says, "I'll go order the pizza."

As he turns to walk back to the kitchen, Neena darts off after him. "I want Giovanni's!"

Dinner runs smoothly even though I'm incredibly tense. It's like my body is aware of Paul; if he moves, I sense it. I practically lose my shit when he stares at the corner of the table and smirks at me, his fingers tracing over my engraved initials in the wood, slowly, as if he's taunting me. There are few opportunities for awkward silence at the table because Paul goes on and on about the places he's been to and the people he's met. Neena is practically panting, her eyes filled with wonder. She's wanted so badly to travel; see the world. But her health has prevented it.

"Have you been to China?"

"A few times," Paul replies before taking a bite of pizza. "Maybe we can go together." He shrugs. Insert awkward silence. Neena leans back in her chair and smiles sadly. Marcus frowns and my eyes well up with tears. Neena may never go anywhere. Not if Paul isn't a match, and even if he is . . . maybe not.

"Who wants cake?" I chirp, standing and rushing to the counter. I need a moment to collect myself, because I don't want to cry in front of her.

Paul seems to pick up on his fubarred comment and clears his throat. "What kind of music do you like, Neena?"

For the next twenty minutes Neena excitedly discusses her favorite bands, ending with her favorite one, *Masters of the V*. I inwardly cringe every time she says the band's pervy name out loud.

She grins from ear to ear before continuing. "I want to meet Zack, and all the guys of *Masters of the V*, soooo bad. They sell these awesome wristbands that mention their current number one hit, *Lick the Cat!*"

Paul frowns and blinks a few times—unsure if he heard her correctly. "Lick the . . . what?"

"Yes," I intervene, giving Neena a stern look. "And I told her I wouldn't let her wear such a thing unless this Zack guy, the lead singer, delivers it to our door himself." Neena quirks her mouth to the side in mild annoyance.

"Well, I think I'll be heading home," Marcus announces as he stands and rubs his stomach a few times. "Excellent pizza, as always," he teases, smirking at me. Tossing the dish towel in my hands at him, I stick my tongue out.

"Paul," he says. "If you need a place to stay, let me know."

"Will do, buddy." They shake hands and as Marcus leaves, he kisses Neena on the cheek. "Night, kiddo."

"Night, Uncle Marcus."

When I hear the front door close indicating Marcus has left, I look to Neena. "Neena you should go get ready for bed, honey."

"Moommm," she whines.

"Neennnaaa," I gripe back.

"I want to talk to Paul some more."

"Maybe I could come hang out with you tomorrow if that's okay with your mom?" Paul offers, cutting his eyes to me.

"I'd love that!" Neena practically squeaks. "Can he, Mom?"

As I gaze at both of them, their matching brown eyes watch me, waiting for my reply, I can't help the feeling of dread that hits me in the gut. *I don't do babies and white picket fences.* Neena said she could handle his rejection—if that's what he gave her, but looking at her wonder-filled gaze, I'm not so sure. Paul has a way about him. It's hard to explain. He draws you in and sometimes you don't even realize it's happened until it's too late. That's how it happened to me. But what if he's sincere? What if he really does want to get to know her? How could I deny my daughter, who may leave this world so tragically soon, this opportunity to get to know her father? I'd be a monster if I did that.

"Sure, we can work something out," I manage through a forced smile.

Neena grins and looks at Paul, who is wearing a matching grin.

She stands and says, "Thanks for coming to dinner. It was really nice to meet you." Then she reaches out her frail little hand to shake his. Paul glances at her hand, his expression somewhere between pain and happiness, before he takes and shakes it.

"Thanks for taking the time to meet me, Neena. I hope we get to know each other a lot better."

"Me, too." Turning to me, she walks toward me, almost skipping, and hugs me. "Thanks, Mom. I love you."

"I love you, too." I squeeze her once. "I'll come up to say good night in a bit."

With a small wave to Paul, she exits the kitchen, leaving the two of us in yet another bout of awkward silence.

"You've done a great job with her," Paul finally says. "She's a wonderful girl."

"Thank you. I got lucky."

He stands and takes his beer bottle to the trash, dropping it in. "And you're okay with me seeing her tomorrow?"

Spinning around, I place my hands on the counter and take a deep breath. "I'm trying to be," I admit. "But honestly . . . I'm scared."

"Of me?"

"Of you making her fall in love with you then jetting off."

He sighs and moves to the counter beside me, leaning against it, facing the opposite direction. "I mean it. I want to know her, Clara."

"Please be careful with her, Paul." He nods once in agreement.

"So how do we find out if I'm a match?"

"I set up an appointment for you. Tomorrow at nine. Are you staying with Marcus? I can text him the address."

"Wow. Okay, that was fast," he sighs. "I'm not sure where I'm staying just yet.""

"Well we're running out of time," I state. "I've spoken to the office on the off chance you'd show up." I grab a notepad and pencil out of a drawer and shove it into his hands. "Here. Write down your number. I'll text you the details and meet you there."

He jots down his number and watches me for a moment after, his eyes fixed on me. I wonder what he sees. Does he see the woman he once shared a bed with; the youthful and determined Clara? Or does he see the shadow of that woman he used to know? Can he see my fear and worry like a map across my face?

"Okay, I'll meet you there. And, Clara?"

Crossing my arms, I ask, "Yes?"

"Thanks for letting me come over tonight. Will Neena be with you tomorrow?"

"No," I answer. "She'll hang with Marcus at the office until we're done."

"Okay. Then I'll see you tomorrow."

He pushes off the counter and I follow him to the door and hold it with one hand as he steps out. He stops and puts his hand against the wood, just as he did when he'd arrived tonight. "This door should go down in history."

I smirk slightly. "Should it?"

He drops his eyes a moment before raising them to meet mine again. "I think that kiss was the first time I ever thought about forever." Wait, what? He's down the porch steps and in his car before I snap out of it. Did he just say that or did I imagine it? Closing the door, I lean my back against it and raise my fingers to my mouth. It may have happened over thirteen years ago, but standing here, remembering it, reliving it in my mind, I can almost feel the tingle on my lips. *And there it is.* The suck. It's been one day and he's already sucking me back in.

CHAPTER TEN

Paul

AFTER I LEAVE Clara's, I drive around for a bit, trying to digest the evening. I have a daughter. It still stuns me every time the thought travels through my mind. I drive for what feels like hours, thinking of Neena and her dire situation, and thinking of Clara and . . . well . . . her beauty. She's definitely held up well after all these years. I can't deny that in the thirteen years I've been gone, I've wondered about her—often. How was she? Had she found someone else? Had she returned to her old life in Texas?

Before I know it, I'm parking my truck in front of Marcus's place and heading inside. Fuck it, I need to unload on a friend. He did offer after all. Marcus lives in a double-wide behind the office that my uncle left to him after he passed away.

When I open the door and step inside, I freeze. There's a tiny Asian woman with huge fake tits sitting on the counter in the kitchen. Her head is back, her mouth open, and she's moaning . . . *pleasurably* moaning. The couch is blocking her lower half, but her dress is pulled down, revealing her sizable chest held up in a purple, lacy bra.

"Good," she cries out in a thick accent. "So good."

The door slams closed behind me and her eyes fly open as her head whips in my direction. She proceeds to spew words I don't understand, a million miles a minute, as she tugs her dress up with one hand and the skirt part down with the other. I'm holding my hands up, about to leave, when Marcus's head pops up just above the top of the couch.

"Paul," he groans, before he runs his forearm across his shiny, wet face.

"Holy shit!" I laugh. "Were you just going down on her?"

The woman continues to yell at me, her arms flailing as she turns to Marcus and starts yelling at him.

"It's Paul," he tries to explain, but it's to no avail. She yells at him some more, then shouts at me one more time before stomping off to the back and slamming a door. Marcus, with his hands on his hips, walks around the couch toward me. He's shirtless and his belt is undone, with his hair disheveled.

"That was Mei-ling," he informs, his tone calm yet edged with anger.

"That's your girl?" I question. "Damn, bro. She's hot."

"And to what do I owe this unexpected visit?" He ignores my compliment as he walks to the fridge and pulls out a beer.

"You said if I needed a place to stay, to let you know."

"Yeah . . . let me know," he points out as he twists the cap off and tosses it at the trash can, missing it by inches. He shrugs and takes a long swig from the bottle.

"That's why I came by. This is me letting you know." I smirk.

"Ever heard of a phone call?" he questions sarcastically.

"If I'd known you'd be going down on your girl like your life depended on it, I wouldn't have just barged in."

"Well from now on, don't barge in."

"Noted."

He does a little backward hop on the couch, careful not to spill his beer, and shimmies back until he's comfortable. "So . . . ?"

"So?"

"How are you? Big night for you."

With a loud sigh, I point to the fridge and he nods. I get myself a beer and return taking a seat on the recliner. "I can't believe she didn't tell me," I admit. I take a long pull from my beer and add, "I can't believe *you* didn't tell me, man."

His head jerks up, his forehead creased with furious wrinkles. "Are you serious?" he asks.

"Yeah. Why didn't one of you come and look for me if you couldn't get in touch with me?"

Marcus slides off the couch, and places his bottle on the coffee table with a thud, causing the liquid to fizz out over the rim and dribble down. He marches to the front door, pushing it open. "Get out."

My head rears back slightly. "What?"

"You heard me. Get out."

"What the fuck, dude? Why?"

He stomps to the kitchen and grabs his T-shirt off the floor, jerking it on. "You left all of us. Not just Clara with a baby on the way. All of us, without *one* fucking word."

"I've always just left without a word," I defend. "It never pissed you off before. And I had no idea she was pregnant."

He rounds the couch and stands in front of me. "You'd leave for a few months, a year at most. Not thirteen fucking years, Paul!"

I can't look him in the eye so I stare at the beer in my hand. Marcus may be a little man, physically, but when he's angry, he's huge. There are truly very few people in this world whose opinion of me matters—to me anyway. Marcus just happens to be one of those few. Taking in a deep breath, I exhale loudly and give a little shrug. "I'm sorry." It's not much, but it's all I got. "But if you think I'm such a dick, why are you still my friend?"

He drops his head for a brief moment and when he raises it again he has this smile on his face, one that anyone, whether they know Marcus well or not, can plainly see whatever he is thinking. "Neena."

Something about the way he says her name hits me hard, causing my chest to ache. He loves her. He loves her like a man loves his daughter. He loves her like I should have been here loving her for the past twelve years. My jaw tightens and my teeth clench as I struggle through the fire burning in my belly. What is this? *Jealousy?* Am I seriously jealous? If I couldn't be here to love and care for Neena as her father, why not Marcus? He's my best friend and one of the best people I've ever known. But still. I hate that he's been here watching her grow up while I didn't even know she existed.

"She's the closest thing I'll ever have to my own daughter."

Fuck. His words are like a bolt to the chest that jerks me to stand. Stalking over to the trash can, I chug the rest of my beer before tossing the bottle in the can. "Yeah. I gotta go," I mumble through a hoarse voice caused by drinking too fast.

"I thought you were staying?"

"Well, I was, until you decided to announce what a shitty friend and father I am."

Marcus's face scrunches up as he snorts in disagreement. "Shitty friend, yes," he confirms. "I didn't say anything about you being a father."

"Which equates to shitty father," I yell back. "I wasn't here, therefore I'm a shitty dad."

"Paul," he starts, his voice laced with frustration. He rubs his forehead with his short fingers. "I'm sorry for what you've missed. Truly. I only meant that I'm grateful for the time I've had with her."

"Do you think that makes me feel any fucking better?" I snarl. "I find out in one day I have a kid just to turn around and find out she's dying!"

He presses his lips together in a flat line and nods once. He hears me. "Well," he finally says, "you're here now. Make the most of it, Paul."

I snatch open the front door, more than ready to leave, and he calls, "Paul. Stay."

"Don't worry about it, Marcus." Even after I get in my rental car, he watches me with his arms crossed as I back out of his makeshift driveway. I know I'm being a dick. I know it's not his fault. But it's not really my fault either. I wouldn't have left if I had known. Right now, it's best for me to be alone. I need time to think. So it looks like I'll be finding a cheap hotel for the night.

CHAPTER ELEVEN
Clara

AFTER PAUL'S APPOINTMENT, he asks if we can chat for a few minutes. He follows me to a small coffee shop not too far from the office. We order our coffee and sit down at a tiny table in the back corner.

As he sips from the white plastic lid, his features are tense; his brows furrowed and his shoulders bunched up. He has something on his mind, but I decide to wait him out. I won't push him. I learned a long time ago Paul James can't be pushed. As I sip my own coffee, I watch him, hating that the years have been so good to him. His skin is still perfectly tan, golden even, he is Italian after all, though his dark hair is painted with the softest and subtlest hints of gray. I can't fathom how it's possible that he's better looking with age, but he is. Over the years, when I've thought of him, I imagined him drunk and looking sloppy—the result of too much booze, drugs, and brothel living. I guess it made me feel better to imagine he was doing horrible.

"What happens if I'm not a match?" he begins.

Clearing my throat, I scoot up a little in my seat. "I don't want to think about that. But if I must . . . We do our best to make her comfortable and make her last days happy."

"Why, Clara?" he asks, his dark gaze fixed on me.

I shrug. It's a question I've asked myself a million times. "I wish I knew that answer, Paul. I've asked myself that many times. Some kids just get sick."

He shakes his head. "That's not what I'm asking."

I stare at him blankly as my chest tightens. I now know what he's asking, but I'm going to make him clarify it anyway. "Then what *are* you asking?"

He sips his coffee. "Why didn't you tell me about her?"

I fight the urge to snap at him. We're adults. Well, one of us is anyway. "I already told you I tried. Several times," I almost bark.

"You didn't really try though," he argues.

"Yes, I did," I growl through clenched teeth.

"No, you didn't. Not really. You could have gotten to me if you'd really wanted to."

Setting my cup down on the table, I lean forward, working hard to keep my voice down. "You told me you didn't do babies and white picket fences. You also told me you didn't do happily ever after. You left, Paul. You left without a word to anyone and you think I should have embarked on some worldwide manhunt to tell you that, *I*, a woman you didn't want or love, was pregnant with your child? Why would I do that, Paul? So you could come home just to abandon her, too?"

"I wouldn't have abandoned her," he clarifies. "I would have come home."

"For how long?" I snap.

"You had no right to keep that from me," he snaps back, pointing a finger at me. "She's my kid, too, Clara. I had a right to know!"

"Well you know now, Paul."

He watches me for a moment before leaning back in his seat. "Listen. I'm sorry for leaving the way I did. I am."

I choke back fresh tears—angry tears. I won't cry in front of him . . . not over this. I want to tell him how crushed I was. How when I woke up and naively thought he had just gone in early, how devastated I was when I realized he had simply left as if the time we'd spent together hadn't meant anything. Not one damned thing. But I won't tell him any of that. "What's done is done," I say, instead.

"She looks like you, ya know?"

"No, she doesn't," I disagree. "She looks exactly like you." The last part comes out as a whisper.

He smiles softly. "The eyes for sure, but the nose and mouth are you."

"She has your wildness in her."

He grins. "And your sassiness. She's quite feisty."

I snicker as my gaze falls back down to my coffee cup. "She is amazing. I know I'm partial, but she really is, Paul."

"I want to know her. I'm not going to run off. I promise."

I lick my suddenly dry lips and nod once. I'm not sure if I believe him, but what can I do at this point? Neena wants to know her father. So I give the only reply I can, praying it's not a mistake. "Okay."

CHAPTER TWELVE

Paul

I FOLLOW CLARA BACK to Sky High, and when we walk in, Marcus is sitting at the table in the front area, tiny glasses on the bridge of his nose, looking at paperwork. He leans back in his chair as we enter.

"How'd it go?"

"Good," Clara answers as she slips her cardigan off. She's wearing this blue, sleeveless top underneath that's fitted to her body. Her jeans are tight, showcasing her ass, which I have to admit looks pretty fucking awesome for any woman, more so since she's almost forty. Her hair is tied up in a loose bun, little pieces falling around her face. She's beautiful. No doubt about it.

"Should find out something in the next week or two," she adds. Marcus nods, his mouth in a tight, flat line. He's worried, too. What if I'm *not* a match? "Is Neena in my office?"

"Yeah. I logged her on to *PornHub*. That should keep her busy for a few hours," Marcus says, earning a scowl from Clara. "What?" he questions. "It's all-you-can-watch anal."

Clara arches an unamused brow.

"She's watching *The Goonies*," he finally admits.

"I'll go check on her and let her know you're here," she tells me.

"Thanks for the time today, Clara," I call out after her. She turns, her gaze meeting mine, and gives me a half smile.

"You're welcome."

When she's out of sight, I look down at Marcus, who is still leaning back in his chair, his arms crossed, watching me. "You know she's the only woman I ever saw you with that I thought might actually have a chance at keeping you."

"She was the only one," I correct.

"Yet, you left anyway."

I rub my hands down my face. "I had my reasons."

"Which were?"

"Unimportant now," I snap. "Has she . . ." *Shit*. How do I ask this?

"Seen anybody?" Marcus supplies.

"Yeah," I grumble, hating the smirk on his face.

"No. Not one guy."

My brows rise in utter shock, and relief runs through me. I know I'm a dick for finding relief in the fact she hasn't been with anyone since I left, but I do. "Really?"

Marcus purses his lips and shakes his head. "No, Paul. Not really," he snorts before he begins to chuckle. "Did you really think she was celibate for thirteen years?" And the bastard laughs harder.

I glare at him. "You're a fucking dick."

"Dude. She's a beautiful, successful woman. Of course there have been other men," he continues.

"A lot of other men?"

He grins widely and chuckles some more. "Wow. Back one day and you're already jonesing for her."

"Fuck off. Just answer the question, Marcus."

He slides out of his chair and starts collecting his papers. "Only a few over the years. None since Neena was diagnosed."

I feel guilty for even asking. "How long ago was that?"

"Four years."

I nod; unsure of how to feel about that. On one hand, I'm glad she hasn't been with a lot of other men. I know I'm asshole for it, but it's true. On the other hand, she's been taking care of our sick daughter. I never meant for her to be alone.

"Why'd you stay, Marcus?" I finally ask. "You hated her when I left. Now you guys seem like best friends."

He looks up at me and sighs. "I stayed because she asked me to."

I want to ask more questions, because frankly, that wasn't an acceptable answer. Clara asked Marcus to do lots of things and he never listened. At least he didn't back when I was around. But before I can delve in, Neena comes barreling down the hall and flings herself on me. "Paul!" I like her spunk.

"Hey, kiddo." I laugh as I hug her. The warmness spreading through me is foreign as she squeezes me. How can I already feel so connected to someone I just met? "You ready to hang out today?"

"Definitely!" she beams.

After we say our good-byes and Clara gives me a thousand instructions of which I'll never remember, Neena and I head out.

"Be careful," Clara tells me in her typical serious tone, as we're about to exit the building. And I know the words mean more. She doesn't mean just be careful while I'm out with Neena. She means to be careful with Neena, period—don't hurt her, inside or out.

"I will," I promise. And I mean it.

CHAPTER THIRTEEN

Clara

I'VE BEEN HOME since five, waiting for Paul to bring Neena home. He's texted me several times throughout the day, letting me know Neena was good and they'd be back around dinner time. It isn't until seven that I hear the front door open and Neena yells, "Mom!"

"Kitchen," I yell back, as I put the last dirty plate in the dishwasher.

A moment later, Neena comes strolling into the kitchen, her face lit up with a huge smile. Seems today was a good day. I love seeing her excited like this.

"Can I use your laptop?" she asks.

"For what?"

"Paul and I want to watch some of his stunts on YouTube." That's when Paul enters.

"I told her it was getting late and tomorrow might be better."

"Please, Mom," she begs.

Closing the dishwasher, I laugh. "Sure. I guess." Neena sprints away, leaving me and Paul chuckling. "I think you have a new fan."

"My *only* fan these days," he jests. His gaze moves to his side and his eyes narrow as he looks at the door frame leading into the kitchen. He glides his finger down the panel of wood, a sideways smirk on his face. He's noticed I kept the engravings, but doesn't speak a word about it. Silence falls between us, before Paul moves to the fridge and squints as he bends down, looking at the pictures Neena has taped to the doors. I stand beside him and when he points to the photo of Neena and Marcus dressed up as Bonnie and Clyde for Halloween, I laugh.

"I bet she had to beg him to do this." Paul snorts.

"Actually, she didn't. To the rest of the world, he's still a grumpy little asshole, but he's different with her. They're like two peas in a pod."

Paul gives a small half nod, his gaze falling for a moment, before rising again. This time, he points to a photo of Neena and me. It's a selfie Neena took one night when we were lying in bed together watching *The Vampire Diaries*. Personally, I think the show is okay, and she loves it, so that's all that really matters to me. "She really is beautiful, Clara," he notes. Then, moving his dark gaze to me, he adds, "Just like you."

My cheeks heat with his praise . . . or maybe it's the sexy gaze, and I have to turn away to hide a smile. *Get your shit together, Clara. He left you.* "Did you guys eat dinner?" I ask, trying desperately to change the subject.

"We stopped and had a sub on the way."

"Good." I nod and turn, closing the dishwasher.

"Got the laptop!" Neena announces as she rushes back in. "Can we make popcorn, Mom?"

I struggle to hide my lack of enthusiasm. It's not that I don't want to make popcorn with my child. It's just . . .the more I'm around Paul, the more I lose my grip on reality. I cannot fall for Paul James again. I simply can't. I don't think I can survive losing him again. My fear of losing Neena, *if* I lose Neena, will kill me. I'm not ready to endure being left by Paul yet again. *You can do this, Clara. You can do this for Neena.* She wants me to get along with Paul, and that's what I plan to do . . . for her.

"You two get the videos going and I'll get it ready," I manage after a moment, plastering a forced smile on my face.

If she notices, it doesn't show. "Come on, Paul," Neena calls. Paul turns to me with a soft and grateful smile. Before he follows her, he mouths, *thank you.*

Nodding once, I watch them exit and inhale deeply. *You can do this, Clara.*

CHAPTER FOURTEEN

Paul

I'VE BEEN BACK in town for a little over two weeks now and I've spent as much time as Clara will allow with Neena. Clara seems to be particularly wound up tight, but I think it's because we're waiting on the results to find out if I'm a match or not. Not being a match would knock me to my knees. She's an amazing little girl.

"Right here," Neena points to a page in a magazine. I've just stopped at a red light, so I look over to see what she's pointing at.

"Corcovado?" I question, surprised. Corcovado is a mountain in Rio de Janeiro, Brazil, topped with a *Christ the Redeemer* statue.

"Brazil would be number one on my list, well, there and China," she mentions excitedly, pulling the magazine back in her lap and staring down at the page.

"I love Brazil," I tell her.

"I know," she says. "Marcus told me. That's one of the reasons I've always wanted to go." She's breaking my heart here.

I clear my throat and hit the gas when the light turns green. I hate that she's grown up hearing about me from other people. That she's grown up wondering about me. Before I can respond, she adds, "I would look at pictures from amazing places and imagine you there. I guess . . ." She pauses. "I guess it made me feel like I knew you. Or maybe, kind of like I was there with you in some way." When I glance over at her, she twists her mouth and darts her eyes back at the magazine. "That sounded so stupid," she says, embarrassment washing across her face.

Gently, I grab her tiny wrist and give it a little squeeze. "No, it doesn't, Neena."

"What's it like there?"

"It's beautiful," I communicate. "You can see jungles on one end and beautiful beaches with blue water on the other. The food is amazing; papayas, tropical bananas, mangos . . ."

"Is that why you like it? The food?"

"That's part of it." I shrug. "I went there for the first time when I was nineteen because a buddy of mine told me that's where the most beautiful women in the world are."

Neena grins. "Is that true?"

I chuckle lightly. "They do have some good-looking women there. No doubt about that."

"More beautiful than Mom?"

I inhale and can't help but smile at her question, but I answer her honestly. "There is no woman in this world like your mother. Believe me, I've looked."

Neena looks down at the magazine again. "Is that where you've been all this time?"

"No. I've . . . kind of been all over."

"Will you go back? To Brazil, I mean?"

"Maybe, one day. But right now, I'd rather hang out with you."

She looks back up at me and gives a halfhearted smile. "Maybe you can take me there, some day." The statement would sound hopeful if it was coming out of a healthy child's mouth. But hearing her say it, it sounds like she knows it'll never happen. But that doesn't stop me from promising it anyway.

"I'd like that," I reply.

When we pull into the office lot, I notice several vans in the parking lot, including the one the news reporter kids from the local high school were in the other day. Several people lollygag around outside on the sidewalk as we park.

"Who are they?" Neena asks. I'm not sure, but I'm sure as hell going to find out. We climb out and all eyes dart to us.

"Paul James?" a woman calls, and then they all swarm us. I take

Neena's hand and pull her to me as I push through the barrage of people throwing questions at me. When we finally reach the front door to the office, Ashley, the high school reporter, opens the door and rushes in behind us.

"I told you to leave," Clara spats at her.

"Neena," Ashley continues, ignoring Clara, "I want to tell your story. All of you." She looks around. "The world just wants to meet her," she says to Clara. "Her ad touched so many people. They just want to know who she is. And I want to be the one to tell this story."

Clara inhales deeply as she struggles to keep her cool. "Ashley," she states simply. "Leave."

Ashley frowns, seemingly hurt, before she looks at Neena. Handing Neena a little card, she says, "Maybe they'll change their minds." Neena takes the card and looks at it as Ashley walks out. We all watch her climb in the van, which has the same kid from the other day, Zane, driving, and they pull away.

"She's relentless," I snort.

"Well, they found us," Clara mumbles as she looks at the five people standing outside the office.

"I'm sorry, Mom," Neena murmurs as she drops her head.

"There's nothing to be sorry about," I assure her. "The important thing is, you guys found me. This . . ." I motion behind me to the people outside, "Will pass."

"Neena, why don't you go rest for a bit," Clara suggests.

"I'm not tired."

"Just for a little bit. Please."

"Fine." Neena turns to me, giving me an eye-roll. I have to fight not to laugh at her. "Bye, Paul."

"Bye, kid." I smile and kiss the top of her scarf-covered head. "See you tomorrow?"

"Will you tell me more about the places you've been to?"

"I think I can handle that."

She waves and scurries off down the hall. When the office door shuts, Clara turns to me. "I'll be meeting with the doctor in the morning for the results."

"Oh?"

Taking a deep breath, she exhales slowly. "I'll call you afterward."

I stare dumbfoundingly at her for a moment. Shouldn't *I* get to be there, too? Neena *is* my daughter, as well. I want to question her, demand to know why I wasn't invited, but I decide now's not the time. She's already frustrated with the reporters outside. "Okay," I answer instead. "I'll talk to you tomorrow."

CHAPTER FIFTEEN

Clara

"CLARA," DR. JONES says. "Would you like to tell her or would you rather I told her?" I know I need to answer him, respond somehow to this devastating news, but my throat is so tight with emotion right now that if I open my mouth I'm afraid I'll melt into a puddle of despair. Standing, he calmly gaits over to the watercooler and fills a small, plastic cup, then sets it on the desk in front of me. I'm sure he's been taught not to show fear or panic, since the patient or the family member he's delivering the bad news to is taking care of that all on their own. I bow my head and nod a thank you before taking the cup and swallowing down a small sip.

Paul is not a match.

Neena is going to leave me.

Oh, God.

My lungs burn, and I'm finding it hard to breathe. "Would you like a few moments, or would you like me to tell you where we go from here?" Dr. Jones asks as he returns to his cushy office chair. I bob my head yes in response. My body is starting to feel numb, preventing me from speaking. "You'd like me to go on?" he confirms. The pressure increases, and with my chest tightening, I nod yes again.

My baby is leaving. No parent should ever have to endure their child passing. I could be run over at this very moment by a speeding semitruck a hundred times and still not feel this level of pain. Staring blankly, I listen as he continues. After he tells me he'll give her meds for any pain or nausea, he gives me a list of local hospice places, reiterating I should get everything in order now, before things get really bad. On the outside,

I'm stoic. But inside, I'm a raging mess, screaming at the top of my blazing lungs. When he finishes, he escorts me to the door and squeezes my hand. I can't help thinking what a shitty job he has, having to tell a parent their child is going to die.

"Call me if you have any questions or if you'd like me to tell Neena." I bob my head once and exit his office. I refuse to break down in the hospital. I won't. I just need to make it to my car. By the time I exit the hospital, I'm sprint-walking, trying to get to my car before the dam of sobs and emotion break loose. When I'm twenty feet away from where I parked, I see Paul sitting on the hood of my car, his arms crossed, his eyes closed. I freeze and watch him for a moment. I know it's wrong, but a part of me hates him right now. He was our last hope. I needed one thing from him. I needed him to be a match.

Neena is going to die. And there's nothing I can do about it.

My breaths come out in fiery gasps and my knees buckle. I fall to the cracked concrete as a wail escapes me. And I bow down, letting my head rest on the cold ground as I cry.

Paul

SHE DIDN'T ASK me to come today, but I wanted to. I wanted to barge in the office and sit beside her to find out what the results were. But she'd probably have ripped me a new one, so I decided not to push. Instead, I found her car and decided to wait outside for her. I'm not a praying man. Not in the least. But I decided it couldn't hurt. So as I waited, seated on Clara's hood, I closed my eyes and prayed for the first time in a long time.

God. I know I'm a piece of shit. I'm not asking for me. I'm asking for the girl, my little girl. Please. Just please, God.

That's when I hear Clara cry out and open my eyes to find her crumpled on the dirty parking lot ground in a mess of tears.

Guess God is giving me my answer.

Standing, I take a moment to swallow back the ache climbing up my throat trying to choke me before going to her. She needs me to be strong.

When I reach her, I don't speak. Nothing I say will make a lick of difference. People passing by are staring, their gazes judgmental, and I want to kick their teeth out. Scooping her up in my arms, I carry her to her car and set her on the back, then I hold her.

Clara

MY FINGERS DIG into his back as I cling to him. His shirt is drenched with my tears where my head rests on his shoulder. His hand cups the back of my head, holding me as I unleash my greatest fear realized. I'm not sure how long he holds me, but eventually my sobs ebb and I manage to pull away from him, and when my gaze meets his, it almost sucks the breath right out of me.

Paul James is crying, too.

I fling myself back into his arms, squeezing him as his body convulses, fighting the anguish he wants to let out. When he pulls away, he wipes at his eyes with his palms and clears his throat.

"I'm sorry, Clara," he rasps. "I'm so sorry. I wanted to be a match. I wanted to save her. I mean . . . it's the least I could do after not being here for her for so long."

Taking one of his hands in mine, I squeeze it. As I'd wandered to my car earlier, a part of me wanted to blame him. The pettiest, smallest part of me. Aside from whatever flaws or shortcomings I see in him, I know he would cut the heart right out of his chest to save her. "It's not your fault," I manage through my own hoarse voice.

"How long do we have?"

"A few months, maybe half a year, if we're lucky."

He bites his lip and nods a few times, then surprises me by cupping my face in his hands. With his thumbs, he wipes at my cheeks. "Will you let me stay? Will you let me have this time with her, too?"

Nodding, I slide off the hood and straighten my shirt. There are so many conflicted feelings when it comes to Paul. But I know Neena wants to know him. I know, deep down in my heart, she would want him close. So no matter my reservations, I have to give this to her. And the only way to trust Paul won't disappear is to keep him right under my nose.

"Why don't you move in with us? You can have the guest room."

"Are you sure?"

Giving him a sad smile, I say, "Honestly, no. But she'll need us both." I don't tell him that maybe Neena isn't the only one that might need him.

CHAPTER SIXTEEN

Paul

AFTER WE TELL the news to Marcus, who takes it pretty rough, we decide the three of us should sit down and tell Neena altogether. I couldn't let them do it alone. Picking Neena up from Marcus's house where she's spent the afternoon hanging with Mei-ling, I take her home while Marcus closes up and Clara heads out determined to buy all of Neena's favorite foods for dinner. I think they both want some time to themselves to process and calm down before Neena sees them.

We pull in the driveway when Neena asks, "What's wrong?"

Feigning confusion, I reply, "What do you mean?"

"You're so quiet."

"Am I?" I hadn't realized I'd been silent most of the way here. I can't stop thinking about how awful it will be to tell her that I am not a match.

She watches me for a moment, her mouth in a tight, flat line. "Please don't lie to me. I hate liars. What's going on?"

Damn she's just like her mother. Intuitive and never settling for an easy answer. "Hate is not a nice word. It's just been a bad day," I admit, rubbing the back of my neck. And that isn't a lie. It's been an awful fucking day.

She turns her head, staring straight ahead, her voice stoic, when she asks, "You're not a match, are you?"

Fuck me. What do I say? I really don't want to lie to her, but I'm not sure I want to be alone when she discovers the truth. I'm chickenshit that way. "Uh, Neena," I begin.

"How did Mom take it?" She stops me.

Twisting her head so her gaze meets mine, I stare back and can tell she already knows. Squeezing the steering wheel, I let out a long sigh. "Pretty bad," I admit. Definitely bad. Atrocious, actually. And she wasn't the only one that felt that way. We all still feel like our worlds were rocked. And not in the good way, but in the shitty this-can't-be-happening sort of way.

She's silent for a long moment before she pulls the purple scarf off, revealing her bald head. She flips the visor down and stares at herself in the mirror, running her small hand over her smooth scalp. It's the first time she's let me see her without the scarf on and I have to admit, it's crushing. She's a twelve-year-old girl. She should be healthy and cutting out pictures in magazines of hairstyles she likes. That's what kids are supposed to do. Letting her head drop, she flips the visor up. "If I tell you a secret, will you promise not to tell anyone?"

"Yeah, of course."

She inhales deeply as if bracing herself for whatever she's about to say. "I'm a little scared to die."

My face tingles as the blood drains from it. I think I just literally felt my heart crack open. No little girl should have to think of things like this. Taking her hand in mine, I squeeze it and clear my throat, the whole time fighting the tears burning in my eyes. I'm not a crier—not by any means, but this kid gets to me. My kid.

"Don't cry, Paul," she warns me. "Please. I just needed someone I could say that to. Mom, she just . . . is always so positive and I know it's just because she loves me and doesn't want to give up, but . . ."

"But what?"

"I just needed to say it . . . or be able to say I'm scared without being told everything will be okay."

I nod in understanding. "You can say anything to me, Neena. I'm here to listen."

"I just . . . want everyone to be okay."

"We will be . . . eventually," I lie, before adding, "that doesn't mean we won't miss you like crazy every single day, kiddo."

The faint smile she gives me does nothing to ease the ache in my chest. I'd gladly take her place, take on her cancer, and keep it for myself if I could. I've lived. Now should be her turn. When Clara pulls up beside us, she lets out a long breath. "This is going to be a long night," she whispers. Then she opens the door and climbs out, leaving her purple scarf behind.

Hours have passed. Marcus and I are standing in the kitchen, drinking beer, when Clara returns from checking on Neena after she went to bed. When she enters, she looks like a ghost; her face pale, dark-lined eyes riddled with pain. The three of us joined here tonight to tell Neena the tragic news and planned to comfort her as best we could. But Neena, the old soul that she is, ended up comforting us. She truly is wise beyond her years.

First she hugged Clara, holding her tightly as Clara sobbed. Then when Marcus got choked up, she sat beside him and rested her head on his shoulder while she held his hand. I managed to hold it together; after all, she asked me not to cry, so I did my best to remain strong for her. This kid could give a lesson in strength. As I watched Clara and Marcus, I could see what Neena meant when she said she was afraid to die. I don't think she meant she fears the actual act—at least not entirely—but she fears its aftermath. I get it. She's afraid of what dying will do to the people she loves. She's afraid of what will happen to her mother when she's gone. She's the strongest kid I've ever met—strongest person for that matter. But even the strongest walls need reinforcement. How heavy the weight must feel to know you are deteriorating, yet feel like you need to remain tough for those you love. She needs me to be her pillar of strength so she can continue to be strong. Maybe she didn't ask for it specifically, but that's what I got from our conversation in the car. Plus, I feel it in my bones. And although I'm crushed, I'll do this for her. I will give her the strength she needs.

"She's asleep," Clara tells us.

"I think I'll be heading home now," Marcus announces as he throws his beer bottle in the trash. "Mei-ling will be crying all night when I tell her the news."

"Thank you for being here, Marcus," Clara says.

"Whatever you need—whatever she needs, I'm here." Then he looks up at me and adds, "That goes for you, too." He shakes my hand, hugs Clara, and heads out the door.

"Did you want to stay tonight and get your stuff tomorrow, or just come back tomorrow?"

Scratching the back of my neck, I answer, "I'll come back tomorrow with my stuff. Unless you want me to stay."

Her eyes seem to droop, her shoulders sagging as well. "If I ask you to lie on the couch with me and hold me, could you do it without thinking it means anything?"

I stare at her blankly for a moment. She's asking me to hold her—lie beside her soft body and hold her? I'm shocked. "I think I could handle that," I reply after a beat.

She exits the kitchen and I follow behind her into the living room. She stands by the sofa, waiting for me to lie down first. I can totally handle this. Can't I? I mean, I think I can. I can handle being so close to her in such an intimate way . . . *shit*. Maybe this isn't such a good idea. But I have to. She asked me to. She *needs* me to. I toe my shoes off and take my place, scooting as far back as I can to allow her enough room beside me. I extend the free arm I'm not lying on, letting her know I'm ready. She inhales deeply, releasing it slowly before she tentatively sits beside me and then lies down. Shimmying back, she curls her body into mine and the smell of fresh linens hit me. The woman still smells the same after all these years. It takes her a few seconds to adjust, but finally she stops moving and seems to sink on the spot. I move my hand awkwardly up and down her body without touching her. It's just dangling midair. My instinct is to wrap my arm around her, pull her further into me, but I'm not sure if that's what she wants. Thankfully, Clara answers for me when she grabs my hand and pulls it around her, holding my fist in her hand, and clutching it tightly to her chest.

"Thank you, Paul," she whispers, her voice trembling.

I squeeze her gently. "You're welcome, Clara." For the next hour or so, her body shakes as she weeps quietly, but she doesn't speak. I haven't always been good with words. And it would be cliché to say, *it's all going to be okay*. Those words in a moment like this would be wasted breaths. It's just like Neena mentioned earlier, she needed someone she could say things to without them spewing pretty words back at her. Clara just needs someone to hold her, let her cry, and let her be angry. She doesn't need me to say anything. She just needs to feel me. Eventually her crying calms, and her body relaxes as she drifts off to sleep. And just before I close my eyes, letting sleep pull me into the uneasy, dark abyss, I whisper, "I'm here, Clara. I'm here for you."

CHAPTER SEVENTEEN

Clara

I T'S NEARLY IMPOSSIBLE to crack my eyes open. I haven't slept so hard in years. But I'm incredibly warm to the point it's uncomfortable, and I have to pee, so I force my lids open and let the morning light leak in. My vision is blurry and I rub my eyes. When I open them again, the first thing I see is Neena with her camera—pointing directly at me. She's wearing a black beanie, her perfect dark eyes peering at me as she holds the camera in her lap, the side screen tilted so she can see what she's filming.

"Sleep well, Mom?" she preens.

"I slept okay," I croak. "How about you, baby?"

She grins. "You're *so* not awake yet."

I roll my head back with a sigh and hit my head on something. I jerk as Paul grunts, placing a hand to his forehead where I just headbutted him.

"Shit," I gasp.

"Language," Neena laughs.

"What time is it?" Paul rasps.

I practically fly off the couch. I didn't mean to fall asleep on the sofa with him. I just needed . . . I don't know what the hell I needed. I guess I just needed to be held and Paul was there. But clearly that was a mistake. I don't want Neena dreaming up some fantasy that Paul and I might reunite.

"It's seven," Neena answers. "Sleep well, Dad?" Paul pushes up, his gaze jerking to Neena before moving to mine. My eyes widen. She just called him *Dad*. I guess noting Paul's reaction, she asks, "Is it okay if I call you that?"

Paul pushes himself up until he's sitting upright. Meeting Neena's stare head-on and placing a hand to his chest over his heart, he replies, "It would be my greatest honor, kiddo."

Neena smiles, then she looks to me. My heart wants to split in two. My beautiful girl is ill, but here she is, smiling. I want to give her a trillion more smiles in the time we have left. And somewhere deep inside where I'd built a wall to protect myself from Paul James, my fortress cracks. He's weaving his way back in. My instinct is to protect her, but I can't anymore. If he makes her smile like this in such a tremendously sad time, I must let him.

"I need to get to the office," I intone after a beat.

"Yeah," Paul adds, and clears his throat as he stands. "Think I'll go get my stuff together later today. The hotel has late checkout. I appreciate you letting me stay here."

"You're staying here?" Neena gasps, her excitement hard to miss.

"In the guest room," I clarify.

Neena springs up and rushes toward me, wrapping her skinny arms around my waist and squeezing tightly. "Thank you, Mom," she whispers. Then she hugs Paul and the biggest grin spreads across his face.

Thank you, he mouths.

I give him a small smile before heading to the bathroom, hoping I'm not making a huge mistake.

"Mom?" Neena questions, her tone dainty as we drive to the Sky High.

"Yes," I reply, before taking a sip of coffee from my travel mug.

"What's it like to have sex?"

I nearly spit my coffee all over the steering wheel and front windshield. Somehow I manage to swallow it, but end up coughing a few times. "Why are you asking me this?"

"Who else can I ask?"

Sticking my mug back in the cup holder, I place both hands on the steering wheel, stiffening my arms, bracing myself for this conversation. "I'm glad you're asking me, sweetie. You can always ask me anything.

I'm just curious *why* you're asking."

She shifts in her seat, her hands knotted in her lap, a nervous habit she got from me. "If I tell you why I'm asking, will you promise not to cry?"

Damn. I don't even know what she's going to say and I already want to cry just because she is asking me not to. I take a deep breath to steady myself. "I promise."

"I'll never have sex." She gives a little shrug. "Not like I want to now, but one day I think I probably would have."

Don't cry, Clara. Do not fucking cry. You promised.

"I want to know what it's like."

Blinking rapidly, cursing the tears that are threatening to spill, I steel myself. "Well," I begin, not at all certain what will come out of my mouth next. "Sex is something that is really . . . wonderful when it's between two people that really care about each other. When two people love each other, being able to connect to one another physically is something truly amazing."

"What about people who have sex that don't love each other?"

I widen my eyes. I definitely have not had enough coffee for this conversation. "I suppose if two adults are consenting to it, sex can be good if they don't love each other, but definitely nowhere near as good as if they do."

"So the sex was *really* good with Dad?"

"Neena," I say, under my breath. "You really want to know that?"

"Not the details, just want to know if that's what it was like with him."

I lick my dry lips and grip my steering wheel more tightly. Flickers of heated moments with Paul pulse through my veins; his mouth, his fingers dancing across my skin, the deep and raspy groans he would let out as we made love. "Yes," I answer. "It was like that with your father."

"Was he the only guy you've ever been with?"

I shake my head. As a mother, I hate to admit to my daughter I've had sex with more than one man. She sees me as this perfect woman. But I don't want to lie to her. "No, baby. He wasn't."

She chuckles a little. I think my honesty surprises her. "How many?"

"Neena!"

"One, two?"

"Four."

She scrunches her face up. "That's not very many, Mom. You're nearing forty. That's only like one a decade."

"Well, what can I say? Ages one to ten were rough years for me," I say, dryly.

"Okay, that's a good point. But it's still a low number."

I can't help laughing. "By whose standards?"

"I don't know. The modern woman," she sasses. "I read in a magazine that the average person has eight to ten sexual partners in their lifetime."

I twist my mouth. "What magazine did you read that in?" Apparently, I'm slacking on supervising her exposure.

"I don't remember," she mumbles.

"Well I don't think a person should feel the need to meet any definite number. Just because some statistic says society meets a number doesn't mean we have to."

"Well, you're below average."

"Sorry my number disappoints you, Neena," I chuckle.

"Do you think Dad has been with a lot of women?"

I snort. I cringe to think of that number. "You'll have to ask him that."

"I can't ask him that!" she shrieks.

Flicking my blinker and turning into the office parking lot, I say, "Then I guess we will never know."

"Are you sad you never got married?"

Parking the car, I turn off the ignition. She's out in full force today, asking me all the tough questions. "I was married," I admit. "Once."

Her eyes widen to the size of saucers. "What? To who?"

"His name was Kurt. It was a long time ago."

"How could you never tell me this?" The look on her face is sheer shock.

"I don't like to think about it, I guess."

"Do you still love him or something?"

I laugh. "No," I answer firmly. "But I did, or . . . thought I did, and he hurt me badly."

Neena deflates a little, her tiny mouth curving into a frown. "What an asshole."

"Neena!" I scold, even though I can't help smiling a little.

She cracks a little grin. "Sorry. But he sounds like one."

I pat her leg. "Do you think less of your mother now?"

She shakes her head animatedly. "No, Mom. I want to know more about you."

"I think I revealed all of my skeletons today," I say, as I open my car door.

Neena climbs out as well, and as I unlock the office door, we both turn at the sound of a van pulling in the parking lot. I sigh loudly. This little girl, Ashley, is relentless. I got us in two hours early in hopes of missing any reporters.

"Hurry up and get inside," I tell Neena. But Ashley practically hops out of the van while it's still moving and rushes in behind us.

"Ashley," I say her name firmly. "Enough of this. The answer is no."

"Actually," Neena says. "I want to give her the story."

I freeze as I stare at Neena blankly. "What story?"

"The story of you and Dad and your lives and how I came to exist."

Ashley, to her credit, remains silent, but I can tell she's fighting a smile. She thinks she's won. "Neena, you don't—"

"I'm dying," she snaps, shutting me up instantly. She's never spoken to me this way. "Maybe if I had a lifetime I'd get to hear the story of my parents bit by bit. Even if you don't want to tell me now because I'm young, you might have one day when I was older. But that's not going to happen, Mom."

"Neena, please—"

"I want to share this story, and I want to hear yours and Dad's."

"We can tell you the story. We don't have to make this public knowledge."

Stepping gingerly toward me, my heart nearly stops when she looks up at me and I see the tears brimming in her eyes. Neena hardly ever cries. Through all of this, the treatments, the sickness, the bad news, she's been strong. "Please do this for me, Mom."

Pulling her into me, and pressing her head to my shoulder, I exhale shakily. My sweet child wants our stories. She wants to know the path that led to her existence. But she's too young to understand how reliving the past can be painful. It doesn't matter though. Not anymore. I have so little I can give her right now other than my love and attention. If this will make her happy . . . "Sure. If Paul agrees, we'll do it."

CHAPTER EIGHTEEN

Clara

O F COURSE, PAUL agreed. Neena has him wrapped around her finger. With one phone call, all it took was a simple *pretty please* and he's on board. I think he'll do anything for her. After the call, he passed by Sky High and picked up Neena before heading to my place to get settled in. The two are two peas in a pod. They've been spending a lot of time together. Even when she appears worn out, she wants to be around him a whole lot. I've learned to give them space. And he's been super patient and delicate with her, especially when Neena pushes herself, so I'm starting to feel better about their time together. She's just so happy when she's near him. How can I not love that?

It's the first free weekend I can afford to sit down to be interviewed, a month after Paul gave it the go-ahead. "You're doing great," Ashley assures me. Mills gives me a thumbs-up from where he stands behind Zane and the camera. Marcus is holding down the fort up front, and Ashley and her crew and I are in one of the more spacious offices, which is usually occupied by both Bowman and Larry, while the guys are out with clients. We've already discussed how Paul and I met that terrible day many years ago when I failed to jump. But now she wants to know the gritty stuff. Stuff I haven't thought about in years. Stuff I hadn't realized I'd have to talk about.

"What happened when you went home to Texas?" Ashley asks. I hate talking about this. It was one of the worst days of my life. But Neena asked for this one thing. A true story of how it all came to be . . . how she came to be. So I start talking.

The flashbacks of thirteen years before, and my first interactions with Paul, coursed through my mind. My attempt—and fail—at jumping left me angry. What a horrible experience. Paul James was an arrogant ass and I wanted nothing to do with him ever again. The whole thing upset me so badly I went straight to my hotel, packed my bag, and headed to the airport. It's official, I would gladly sell my half to Paul after that experience.

In the cab ride to the airport, I called Kurt, but it went directly to voicemail. *He must be in a meeting*, I'd thought. *Shocker.* I'd call him later.

It took eight hours to make it home with layovers and such, and by the time I'd hit that blessed Texas soil, I was beat. The only thing I wanted was a warm bath and my husband. So I really hoped he was home. Through the hours of the long journey home, I was overwhelmed with gratitude. No matter how terrible life could get, I had my health, my friends, and Kurt. Our marriage wasn't perfect, but I loved him and I knew he loved me. He was extremely busy, but I could always count on that. Always.

After paying the cab driver, I drudged my achy feet up the stairs to our apartment, dragging my gigantic suitcase behind me, wondering what in the hell I packed. Unlocking the door, I pushed it open, yelling, "Babe!" It wasn't until I was inside that I bothered to look around and saw candles lit. Then I saw Kurt standing near the love seat, hands in the pockets of his slacks, watching me.

My eyes teared up. I hadn't realized the toll this trip had taken on me emotionally until then. The man that killed my parents left me half his business. I couldn't get over that fact. What a mind trip. My heart swelled as I took in the room, the beautiful candles, and my handsome husband. He was my rock; my steady.

"You're home," Kurt sputtered, his tone uncertain.

"Yeah," I sighed as I shut the door and flung myself on him. His arms gingerly wrapped around me. "I love you so much. Thank you for this."

"Clara," he grumbled my name as he peeled me away from him. "We need to—" The sound of the toilet flushing in the hall bathroom interrupted him, causing me to jerk back. Did I just hear that?

"Who's here?" I asked as the sink cut on for a moment before cutting off again.

Kurt dropped his head and pinched the bridge of his nose. "It's not what you think, Clara."

I stared at him a moment, waiting for him to clarify, but he didn't have to. The tall, leggy woman with long, brown hair that emerged from the restroom and froze when she saw me was enough clarification. Her eyes darted to Kurt, then back to me, then back to Kurt.

"Yes, that's right," I finally said. "I'm his wife who showed up unexpectedly. And you would be . . . ?"

"You should go Daisy," Kurt interjected.

"Her name is Daisy?" I asked in disbelief. Daisy, to her extreme credit, grabbed her purse and left. Kurt immediately turned the lights on and started blowing the candles out. My heart sunk realizing what a fool I was. I thought this was for me. But how stupid was that? Kurt didn't even know I was coming home. Of course it wasn't for me.

"Who is she?" I quietly gritted out.

"A friend," he mumbled as he lowered his head.

"How long have you two been seeing each other?" My anger anchored me, allowing me the strength to question him without breaking down right away. My voice was calm and steady, my gaze direct even though Kurt looked anywhere else but at me. *Coward.*

"I haven't slept with her," he stated as he picked up two candles and walked past me to the kitchen. "She's a friend."

Turning, I crossed my arms, my blood pressure rising as each second passed. "So you always hang out with your female friends in candle light?"

Shoving the candles into the cabinet, he shut the door and leaned his head against it for a moment before turning to face me. My stomach flipped when his gaze met mine. I could read his thoughts before he even spoke. He didn't love me anymore. Not like a husband should love a wife, anyway.

"I haven't cheated, Clara. I need you to know that. But if I'm being honest . . ." He paused and clenched his eyes closed before opening them again, "I've wanted to," he finished.

I blinked furiously in an attempt to stop the tears, but they fell anyway. "I thought things were better. I thought *we* were better."

Running a wide palm down his face, he squeezed his eyes closed and groaned. "I don't want children, Clara."

"But you wanted to try too. You agreed. We spent a year trying—"

"I wanted to make *you* happy," he interrupted. "You wanted a baby and I thought if it makes you happy, why not? But then when we got into it and it didn't happen . . . you changed."

"And I put it off to work on us," I defended, my voice raspy with hurt.

"Yes, but it feels like you're only going through the motions. Yeah, we hang out and have sex, but I can feel it in you. You're biding time until we can get back to trying again."

"That's not true," I cried. "I've given it my all."

He walked around the counter until he stood two feet before me. "And so have I," he said quietly. "But sometimes," he sighed with a frown, "that's just not enough."

"Kurt," I whispered his name ever so quietly, the word a plea for him not to do this. And even though I could reach out and touch him, I could hug him, claw him, or tear into his flesh with my teeth . . . it wouldn't have mattered.

He was already gone.

"I'm going to go stay with my parents for a while. I'd like to keep the apartment, but I know you'll need some time to make arrangements."

With that, he walked back to our bedroom and began packing his things. I sat on the couch, crying, holding my face in my hands, wondering if anything could possibly hurt as much as this. *Little did I know, many years later, I'd discover what pain really was.*

Ashley scoots back in her seat, visually uncomfortable, her mouth in a tight line. She's so young; only a senior in high school. I doubt she can even comprehend the magnitude of the story I just told her. Or, maybe she can. Maybe she wasn't expecting this kind of brutal honesty or so much detail.

"Kurt sounds like a dick," she surmises.

I almost choke on my saliva as I laugh. *So she does understand . . . kind of.* There was a time when remembering that conversation with Kurt would send me into a fit of tears, but now, it seems like something that happened in another life.

Seeing my reaction, Ashley chuckles, but she's determined. She wants the story, so she goes on. "So what happened after that? What brought you back to Virginia?"

"I guess I decided I needed a change." I take a sip of coffee before I continue.

Two days later, on Monday morning, I was back at work, but only in the physical sense. My mind was elsewhere. I worked at a prominent orthodontics office in the Dallas area. I loved it there. It was special to watch someone come in with a smile they hated and get to see them the day they got their braces off. Especially the adults. Those were the people who spent their lives hiding their teeth, hand cupped over their mouth, afraid to smile genuinely, who now left the office feeling like brand-new people. Seeing the kids was great, but adults appreciate it so much more. They knew how much it meant. The work aside, I *loved* my coworkers. They were nuts and it made each day, even the bad ones, fly by.

"You look like you're wearing clamdiggers, Vanessa," Ally noted. Vanessa looked down at her pants where she stood in front of the microwave, heating her soup. Vanessa stood at 5'8, with her legs making up most of her height. She chortled at Ally's statement, her big, bright, white smile beaming against her mocha skin.

"They shrunk in the dryer," she argued.

"You sure you're not wearing one of your kid's pants?" Ally continued.

"Shut up, Ally," Vanessa laughed. "They started as pants and now they're capris. You're just jealous I don't have to get a stepladder to reach anything over four feet tall."

"I'm not that short," Ally pointed out, and chucked a potato chip at Vanessa as she sat down with her sandwich. The chip landed on Vanessa's chest, her ample bosom preventing it from sliding off.

They both burst into hilarity before Vanessa took the chip and popped it in her mouth. "Thanks for the chip."

Ally unwrapped her turkey sandwich. "I almost don't want to eat," she told us. "I had Benji Rickman as my last patient this morning."

"That's rough," Vanessa noted as she gently blew on the spoonful of soup.

"I swear, I don't think the kid ever brushes his teeth," Ally said, her southern accent thick, especially when she was worked up about something. "I picked enough food out of his brackets to feed a third world country. And I'm pretty sure he ate SpaghettiOs for breakfast."

Vanessa dropped her spoon in her bowl of soup, cutting Ally an annoyed look. "Do you have to talk about that while I'm eating? For real?"

Ally snorted around the chip she had just popped in her mouth, her blue eyes filled with mirth. "Sorry. I wanted you both to share in my pain." She shrugged. "His gums were swollen over the brackets. Bled like a stuffed pig."

Vanessa leaned back in her chair and crossed her arms under her ginormous breasts. Ally threw her head back, laughing her ass off. What I loved most about my coworkers was we could say anything to each other. There was no shame. "She's about to make me lose my religion," Vanessa said to me. I smirked a little to show her I heard her, but I really wasn't listening. I felt like a zombie. The usual hysterics just weren't cutting it today. All I could think about was how my life was rapidly disintegrating.

Silence fell between us and when I looked up, I saw Vanessa giving Ally a pointed look while Ally shook her head no.

"What?" I asked. They both looked at me then back to one another. "What? Spit it out," I demanded.

"Tell her," Vanessa insisted.

Ally dropped her head and rest it on the table for a moment. When she raised her head again, uncertainty was rich in her eyes. "Um . . . When you were gone last week . . ." She paused, inhaling and exhaling awkwardly. "Jeb and I went down to Ft. Worth. We stopped for lunch and sat at the bar while we waited for a table. Jeb saw them first."

I cocked my head to the side as I stared at her through narrowed eyes. Jeb is Ally's husband. They're disgustingly in love and right now I hate them for it. Well, not really, but kind of. I refused to ask her who Jeb saw. Deep down, I already knew.

Ally gave Vanessa another awkward look. "They saw Kurt with a brunette," Vanessa finally stated, earning a dramatic eye-roll from Ally.

"Damn, Nes."

"What?" Vanessa asked, chewing the saltine in her mouth. "There's no sugarcoating that."

"I was trying to put it delicately." Ally moves her attention back to me. "Jeb and I could be way off base, Clara, but they looked . . . cozy."

Pushing my salad away, I sat up rigidly.

"You already knew, didn't you?" Vanessa questioned, reaching across the table and squeezing my arm.

"Did you?" Ally asked, her eyes widening.

"He told me Friday night. Or, rather, I walked in on them and then he told me."

"What a piece of shit," Ally gasped. "He had her in your apartment?"

I nodded then made a *pfff* sound. "He swears they haven't slept together."

Ally's mouth hung open. "Let me walk in on Jeb in our house with another woman. It's gonna be some Lorena Bobbitt shit all over again."

"That dude ended up in the porn business. You know, after it was reattached. Not sure that turned out like Lorena thought it would," Vanessa argued.

"I'm pretty sure a man getting his dick cut off is punishment, no matter how much porn snatch he got in the end," Ally pointed out.

"Ally," Vanessa snorted, lowering her head to hide her smile. "You are so . . . wrong, on so many levels." Most of the time, Vanessa was a woman of high regard. On the rare occasions, she slipped. I imagined she was more like Ally and I before she had children, but her kids were her life, and she worked hard to live right in both thought and action. She tried to provide examples not only to her children, but to everyone. Ally just knew how to push her buttons. Regardless, I admired Nes. Watching her with her kids made me want one of my own so desperately; to not only feel that level of love, but to give it. It was beautiful. Ally, also a wonderful person, had a dirty ass mind. But she was by far one of the brightest people I had ever met—both in mind and spirit. She could take the worst situation and bring laughter to it. I cherished them both as friends. It's rare to find people you can tell your darkest secrets to and know that not only will they not judge you, but will help you find the bright side.

"I don't plan on removing any of his appendages, ladies," I cut in.

"So . . . what happened?" Ally asked. My eyes teared up with the question, and I wiped at them quickly.

"He isn't in love with me anymore," I rasped, my bottom lip quivering. "We're getting a divorce." It was in that moment I realized the hell the next few months of my life would be . . . maybe even years. Of course, people I knew would run into Kurt with his new girlfriend and report back to me. Especially friends. And even if they didn't, it was only a matter of time before I ran into them myself, and that was something I just couldn't bear.

I glanced up at my girls. Neither really knew what to say. Instead of speaking, they scooted their chairs closer to mine and took turns hugging me while I cried. When I managed to calm down a bit, I told them about my trip to Virginia and the business that was left to me.

"Now what the hell am I supposed to do?" I hiccupped.

CHAPTER NINETEEN
Clara

"WELL CLEARLY YOU decided to come here," Ashley notes as she looks at the notebook she's been writing in. "How'd that come to be?" They all wait for my reply.

I've been sitting in one position for far too long. I adjust in my seat and clear my throat. I can't help smiling a little, even though at the time I felt like my soul was being crushed.

"Who farted? Vanessa?" Ally questioned as she twisted her neck and looked back at Vanessa.

"It wasn't me," Vanessa mumbled. She was sitting in the backseat, her head laid back on the headrest, as she dozed with one of those sleep masks on.

"This traffic is horrendous," I groaned. We were thirty minutes away from Sky High Skydiving when we hit traffic and hadn't moved in over an hour. I was grateful for their company on the trip, especially since they were only able to stay two days because they'd have to get back to work. When I'd told them my plans, there was no question for them—they were going to help me. At first, I wasn't comfortable with imposing on either of them. But Ally had quickly reassured me, stating, "Jed is a grown ass man. He can hold his own for a couple of days." Vanessa was also on board. Knowing how—understandably—attached she was to her kids, I waited till the weekend, when her husband volunteered to visit with the grandparents.

"We could've flown if someone wasn't scared shitless of planes," Ally said, twisting her mouth. It was obvious she was talking about Vanessa who was terrified of flying.

"I don't want to die," Vanessa murmured.

"There is, like, a one in a million chance you'd die in a plane crash. You're more likely to die in a car wreck," Ally argued as she lowered her window and spit her gum out as if she were hawking a loogie.

"That was ladylike," I said dryly, to which Ally stuck her tongue out at me.

"But a car is on the ground," Vanessa muttered, getting back to the previous topic.

Ally looked at me and shook her head. She had huge brown sunglasses on that made her head look mutant and tiny and even though I couldn't see her eyes, I knew she was rolling them. I somehow managed to laugh quietly.

"Stop talking smack, Ally," Vanessa warned. Even with the mask on she knew we were laughing at her, which only made us laugh more.

We both burst into laughter as I put the car in drive because traffic started moving. Unfortunately, we only moved a tiny bit before stopping again. But, yay, we were getting closer. "It's good to see you smile, Clara," Ally said. "It's been a while."

For some reason the statement made me want to cry, but I fought it. It had been five weeks since Kurt abandoned me. And I wasn't feeling any better about it. Yeah, he was a major asshole, but I missed him. I hated the thought of divorce. I hated I'd failed—or rather *we* failed. He was my husband. I loved him. I wasn't ready to give up on him. I hadn't left when we'd failed at having a baby. And our failed marriage was something I stupidly would have worked on. So I didn't leave without giving it one more shot. I had to try. So I called him. He didn't answer. Then I called him again. No answer. At that point, I was not going to sugarcoat it . . . it hurt like hell. After three weeks and three voice mails, he finally returned my call and agreed to meet me for coffee.

I got to the Mean Bean Coffee Shop twenty minutes early. He was thirty minutes late—as if I wasn't already feeling pathetic enough for begging him to meet with me. As he sat down, he wouldn't even make eye contact with me, and it crushed me.

"Thanks for meeting me," I managed.

"I only have ten minutes. I have to get back to work."

The blood drained from my face as a new wave of pain set in. Ten minutes? That was all he could spare for me? Damn, that hurt. I'd never felt so shunned in my life. Even if he didn't want to be with me anymore, couldn't he show some kind of . . . feeling? Some respect? I was his wife, and we'd spent years together. Didn't I deserve that?

I pushed down the hurt and inhaled deeply. "I miss you." It was hard to say. Not because it wasn't true. It was *so* true. Why I missed him, I had no idea, especially when he was acting so cruelly. Scratch that. I knew why this was so difficult to swallow. I'd lost my parents through a cruel twist of fate. I didn't take being left very well. I was lonely. It was also hard because I was opening up to him. I was handing him the power to intentionally hurt me more by dismissing me or belittling my feelings. Not to mention my pride. His rejection would be the final blow to what dignity I had left.

He closed his eyes for a minute before opening them again and meeting my gaze, as if I was exhausting him. "Daisy is pregnant."

I went numb.

Sometimes, something hurts you so badly, and the pain is so much, your body and mind somehow shut down to it. So *this* was what it meant to be shocked. I was in full-on shock. His face contorted. He knew what that news was doing to me—how it was killing me.

"It's still very early," he continued, without a care in the world. "Only a couple of weeks. She just took the test yesterday. I thought you should know. Maybe now the calls will stop."

When I didn't respond, he must've realized how cruel he had sounded. He made me sound like a pesky telemarketer. *Maybe now the calls will stop.* He went on to assure me they hadn't slept together until after he and I had split. But just as quickly as his integrity had shown up, it went away in the snap of a finger, and he informed me that she was going to move into our apartment with him. That I was to look for a new home because he was tired of staying in her tiny studio. I guess he didn't stay with his parents like he'd said he would. At some point, in spite of my inability to respond to his news with words, my body shook and my eyes teared up. This was when he decided to make his exit.

"I'm sorry, Clara, but I have to go." Yep. I was on the same level of importance as a goddamn telemarketer. Standing, he pulled a large manila envelope out of his briefcase and placed it on the table. "We can save a lot of money if the divorce isn't contested. I'm happy to pay for it, if that's the case. I just need your signature for the separation agreement."

When he turned to go, I panicked. I didn't want him to leave, but I knew it was over. He didn't want me anymore. And even if he had, there was no going back. He'd made irrevocable decisions. It didn't matter how much I loved him, there were just some things a person couldn't overlook. I panicked because I couldn't bear the thought of him leaving believing I was pathetic; believing I was just going to be sitting around pining over him and crying myself to sleep every night. I couldn't bear to look that weak.

"I'm moving to Virginia," I blurted out. He turned back, tilting his head to the side in question. "I'm not selling the business. I'm moving there and starting fresh." In my brief time with Paul James and his small friend, I hadn't realized my capacity to hate a situation. They were nitwits running a business half-assed. But as awful as they were and as scary and risky as it was to move to Virginia to start over, it paled in comparison to how truly awful staying in Texas where Kurt and his expecting girlfriend would be.

"I thought you didn't want to work there—that it was too painful?"

Standing, I picked up the envelope and approached him. I was trembling, barely holding it together. His news had destroyed me. It took all of my strength to hold strong; to stop my body from shaking with emotion. But somehow I managed. I ignored his statement. He didn't get to know my feelings anymore.

"I'm leaving at the end of the month. I'll be out of the apartment by the twenty-ninth. Then you and Daisy can move in and start your lives together. I'll make sure your attorney gets my forwarding information."

"Clara," he said my name as if he didn't understand.

My grandmother, who raised me, always said in moments like this, when you want to scream and yell, you should take the high road. *Kill them with kindness,* she'd say. I'd like to say I heeded this advice often, but that would be bullshit. Frankly, I rarely took the higher road, but this time, I did. Standing on my tiptoes, I held his shoulder with one hand as I kissed him chastely on the cheek. Leaning in so my mouth was to his ear, I whispered, "I wish you all the happiness in the world."

I walked out and didn't look back. The moment I got home, I called Richard Mateo and informed him I would not be selling my half of the business.

"GPS says ten minutes," Ally said, pulling me from my memories.

"Praise Jesus," Vanessa moaned. "I have never had to pee so bad in my life."

"Except for the last time you needed to pee two hours ago when you said the same exact thing," Ally replied, as I glanced in the rearview mirror. Vanessa whipped off her mask and chucked it at Ally, hitting her on the shoulder.

"Okay, guys," I interrupted. "Get ready. Traffic is moving again, so we'll be there soon. And these guys are douche bags."

"Do they know you're coming?" Vanessa asked.

"Unless Mr. Mateo told them, no."

"Well," Ally sighed. "This should be interesting."

CHAPTER TWENTY

Paul

IT'S TWO WEEKS after Clara's first interview, on a Wednesday evening, and I'm sitting in front of the pimple committee, about to recount my past. "You seem nervous," Ashley notes as Mills slips the tiny mic on the collar of my shirt.

"Do I?" I snort. "Done a lot of interviewing in your vast career of journalism? Who's the last person you interviewed? The lunch lady? Covering the hot story of high calories in school lunches?"

She narrows her eyes at me. "It's not my interviewing experience that leads me to believe you're nervous."

"Oh, no? Then what makes you think I'm nervous?"

Raising one cocked brow, she sasses, "The sheen of sweat across your forehead. The way the light is hitting it, it's almost blinding me." The guys snicker.

I can't help smiling slightly. For such a young girl, she sure is a smart-ass. "So . . . how does this work?"

"I ask a question, and you answer."

"How'd Clara do?"

Ashley smiles sadly. "She did well. We covered a lot of hard . . . topics."

"Oh, yeah?" I raise my brows, wondering what *hard topics* she spoke of.

I saw Clara just before I came in here for my part, but she wouldn't make eye contact with me. She'd walked out mentioning she had some errands to run, which I knew was bullshit, and that she'd meet me later on at her house. Since I moved in, things have been a little . . . off. I thought maybe she was still feeling awkward about us falling asleep on the couch together. That would be my only guess as to why she's been avoiding me. Neena had insisted on staying here with me but after a few minutes she got tired so Marcus took her back to Clara's office so she could nap.

"Well, where do you want me to start?"

"How about . . ." Ashley taps a pencil against her chin as she answers, "The day she came back to Virginia and you discovered she was your new partner."

I lean back in my chair, releasing a long breath. What a day that was.

"So, just start telling it?"

"Yep. I'll stop you if I have any questions."

We'd just gotten in from our last dive of the day. Marcus was waiting in the front with everyone's checks. Bowman rushed in, grabbed his, and split with a wave to us all. He had a date that night and was in a rush. Sap moseyed in behind me, taking a long swig from his flask as he did. Without a word, he walked up to Marcus and offered it to him. Marcus took the flask and Sap took his check. Sap had worked here since my uncle began and ran the joint, and I imagined the old goat would never retire. He liked this shit too much. Marcus threw his head back and barely managed to choke down his sip before he began coughing and hacking.

"What the hell is it?" I asked.

"That's some shine my cousin made," Sap laughed as he slapped Marcus on the back a few times. His face had turned fire engine red.

"Maybe a little warning next time, you old bastard," Marcus managed. "I thought it was bourbon." He slid a piece of paper across the table to me. "Found this today. Looks like you have a new partner."

I hadn't heard from Richard in weeks, and last we'd spoke, he'd said he believed my potential co-owner of Sky High Skydiving was going to sell. "They decided not to sell?"

"The envelope was postmarked two weeks ago. Might have known if you'd open the damned mail once in a while."

"I do the labor here," I argued. "Not the paperwork. Besides, I thought you would do it once Dennis passed."

"I'm an accountant/business advisor. Not a secretary." Marcus had worked for my uncle for years before I did. He was a foster kid that had been bounced around from home to home. Supposedly, Marcus was an emotional kid. Growing up with his condition earned him a lot of unwanted attention and undeserved bullying. He'd come into my uncle's office, begging for a free dive. When my uncle said no, Marcus returned that night and broke every window in the front office. This was Marcus's second arrest and by all means, my uncle should have pressed charges. Instead, he adopted him. Dennis Falco was a man I respected on so many levels. He'd always treated me like his own son and helped my mother— his sister—when my father bailed. When my career ended as a stunt man, he'd welcomed me here with opened arms. Skydiving was an amazing rush; something I'd needed badly at the time. This was the perfect fit for me.

"Pretty sure the will stated you became secretary when he died," I jested.

"Maybe we need to hire someone," Marcus ignored my joke and continued yapping.

"Yeah, maybe," I snorted. "But no hot ladies," I warned. "We'd never get Dirty Sap out of the office. He'd be in here flirting with her all day. Isn't that right, Sap?"

But Sap wasn't paying attention. He was looking out the large front window into the parking lot, a grin slowly spreading across his stubble-filled, wrinkled face. "Well I'll be . . ."

I dropped my pack as we watched Clara, aka Ms. Chickenshit, and two other women walking toward the door.

"Oh shit," Marcus groaned. "I wonder what she wants." The woman was sure one to leave an impression. After Clara had stormed off that day not so long before, we'd had a good laugh about it. What else could we do? It was obvious to us she simply had no sense of humor and a very large stick stuck up her ass. One of the women with her, a tall, dark-skinned woman, zoomed past her and rushed in the door.

She was bouncing like a two-year-old as she asked, "Bathroom?"

"For paying customers only," Marcus replied as he slid off his chair and moved to stand beside me.

"I have to pee so badly, my eyeballs are floating, sir," she argued with a hint of attitude. "So unless you want me to go right here on your floor, I suggest you tell me where in the h-e-double hockey-sticks the bathroom is."

Marcus and I cut a look to each other. Was this chick for real? Who in the hell says, 'h-e-double-hockey-sticks'?

"Third door on the right, down this hall," Sap replied, his face still lit with a grin. Dirty bastard. As the woman bulldozed through us like a defensive lineman, Clara and the other woman entered. Clara had her hair up in a messy knot and she wore those weird capris sweatpants things, with a white tank top. The tiny woman with her wore a pair of black shorts that I later noticed had *Juicy* written across the back, with a huge sweatshirt with a picture of a skull on it. When they walked in, the small woman looked around. Clara met my stare dead-on and squared her shoulders.

"Mr. James."

I'd almost called her by my favorite nickname. For the few days we laughed about her after her failure to jump, we'd called her a shrew. I doubted that would go over well just then, so, crossing my arms, I replied, "That'd be me."

Darting her gaze to Marcus, her mouth twisted, and she rolled her eyes before looking to me again. "I'm sure you remember me."

"I remember you," Sap piped up, flexing his eyebrows up and down a few times.

The woman standing beside Clara snorted a laugh out at his words. Just then, the tall one came back in from the bathroom. She stopped, looked to Marcus, and said, "You're out of toilet paper."

Marcus scowled at her. "We'll get right on that."

"So this is it?" the tall woman asked as she took a slow spin around, taking in the room. "It does need a little revamping, but you'll get it there."

"Excuse me?" I laughed at her absurd statement.

"Just needs some TLC," Clara sighed, as she too looked around.

"Where's the bathroom, Vanessa?" the short woman requested.

"Down the hall, third door on the right. But they need to put some TP in there."

The short woman looked to me, then to Marcus, where we both stood with our arms crossed. Neither of us offered to restock the bathroom for her, nor would we. Who in the hell are these women and why did the shrew come back here?

"Come with me, darling," Sap told her as he gestured a hand down the hall. "I'll get you what you need." Goddamn it, Sap! As he led her down the hall, he walked about two steps behind her, stopped, twisted his head, his brow wrinkled in confusion. "Juicy?" he almost mouthed the question before turning back and following her. Marcus gave me a sly look as his mouth curled up on one side in humor. Obviously he was checking out her ass. Sap was a dirty old man, but we loved it.

"So this is the guy?" the tall one questioned as she jabbed a thumb in my direction. Before Clara could respond, she added, "Great day, girl. You weren't lying about how hot he is."

Clara's eyes nearly bugged out of her head as her cheeks flamed red. "Vanessa!" she hissed as she slapped her friend's arm.

"What?" Vanessa whined as she rubbed her arm. "You said it."

I couldn't help but take a stab at her. "You hear that, Marcus? I'm hot."

Clara closed her eyes and breathed deeply, willing herself not to respond to me goading her. Marcus fluttered his lashes at me and chuckled, and started coughing because he wanted to outright laugh, but was fighting it. The one we now knew as Vanessa bolted toward him and raised his arms above his head, smacking him on the back. "Get it out, little man," she said.

Marcus immediately jerked free and backed away from her. "What the hell are you doing, lady?" he choked out.

"When my kids cough like that, I raise their arms above their heads and it helps them get it out."

"I'm not a kid, lady!" Marcus wheezed.

"She was only trying to help," Clara defended her friend, her hands on her hips.

"Well, I don't want her help," Marcus argued.

Clara shook her head in disbelief. "Okay, Vanessa," she said sternly. "Why don't you and Ally go grab a bite while I look around? I saw a sub shop up the road." Then moving her gaze to me, her mouth quirked up in a small smile, as she goaded, "I need some time to get to know *my* new business partner."

Widening my eyes, I let my mouth drop open. *Fuck*. Marcus looked to me, his eyes rolled back as if they were stuck in the middle of an eye-roll. "No fucking way," he droned out.

The room fell silent for only a split second until Sap's hoarse and raspy laugh bellowed from down the hallway, killing the quiet. Apparently he overheard Clara's last statement and found something about it incredibly amusing. He walked in, still chuckling. His body shook as he attempted to control his laughter, his gaze darting between Marcus and me. Taking a few steps toward Clara, he tipped his worn-out Chevy hat and rasped, "Well, welcome to the family, sweetheart."

"So you had no idea who inherited the other half of the business?" Ashley asks, staring at her notebook.

"My uncle wanted it kept private until Clara made her decision. I wouldn't figure out until much later why that was."

Ashley peeked up slightly, her head still down as she continued to scribble on her pad. "And why was that?" I hate—and have always hated—knowing exactly how my uncle was affiliated with Clara. It repulses me to know why he left her half of his business. Rubbing my palms on my pants, I answer, "I think that's a story for Clara to tell. Not me."

"Fair enough." Ashley nods. "So Clara arrived, you found out she's your partner . . . and what happened next?"

I gave her a less than thrilling tour of the office and a basic description of everything. She listened, took notes on a legal pad, and didn't speak a word to me. At the end of the tour, we walked in to the back office and I plopped down in the chair, putting my feet up on the desk.

"I'm curious," I began. "Why did my uncle leave *you* half of his business?"

"I've asked myself that a few times," she snorted.

"Were you his . . ." I didn't finish my thought. *Lover?* No. Even then I knew that couldn't be. Uncle Dennis was a stud in his prime, and it was weird he'd kept something of this caliber to himself, almost sub rosa, for so long, but I doubted he could've pulled in a woman of Clara's youth and looks at his age and no one be the wiser. But what else could it have been?

Clara narrowed her eyes at me. "His what?"

I shrugged, somewhat uncomfortable with what I was asking, but not at all afraid to ask. "His lover?" I finished.

Her mouth pinched into this weird thing where she seemed to be fighting a huge, crazy smile of disdain. The look she gave me said: *No. I was not his lover. You're an asshole.*

"I'm just trying to understand here. Who are you? How did he know you?"

Walking over to the back wall where we kept a bulletin board of photos from jumps, she crossed her arms and stared. Most of the photos in the front of the office where customers entered were of me. This board, however, held mostly photos of my uncle.

"He looks like he led a very full and exciting life." The way she said it raised my hackles. She said it as if it made her mad he'd lived a happy life. Putting my feet down, I stood and rounded the desk while I watched her. For some reason, I felt the need to defend Dennis even though I had no idea what I was defending him against. In the short time, and very few interactions I'd had with Clara, I'd seen very few dimensions to her. She was a ballbuster, definitely. But oddly, I found it attractive. She was uptight; her sense of humor nonexistent, it seemed. But in that moment, while she stared at the photos of my uncle, I saw pure and unadulterated vulnerability. Something about looking at those photos broke her heart. And for the briefest of moments, her façade of being unbreakable slipped away, revealing what lay beneath.

"He was a great man. He led a great life," I pointed out.

Turning back to me, she dropped her arms. "I bet," she murmured, but the words didn't sound authentic.

Then it hit me. I stood to my full height. "Shit," I mumbled. How could I not have thought of it before? "You're his daughter?"

This time, she put no effort into hiding her displeasure. Her expression read: disgust. "No. I am most definitely not *his* daughter."

I didn't respond. I had no idea what to say. Clearly, this woman, my new business partner, not only hated my uncle, but loathed him. So why would he leave her half of his business?

Clara, apparently tired of discussing her affiliation with Uncle Dennis, moved on. "I hope we can work together to make this business flourish."

"It does pretty well as it is," I defended. I didn't need her help, and for a woman who couldn't even find the courage to jump out of a plane, even in tandem, I wondered how in the hell she could possibly think she had anything to offer this business.

"There's always room for improvement," she answered simply.

I snorted. "Well, since you're such an authority on skydiving," I added dryly.

"Can I use this as my office?" She ignored my smart-ass comment.

"We can share it. I guess. I'm not in here often," I grumbled.

"Good," she acknowledged. "I need a key. Where can I get that?"

Begrudgingly, I rounded the desk and opened the top drawer, pulling out my uncle's set that had been in there for weeks. "These were Dennis's. Feel free to take off the engraved key chain." I didn't even know what in the hell they were. Initials and a date. I tossed them to her and she caught them, staring at the key chain in the palm of her hand. She was frozen as she looked at it. At that point, I was pissed off and tired. In the span of a day, I'd gone from thinking I would own this business solo, to finding out I had a very unwanted, uptight business partner that knew nothing about skydiving. I was done.

"We good?"

Closing her fist around the keys, she clutched them to her chest. "I'll see you in the morning."

That first week after Clara arrived was hell. We hated her. Marcus especially. She demanded to see all the financial information and wanted to get new software to help manage the business's spending. Marcus had a system, even if he was the only one that could understand it, and he was pretty damn efficient. He didn't like having her come in and start taking over what he felt was an already well-oiled machine. She stated we would have a biweekly meeting with the staff. At the first one, she informed everyone they would be needed Sunday evening to help "revamp" the office. Sap was excluded as he had a bad back, but everyone else was required to show. She needed painters. *No one* liked that idea. That's because her little idea was pure bullshit. Why would they want to give up their Sunday evening?

"The guys are paid to jump," I pointed out as I followed her into the office after the meeting had concluded. She plopped her notebook on the table and started fingering through a stack of papers.

"And this office as a whole is the first impression. It looks awful. This is where they work and asking them to help out one night is not that much to ask."

"We can hire painters," I protested. "Or you can call your little friends to come back and help you."

She laughed, ignoring my dig. "No, we can't. We need to save as much money as we can for advertising."

"We have a budget for that."

"Not a big enough one."

"Look," I affirmed. At the sound of my tone, she stopped shuffling through the papers and gave me her undivided attention. "Painting the office and making it look "pretty" isn't going to do shit. People come here to jump. For the experience. Not for pretty-colored walls and comfy couches. This isn't a fucking showroom."

"It's funny you think the experience is solely the jump. Yes," she agreed, "the jump is the biggest part, the finale, but it's not everything. We can give our clients, from start to finish, an incredible day starting with entering a clean, well-managed office with a friendly staff."

"What the fuck is wrong with the staff?" I huffed. "We *have* a friendly staff," I argued.

She scoffed at me. "You have Marcus playing pranks on paying customers, Sap eye-fucking anything with tits, and *you* with shitty manners."

Damn. She was crass.

I shook my head and groaned in annoyance. "Tell me something, sweetheart. You say we're doing all of this wrong, yet somehow we make a profit. Explain that."

She walked up to me, inches away, and put her hands on her hips. "Luck."

I took a step toward her, so our faces were merely an inch or two away. *That was a bad move.* She smelled incredible, and how had I not noticed before that her eyes had little flecks of green in them? "Um. Well, it's working."

"Did you know there are three other skydiving businesses in Virginia?"

"I am aware," I mumbled, narrowing my eyes at her. "What's your point?"

"Do you know what your referral numbers are?"

"Not off the top of my head."

"Based on the website bookings alone, where a majority of your jumps are scheduled, they can enter how they heard about us, and referrals are only at two percent. That . . ." She gave my chest a hard poke, "Is shameful."

My blood pressure was rising. "We work our asses off here. And we've made it work. Dennis built this business from the ground up."

"Paul," she snapped. "I don't give a shit about who did what or how they did it. I see a business with potential to grow, to profit more. Are you really going to complain about the possibility of making *more* money?"

"No," I argued. "I'm complaining about working with a goddamned tyrant. You're set to suck all the fun out of this place."

"Painting some walls and replacing some furniture is not sucking the fun out of anything. Expecting everyone employed here to be polite and do their job is exactly that . . . their job!"

I threw my hands up. "Fine. Do what you want. I'm out."

"You'll be here Sunday, won't you?"

Giving her a bogus Army salute, I sarcastically said, "Sure thing, Sergeant." What was this chick smoking? There wasn't any way anyone could have misinterpreted what I was really saying, but just in case, I added, "If you want to paint this place, fine. But I'm not spending *my* night off doing it."

Shaking her head, she turned away from me, and I left. I hadn't realized after our meeting the entire staff was still sitting in the front office, listening to every word we'd said. A few whistled and clapped as I stormed out. I wasn't sure I liked that. I didn't think Clara fit, and I didn't want her for a partner, but at the same time, she *was* my partner and these people were her staff. I had just said I wouldn't be there Sunday, and now they thought they wouldn't have to be there either. Looking back, I wish I would have said something to them, but Clara got under my skin. So, I let them treat her badly. I let them disrespect her.

Maybe she'd leave if she saw they hated her.

Ashley stares at me, her expression stoic.

"Not my proudest moment," I admit.

"No, I would hope not," she agrees quietly. Mills excuses himself and makes his exit. Lucky bastard.

Shame floods me. I was a young, stupid man. But I guess it doesn't matter that I've matured . . . well, mostly.

"Well, I think that's all for today. Same time next week?" Ashley asks.

Fuck it. Why not? "Yeah, sounds good."

I shut the door behind me as I leave the office, letting Zane and Ashley clean up. I'm halfway down the hall when I hear Neena giggle.

"They're playing at the National next month."

"I love Masters of the V," Neena gushes as I round the corner into the front.

"Yeah, they're one of my favorites, too," Mills tells her. They're sitting on the love seat, sharing a set of earbuds and staring at Mills' iPhone. Well, Neena seems to be staring at Mills while *he* stares at his phone.

"They're ready for you to help clean up in there, Mills," I snap, causing him to jerk up, the earbuds falling out of both of their ears.

"Oh, ah, yeah, cool. Good seeing you, Neena," he mumbles as he gives a little wave and clumsily rushes down the hall. Neena lets out a long sigh as she watches him exit. Looking at her better, I notice something different. Her lips are pink and glossy.

"Are you wearing makeup?"

She immediately crosses her arms and scowls a little. "Yeah. So?"

I scratch my head. "Just curious . . . You ready to go, kid?"

"I'm not a little kid, Dad," she retorts.

I lift my brows in shock. I've called her a kid quite a few times and she's never complained. I want to point that out to her, but Ashley, Zane, and Mills enter the room, carrying their bags with them.

"Later, guys," Zane calls.

Mills is the last one to leave and he gives Neena an awkward little nod as he pushes through the doors to the parking lot. Neena waves, her pale cheeks turning the slightest shade of pink as she smiles at him.

Why do I feel so . . . angry right now? Not really angry, just . . . protective. She just waved at him. And he didn't do anything. There's absolutely nothing to get upset about.

"Now are you ready to go, princess?" I had to add the last part just to mess with her.

"Daddddd," she groans as she drops her face in her hands.

"What?" I mock confusion. "You are my little princess."

"And I thought Mom was the embarrassing one," she murmurs as she stands, her eyes glued to the parking lot as Ashley, Zane, and Mills load up the van.

"No, she's just the mean one." When Neena looks up at me and sees my grin, she giggles because she knows I'm joking.

"I'm telling her you said that," she threatens.

"No!" I gasp, clutching my chest. "Please. Anything but that."

"I'm sorry, but you did this to yourself, old man." She smirks.

I pull out all the dramatics. "Your mother will end me. I'll never see the light of day again!"

"I'll keep this between us on one condition," she offers.

"I'll do anything. Whatever you want," I say, animatedly. "I'll run outside naked and dance on their van if that's what it takes!" And I point out the window.

"Oh my God, please don't do that."

"Then tell me, Neena!" I drop to my knees and crawl toward her, my hands clasped together as if in prayer.

She laughs hysterically when I grab her and hug her tightly, while continuing to plead. "Okay, okay!" She gasps for breath after laughing so hard. "You can call me kid, kiddo, or princess, whatever you want, just not in front of other people, okay?"

"Can I call you princess-kid?"

"You're so weird, Dad," she snickers as I squeeze her harder. "Princess-kid . . . just not in front of anyone, okay?" she reiterates.

I sit back on my heels and chuckle, my chest tightening at the sight of her. I've been around the world and seen some of the most beautiful places, but nothing compares to seeing her laugh. "Okay, kid. It's a deal."

CHAPTER TWENTY-ONE

Clara

"I'M GOING TO go take a shower before dinner, Mom!" Neena yells to me from the front door as she and Paul enter.

"Hello to you, too!" I yell back.

"Hi, Mom, love you," she responds before I hear her footsteps as she charges up the stairs.

When Paul enters, he stands in the doorway of the kitchen, frozen. His hair is a bit of a mess and his face has that day-old scruff, the trace of gray lightly lacing through the dark, coarse hair. I hate that he looks sexy even when he looks like shit. It takes me a few seconds to stop staring at him. I guess I'm getting my fill since I fled from him earlier. "You're cooking?"

"Ha-ha," I mock dryly. "I can cook."

He stares at me blankly.

"It's macaroni casserole," I grumble. "Any idiot can make it." Why do I feel the need to explain myself? I *can* cook, a little. His face lights up with his signature grin, showing all of his stupidly white teeth, and I can't help smiling a little. He's laughing at me. "I hate you."

His laugh fills the room and I feel a rush go through me. The man's smile is lethal; pair it with his laugh—and it's game over. Here I am, back in the *suck*. Falling into the Paul James trap . . . *again*. "I got an already made rotisserie chicken from the store. Made a salad, too."

"You're a regular *Betty Crocker*," he quips as he plucks a cucumber off the salad and pops it in his mouth.

"How did it go?"

Paul reaches in the fridge for a beer and sighs. "I didn't realize how . . . hard it would be to talk about the past like that. Especially to a teenager."

"Tell me about it," I chuckle.

"You know, Clara . . ." The way he says my name causes me to look at him. "I'm sorry for the way I treated you when you first got here."

I'm stunned. I wouldn't have expected him to say that in a million years.

"I was an asshole." That either.

"True," I can't help adding, to which he owns with a few dips of his head.

"And I should've never let the staff disrespect you the way they did."

I swallow a few times because, damn it, it was hard, and turn back to my casserole. "I managed, and got through it," I reply. These are the days I hate to think about. I was fresh blood. Starting here was awful, but at the time the alternative—staying in Texas and possibly seeing Kurt with his new family—was far worse.

"I know. And you were right about so much. But I know that had to have sucked. If I had known what happened, why Dennis left you half, it would've been—"

"Different?" I sneer, cutting my gaze to him. "Wasn't it easier to assume I was his mistress or illegitimate daughter?"

"You should have told me," he replies calmly. "I understand why you didn't at first, but after we . . . when we were . . ." He pauses.

"You can't even say it," I challenge him.

He narrows his brows. "Why are you getting angry? I'm trying to apologize."

This time I spin toward him and put my hands on my hips. "For what exactly, Paul?" My skin heats as my tone thickens with ridicule. "Being a dick to your new business partner or for running off on me with no rhyme or reason? Or for not loving me? Which is it?"

He runs a hand through his thick, black hair. "I . . . thought you wanted other things."

"Maybe you should have asked me." Popping the oven open, I shove the dish inside and slam the door shut.

I spin around intending to stomp out of the kitchen, but he's here. Right here. I jump, startled, but he quickly grabs me and pulls me to him.

His body is still hard, not like it was years ago when he had that blessed gift that is the youth of your twenties, where you look at the gym and have a six-pack, but still, for a man his age, his body is primed. Tracing his fingers up the back of my neck, he fists my hair gently, forcing me to look at him. "Look at me. I fucked up," he rasps. "I know it. I've always known it. But I *did* love you, and I've never stopped. Hate me for leaving. Hate me for being a dick. But don't hate me because I didn't love you."

Then he kisses me. Soft and quick, long enough for his light beard to scratch against the delicate skin of my face, before releasing me. Stumbling back, I hit the counter and hold myself. I'm going to need a minute to process what just happened.

"On another note," he moves on. "I think Neena might have a little crush on that Mills kid."

I stare at him. He still loves me? He kissed me. I'm still processing the kiss. What's he talking about?

So he continues, "She got all excited when I called her a kid in front of him."

I manage to move robotically and make my way to the fridge, snatching my own beer. It's probably best we change subjects because I have no idea what to say about what just happened. Clearing my throat, I respond, "She's got good taste. He's a cute guy."

"What?" Paul snorts. "You're not bothered by this?"

Rolling my eyes, I twist the cap off my beer and take a quick sip. "Why would I be?"

Paul shrugs, his expression changing with his thoughts. "I don't know. Because she's our little girl and he's . . . a guy . . ."

I give him a pointed look, waiting for the real issue to come out.

"With a penis," he finishes.

I can't help the laughter that explodes from my mouth. "Boys do have those pesky things, don't they?"

"Are you laughing at me?"

I look up to the ceiling in thought. "Yes," I chuckle. "Yes, I am."

Paul purses his lips in annoyance.

"It's not like they're doing anything. There's nothing wrong with her having a crush on an older guy."

"Wow," he surmises. "I thought I was the cool parent."

"You are," Neena chimes in as she enters the kitchen. "What are we talking about?"

"Wait. Why am I not the cool parent?" I fake offense.

Neena shrugs. "You're just cool in a different way," she replies, stealing a cucumber from the salad on the counter, just like Paul did a few moments before. I'm starting to see she's a lot like him.

Paul does an obnoxious, silent mocking laugh, directed at me. I flip him the bird when Neena isn't looking. "You know, if you want to be cool like me, I could give you some lessons."

I pretend to gag. "Thanks, but I'm good on my own."

"I wouldn't charge much," Paul continues.

"Is that so?" I ask as I slightly pull the oven door open and peek inside.

"What should my fee be, Neena?" he asks.

When I turn back, Neena has her mouth twisted in thought. Then her brows perk up. "A date."

I'm holding my breath as Paul and I awkwardly make eye contact. I cannot have her thinking we will date. "I'll make you a cake," I finally answer.

They both twist their mouths. Neena opens her mouth to speak, but for fear she'll mention Paul and I dating again, I speak before she can.

"Your dad wants to beat up Mills because you like him," I announce nonchalantly.

Cue matching father-daughter facial expressions. They both look like they want to die of embarrassment.

"I didn't say beat him up," Paul clarifies, looking to me. "And thanks for throwing me under the bus, by the way."

I raise my hand and pull down twice, bellowing out an obnoxious, "Honk-honk."

"I don't like him," Neena protests, her face bright red.

"There's nothing wrong with you liking him, Neena," I clarify. "Paul is just having a father moment. This is classic."

Neena smiles faintly as she meets Paul's gaze. "Please don't say anything to him."

Paul throws his hands up. "I never said I was. Your mother is embellishing. Big time."

Her smile slowly fades and she plops down in her seat at the kitchen table. "Doesn't matter anyway," she sighs sadly. "I'm just the ugly sick girl. He'd never like me."

As a mother, who loves her child so fiercely, and who sees all of her beauty, inside and out, that statement just crushed me. On instinct, I move to approach her, comfort her, but Paul holds his hand up, stopping me. I want to be angry with him for it, but when he kneels down in front of her, my heart melts a little.

"Look at me, Neena." When she does, he tells her, "You are so damn beautiful. I know I'm your father and you think I'm just telling you this, but it's true. Inside and out, kid. Beautiful. I've been to a lot of places, seen a lot of faces, and none in this world are as beautiful as yours."

"I have no hair. Guys like girls with hair."

"Guys like girls that are awesome, and you're clearly that. Even without hair, you have killer eyes, like your dad," he adds with a wink, "and you've got your mother's head-turning smile."

He knows damn well she has his awesome smile.

Standing, he looks down at her. "And Mills is a lucky bastard if a girl like you wastes even a second thought on him."

Neena nods and perks up. It's not her style to feel sorry for herself, and I wonder if maybe she's starting to get depressed. The doctor gave us a prescription for anti-depressants, just in case. I just didn't think she'd need them. And maybe I'm misreading her reaction just now.

"Can we eat?" she asks. "I kind of want to go to bed early tonight."

"Ten minutes, sweetheart."

As we eat dinner, Paul and I try hard to keep things light, to make her laugh. She works just as hard to keep up, but it's not difficult to see her heart isn't in it. When she kisses us good night, I hold her and squeeze her tight.

"I'm okay, Mom. Really. I'm just tired."

Letting her go, I bend and kiss her forehead. *No fever.* I try to hide my sigh of relief, but she snorts and shakes her head.

"No fever."

"I know."

"What?" Paul asks, causing us to giggle. I'm so busted.

"Nothing," Neena replies. "Mom's just over here using her lips as a thermometer."

"Well, I thought I was subtle," I sigh.

Neena smiles. "Night, guys." She waves and heads up the stairs.

With nowhere else to look, Paul and I look at each other. I have no idea what to say about our kiss. So, for now, I'll avoid it.

"About the kiss," Paul says.

Scratch avoiding it.

"Let's table it until tomorrow," I pipe up. "It's been a long day. We're all tired."

He nods once, sliding his hands in his pockets. "Okay. Well, you go on up to bed, I got the dishes."

"Are you sure?" For some reason, no words have ever sounded sweeter. I can't remember the last time someone did the dishes for me. Even if it means just loading the dishwasher or clearing the table.

"Yep. I'll see you in the morning."

I trudge up the stairs. Climbing into bed, I flop down and bury myself under the covers. I try counting sheep. I try naming all fifty states in alphabetical order. I try it all. But sleep escapes me because my mind keeps turning back to Paul and the kiss, and how he confessed he still loves me.

And how I still love him.

He's getting to me.

I'm officially in the vortex of the suck.

CHAPTER TWENTY-TWO

Paul

"**L**AST WEEKEND WE left off where you and Clara were butting heads about her new . . . managerial methods."

"Is that what we're calling them?" I chuckle.

"Did anyone show up for the paint party?"

I scrub the length of my face with the back of my hands a few times, applying pressure with the knuckles, and prepare myself for the trip down memory lane.

When Sunday evening rolled around, Marcus and I were three-beers deep at a bar about ten minutes from the office. I'd driven by the office on the way to the bar about twenty minutes before everyone should have been there. Clara's car was the only one in the parking lot. Being a young, arrogant ass, I continued on even though I knew deep down what I was doing officially made me an asshole. But I told myself she deserved it. Even after three beers, I was working hard not to think about Clara; willing myself not to think about how none of the staff probably showed up. I was trying not to imagine how she was undoubtedly going to ream me when I saw her again, and how I probably deserved it . . . sort of. I hated that maybe, deep down, I felt bad. There was absolutely no reason for me to feel bad. She was kind of an asshole, too. Just in a different way than me. I needed to get my mind off things; find a distraction. The two women that had just taken seats across from where we sat at the bar did the trick.

115

Distraction found.

With a jut of my chin, I motioned for the bartender to put their drinks on my tab.

"Which one are you going for?" Marcus asked as he lifted his glass in a silent toast to the ladies. The women smiled, glancing at each other before looking back at Marcus. You would think his height would make it difficult for him to get women, but it was quite the contrary. There would always be one intrigued by the idea of hooking up with a little person. He was at perfect eye level, after all. Maybe they were just curious. The list of women interested ran a mile long. But I'll be damned if more often than not, that one hookup would turn into several. Marcus always joked he had a cock of gold, and I didn't doubt it.

"Either one will do." I shrugged. Women were all the same to me then. I had no desire to settle down . . . at all. Settling down meant losing my freedom, and my freedom was too precious to me. I needed to be able to pack up on a whim and hop a plane to Brazil, or anywhere, if I felt the need. Having a girlfriend or wife wouldn't allow that luxury.

"What's with you today?" he asked, his face scrunched up. "You seem . . . off."

Sitting up straight, I widen my eyes in an attempt to look full of pep. "Nothing."

Marcus eyed me with an inquisitive brow. "You worried about the shrew?"

"Pfft. Why would I be?" I feigned.

"She's going to breathe fire in our faces tomorrow," Marcus grumbled before popping the peanut he just shelled into his mouth.

I gave another nonchalant shrug. I wished he'd stop talking about her already. "She'll get over it." The side of his mouth quirked up as if he didn't believe me. I did *not* want to discuss Clara with Marcus. I needed to change the subject. "I'm hungry, bro. You wanna order some food?"

He tilted his head as he snorted and took a swig of his beer. I wasn't fooling him. But he didn't push. After eating some cheap, grease-filled dinner, having two more beers, and playing a game of darts, I drove Marcus to his home behind the office. It was just past ten when we passed the front of the office and noticed only Clara's shitty little car in the lot.

"Looks like no one showed up," Marcus pointed out, snorting out a laugh.

"No surprise there," I murmured.

When I parked my truck and he started to open the door to climb out, he turned back and said, "It's too bad she's such a stick-in-the-mud. She's actually pretty fucking hot."

I nodded in agreement as I stared ahead. He wasn't kidding. Clara was extremely attractive. Not in an obvious, needed to wear slutty clothes and lots of makeup kind of way, but in a soft way, almost as if she didn't even know how beautiful she was. Too bad her looks were shadowed by her tyrannical personality.

When I glanced back to Marcus, he was smirking at me, and shaking his head. "You want to sleep with her." He wasn't asking, he was stating it. What the fuck ever.

"Pfft. She'd likely rather get mulled by a bear than hook up with me."

"That wasn't a no, Paul."

"It wasn't a yes, asswipe," I argued.

"But still not a no," he snickered. "Really, Paul? You'd do the shrew?"

"Get out of my truck," I grunted. "We gotta work tomorrow."

Shaking his head, he sighed, "Yeah, okay. See ya." Then he slid off of the seat slowly until he hit the ground, shut the truck door, and went inside.

I rounded the building. As I approached the office's lot, I still didn't know why I pulled in. I told myself I wanted to see her suffer; see how she looked when she realized she couldn't just whoosh in here and change everything. This was my fucking domain. I wanted to see her broken. But, I know now, no matter what I told myself then, I just wanted to see *her*.

When I entered, the intense paint odor hit me at once. She'd successfully painted one wall and was standing near a table looking through some of the framed photos she'd taken down as she placed them in a box. Her head whipped around when she heard me enter. Her surprised expression faded quickly into a look of annoyance. "Here to gloat?"

"Maybe," I teased as I approached. She was wearing a pair of sweats that did absolutely nothing for her ass. Her hair was tied up in some weird bird's nest looking thing and she was wearing a faded Michael

Jackson T-shirt that was two sizes too big for her. *But damn.* Even amidst the paint fumes that smell of clean linens found me. "You're not throwing those out, are you?" The photos were of me, some of the few I still had from my short career as a stuntman. Those photos were some of my prized possessions. Once upon a time, people thought I'd be the next *Evel Knievel.* I was hot shit . . . or at least they thought I was.

"How'd you get into that kind of business? The stunt business, I mean."

Small talk. Really? Tilting my head, I studied her, searching for a hint of sarcasm, but didn't find a trace. *Shit. Did she really want to know something about me?* "When I was a kid, I was always skateboarding, snowboarding, biking, and causing my mother to panic." I chuckled as the memory of my mother worrying her head off came to mind. The things I put that poor woman through. "When I was eighteen, I attended this motorbike event in California and won. Someone there was a director and they liked what they saw." I shrugged one shoulder. "Voilà. I became an instant stuntman for movies." I was invincible. Fearless. "They were the best days of my life," I admitted as I picked up a photo of me riding a bike off a burning building.

"Why'd you stop?" Clara asked as she placed more frames in a box.

"Got injured." I shrugged. "Too much risk after that."

Her gaze flicked to mine, with a hint of sympathy in them that quickly vanished. Her lips were tight, in a flat line, before she asked, "What happened?"

I could tell she hated herself for asking the question. After all, asking indicated that she gave a shit, and she didn't want me thinking that. Remembering what happened, what caused me to retire, wasn't something I liked to think about. Oddly enough, it wasn't a stunt that ended my career.

"Betty Lee Ozman."

She furrowed her brows in confusion. "What?"

"I was changing a tire on the side of the Interstate and I got clipped by a car."

Her eyes widened with disbelief. "Are you serious?"

"Yep," I confirmed with a sad chuckle. "Little old granny didn't see me. Luckily she wasn't going the speed limit. She might have killed me."

"Damn," Clara muttered. "How bad were you hurt?"

"I was unconscious for a week. They weren't sure I'd even wake up, and when I did, they informed me one more blow to the head could kill me. My mother made me swear I'd quit the stunts."

Looking down in the box, she frowned slightly. "I'm sorry, Paul."

It was one of those weird moments in life. I hated her. She hated me. But she was being nice to me. At any moment a series of phenomenons; hurricanes, tornadoes, or tsunamis, would ensue.

I quickly changed the subject. Spinning around, I gave the room another once-over. "You just went ahead and started painting by yourself, huh?"

"Yep."

"You'll never finish this tonight."

"Oh, I know," she answered cheerily. "But I have a good start."

Collecting her paintbrush and can, she headed toward the back. I took the ladder and folded it. "Thanks," she murmured politely.

Seeing her seem so okay, happy even, made me nervous. The woman I had come to know in the past few weeks would've had steam coming out of her ears right now. "You seem . . . not angry no one showed up."

She shrugged. "It'll get done, one way or another."

While she rinsed her brushes and roller in the bathroom, I put the ladder up and turned off most of the lights in the back. I waited for her, and when she entered the front of the office, she froze when she saw me.

"You're still here," she stated, more than questioned.

"Just want to make sure you got to your car okay."

Her mouth quirked up on one side, her expression suspicious. "Okay."

I held the door open so she could exit, then waited while she locked it. I noticed she hadn't removed Dennis's keychain on the set of keys I gave her. "You need help getting that off?" I pointed to them.

Looking at them in the palm of her hand, she frowned. "No. I'm keeping it on, but thanks."

I stood at the office door and watched her unlock the driver's side door of her vehicle. "Night, Paul," she called just before she climbed in.

"Night." I waved, but felt off. I expected her to blow up at me when I walked in, but she didn't. Why? It didn't make any sense.

The next day, my house phone rang bright and early. And when I rolled over in bed, cracking one eye open, the clock said it was ten in the morning. Hey, that's early for me. After clumsily slapping my hand around a few times, it landed on the receiver and I answered.

"Hello," I managed, my voice hoarse.

"You better get down here, Paul," Marcus grumbled.

"My first jump is at three."

"She's canceled all jumps today."

My eyes opened, blinking a few times against the harsh morning light. "What?"

"All jumps—canceled. The guys are pissed."

I released a long and aggravated sigh. "I'll be there in a bit."

After tugging on some twice-worn cargo shorts and an old Sky High T-shirt, I made my way down to the office. Marcus, Bowman, Sap, and two other employees were waiting out front, leaning against the building when I pulled up.

As I advanced, they all stood straight. Marcus spoke first. "She's closed the office for remodeling. Canceled all jumps until it's finished."

Running a hand over my face, I let out a tired and frustrated growl. I guess she had this planned last night and that's why she didn't blow up at me for not showing up. I walked in the office, leaving them to brood outside.

Country music blared from the back of the building, so I followed the sound until I found her in the bathroom, rinsing brushes. She was shaking her hips and singing with the tune, clearly unaware I'd entered. I was pissed. Rightfully so. But that didn't mean I didn't take a second to appreciate the cutoff jeans and tight tank she was wearing. Her attire pissed me off even more. How dare she screw us out of money and look sexy as fuck while doing it. Every other time I'd seen her, she was wearing her less than form-fitting clothes that hid her body. This little . . . sexy outfit was distracting me.

Focus, Paul.

"What the hell do you think you're doing?" I snapped, causing her to jump because I startled her.

One side of her mouth curled in annoyance. "It's called work," she sneered as she turned off the faucet.

"You canceled our jumps?"

She shrugged as she picked up the bucket of paint at her feet and shoved by me, heading to the front. "Figured since I'm doing all of this painting by myself, it might take a while and we can't have our clients coming in here with wet paint all over the place."

I closed my eyes and willed myself to calm down. This woman was driving me mad. "How are we supposed to get paid if you cancel the jumps?"

Placing the bucket on a plastic-covered table, she turned to me, sticking out her lower lip—a look I found sexy-as-fuck on her even though she was mocking me—and she pouted. "Well I guess everyone should come in here and help. The quicker it gets done, the faster you guys get back to doing dives."

"Are you fucking kidding me, Clara?" I asked, exasperated beyond belief. "The other day you were bitching about us needing to make more money and today you cancel our jumps? That makes no sense."

Whipping her head around, she glared at me before stomping to the front door where the guys had been watching us through the window. Opening it, she boisterously called, "Come on in, boys. Might as well hear it straight from the horse's mouth."

Reluctantly, the guys moseyed in, their gazes flicking to me in question. I had no idea what the shrew was about to say, so I rolled my eyes in answer. Marcus entered last, remaining by the door, leaning against it to hold it open, his arms crossed over his chest. I wanted to laugh—defiant little fucker.

"I asked all of you for four hours on Sunday evening," she began. "None of you showed up or even bothered to call."

"It was our night off," Bowman protested.

"It was my night off, too, yet I was here," Clara muttered.

"Yeah, but you have no life so . . ." Marcus interjected, earning an exasperated sigh from Clara.

"Let's be clear," she ignored him, taking the high road, and continued,

"I am a college educated woman. I can find another job if I want to."

"So why don't you?" Marcus pushed.

"Because I love working with tiny little assholes," she snapped. I guess she detoured off the high road.

Marcus glared back.

Clara tilted her head as she looked at each and every one of us. "Because this," she motioned her hand around the room, "was left to me. Half of it, anyway. Now I'm here trying to make it bigger and better, trying to grow this business and y'all seem to think you can ignore me. Well here's the deal . . . no jumps until we get this office done. If you won't take me seriously, maybe you'll take your loss of income seriously."

"On that note, I'm heading out," Sap announced. "Good luck, Clara," he mumbled. I couldn't tell if he was annoyed with her or me as he marched out the door.

I turned my attention back to Clara. "You can't do that," I argued.

"Yes, I can."

"We'll schedule around you."

"She changed the password to the schedule log in the system. I already tried," Marcus informed me.

Clara looked at me, her hands on her hips, one brow lifted in a perfect arch. She was pretty damn proud of herself.

I stared blankly at her. "Are you serious?"

"You left me no choice." She shrugged.

"I didn't realize stopping our income was a choice."

"We're partners," she scolded. "You should be backing me up. I would do it for you."

"Partners discuss things and make plans together. That's not what happened here," I argued.

"You won't listen to anything I say." She threw her hands out in frustration. "Every time I come to you with an idea or plan, you shut down and ignore me." The room was quiet, everyone hanging on every word we spoke.

I could've fought her on it. Somehow. But at that point I just wanted to shut her up. If painting the walls did that, I figured let's get it over with. "All right, guys, we're painting today."

They rolled their eyes and groaned, but began looking around trying to figure out where to begin.

"Happy now?" I taunted, giving her an obnoxious bow like a servant would to their queen. "We're all here, doing as you bid, your majesty." But it came out rougher than I intended.

Clara's eyes glossed over a little and she almost seemed to frown. I was being a dick. We all were. At that time, I thought she was just hell-bent on bulldozing us, forcing us to bend to her whims at any cost. Now, I know she wanted to be a part of the business. She wanted to make her mark and feel useful. She was trying to find her place.

We all took our tasks and got to work, ignoring her. Even when we broke for lunch, we left and didn't invite her. She stayed at the office and kept working. By evening, we'd finished the painting and even though everyone complained and made it clear they hated her for making them be here, she thanked us all, one by one.

We bullshitted in the parking lot for a few minutes while she remained inside and when everyone left, I went back in, realizing I had left my keys on the desk. She was in the office on the phone when I found her. Unaware that I had returned.

Her back was to me as she sat in the office chair, one elbow propped on the desk, her head resting in her hand. "Yes, I've looked the papers over and I'm still deciding," she spoke in a monotone voice into the receiver. Her tone didn't match her stature; to hear her, you'd have thought she was discussing something irrelevant—something that warranted no emotion. But the way she held her head, her eyes clenched closed, said something entirely different. She was hurting. Badly.

"I'm aware you're ready to get this done."

She listened for a moment to whomever she was speaking with before her head shot up and she snapped. "Well you can tell *Daisy* I have been your wife for the last five years and I'm sorry that our divorce is getting in the way of your romance."

I was stunned, and my brows rose as a reaction. Shrew was married? She's getting a divorce? I had been racking my brain wondering what in the hell inspired her to move here and jump into this business she knew nothing about. I guess I'd found my answer.

"Well I'll sign them when I'm ready," she stated in a calmer voice. "Give Daisy my best." Slamming the phone down, she hung her head, her hands clenching the armrests of the chair as she tried to calm herself.

I decided to let my presence be known. As I entered the office, I cleared my throat, causing her to jump, yet again. She stood, wiping at her eyes quickly, before clearing her throat. "I thought everyone left?"

"Forgot my keys," I said as I grabbed them off the desk and dangled them for proof. "You okay?" I asked. Maybe I didn't like her. Maybe I didn't want her there, but I'm not a complete tool. I hated to see a woman cry. Especially one that had so much fierceness to her. Wild animals aren't meant to be broken. And neither was she.

"I'm fine." She grabbed her purse, and met me at the office door. I flipped the light off as she passed by me and headed up front. As she locked the front door, I had to ask one more time. "You sure you're okay?"

"Paul," she sighed, brushing a loose strand of hair from her face and pushing it behind her ear. "I appreciate you asking, but we both know you don't give a shit about me. Let's not pretend."

I groaned through clenched teeth in annoyance. "I may not like you," I clarified, "but that doesn't mean I want you to suffer."

Shaking her head, her mouth quirked up in a sad smile. "I'm fine. Have a good night."

She hurried to her car and climbed in. When she started her vehicle, the engine groaned in protest before it sputtered out. She turned it again, but this time it didn't even attempt to cut on. With her doors and windows closed, I couldn't hear her, but with the well-lit parking lot, I could read her mouth when she said, "Fucking piece of shit."

Thudding her head against the steering wheel, her shoulders rose as she inhaled deeply. Damn. She was going to need a ride. More alone time with her. Great. Just great.

I decided to give her a minute, knowing she'd get out of her car at some point and ask me for a ride. But she didn't. When I got tired of waiting, I gave her passenger side window an aggressive rap to get her attention. Cutting a sharp glance to me, she mouthed, *What?*

I glared at her. She wasn't my favorite person in the world either, but I was willing to give her a ride and this was how she acted?

"I'm leaving. If you need a ride, I suggest you move your ass." With that, I went to my truck and climbed in, giving the door a hard slam. Still, she didn't budge. Shaking my head, because, unbelievable, I fired up my truck and put it in drive. At the sound of my engine, she hopped to and got out of her car. But she didn't rush. In fact, I think she forced herself to move slower as she locked her car, then walked across the parking lot. Like I said, unbelievable. This chick had balls. I wanted to laugh and strangle her simultaneously.

Opening the door, she climbed in, and slammed the door, clearly imitating me.

"Take it easy on my baby," I jested, trying to lighten the mood.

Crossing her arms and letting out a huff, she pointed and murmured, "That way."

Shifting the truck into drive, I mumbled to myself, "That way." Even my mocking was high-pitched. For the next ten minutes we rode in silence with the exception of Clara directing me. When we finally reached her house, I didn't throw her out like I wanted, instead I parked, leaving my headlights on as I surveyed the property. The place was a shithole. The yard was overgrown; the grass looked like it hadn't been cut in ages, and one of the front windows had a cardboard box taped over it, possibly meaning broken glass was the culprit.

"You're living here?" I probed in disbelief. "By yourself?"

Clara opened her door as I cut the ignition. "Yes. By myself." Sliding out, she huffed deeply. "Thank you for the ride."

I opened my mouth to respond when the sound of glass breaking sounded out, causing her to jerk her gaze to the house.

"What was that?" I asked as Clara narrowed her eyes.

"I don't know," she mumbled as she dug through her purse, retrieving a large revolver.

My eyes widened. What the fuck? "You carry a gun?"

She didn't look at me as she popped the chamber open, spinning it, before popping it back in place. Damn. My dick twitched a little. She handled the weapon like a pro, it was sexy as hell. "Sure do." Without another word, she left the truck door open and made her way toward the house. I hopped out of the truck and rushed beside her, refusing to look like a pussy by letting her enter the house alone.

"You can go, Paul. I have this."

"What if someone is in there?"

"If someone is, they'll be sorry," she replied as she took the first step to the porch, which groaned in protest from her weight. Her face tightened and she winced at the sound, fearing it alerted anyone that might be inside to her approaching. I followed behind her, the stairs creaking loudly with my additional weight. Her hand, the one not holding the gun, had just found the doorknob when I took the final step onto the porch. At that exact moment, as she opened the door, I fell through the porch floor, the aged and weak wood having given out from under me.

The sound of the wood splitting was loud, causing Clara to whip around, and she pointed the gun in my direction.

My stomach felt like it dropped out of my ass. "Don't shoot," I shouted. She immediately dropped the gun to her side, pressing her mouth in an angry and frustrated flat line.

"Jesus Christ," I muttered, clutching my chest, my heart racing. She almost shot me.

"I almost shot you," she growled as if it was somehow my fault.

"No shit," I snapped as I took inventory of myself. No missing body parts; no injuries. Climbing out of the hole, I treaded gently on the porch, fearful I might fall through again. "Give me the gun," I ordered her.

She scowled at me. "No."

I glowered back. "I'm going in first so give me the gun." I held out my hand as I gave her a stern look.

Quirking a defiant eyebrow, she snickered, "Do you even know how to use a gun?"

"Of course, I do," I lied. I had fired guns before, but I was no pro. All I really wanted at that moment was to make sure she didn't kill me by accident.

Rolling her eyes, she handed it to me. "Be careful with that."

I shook my head in annoyance, cursing this infuriating woman to myself as I entered the house. The weight of the gun surprised me as I held it by my side. This was a heavy gun for a girl. I almost said that to her, but decided against it since it might earn me some kind of feminist lecture. My steps were slow, and light, but the floors still creaked with each one. She was right behind me as I blindly made my way down the dark and unfamiliar hallway.

Something thudded and I stopped, causing her to bump into me.

"Damn it, Paul," she muttered.

"Shh," I ordered hastily, extending my neck slightly to listen. Scratching sounds, like nails on a wall. I was relieved it was only an animal . . . we just didn't know what kind of animal.

After a moment of quiet, she whispered, "It sounds like it's coming from the kitchen." She nudged me forward, and we crept toward the back of the house, toward what I assumed was the kitchen. We reached the doorway and Clara weaved her thin arm between me and the doorframe before I had a chance to understand what she was doing. In a flash, the kitchen light blazed on, shocking my eyes. A loud hiss mixed with a frantic meow made me jerk when something small and black jumped. It scared the shit out of me and I reacted, jerking my arm up to point the gun, which accidentally went off with a loud pop that kicked my heartbeat into overdrive.

"Shit," I gasped, freaked out that I had just accidentally fired the gun. The bullet split through a vase on the kitchen table, destroying it into hundreds of pieces. The small black thing, I now knew was a cat, as I watched it haul ass out of a tiny fold of cardboard on the back window, seemed just as freaked out as me. Apparently there were multiple windows busted in this house.

"Motherfucker," I yelled as I tried to catch my breath. I wasn't scared of a cat. Okay, maybe it scared me for a second because of the sheer shock of it. Clara's laughter pulled me from my shock as I turned to see her bent over, holding her stomach, laughing.

"You think this is funny?" I sneered.

Her body shook as she tried to get her laughter under control. "Not you shooting my vase," she finally answered, "but your reaction was priceless."

"Why do you even have this?" I asked, darting my gaze to the gun in my hand.

"Give me that," Clara demanded as she pried the gun from my hand. Passing by me, she placed the gun on the counter, closing her eyes as if she needed to calm down herself. "Fucking cat," she muttered under her breath, still chuckling.

"I'm not going to lie," I piped in, a little out of breath. "That scared the shit out of me."

"Gee, I couldn't tell," she said dryly.

12

"You need to get new windows," I pointed out.

She huffed, something that held a hint of disdain. "New windows cost money."

"This place isn't safe with cardboard as windows."

"Thank you, Paul. I didn't realize," she griped sarcastically.

"When did you move in here?"

"About a week ago," she sighed as she crossed her arms and turned, letting her gaze travel the room. There was no stove, half the cabinet doors were missing, and the linoleum on the floor was ripped in several places. And this was just the kitchen. I cringed to think what the rest of the house looked like.

"Did you get it for free, because short of that, I cannot imagine why you'd move in here?"

"Guy gave me a lease-to-own option, it was super cheap, and I liked the idea of . . ." She twisted her mouth in thought before she continued, "Putting life back into it. Someone gave up on this place a long time ago. Maybe I just don't like giving up."

I had the feeling she wasn't just talking about the house anymore. I fought the urge to scrunch up my face in humored skepticism. This sounded just like a woman to me. They're all so sentimental. She was insane. This house was a money pit. And it would take her forever to get it to standard, suitable living conditions. "Look here," she pointed as she approached. I stepped aside when she reached the doorframe and ran her hand down the wooden panel. Engraved in the wood were initials and dates with height measurements beside them. "This was a family. Someone's kids grew up here. Someone's life started here."

I narrowed my eyes as I watched her tiny finger run over the etched wood. "But not *your* life," I pointed out. "There are better places around here that need far less work."

"That's my point, Paul. Someone gave up on this place. They built it and then they just let it go and didn't look back. They simply threw it away like yesterday's trash." Her gaze lingered where her fingers brushed the wood, a sadness seemingly seeping out of her, but she quickly recovered.

Lifting her face to meet mine, she gave an awkward smile. "Thanks for the ride, Paul."

I realized she was telling me it was time for me to go. "Oh, yeah," I sputtered. "Sure." She followed me back down the hall to the front door and before I exited I turned and asked, "Aren't you scared to be here by yourself?"

"Why?" she snickered. "You think I should be?"

"Hell yes," I asserted, widening my eyes in emphasis. "We're here together right now with a big ass gun and *I'm* scared."

She laughed. Like really laughed. Her smile stretched across her face, her mouth opened, her teeth in full view. She could be such a pain in the ass, and it drove me fucking nuts. But in that moment, knowing I made her do that, laugh that way, it was like a thrill—just not the kind I was used to. Thrills were my life, and I was addicted to them; the rush of doing something dangerous always gave me a high I had never been able to replace. Until that moment.

When her laughter ebbed, it faded into a grin, before shrinking to a small smile. Our gazes locked for a moment, and I wondered if in that brief span of seconds she felt what I did. Did she forget for a small time that she hated me, that she thought I was an asshole? Was I the only one feeling this way? I felt like maybe she did, the way her bright eyes seemed soft as they were fixed on mine. But as quick as the moment came, it seemed to disappear even faster.

Pulling her gaze away, she cleared her throat and said, "Good night, Paul."

With a nod, I left, careful to walk delicately on the porch so I wouldn't fall through again. When I climbed in my truck and fired it up, I stared at the house for a moment, still not able to wrap my head around it all. She moved to a new state, started a new job, and bought a house that needed a ton of work. Was this woman afraid of nothing?

CHAPTER TWENTY-THREE

Paul

ASHLEY IS SMILING at me, while Zane is staring at me from where he stands behind his camera on the tripod. Mills is leaned against the back wall and looks as if he's so bored he may pass out.

"Should I keep going?" I ask, unsure. I feel like I've been talking for hours. This damn room is becoming claustrophobic.

"I think that's enough for today." I almost let out a huge breath of relief. Closing her notebook, she scoots forward in her chair. "Clara is quite a woman," she notes.

"Yeah, she is," I admit.

"So, we'll see you tomorrow?"

"My turn again, huh? Yeah. Sure thing."

We say good-bye and I head out of the room, taking in fresh air. Marcus is in the front, reading the newspaper, waiting for the guys to get back from their last jump of the day. I plop down on the couch beside him, letting my head fall back. He's quiet for a moment, the paper hiding his face, when in a sultry, deep voice, he says, "Knowing I made her laugh that way . . . it was a thrill." The paper shakes with his body as he tries not to burst out laughing.

"You little shit," I grumble. "You were listening?"

"You have a way with words, Paul," he snorts through his laughter, which he no longer tries to hold in.

"You're such a dick."

The paper is now crumpled in his lap, revealing his bright red face as he laughs so hard he can't breathe.

"That's it," I growl, wrapping my arm around his head, and locking it.

"Let me go, you asshole," he demands, even though he's laughing.

I ball up my fist and rub the top of his scalp, giving him a proper noogie. His little hands grip my wrist, trying to free himself, but I'm too strong.

"Is *this* giving you a thrill, Paul?" he howls with laughter, mixed with a few grunts.

"Sure does." I laugh, too.

"You better stop or I'm going to punch you in the balls," he warns. Just before I move to extend my body out of his reach, he swings his hand and hits me right in the family jewels. We both fall to the ground as I clutch my nuts, groaning in pain. We're both huffing, our age rearing its ugly head. The young men we used to be would've popped right up off of the floor and gone at each other again. But now, wrestling feels like a full cardio workout. Marcus is able to stand before me, but he uses the armrest to pull himself up.

A soft giggle makes our heads snap in its direction. Neena is standing in the hallway with her camera, filming us. Clara stands behind her, smirking, as if she thinks we're ridiculous. Which we are. Flicking my gaze to Marcus, his hair seems to be standing straight up like he just got out of bed from a night of rough sex. I'm still on the floor, cradling my manhood. This doesn't look good.

"Neena," I gasp. "Would you mind turning that off, princess?"

She quirks a warning brow, something she definitely learned from her mother. I called her princess. I'm not supposed to do that. At least not in front of other people.

"I mean, please."

She flips the screen closed and clutches it to her chest. "You guys are funny."

"They're something, all right," Clara murmurs. "You guys are taking her home and cooking dinner, yes?"

"We will have it ready by the time you get home," Marcus assures. "Mei-ling is coming over too. We have big plans for tonight."

Clara eyes him inquisitively. "Please elaborate."

"I can't." Marcus winks at Neena. "Paul and Mei-ling have been working on this for a few days."

Clara's dark eyes dart over to mine, a look of uncertainty and excitement mixed in them.

"You'll like this," I assure her. "But Neena will like it more."

She bobs her head once in compliance before she kisses the top of Neena's head. "Good luck with these two knuckleheads."

As Clara leaves to be interrogated by Ashley and crew, Neena smiles, and it's sincere, but something is off. Her usual smile that lights up her whole face isn't quite there. And now that I'm really looking at her, she's paler.

"You okay, hon?" I ask as I roll on my stomach preparing to stand.

"Just a little tired," she answers, and I center in on the small dark circles forming under her eyes. No matter how much she sleeps, her skin has paled considerably, making her appear as if she's hardly sleeping.

"We don't have to do what we have planned tonight if you're not feeling well," I tell her. Entertainment be damned if my little girl isn't feeling up to it.

"I'm fine, Dad," she replies, raising her voice an octave as if by doing so she will sound peppier.

"Okay," I answer uneasily. "Why don't you sit down for a bit?"

"The guys should be back any second now. It's an early day. We'll be leaving in twenty," Marcus tells her. She nods and flops down on the couch, sitting cross-legged, flipping her camera lens open again, and watching what she's just recorded.

"Get up," Marcus grunts as he passes by, giving me a hard kick in the ass.

"Asshole!" I groan after him, earning a little chuckle from Neena.

CHAPTER TWENTY-FOUR

Clara

"**P**AUL TOLD US about the first time he saw your house," Ashley chuckles, pushing some of her dark hair behind her ear as she folds her legs beneath her, sitting cross-legged.

I huff out a little laugh at the thought. "Did he tell you he accidentally fired the gun, too? At a poor cat."

She grins. "Yeah, he did. That night seems to have been a pivotal point in the dynamic between you two, at least as far as he's concerned."

I tilt my head in thought. "I think . . . it was the first time we really ever laughed together. Laughter is like the old grandmother in every family," I note, "it brings everyone together. Even people that hate each other."

"Did you really hate Paul?"

I wince with her question. "Hate is a strong word," I surmise. "I hated him as a business partner, I guess. As a person . . . he was okay."

"Were you attracted to him? I mean, I know physically you were, but . . . otherwise?"

I exhale loudly, widening my eyes. "Truthfully . . . I was a mess at that time. Thinking about Paul or anyone else that way seemed impossible. I was still very hurt with the loss of my marriage."

Her brows perk up. "You still wanted Kurt back?"

Adjusting in my seat, I answer her. "I wanted my life back. I wanted him back. But at the same time, I really didn't. I wanted who I thought he was back. Having people ripped from your life is hard."

Her brows furrow as if she doesn't understand. As if she thinks Kurt didn't deserve any consideration whatsoever from me. And she's probably right. But I didn't feel that way back then. "He was my husband. Life was comfortable, familiar. I knew him, or I thought I did, and I felt safe knowing he mostly knew me. He knew how I liked my coffee, how I'm grumpy when I first wake up. He knew how I cried at sappy movies or sad stories no matter how many times I'd seen them. He knew I liked fountain Coke from *7-Eleven* with lots of ice—he had my habits down to a T. Once upon a time, he loved me and all my quirks. That's hard to let go of."

"So . . . you didn't want him back?" She cocks her head to the side in question.

"I wanted the man I married back. But he'd left me long before then. You're so young, Ashley," I explain. "This probably doesn't make any sense to you. I was grieving. Marriage feels like a living and breathing thing, and when you lose it, it's like losing a family member. There are all these memories you're left with, good ones that you can't really look back on fondly because you know it's ended. And just like death, once it's gone . . . really gone, you can't get it back. My marriage was gone. I wanted it back. But I knew, no matter what, it would never return. Even if he'd come back crawling on his hands and knees, too much had happened. He'd lied and disrespected me too many times; betrayed me too much. And even though I knew that, that still didn't make it any easier."

"How were you coping with the news about Daisy?"

I let out a long groan. "I wanted to hate her. She had the life I'd wanted. I was so sad, and I wanted him to feel that, too. I wanted him to hurt like he'd hurt me. And I felt like Daisy was keeping him from feeling any pain. She was his distraction. But I didn't hate her. I refused to. Hating her would make me a smaller person, a petty person."

"So how did you do it? Moving away from your job, your friends, and your life. It doesn't sound like you had a great welcoming committee here."

I run my finger along the arm of the chair. "No, I didn't."

"Did it get any better?"

"Over time. It took a few months. I think he started trying harder, but we still butted heads on quite a few things."

"Well Paul described the gun incident night as a turning point for him.

What was yours?"

I'd lived in Virginia for a month and a half. I had no friends. My staff hated me. Marcus *really* hated me. I'd put an end to his shenanigans with our clients and he did not take it well. With Paul, it was day to day. Some days we got along just fine, others, he thought I was a raging bitch and I thought he was an entitled asshole. I sold my shitty car to the junkyard and bought another shitty car that looked way uglier. At that point, I didn't really have anywhere to go, so the appearance of my vehicle didn't matter much so long as it ran and got me to work and back home every day. I was more alone than I'd ever felt in my life. But I had my house. My beautiful, shitty house. When I wasn't at work, I worked on my house. Business was good, thanks to some new methods I'd implemented, and I was finally starting to get a paycheck and since I had no life, my money went to my home.

With each job; painting walls, replacing windows, and so on, slowly, I felt myself finding peace. It was a Saturday, the first one I'd had off since I moved to town, and I'd planned an "exciting" day of staining cabinets for my kitchen. The weather was unseasonably hot for April in Virginia, or so everyone said. Every window in the house was open, box-shaped fans in them, since I hadn't had enough money to add central air and heat yet. The oil heat got me through the cold nights, but eventually it would have to go. With my stereo blasting and the fans running, I didn't hear Paul's truck pull in, nor did I hear him enter my home. I was standing on my counter, smearing wood stain on the cabinets, when he touched my leg. I nearly fell off of the counter, it scared me so bad.

"What the hell?" I hissed, my chest rising and falling dramatically as I attempted to catch my breath.

When he laughed, I couldn't hear it because the music was too loud. He turned and hit the power button, then I could hear him chuckling.

"What are you doing here? You're supposed to be doing dives this afternoon."

"Well, hello to you, too," he said dryly.

"Hi, Paul," I uttered exaggeratedly. Then, putting a hand on my hip, I asked, "Again. What are you doing here?"

"The last group canceled today. Their church bus broke down and they couldn't make it."

"Damn," I sighed. "That sucks." That was a lot of money we just missed out on.

"Good news!" He beamed. "The day is not lost. I come bearing gifts. Well, a gift."

I narrowed my eyes at him. He brought me a gift? What kind of gift would he have brought *me*, and why?

"It's in the back of my truck." He stared up at me, his dark eyes flicking down for a moment to my legs, before meeting my eyes again. I pretended not to notice. When I didn't move, he asked, "Would you like to see it?"

"That depends. What is it?"

"You have to come outside and see."

Rolling my eyes, I bent down and hung my stain rag over the edge of the bucket and climbed down. I hated that he showed up unannounced, for the obvious reasons, like, we weren't friends. But another reason, which I hated to admit, was I knew I looked like hell. And staying true to Paul James, he looked amazing, as always. I was covered in sweat, no makeup, and my hair was knotted up on the top of my head. I'm pretty sure with the heat and the massive amount of sweating, my deodorant had already worn off since I had applied it that morning. So I probably didn't smell that great either. He was finding something funny as he watched me, a humored smirk across his face.

"Something funny?" I sassed.

"You're just cute when you're annoyed."

Cute? Why didn't that word feel quite right? No woman wants to be cute—not really. Cute is for little girls and babies. Women want to be beautiful; sexy. Deciding not to acknowledge it, I followed him outside to his truck, noticing what looked like a table in the back. Dropping the tailgate, he spun around to me with a grin and motioned his hand as if to say, *look at this.*

"It's a table," I noted. It looked like a nice table, newly built, without any finishing to it. But what was I supposed to think about it?

"It's yours," he said.

I looked at him like he was nuts. "Mine?"

"I built it for you."

I made an effort to school my expression. Was he serious? "You built this?" I asked, pointing to the table.

Scratching the back of his neck, he released an awkward chuckle. "You don't like it?"

"No," I quickly but calmly replied. "I'm just . . . confused."

He cocked his head, twisting his mouth to the side. He knew what I meant. He knew all things considered, it was weird that he built *me*, of all people, a table. "You've heard I'm kind of a wanderer, right?"

"Uh . . . yeah," I answered, severely confused. We were just talking about a table, now we're talking about traveling?

"Staying in one place makes me restless. Diving sates my need for adventure, somewhat, but not completely."

He looked at me then turned back to his truck, eyeing the table. "I've been trying to keep busy, stay distracted. Woodwork is my latest distraction."

"I see," I murmured.

"I built this same table three other times, but this one . . . this one I had trouble with."

"It looks like a nice table," I offered. "But . . . why are you giving it to me?"

"Well . . ." he chuckled. "I don't need it, and I thought maybe you did."

"Why'd you build it if you didn't need it? Why not build a desk or a chair or something?"

"I don't know," he snapped a little, annoyed at my questioning. "If you don't want it just say so."

I gritted my teeth, biting the urge to snap back at him. Could he really blame me for being skeptical? Climbing up into the bed of the truck, I ran my hand across the wood. It really was a nice table. I couldn't really see what he thought was wrong with it except for the rings with dark growth. Some people might not like that. The table was nothing fancy; it was simple. I liked simple. Simple could be elegant. Then I realized I could stain it to match my cabinets. "How much do you want for it?"

Paul dropped his head as if he was exhausted by me. "Nothing. I'm giving it to you. It's a gift."

I lost my patience. Was this a joke? Was he messing with me? "Why? Why me?"

He tilted his head to the side as he looked up at me. "Because I didn't give up on this one. And I like the idea of giving it to someone that won't give up on it either."

My gaze dropped. I didn't like that he saw this vulnerability in me. I hadn't realized he was actually listening to me the night he brought me home as I babbled on about not giving up. I must've sounded like a nutjob. It was obvious, at least to me anyway, that I was going crazy latching onto a house that I had no ties to with such intense sentimentality. I wondered if he saw it, too. Or was he just taking pity on me?

"Are you sure?" I asked, my tone not hiding one bit of the uncertainty I was feeling.

"I wouldn't have brought it over here if I wasn't," he argued.

I climbed out of the truck and together we pulled the table down, setting it near the porch. "I'm going to grab the wood stain I have in the kitchen. It'll match the cabinets," I told him.

"Wait," he called as I spun around to go. When I turned back, he was unfolding a pocketknife before extending his arm, handing it to me.

"What is that for?"

"To make your mark."

I blinked a few times, realizing what he meant.

"This is yours now. You'll love it and take care of it."

Taking the small knife and rounding the table, I looked for a good place to engrave the wood as I bit my lip in concentration. I decided on a corner. My letters were small and when I blew the wood shavings and dust from it, I smiled a little as I met Paul's gaze. Then I held the knife out to him.

"Your turn."

He looked stunned. "You want me to mark *your* table?"

"You built it," I answered. "You're part of this table's history."

Taking the knife, his mouth partly curved upward, as he scouted the surface of the table, looking for the perfect place to engrave. I'd like to tell you he picked a corner, just like me. An area that's small. Something modest, yet meaningful. But, no. He picked the center of the table.

Dead center.

When he finished, he smiled down at his engraving. *EPIC.*

"Center of the table?" I questioned dryly. "Very subtle."

He laughed as he folded the knife and slipped it back in his pocket. "Life's too short to be subtle."

Bending over, he blew away the dust and ran his hand over it once more. "Besides," he added with a sideways smirk that told me whatever was about to come out of his mouth would be sarcastic. "I kind of like the idea of you seeing my name there every day and thinking of me."

"I'm sure you do," I snorted. "Good thing I brought some tablecloths from Texas with me. They'll fit perfectly on this."

He laughed as I spun around and headed inside for the wood stain. When I returned, he was shirtless. Really? Couldn't he at least keep his clothes on? Perched on the table, his back to me, his arms were crossed and his warm skin glistened with the slightest sheen of sweat. Even from behind, he looked delectable. Shit.

I chucked a clean rag I'd grabbed from inside at him. "Tables are for glasses, not asses."

He slid off the table with ease and turned to me, his dark eyes squinting against the bright and unrelenting sun. At the sight of his front side, I rolled my eyes. Stupid, stupid, muscular sexy chest. And arms. Those were stupid, too. Oh, and the dark hair on his chest that seemed to angle down perfectly until it thinned out, disappearing beneath his shorts. I'd never dated a guy with that much . . . hair. Not that Paul had too much, or that I thought about dating him or his hair, but Kurt had very little and the little he did have, he shaved. I had never developed an opinion on the whole hair thing with men, but on Paul I found it very . . . virile. It was alluring. I wondered what it would be like to run my fingers over it. Then I wondered why in the hell I was thinking about running my fingers over Paul's chest hair. What was wrong with me?

"It's hot as hell out here," he noted, raising one hand up and running it through his dark hair.

"Are you staying?" I asked, snapping myself out of it.

"Thought you might want some help with staining it and getting it inside."

"You don't have to do that, Paul."

Beaming a smile at me, he shrugged one shoulder. "Call it a peace offering."

I didn't know how I felt about that. Was a table supposed to buy my forgiveness for him treating me so badly when I'd first arrived? Or rather since I arrived. Either way, I didn't question it. If he was willing to call for a truce, I'd take it. At that point, I was exhausted in every way. Having one less enemy at the office would be wonderful.

"So we're partners, right? No more bullshit?"

His gaze flicked down and he moved his hands to his hips, before meeting my eyes again. In his deep and husky voice, he said, "No more bullshit." Then he came to me, stood in front of me, and extended his hand. I took it, and we shook.

He stayed all day. After we stained the table, he helped with the cabinets. After the cabinets, he helped me remove the toilet from the downstairs bathroom. By the time night fell, I was thoroughly exhausted. We sat outside on a blanket and ate tuna fish sandwiches with Cheetos and Coca Cola.

Before he left for the night, we stood by his truck awkwardly. Finally, he stunned me with an awkward one-armed hug, before he slid in his truck and drove away.

Ashley's mouth twists as she taps her pencil against her notebook. "So . . . nothing really happened?"

"What do you mean?" I ask with a snicker.

"No kiss? Not even a hug?" Zane is watching me, his brows raised as if he is waiting for my answer. Apparently he's finding my story quite intriguing.

"Well, there was a one-armed hug, like I said," I point out. "But nothing major yet."

Ashley gives a weird smirk, clearly disappointed with my answer, but decides to move on. "Was there peace? Did you two start getting along?"

Sighing, I say, "With Paul and I, yes. With Marcus . . . no. The others started to warm up to me, but it was slow going, and Marcus' attitude toward me wasn't helping."

"We'll get to Marcus in a few minutes," Ashley insists. "I want to hear more about the budding friendship between Paul and you."

CHAPTER TWENTY-FIVE
Clara

WE WERE AT the race—Richmond International Raceway. I'd never been to a *NASCAR* race. Texas Motor Speedway wasn't an unknown concept to me when I resided in Texas, but racing had never really interested me. But in Virginia, racing was a big deal. And as we walked around, I was definitely feeling like a human dropped on a foreign planet, forced to walk among a different species. Girls walked around in bikinis donning the controversial confederate flag; others wore cutoff jean shorts with their ass cheeks hanging out. Men walked around sporting T-shirts with their favorite racers on them, and with helmets that held beer cans with long straws in their mouths. There was porta potties everywhere and the heat didn't help to keep the stench down as we passed by them. As if all that wasn't enough, Marcus decided to wear a T-shirt that had *I'm with the shrew* on the back of it, just above an arrow pointing to the side. He'd made a point to remain to the left of me all day just so that arrow would point at me.

My new tactic in dealing with him was to ignore him. I thought if I didn't react, maybe he would stop. "You're a dick," I told him. On that day I failed.

He shrugged, feigning ignorance. "Whatever do you mean?"

I ignored him and huffed annoyed that we were waiting on Paul who was taking forever to talk to a group of women. "Is he planning on talking to every woman with huge tits today?"

"Sex sells," Marcus pointed out. "He's good at seducing women into adventure."

I stuck my finger in my mouth and pretended to gag.

"Are you offended, Queen of Prudes? I'm sure those lovely painted walls in our office will sell more dives than an attractive man who actually jumps."

I flipped him the bird because I couldn't come up with a witty comeback.

"No one is making you do it, Clara, so why do you care?"

"Because it's . . . tacky." How could he not see that?

"So what if it is? If you're going to stand around all day with that face, just go back to the RV."

"What face?" I asked in offense.

"Like you need a giant enema. Chill."

For a moment, I wondered if I was strong enough to punt him across the track like a football. He really knew how to get under my skin.

When Paul finally joined us again, he pretended to ignore our spat and focused on trying to earn clientele. Somehow that involved only stopping at groups including attractive women.

"Uncurl your lip," Paul ordered as we left one group. "This is big money for us."

"I get that," I griped. "But why do we have to be here all day?"

Cutting me a look that said, *watch this,* he turned off the gravel path and walked right over to a group of young men and women, dancing as they blared country music. The women flocked to him, puffing out their chests so their bosoms would stick out more. Paul, in his straw cowboy hat and tight, black T-shirt, flashed his smile, the one I had come to know as the hook, line, and sinker smile. Stupid smile. I hated it. I hated it mostly because it had the same effect on me as it did every other woman.

For the next twenty minutes I stood to the side while Paul drank beer with his new posse and at the end of it, he handed all of them a brochure and told them to watch for him because he'd be skydiving into the race. I tried not to be annoyed when one of the women wrote her number on the palm of his hand. As we walked away, my aggravation was rolling off of me in waves. Paul sensed this because he said, "What?"

"You shouldn't drink before a jump," I griped. It was the only thing I could come up with. Marcus hadn't quite finished with the last group and remained behind as we moved on.

"It was two beers and I've been chugging water all day," he argued as he shook his water bottle in my face. I knew he had been, but he still shouldn't have drunk anything alcoholic. Period. "What's really the problem here?"

"Nothing." I shrugged. "I just think you're trying to say flirting is promoting and it's not."

"I flirt to promote," he argued.

"Or to get laid," I quipped.

He laughed and wrapped an arm around my shoulders, squeezing me to him. My body tensed so I immediately pulled away. He held his hands up as if surrendering. "Sorry."

I clenched my jaw and looked away. I didn't like him touching me because, actually, I *really* liked him touching me. It had been happening more and more; his arm resting against my arm as we looked at something on the office computer together; his hand brushing mine as he handed me something. Small touches, yet never really simple. I refused to fall victim to his charm because the truth was it was all bullshit. It had to be. He was handsome and charming and his smile captivated everyone, and all of those things coupled together were lethal. Somehow those things directed at me made me feel . . . special. Which was why it was all bullshit. No one was special to Paul James. He'd share that lethal combo with anyone.

"You have got to loosen up, Clara," he chuckled as he adjusted his straw hat.

"Do I now?" His statement agitated me. I didn't consider myself an uptight person. Not at that time anyway. Okay, maybe I was guarded. But I had just been through hell in the last few months and guarded was the only way I knew to survive. But I wasn't stuck-up.

"I just mean you need to have some fun."

"Is your definition of fun walking around a racetrack half naked? You want me to act like all of these women out here; desperate for attention?"

He let out a long sigh. I guess I was exhausting him as well. "No, not half naked. I just mean, it's okay to flirt with a guy even if you have no interest in him."

"Some men would call that a tease," I pointed out.

"Only stupid ones."

I shook my head in disbelief. "You mean flirt to sell?"

"And so what if you did? You're the one always preaching about presentation. *It's not just the jump,*" he imitated me, his tone high-pitched, mocking me. *Do I really sound like that?* "You can flirt without acting like a . . . ya know."

I raised my eyebrows. "No. I don't *know.*"

"Like you're easy or something."

"Jesus, Paul. You're unbelievable."

He laughed. "I know," he said sarcastically.

"Should I go and flirt with those guys over there?" I pointed to a group near a jacked up Chevy truck.

"Well, we've made changes and tried new things that you've wanted to implement. Maybe you should try something of ours?"

"You want me to try acting like a ho?"

He took a long swig from his water bottle. "Jeez, Clara," he groaned. "You're being extreme. Obviously I don't think you should go over there and rub your tits in their faces."

"Then what do you want me to do?" I snapped.

"Can't you just go over there and act like you like them and then slip in the fact that you own a skydiving business and how thrilling it is? Fuck." Then he took a stab at me. "Not that you would know."

I narrowed my eyes at him. "I don't have to jump to know it's thrilling."

"Do you know how weird it is that you own a skydiving business but refuse to jump?" The answer to that question was *yes.* I did know. And even if I didn't know, or I'd somehow magically made myself forget that fun little fact, Marcus went out of his way to remind me every chance he got how asinine it was.

"I will jump," I argued. "One day."

"It's okay, Clara. If you can't do it, you can't do it." He shrugged as if it was no big deal.

"What? Jump?"

He cut me a look that said, *you're an idiot.* "No, babe. *Flirt.* It's okay if you can't flirt."

I stopped on the dusty gravel path we'd been following and stared at him dumbly. *Was he serious?* It took him passing me a few steps before he realized I was no longer beside him. When he turned around and saw my expression, a wide smile spread across his face. "What'd I say?"

"Oh, I don't know," I said dramatically, throwing my hands up. "Apparently I'm a mutant incapable of seducing a man."

He threw his head back and snorted out a loud laugh. "Wow. Got all that out of what I just said, did ya?"

"Shut up, Paul," I mumbled as I walked by him, shoving him with my shoulder, which only made him laugh more.

"Are you saying you can do it?" he yelled after me.

Spinning around, I crossed my arms. "Of course, I can do it!" And I could. That's not to say I could do it well, however, I had two things that men liked; ass and tits. Oh, make that three. I was breathing. Those three attributes were my key to success in the art of flirting.

"Prove it," he challenged me. If a look could convey hatred, then the one I gave him did. Bastard.

Looking down at my attire, I twisted my mouth. I didn't exactly look like the other women walking around. They looked sexy . . . well, some of them did. The ones that were trying too hard looked trashy. I mean, really. They were wearing bikinis for God's sake. There wasn't a body of water or pool for miles.

Modest.

That's the word that came to mind when I thought of myself.

I looked modest.

And as much as I absolutely hated to admit this, I didn't want Paul to see me as modest. I didn't want him to see me as trash either. I held Paul's gaze as he approached me and I tugged up the front hem of my blue T-shirt and looped it through the collar. I pushed the material up so it was wedged under my bra. My separation from Kurt had a lot of shitty things that came with it, depression for starters. But while depression sucked majorly, the weight I'd lost was the only bright side. My tummy was flat and as I pushed down the waist of my white shorts slightly, I could tell Paul was liking what he was seeing when he widened his eyes and his mouth quirked up on one side into an appreciative smile. I couldn't see myself, but the whistles coming from men passing by us was all I needed. The slight tweak to my outfit paired with my cowboy boots, and I was prepared to flirt. God, I felt like such a hussy. I mean, who does that? But the way Paul licked his perfect lips, his tongue darting out, wetting them as he stared at me, I kind of forgot to feel bad about being a hussy.

Tugging the tie from my hair, I shook it out, letting the length of my hair fall down my back and cascade over my shoulders. Paul's smile faded.

"What?"

"I didn't mean you had to do . . ." he waved his hand, motioning it in front of my body, "all that."

"Do I look bad or something?" I asked, second-guessing myself.

"No," he mumbled. "You look fine."

Fine?

He told me I looked *fine*.

He might as well have said I looked mediocre.

Plain.

Unexciting.

Maybe pathetic.

"Gee, thanks, Paul."

"Oh for Christ's sake, Clara." He clenched his eyes closed. "You know you look hot as fuck." With a wave of his hand, a frustrated gesture as if he was dismissing me, he passed by me, grumbling to himself. I smiled to myself where he couldn't see. Moments later, I sashayed over to a small group of men playing cornhole.

"Can I get in on the next game?" I asked, twirling a lock of my hair between my fingers.

They welcomed me most enthusiastically. Within a minute, I had a cold beer in my hand and the attention of two decent looking, yet sweaty men. Paul bullshitted with the guys on the other side of the game and from time to time I caught them looking at me or pointing at me. At one point, I puckered my lips at Paul and he rolled his eyes. As we played, I asked the men around me about their jobs, their lives, their girlfriends, and so on. Then came my opening.

"What do you do?" one of them asked as he stared at my chest. Eyes up here, buddy.

"Me?" I threw my beanbag, sinking it, and earned a loud groan from the guy standing next to me. His partner and mine were on the other side. "I own a skydiving business."

"Are you serious?" he snorted.

Tilting my head, I looked at him. "Is it so hard to believe?"

"Why don't you tell him in detail what it's like to dive, Clara," Marcus interrupted. I looked down at him, glaring. Where the hell did he come from? He must've just caught up to us. I shot Paul a quick glance, but he didn't seem to understand that my look was saying, *get your ass over here and take your asshole friend away.*

"Clara is our best diver," Marcus continued.

"I wouldn't say that," I laughed nervously.

"She's just being modest. Go on now, tell him all about it." Marcus' mouth curled. Asshole.

I could do this. I didn't have to know the technical details. I only had to sell the idea of the thrill of diving. Licking my lips, I let out a soft sigh. I was aiming for schoolgirl sultry, but I wasn't sure I pulled it off. Acting like a slut to sell wasn't something I really wanted to do, but Marcus needed to be proved wrong. I was fearless. I could do anything. I hoped.

"How can I describe the rush of diving?" I mused as I trailed my fingers lazily down the collar of my shirt and stopped just before I reached my cleavage. "No matter how prepared you are, you still feel nervous. Kind of like . . . making love to someone for the first time." I glanced around and realized everyone was watching me, listening, even Paul who had moved over to our side. Marcus was standing with his arms crossed, clearly convinced I wouldn't pull this off. "As they take you up in the plane, the engine roaring, that pressure building as you get higher and higher . . ." Lifting my hair up, I rolled my cold beer over the back of my neck and then my chest. I could feel everyone's eyes upon me, burning into me. I really did feel like a slut. "Your heart is beating like a drum, your blood pumping because the anticipation is killing you. Then you're at the door, the cool air whipping against your face, the earth spread out beneath you. It's breathtaking."

"Then what?" Marcus asked, trying like hell to trip me up.

"Then . . ." I paused. I had to continue. "Then you're right there . . . on the precipice of the big finish." It's amazing how you could almost describe anything using sexual innuendo. I was nailing this. The men around us were hooked; a few of them had moved closer and closer as I spoke. They seemed to be hooked, anyway. I couldn't be sure if I was selling to them or if they were just horny bastards acting like dogs panting over me. Or maybe they were both. I let out a soft moan for emphasis.

"Then you fly," Paul intervened. "You feel free and weightless. The adrenaline rush is intense."

"It sounds intense," the one standing closest to me said, his gaze fixed on me. "Maybe I can get your number and you can tell me some more about it?"

Before I could respond, Paul whipped a brochure out of his back pocket and handed it to him. "Call that number there or visit our website." With that, he took my beer and threw one arm around me, placing his hand on the bare skin of my side. I was stunned. Marcus was too, apparently, as his mouth twisted even more. The one that asked for my number backed away, holding his hands up as if surrendering. I moved to jerk Paul's hand away, but his grip tightened. Then he said, "You guys enjoy the race." Paul led me away, his arm still around me, his hand gripping my waist. When we were about twenty feet away, I got my wits back and shoved him off of me. He laughed as he stumbled to the side.

"What the hell was that?" I hissed.

"They were about to mount and start dry humping you."

"You're the one that told me I should flirt to sell!"

"Yes, flirt. Not look like you were auditioning for Playboy."

I rubbed my forehead. This conversation was killing me. But deep down, I knew what he was saying. He thought I went overboard; went too far. And I did. I knew that. But I was so tired of him and Marcus and the guys making me out to be this shrew with a stick up my ass. Just because I didn't walk around and act like a bimbo and fawn all over every attractive man I saw, didn't mean I was incapable of doing it. Looking back, it was stupid. I was an intelligent woman. And I reduced myself to prove him wrong. The feminists of the world would have hung their heads in shame if they'd witnessed it. But on the other side of that, there was this: I wanted to make Paul see me in a different way. I wanted him to see I could be sexy. However, I would never have told him that. So I played dumb. "You said to *flirt*. You challenged me to prove I could do it."

He chuckled disdainfully. "Well, I didn't know you'd go over there and act like a sex kitten," he grumbled.

Shaking my head, I asked, "Sex kitten?"

"What was with rubbing the beer all over you like that?"

I laughed. Like, really laughed. "I thought it was a nice touch."

"All you needed was some cheesy music and you'd have had the start of an amateur porn movie."

I rolled my eyes. "Now you're exaggerating."

"Dude was about to bend you over the cornhole boards and go at it."

"Paul!" I shrieked, looking around to see if people passing by heard him. "You're being disgusting."

"It could have been titled: *Corn in The Hole.*

"You're so gross!" I groaned as I tugged my shirt back down, my modesty having returned full force.

"No," Marcus piped in, making me jump. I hadn't noticed him behind us. What was it with this guy? "He's not so *gross.* He's so jealous."

I pressed my lips together, unsure of how to respond to that. Was Paul really jealous? As for Paul, he pretended not to hear Marcus. Instead, he immediately beelined for another group of people and stopped right in front of a woman with huge boobs wearing a white T-shirt. And she had no bra on. Paul was like white on rice. Maybe he wasn't jealous after all.

Ashley watches me, the slightest smirk on her face. "He was definitely jealous."

I snicker. "He was the most confusing man I'd ever met." Looking at my watch, I realize I'm already late for dinner. "Are we done for today? I'm late."

"Oh, sure. Same time next week?"

"See you then."

CHAPTER TWENTY-SIX

Clara

WHEN I GET home after Ashley releases me, it's already close to seven. As I climb the stairs of my porch, the front door opens and out steps Mei-ling, donning a Chinese Hanfu dress. It's red, with gold flowers embroidered into it. Her black hair is tied up in a seemingly loose bun, sticks crossing in the back of it. She looks like a China doll, her skin flawless, lightened with makeup and rouge added to her cheeks.

"Ni hao," she greets me, bowing slightly. I stare at her a moment, slightly stunned. I was expecting to come home and eat pizza and pass out on the couch while watching some corny movie with everyone, not to be greeted at the door this way. From the open doorway, beautiful music plays, beats and twangs of instruments I'm not familiar with, but the sound is amazing. Foreign.

"Hi, Mei-ling." I give a little wave.

"Ni hao, Mom!" Neena appears in the doorway. I'm glad she's so excited. She, too, is wearing a Hanfu dress, but hers is light blue with white embroidery. My little doll. Her face is made up, same as Mei-ling's, with lighter rouge on her cheeks, and she's wearing a wig that matches Mei-ling's hair. Earlier today, she looked tired and worn out. But now, she seems so happy and peppy, with a giant smile on her face. My mouth quirks up as I stare at her.

"You look beautiful, Neena."

She looks up at Mei-ling, pleased with my compliment.

"You always do," I quickly added, because it's true. "What's going— " My words are halted as Paul appears just behind her. In a men's black Hanfu lined with silver, he looks incredible. The silky black fabric against his deeply golden skin, matched with his salt-and-pepper hair is sexy as hell. I swear, the man looks good in anything. And in nothing at all as well. It's really not fair. I center in on his mouth. Suddenly the memory of the kiss we shared snaps through my mind and I can't help licking my dry lips. It's rolled through my mind on repeat since it happened; how he held me, how he silenced me, how he sucked the breath right out of me. My life is filled with worry and dread. I don't know how things with Neena will turn out. That scares me. I have so little power. So little control. The not knowing is awful. I fear the unexpected. But Paul kissing me was definitely unexpected—in the best way. He made me stop thinking for a brief moment. And I find myself craving more.

Paul must recognize my reaction because he tightens his mouth, fighting a smile. He knows the look. He knows I'm attracted to him. Even when I've hated him, I've always found him attractive. "Ni hao, Clara." He dips his head in greeting, his hands behind his back. When he raises it again, his eyes find mine, and there's a heat in them that hits me everywhere below the belt. I swear, one look has my insides fluttering. Tingling. It's his superpower. And it's my kryptonite.

"Hi," I say, dumbly, before swallowing the dry lump in my throat and tearing my gaze from his. "Looks like I'm late to the party."

"Actually, you are just in time," Mei-ling tells me, as she steps to the side and motions a hand for me to enter. Neena and Paul move as well so I can step inside, but Mei-ling touches my arm, stopping me. "It is tradition to take your shoes off before you enter." Looking down to my right, I see everyone else's shoes lined up nice and orderly.

"Oh, sorry." I quickly slip my shoes off, placing them next to Paul's, then step inside. The stairway to the second floor is lit with beautiful Chinese lanterns, but the living room is covered with giant, wall-sized pictures of what appear to be Chinese buildings.

Neena takes my hand and squeezes, resting her head against my arm. When I look down at her, she's smiling as she stares at the photos. "Dad said since I can't go to China, he'd bring China to me."

I blink fast. *Don't cry. Don't cry.* She's always wanted to travel; see the world. Paul's need to be free and seek adventure is definitely genetic. With her being so young, her poor health, and money being so tight paying medical bills, traveling hasn't been possible. Paul is standing on the other side of me now, but I can't look at him. If I do, I'll definitely cry. Instead, I slip my hand in his and squeeze. It's the only way I can communicate how much this means. Not just to Neena, whom it means the world to, but to me. When he squeezes back, he continues to hold my hand.

Neena points to the huge picture in front of us. "This is the Tiananmen. It's known as the *Gate of Heavenly Peace.*"

"Wow," I manage with a husky voice, my throat still tight with emotion.

"Mei-ling says it's like their national symbol."

"Should we have her dress and then we can give her a tour of China?" Mei-ling asks. I spin around. Her tone is so demure; not like how she usually speaks. Normally, she is loud and straightforward. Now, she's . . . soft. I guess she's taking this presentation pretty seriously.

"Dress?"

"Oh, yes," Paul chuckles. "We have a Hanfu for you as well. It's on your bed."

"I'll help you," Mei-ling adds.

"And hurry up," Marcus cuts in as he enters the room. His hair is tied back and he's wearing a black Hanfu, just like Paul's, minus the silver. I can't help grinning.

"Shut it, Clara," he grumbles. I know deep down he hates this. But he loves Neena more. Like Paul, he'll do anything for her. "The dumplings are almost done."

"Don't ruin them!" Mei-ling yells from halfway up the stairs, sounding like her old self. I try to muffle my snort of laughter. *There she is.*

"Be right back," I call as I follow her up. As I climb the stairs, I look down and see Paul is watching me. And just before the wall from above blocks my view of him, I mouth, *thank you.*

"I want to help Mom get ready, too!" Neena calls as she follows me up the stairs. "We'll be right back." I gaze back and notice she's limping slightly and her face cringes a little when she's halfway up the stairs, but she quickly notices I'm staring and smiles. Her joints must be hurting. She wants this so much, I'm afraid she's hiding how exhausted and pained she is at the moment.

CHAPTER TWENTY-SEVEN

Paul

W HILE THE LADIES return, Clara looks incredible in her Hanfu. It looks like mine, black with silver lining. Her hair is up, just like Mei-ling's, but she must've decided against the makeup. The way the dress is cut, how it fits her body . . . she looks beautiful.

Clara is unusually quiet as Neena leads her through the rooms, explaining what she's looking at; the Temple of Heaven, the Great Wall of China, and so on. Clara gets a thorough history lesson and by the time Neena is done, it's time to eat. She hasn't been too hungry lately, and I'm hoping she's up to eating the foreign cuisine. The table is set, with chopsticks to the right of the plate, and glasses are out.

"In proper Chinese etiquette, the guest of honor sits facing the doorway," Mei-ling explains. "This is not our house, but as Marcus is cooking and we are technically hosting, he will sit in the seat closest to the kitchen, facing Neena."

Mei-ling directs us to our seats and when Marcus enters, he's holding a tray with some kind of fancy dish with a lid.

"Ooh, what is it, Marcus?" Neena asks, as she raises her head in an attempt to peek.

"This, my dear Neena," Marcus begins with his best imitation of an Asian accent, "is a Chinese specialty. We have made only the best for you, young grasshopper."

"Oh shit," I murmur. "He's going Mr. Miyagi on us."

"Who is Mr. Miyagi?" Neena questions, her face scrunched up.

I look at Clara like she's insane. In a serious and intent tone, I ask slowly, "She's never seen *The Karate Kid?*"

Clara appears to be spacing out for a beat and then rolls her eyes at me and chortles. "Afraid not." Maybe she's forgetting how much of a cult classic this movie is.

Turning to Neena, I meet her gaze head-on. "Neena, after dinner I want you to go upstairs and pack a bag. I'm taking you out of this home immediately. Clearly you have been deprived of any real culture and your mother needs to have her rights taken away."

Neena giggles and Clara shakes her head at my ridiculousness.

"And you!" I point to Marcus. "How could you let this happen?"

"I'm sorry," Marcus feigns crying. "I've failed you as a friend."

"Mr. Miyagi was Japanese, not Chinese," Mei-ling points out, seemingly annoyed.

"But he played a Chinese man in the movie," Marcus adds.

"No, he didn't," she argues.

He laughs. "He was badass, nonetheless." Then looking down to Neena, he says, in his best Miyagi voice, "First learn stand, then learn fly. Nature rule, Nanson, not mine."

"Another Mr. Miyagi quote," Clara says, a little dryly. At least she's talking more now. I'm starting to wonder what has her so off tonight.

"Marcus," Mei-ling says his name, her thick accent rising an octave the more annoyed she gets. "The food."

"Oh, yes." Marcus nods, still holding the tray. "Tonight we have made a very special meal for you. You are going to love it. Your parents are going to love it." Marcus is purposely taking forever, enjoying riling Clara and Mei-ling up.

"Spit it out, Marcus," Clara groans.

"Silence!" he snaps at Clara, still in an Asian accent, making us laugh.

"For you, tonight," he sits the tray down slowly, "we have . . . the pupu platter."

Neena's head rears back as her mouth twists. "Poo poo?"

"Oh, yes, so much pupu," he replies, laying heavy emphasis on the pupu.

Neena looks at me, eyes wide, sheer shock and disbelief in her gaze, and mouths, *poo poo?*

The room roars with laughter, to which her face turns bright red. Even Mei-ling is laughing with us.

"What?" Neena asks, looking utterly confused.

Clara leans against me as she laughs, unable to stop. Leave it to Marcus to make everyone laugh. I wrap my arm around her and pull her to me as our bodies shake. It feels good to hold her this way, when she's happy. I constantly see her mind working overtime. When she finally pulls herself up, she is wiping under her eyes she's still laughing so hard. "Not poop, babe. I promise," she cackles, before chuckling softly. "It's just the name of the dish."

Neena cuts Marcus a sassy look, even though she's smiling. I swear this kid has the best sense of humor. She just rolls with things. She knows how to laugh at herself. "Very funny, Marcus."

"You really think I'd feed you poop?" he asks as his laughter ebbs.

"I don't know," she answers honestly.

Marcus lifts the lid off the dish and in true Chinese etiquette, begins serving us. "Well, if it makes you feel better, this pupu platter is probably going to make me poo poo later, for real."

"Marcus!" Mei-ling shrieks. Then she starts fussing at him in her native language that none of us, not even Marcus, understands.

"You. Are. Gross," Clara tells him while I try to bite back my roars of heavy chuckles.

"Just don't use my bathroom," Neena insists as she practices with her chopsticks. "You clogged it last time. We had to hire a plumber."

"Oh yeah," Marcus mumbles as he looks off to the side as if remembering.

"Real classy, dude," I interject, but he simply grins.

Marcus continues to serve the food as he speaks to Neena. "I think your mother actually cooked that night. Must've been food poisoning. Sent me straight to the shitter."

"Language, Marcus. And it was not *my* cooking," Clara defends. "And are we seriously talking about Marcus taking a dump right now? I mean . . . right now at the dinner table?"

"Ironic, isn't it?" Marcus looks at Clara thoughtfully before turning back to Neena. "We're discussing poo poo, while eating pupu, kid."

What is it about gross stuff that makes kids laugh? Neena's face lights up as she laughs as hard as Marcus. There's not a single person in this room that isn't touched by her smile. It's captivating. And I know, without a doubt, we'd all do anything to see it. Even if that means talking about poop when we're about to eat. As I watch her, my heart tightens, and I feel Clara's hand rest on my leg and squeeze as she watches Neena thoughtfully. I place mine on hers as our eyes meet. It's one of those moments, and I know I'll never forget. I wish I could freeze it, or somehow box it; trap it so we never lose it. Here we are, with our friends, and our daughter. Our daughter is sick, weakening before our very eyes, and she's laughing. How many of these moments do we have left? How many more might we get? I'd give anything to see that smile forever. That thought chokes me. And angers me. I've missed a lifetime of these moments . . . *her lifetime* of moments. It's not fair. And suddenly, I'm fuming. I'm angry I was denied this. Seeing my little girl every day. Watching her play, so carefree, without a single fear in the world. It's not fucking fair. I'm not ever going to be ready to say good-bye to my child. Why didn't Clara tell me? Why didn't she try harder to find me? I know she emailed . . . but is that really trying? She robbed me of precious time.

I scoot away slightly. I can't touch her right now. Her hand slips off my thigh, and I refuse to look at her. I already know how she looks. Confused. A moment ago I was relishing her body against mine as we laughed. We were a unit. Now, I can't even look at her. I plaster a smile on and try to focus on the moment. This moment. With my daughter who is smiling. One of the few I have left.

After an incredible meal consisting of the pupu platter, Chinese dumplings, and snacking on Tuckahoe pie, we're stuffed. Clara and I decide to do the dishes while Marcus, Mei-ling, and Neena plop on the couch and digest for a bit.

Clara is washing a pot as I stack the last of the plates by the sink. "I think Marcus used every dish in the house."

I snort. That's the only thing I can do. Only it comes out like a growl.

She slams her hand down on the faucet, shutting off the water. "What is it, Paul?"

"What's what?" I play dumb.

"This," she motions a soapy hand at me. "You went from hot to cold in a matter of seconds with me. What is it?"

"Nothing," I answer, gritting my teeth. I want to lash out at her, but I know I shouldn't. It won't change what happened and it won't change what is happening. I missed the first twelve years of Neena's life. And now she's dying. Those are the facts. Yelling at Clara, no matter how angry I am with her, won't change that.

"Fine." She flips the faucet back on and starts scrubbing the pot again. Under her breath, she mumbles, "Ruin a great night with your little head trip."

I lose it. My heart thunders as my rage pumps through me. I hit the faucet, causing her to jump. When she twists her head and sees me, she narrows her eyes, glowering at me, but doesn't back away.

"Ruin a great night?" I snort with disdain and derision. "How many good nights with her have you gotten?"

"What?" she questions, appearing angry and confused.

"Twelve years," I answer for her, stepping closer. She doesn't back away because . . . well . . . it's Clara. She backs down to no one. "Twelve years you saw her grow, laugh, and play, and twelve years of fucking hugs, Clara. Of laughter and pure and sweet smiles. You got all of that. And what do I get?" I ask her, my voice cracking slightly with pain and emotion.

Clara's enraged expression ebbs in to what almost looks like shame.

"You denied me that. You denied me what little time she has had."

Her expression morphs back to raw anger.

"You denied yourself that, Paul," she hisses quietly. "You took off. Not me."

"You could have found me. You know you could have. I mean, here, only when you were at your most desperate time, you found me. Why not before, huh?"

She finally steps back, her forearms and hands soapy, dripping water on the floor. "The same reason you never came back. You never called. You never wrote. Not me. Not Marcus. You disappeared. So let's be real here," she growls. "You didn't want to be found because you didn't want to come back."

"You were having my baby!" I boom. "I deserved to know that!"

"You are ridiculous!" she booms back. "You leave and I'm supposed to chase you? And for what? So that you'd hate me for trapping you here?

Or you'd play part-time father in between your world travels and fucking adventures?" She pulls a dish towel off the counter and wipes angrily at her hands. "While you'd been skydiving in Brazil and backpacking through jungles, and screwing exotic women, I've been running a business, which by the way, funds your fucking adventures. Oh, and I've been raising a child by myself . . . who happens to be dying. Don't you think that destroys me? Occupies all of my time? Yes, you missed some pretty amazing times in her life. I won't lie. She has been my world and I wouldn't trade a second of it. Those moments are more valuable than anything to me." She places a hand over her heart.

I wince as her hand trembles. But her words are like a knife in my chest. I should have had those moments, too.

"But you also missed the blow of finding out your eight-year-old child has cancer. You missed watching her go through radiation, chemo. You missed the nights when she was so weak she couldn't get out of bed and puked all over herself. You missed watching your healthy, vibrant daughter lose her hair and cry when people stared at her. You missed watching her fall behind in school, unable to keep up with her peers. You missed having to choose whether to do more chemo or let things go. You—"

"Wait," I cut her off. "What?"

Clara pauses, unsure of what I'm asking.

"More chemo was an option?"

She sighs, exhausted by our argument. Tears are streaming down her face and she uses the dish towel to wipe them away. "Not to cure her. It may have bought us more time with her."

I back away from her and fist my hair. "And you didn't do it?"

Clara's head snaps up, her narrowed gaze fierce with fury. "We decided together what was best."

"You let a child decide this?"

"We decided together," she growls at me.

"Are you fucking kidding me?" I shout. "Why would you decide to not have more time with her?"

"Because I'd be miserable," Neena cries from the kitchen doorway. Her makeup is smeared from her own tears and she's holding her wig in her hand. Watching your kid slowly dying has been fucking awful. But watching your dying kid cry tops the list of the worst things ever.

"Oh, baby," I whisper, swallowing past the lump in my throat.

Marcus is behind her and he gently pulls her arm, trying to lead her away. "Come on, Neena."

Neena weakly jerks her arm away and steps into the kitchen. "What would more time mean if I'm too tired and sick to live?" she asks through trembling lips. "They said my heart and kidneys would suffer. And chemo, Dad, it's awful. I would have done it again if they'd said I'd live . . . but I wouldn't. It would just . . . delay my death. I'm so sick and tired of dying. Can't you understand that? I'm tired, Daddy."

My eyes are burning with tears. Clara is holding her fist to her mouth, and she says nothing as her body shakes. She's trying to contain herself. But Neena isn't done with me yet.

"She should've told you about me." Then she looks at Clara. "You could've tried harder, Mom. I needed my dad." Clara eyes well up more and she nods in confirmation.

"I could have," she manages, her gaze meeting mine.

But then Neena looks to me and my heart stills. She's disappointed. My own eyes are staring back at me with offense. "You can be mad at her for not finding you sooner. But, Paul . . ."

I stop breathing. She called me Paul. Not Dad. Not Daddy. "Do not ever yell at her again about what is happening to me. It's not her fault I'm sick." Tears are steadily falling down her face and I want crawl into a deep black hole. I did this. I'm such an asshole. I pull on my hair some more. Fuck. Fuck. Fuck.

"She hasn't lived because she's been trying to save my life. She's done everything for me. Please . . . don't yell at her." Then she goes to Clara and hugs her. These two ladies that I love more than anything in the world are crying and hugging, because of me . . . well, I am officially the biggest piece of shit in the world.

"I'm sorry," I say, my voice husky. "I need . . . I need to get some air." Marcus calls after me, but I don't look back. I'm out the back door in a flash. As soon as the night air hits my heated face, I gulp deep breaths. What the fuck just happened in there? Am I insane?

"Well that was fun," Marcus mumbles from beside me. I didn't even hear him follow me.

"Shut up, Marcus," I groan.

He shifts beside me. He has no idea what to say. No friend likes telling another friend that they're an idiot. Normally he'd come out with it anyway, but I guess with the subject matter being a delicate one, he's holding back. His voice lowers. "You okay?"

"Other than making my sick kid cry on what was otherwise a perfect night? Yeah, I'm okay. Just fucking peachy."

He pats the lower part of my back because that's as high as he can reach. "Okay. You had a moment. We all do. Now it's done. It's out of your system."

"I feel horrible for what just happened in there. I just feel so . . . gypped. It's not fair."

Marcus snorts. "I know you're hurting, brother. I'm sure you feel gypped. You feel slighted. You feel like you were denied something you should have had."

"Exactly," I exclaim loudly.

"I'm sure Neena can relate."

And there it is. Like a truck to the face. The only one who should get to act like a giant jerk because they feel robbed is Neena. Because she *is* getting robbed; she's getting deprived of life, of time. I nod a few times, letting Marcus know I've heard him loud and clear. It was exactly what I needed to hear; a hard punch of reality to the nuts.

"So let's go do the dishes since you've made all the ladies in the house cry tonight. Even Mei-ling has joined in."

"When I fuck up, I go all out, don't I?" I jest even though the humor isn't there.

"We all have our gifts, my friend."

Clara and Neena never come back down, even when Marcus and Mei-ling leave. Marcus and I had taken down all the pictures and lanterns, cleaned the kitchen, and put away the leftovers. Now the house is silent. As I finish climbing the stairs, I see Clara is in her room, lying on her bed. Her eyes are open as she stares ahead, lost in thought. I gently tap my knuckle on the door and her head pops up.

"May I come in?"

"Yeah," she says as she clears her throat. "Shut the door behind you. I don't want to wake Neena." I do as she says and move so I'm standing in front of her where she's now sitting on the bed.

"How's Neena?"

She inhales and lets it out slowly. "She's okay. She just hated seeing us fight. She's asleep."

Her red and swollen eyes meet mine and my chest aches so fucking bad. I drop to my knees and grab her hips, pulling her to me. Her hands find my shoulders and hold me so I can't pull her closer.

"What are you doing?" she asks.

"I'm getting on my knees and begging you to forgive me for being a giant asshole."

She snorts.

"Not just tonight. But thirteen years ago. When I left."

Her mouth tightens as she looks down at me. "I'm sorry, Clara. I love you. I loved you then. I love you now. I love Neena. And all I want, more than anything I've ever wanted in my entire life, is to love you both and be with both of you. I know you've fought for her—that you're still fighting for her. I know you've done everything you can. Please forgive me."

She looks away and I wonder if she can't. Could I blame her if she couldn't forgive me? But then, she sniffs once and pushes me back gently as she slides off the bed to her knees. I scoot back to give her room.

"I'm on my knees, with you, Paul. Neither of us are perfect. We've both made mistakes, and . . . I can forgive you. I *do* forgive you. Can you forgive me? For not finding you sooner."

My eyes widen in shock.

"Yes," I whisper. "I forgive you."

Our eyes lock as we watch each other, our chest heaving up and down slowly. When her eyes move down to my mouth and her tongue darts out, wetting her lips, I can't stop myself. I lean in, wrapping her in my arms, pressing her lips to mine. Her hands slide up my chest to my shoulders until her fingers are threaded in my hair and she holds it in her fists as I push her back against the bed and kiss her. When her hands move to untie the belt on my Hanfu, I grab her wrists, stopping her. Her brows furrow and her eyes are instantly filled with confusion and embarrassment.

"I want to," I tell her. "So fucking badly." I let out a frustrated breath. "But not tonight. I don't want it to happen like this." I *do* want it. But I want her to be happy, not with red eyes and a puffy nose because I'm a dick and I made her cry.

She nods a few times in understanding. I stand first, then hold a hand out, helping her to her feet. When she pulls at my shirt, I hold her wrists, questioning her with my eyes.

"No sex. Just sleep with me. Please."

Releasing her wrists, I hold my arms up, and awkwardly we get my Hanfu shirt off. We take our time, removing each other's clothes until I'm in nothing but my boxers and she's in her panties and a white tank top. Her body hasn't changed much, still lean, her skin still like silk. We climb into bed and she lays her head on my chest, just above my heart. We don't speak as I hold her. There are no more words. Because there isn't a need for any. Too much has already been said tonight.

CHAPTER TWENTY-EIGHT

Clara

"MOM," NEENA WHISPERS my name. When I open my eyes, she's standing beside my bed, a grin on her face, the camera on and pointing at me. I give a small wave to the camera before throwing the pillow over my face.

Mumbling through the material, I announce, "I look like a mummy. Don't I look fabulous?"

"You've looked worse," she laughs.

I poke my head out. "Thanks. Turn it off, Neena," I groan.

Smirking, she flips the screen closed, and sets the camera on my nightstand. She's still wearing her favorite pajamas; fleece yoga pants with a ratty *AC/DC* T-shirt of mine she's now the proud owner of. I roll over slightly. There's a weight on me and it takes me a moment to realize it's Paul's arm.

Neena waggles her brows. "Sleep good last night?"

I decide not to react. She's already caught us in bed together, even though technically nothing happened, I won't bother trying to explain. At closer examination of her, I notice she seems quite pale this morning. More than she did last night. This worries me. She isn't wearing her scarf, so the dark fuzz that covers her scalp from where very little of her hair is starting to grow back adds a deep contrast against her pale skin. "You okay?" I ask. I try not to pester her, since my one goal now is to keep her as happy and healthy for as long as I can, but every day it seems she fades more and more.

"I'm fine," she dismisses me as she turns and walks to my dresser, grabbing a tray. "I made you guys breakfast." Oh. The tray is actually a metal cookie sheet covered with one of my less-stained dish towels to hide the burn marks on it. She even added a little flower in a tiny vase.

My brows perk up. "Oh, honey . . . You did?"

"And coffee, too."

"Did I hear coffee?" Paul grumbles, not bothering to lift his head.

"Breakfast in bed, Mr. James. Aren't we the spoiled ones?"

Paul rolls over, his eyes squinting against the morning light. "You made us breakfast, princess?"

"Dadddd . . ." she moans.

"Your mother doesn't count as other people," he grunts as he sits up. "Pretend she's an inanimate object."

"You know how to make a lady feel real special, Paul," I say, sardonically, as I sit up, pulling the blanket to my chest.

"Okay, Mom doesn't count," Neena confirms as she sets the tray on the end of the bed.

"Aw, thanks, honey," I remark with a smirk.

Neena places paper plates on our laps with two pieces of almost-burnt, buttered toast and paper napkins. "Here's your coffee." She hands us each a mug. "I made it the way you both like it."

Paul's mouth quirks up slightly as he looks down at his mug. There are little coffee grounds floating on the top, with chunks of creamer that didn't dissolve. Taking a sip, he moans as if it's the most delicious thing he's ever tasted. Neena grins with pride, picking up the cookie tray.

"I have to get dressed," she informs us as she sets the tray on the nightstand after removing her camera. "Yell for me if you need anything." She exits slowly, the slight limp noticeable again, and my heart hurts a little. My baby is in pain. Millions of dreaded thoughts fill my mind. Mostly, is this the beginning of the end?

"Thank you for breakfast, sweetheart," I tell her as I bite into my toast and feign a smile of enjoyment.

When she leaves, as I chew, I glance at Paul. He's holding his burnt toast, his mouth twisted to the side. "Clearly she gets her cooking skills from you. But you know what? It's the best damn breakfast I've ever had, because it was made with her little hands."

I smile genuinely. This is as hard on Paul as it is on me. He continues to chew and I can't help but chuckle a little, but when I do, I choke on the toast in my mouth and start coughing. Taking a sip from my coffee, I get it down, but then there's the issue of the coffee itself.

"I know," Paul murmurs, taking in my expression. "It's awful. Her own original recipe," he adds and laughs.

He is having way too much fun pointing out Neena gets her culinary skills from me. I shush him as I giggle quietly, worried Neena might be listening. "You seem to be getting it down just fine."

He shrugs one shoulder before taking another sip. "My little girl made me breakfast in bed. If she'd bought me a burnt turd and a cup of toilet water, I'd choke it down."

"Eww. Nice, Paul. That's almost poetic." I'm giving him a hard time, but what he said, although disgusting, melts my heart. He loves her. And making her dad breakfast is just as special to her as it is to him. Shaking my head, I add, "A turd and toilet water. Really?"

"Sorry, your morning breath made me think of it."

I smack his chest before plopping my plate on his and flinging the covers back as I set my mug on my nightstand. But Paul is quick. He grabs my arm and tugs me back, managing to keep the coffee in his mug from spilling. As he holds me in place, he twists his other arm back and places the cup on the other nightstand closest to him before moving the stacked plates there as well. In a flash, he has me back in bed, pinned beneath the weight of his body. I don't fight too hard; it feels too good to have him on top of me like this, his mouth now dancing kisses along my shoulder and neck. But when he tries to press his mouth to mine, I twist my head.

"Sorry, but my breath smells like a turd. Remember?"

He laughs haughtily. "I was just kidding. It doesn't smell like a turd." Then with an apologetic smile, he adds, "Toilet water, maybe. But that nice floral-scented water."

"Dick," I mumble. He laughs some more.

Taking my face in his hand, he turns me so my eyes meet his. And though I'm pouting, our gazes lock and we watch one another, both of us recognizing what's happening. We're coming together again. But why? Is it that there's something really here? Is there real chemistry? Or are we both afraid to be alone as we watch Neena leave us? I don't think I realized I needed someone to help me get through this. Not until Paul came back. Of course, I've had Marcus and Mei-ling and the guys at work, but maybe I needed more. There's something to be said about the distraction of a budding romance. And maybe that's what this is. Or maybe it's only two people seeking solace in one another. One thing's for sure. It's scary as fuck. There's so much history, yet there's a big gap in it. Neither of us are who we were thirteen years ago, but we're not entirely different either. He wants me. I can feel it. His erection is pressing against my leg, his dark eyes are rich and hungry with desire. This time, when he leans in to kiss me, I let him. It starts off slow and I moan in his mouth as his hand slips down and finds my breast, groping it gently. But then, we're frantic. In seconds he has slipped my panties down my legs and has my legs over his shoulders. With the first flick of his tongue, I moan again, pleasure shooting through me like a bullet.

"Shh, Clara," he warns me as I mew with pleasure. I pull a pillow over my face knowing I need to be quiet because Neena might hear, but not sure I can. It feels so good to be touched like this. By him. When he dances his tongue over my clit, quick and soft, my hips buck up, my body begging for more. His large hands hold me still, working his magic, humming deeply, and just as I'm about to hit that sweet, sweet moment of release . . .

"Mom!" Neena shouts. Her voice sounds like she's close to my room. Paul practically hits the ceiling as he jumps up and flips so he's sitting beside me, yanking the blankets over us. I hurriedly run my hands over his beard, slick with my arousal, before trying to smooth the blankets as the bedroom door flies open.

"Where's my purple scarf?"

"Dryer," I tell her, a little too eagerly. Her gaze darts between me and Paul, then falls to the floor where Paul flung my panties moments ago. Her eyes widen with realization. She quickly shuts the door and her heavy footsteps taper off down the hall.

"You think she knows?"

"I'd say so . . ." I mumble. "She looked pretty freaked out."

"Damn." He rubs his face with both hands. "So this is what it feels like to be cock-blocked," he chuckles, handling his erection under the blanket.

Smiling at him, I lean my head on his shoulder. "Welcome to fatherhood, Paul."

CHAPTER TWENTY-NINE

Paul

I'M STANDING IN the bathroom, shaving my neck, where my beard has grown down to. Neena has been watching me, oddly fascinated with the task. A part of me wonders if this is just her hanging out with me, or if she needs to talk.

"Something on your mind, princess?"

She fidgets a little from where she sits on the edge of the tub. "I wanted to ask you something."

"Shoot," I tell her.

"It might upset you. It really upset Mom when I tried to talk to her about it."

Crap. Is this about finding Clara's underwear on the floor? Placing my razor on the sink, I kneel down and give her my undivided attention. "I promise. I won't get upset."

She licks her dry lips. "I want to be cremated."

My face falls. I'm not expecting this. This topic hits me right in the gut, mostly because it's a reminder she will leave us one day not too far in the future. And that destroys me. Secondly, because it's unfair a twelve-year-old is trying to discuss her funeral arrangements. Neena knots her fingers in her lap and looks down at them.

"I told Mom. She got so upset, we never really discussed it."

I fall back on my ass and rest my arms on my knees. "Your mother just . . ." I let out a long breath. "That's hard for a parent, Neena."

"I know," she assures me. "But I need someone to know, and

acknowledge what I want. You told me I could tell you anything and you wouldn't make me feel bad about it."

"I did. And I mean that. But I hope you know Clara doesn't mean to make you feel bad, hon. She just loves you so much."

"I know. I do. But . . . that doesn't make it easy."

I sigh deeply, bracing myself. This won't be easy to listen to. But I have to. Neena needs me. "So tell me what you want, princess," I whisper.

She leads me through her wants, the plans she's made by herself, and asks me to make sure they're fulfilled. Her plans are touching, and there's meaning behind each step and action. Some things hurt more than others to hear, but I stay strong and listen intently. There's a part of me that feels immense guilt. I'm promising Neena something that Clara will no doubt want control over. She'll be grieving her loss and then I'll be trying to take over Neena's funeral. Maybe Clara will be okay letting me handle it. After all, she's already done so much. Maybe she will let me do this for our daughter. But a part of me suspects it won't be that easy.

When she's finished, I tell her, "I'll do my best. I promise you that."

"Thank you, Dad."

I stand and brush off my pants, and bending, I wrap my arms around her and we hug before returning to my shaving. The whole time, I was careful not to get cream on her.

"What's it like to shave?" Neena inquires, still on the edge of the tub.

I rinse my razor in the sink full of water and look at her. "You've never shaved?"

She shakes her head no. "Haven't had any hair in a while. And the baby hairs I have on my legs aren't even noticeable."

I want to smack my forehead. I should have thought of that. "It's not my favorite thing to do."

"Do you like having a beard?"

I snort. "It's okay. I'll probably shave it soon."

"Can I shave it? I mean, when you're ready to?"

I tilt my head, meeting her gaze. "Sure, princess. Let's do it now."

"Really?" she asks, her features perking giddily.

"Why not? It's about time to take it off anyway."

I give her the electric trimmer and take a seat on the toilet. "Let's shorten it before we shave it so it's a little easier."

"You sure?"

I nod with a smile. "Let's do this."

Neena stares at the trimmer a moment before she shakes her head. "No. I'm afraid I'll cut you. I haven't done it before."

"What you need is practice," I mention. I widen my eyes as an idea hits me. "Clara!" I shout like a madman. "Clara, help me! Help me!"

Loud stomps rush up the stairs and Neena looks at me, her eyes wide as saucers. "Ooh, you're in trouble. She's going to murder you."

I grin. "I know."

Clara flies into the bathroom, the front of her shirt soaked with something, breathless, her eyes filled with fear. "What's wrong?" She grabs Neena and runs her hands over her. "Are you okay? What happened?"

Oh, shit. My stomach drops. I didn't think she'd think I was calling for Neena. I thought she'd think something was wrong with me.

"Nothing," Neena whines, pushing her hands off. Then she points at me. "Dad was just playing a joke."

Clara's gaze fixes on me, the wrath of hell burning in them. "Are you serious?"

I back away with my hands up. Almost as if waving the proverbial white flag. "Have mercy," I beg. "I wasn't thinking you'd think it was her. That was dumb. I'm so sorry."

"It was just a joke, Mom," Neena insists, tugging at Clara's arm. "Please don't be mad at him."

Clara spears me with a look that says, *if she wasn't here right now, I'd remove your balls*. She lets out a long breath, plastering on a tempered smile, attempting to gain her composure. "Please don't do that again," she tells me.

"Promise."

"Was that all you two needed? Just to give me a heart attack this morning? You scared me so bad I spilled coffee on my shirt." She looks down at her soaked front and twists her mouth. "I think it burned my skin."

"Sorry about the shirt," I say. "But we need a guinea pig." Clara looks to Neena for explanation, but I continue. "Neena wants to shave my face, but she's scared. I want to show her how to do it."

She's staring at me. "Okay . . ."

Apparently she needs some clarification. "I want to show her on you."

"I'm not letting you shave my face, Paul," she laughs.

"Just sit down," I huff playfully. "I'm going to shave it with a razor with the cover on. I won't really shave your face. She just wants to see the technique."

"Please, Mom," Neena begs before Clara can answer, a small smile on her face because she knows Clara will do this for her even though she doesn't want to.

"Okay," she mutters. Grabbing two hair ties off the sink, she yanks her blonde hair up and twists it into a knot on her head. Plopping down on the toilet, she watches me as I fill the sink with clean water and grab a razor with a plastic cover from the medicine cabinet.

"Oh," Neena beams. "I need my camera."

"Great," Clara says.

"Hey, this is making her day," I tell her. "Thanks for doing it."

"I'm glad to do it. I'm worried though. She seems to be slowing down, don't you think? Moving slower. Not quite as perky or energetic."

"Yeah," I mumble, my chest aching. "I've noticed too."

"Thanks for doing this, Paul," Clara says, sincerely. "I just feel like the happier she is, the more time we have."

I nod. "I agree." It's our own personal form of denial. Then the thought of last night hits me; our fight; the terrible things that were said. "I'm sorry about last night." It's been said already, but it needs to be said again. She grabs my hand and squeezes.

"I'm sorry for so much. But we're a team in this now. And I'm glad you're here."

Looking down at Clara, her blue eyes fixed on me, deep with sincerity. I can't help myself. Leaning down, I kiss her lips softly. When I stand again, I say, "You're beautiful."

"You really are, Mom," Neena chirps softly from the doorway, camera in hand, filming us.

Clara blushes. "Only because I shave my face daily," she jokes.

Neena continues to film as I cover Clara's face in shaving cream, and she even makes me kiss Clara, explaining how cute it will look. *My daughter, the romantic.* As I glide the plastic over Clara's delicate skin, I explain to Neena the technique and where the sensitive spots are. When we're done, Clara towels off her face and poses. "How do I look?" she asks in a deep and masculine voice.

"Handsome," I confirm. "Manly."

Clara looks at the camera and does some kind of obnoxiously loud kiss after flexing her arms, like she's a dude kissing his bicep. "Yeah, I'm a stud." Neena rolls her eyes, but giggles because her mother is a loon.

"I'm going to go have a burping contest with myself in the other room," Clara tells us as she heads for the door.

"Don't act like that's just a guy thing," I call after her. "You know you do it, too."

"I'm going to change my shirt and make myself a fresh cup of coffee," she calls back, ignoring me.

I grin at Neena. "See how she didn't deny it?"

After she leaves, I clean the sink and prepare for my shave. When it's all ready, I take a seat and hand Neena the trimmer, but she stares at it for a moment before handing it to me. "Hold on one sec." She scurries off and when she returns she has her cell phone. "We need before and after pics." She snaps two of me before I grab her and set her on my knees as I lean in from the back. "Now one of us together."

She shakes her head no and tries to stand, but I hold her in place. "Why not?"

She won't look at me when she replies, "I like taking video and pics of others. Not of myself. I hate how I look."

"You look beautiful," I state. "Don't ever forget that. Please, just one for your old man?" I beg, squeezing her.

Her shoulders droop, but she extends her arm out with her phone, the screen facing toward us. "On the count of three," she warns. "One, two, three."

Just before she clicks the photo, I kiss her cheek and she giggles. The picture is perfect, capturing her amazing smile. "Dad!" she groans tiredly.

"Okay, one more. I'll be good this time, I promise." I take the phone from her and hold it away from us. Then I count, just like her. But when

I reach three, she turns and wraps her arms around my neck and kisses my cheek.

Okay, I lied. *This* picture is perfect.

I kiss her head and hand her the phone. "I better get copies of those," I inform.

"Or what?" she challenges me, feigning playing tough.

"Or I'll ask your mother to cook dinner tonight."

Her mouth drops open in mock horror. "You wouldn't dare."

"Try me." I narrow my eyes, holding back laughter.

"Fine," she answers, pretending to be miffed. "You'll get the pictures," she ensures me. "I promise."

For the next twenty minutes, she trims my beard. Then she slathers shaving cream on and slowly shaves my face. At some point Clara walks in, and as she strolls to us she's armed with Neena's camera and tapes us. I never even noticed her picking up the camera. She's smooth like that. There's shaving cream everywhere and when Neena finishes, she towels off my face and smiles. "You look really handsome, Dad."

"I agree," Clara adds.

Neena looks from me to Clara. "This feels . . . good." She grins. "Like a family."

Standing, I hug her and reach one arm out for Clara, who joins us. "We are a family, kid." I kiss the top of Clara's head as it rests on my chest. Then Neena's. These two. They're my world. I never imagined I could find such peace in this type of life. I never imagined feeling like a family would satisfy me. But it does. It's everything. *They* are everything. And that's what I tell them when I whisper, "Everything that matters is right here in my arms."

CHAPTER THIRTY

Paul

"I HEARD THE Chinese feast night last week had an interesting turn of events," Ashley mentions casually as Mills clips my mic on. I narrow my eyes. She's talking about the fight between Clara and me.

"Who told you that?" I ask, unable to hide the annoyance in my tone. We may be here sharing our past with her, but that doesn't make her privy to every detail of our lives.

Without batting a lash, she replies, "I have my sources."

"What sources?" I question suspiciously. "You're fifteen."

"Seventeen," she corrects me.

Mills clears his throat loudly, turning away from me. "He's all set."

I twist my mouth in thought. Did Neena tell Mills about our fight that night? Are they talking on the phone? I decide to wait until Ashley is done with me before I try and figure out what's going on. A high schooler has no business messing with my daughter.

"Clara told us about the race."

I scratch at my stubble, wondering if my expression shows my shock. "She did?"

Ashley tilts her head, watching me carefully. "She did."

"Where'd . . . she leave off?"

A small smile breezes across her lips. "The part where you got jealous when she flirted with the guys."

A husky laugh escapes me. "Yeah, I guess I did."

"Did it surprise you?"

"What? That I got jealous?"

"No," she laughs. "Men are idiots." From behind her, Zane raises his head and rolls his eyes. "There's nothing surprising about that," she continues. "Did it surprise you she could flirt so well?"

"Maybe," I admit, leaning back in my chair.

"Why?"

"Because I'd never seen her do it."

"Flirt?"

"Yeah," I confirm. "With anyone. Not with the guys that worked for us. Or any of the male clients that came in."

"Not with you," she adds, her tone speculative. Nosy little brat. "Did it surprise you she never flirted with you?"

I let out something between a laugh and a snort. I know what she's implying, but I play dumb anyway. "What do you mean?"

Ashley shoots me a look that says, *you know exactly what I mean.* "Because you were you. Paul James. Epic. You're an attractive man," she goes on and Zane narrows his gaze at the back of her head. Interesting. "Women, on the norm, flocked to you. Did it surprise you Clara didn't?"

I stare at her blankly. Oh.

"Come on, Paul," she grumbles. "Don't be coy. You were a hotshot, an adventurer with good looks. Women loved you. They probably threw themselves at you." *Does that mean I'm lame and look like shit now?* I ponder it for all of two seconds. Then holding one finger up as if to emphasize her point, she adds, "Except for Clara."

I grin with insult. "You make me sound pretty damn vain, Ashley."

"Because I'm describing you accurately?"

Jesus. This kid shows no mercy.

Turning my head, I scratch my stubble again, buying myself some time. If I'm being honest, it did surprise me. Even though my initial thoughts were that Clara was just a stiff and incapable of flirting, but after I challenged her at the race, I knew differently. She *could* flirt. She *could* show a man she was interested. But she hadn't dropped *me* any signals.

Finally, I decide, fuck it, I'll be honest. "It surprised me," I admit. "But I think that kind of made her more attractive to me." And it did.

178

Because once I saw her draw every man's attention in that group by simply rubbing a cold can of beer over her chest and neck, I never wanted her to flirt with anyone ever again.

Except me.

Ashley smiles wide and jots something down in her notebook. "Why the smile?" I ask.

"I just love this story." She chuckles. "Okay, let's move on. After the race, how were things? Not just with you and Clara, but in the office, too. Was the atmosphere still volatile?"

That's an understatement, I think to myself.

Two days later, I'd strolled into the office for my afternoon jumps. While I'd initially hated Clara and fought her on the changes she was trying to implement, I had to admit, life was pretty good for me. Marcus handled all the financials while Clara handled scheduling and advertising. That meant all I had to do was the only thing I wanted to do. Jump.

When I walked in, Bowman was heading out, giving me a wide-eyed look in warning as he passed by.

"What?" I asked.

"It's like World War III in there, man. I swear this is like an everyday occurrence now."

I froze, and let my head drop back in frustration. That could only mean one thing. Marcus and Clara were fighting. *Again.* Sometimes my job required wearing another hat. Referee.

I could hear them shouting as I approached the office.

"Clara. *Fucking.* Bateman." Clara seethed. "It's clear as day on the envelope."

"You are the one that assigned me the duties of opening the mail," Marcus argued.

"Yes," she hissed. "Sky High mail. Not *my* mail!"

As I entered the office, they both turned their heads to look at me. "Morning, all," I gushed cheerily. "Beautiful day, isn't it?"

They both stared at me, seemingly wishing they could kill me with their eyes.

"Why yes, Paul," I answered myself, imitating Clara in a feminine voice. "It is a lovely day."

"Hey, Paul." I moved on to imitating Marcus. "How are you?"

"I'm good, man," I answered myself. "Thanks for asking."

I got nothing. Neither of them even cracked a smile. Letting out a long sigh, I pulled one of the folding chairs from the wall and flopped down on it. "What is it this time?"

"I accidentally opened Clara's mail and she's lost her shit about it."

"It had *my name* on it! He had no right to open it."

"Okay," I replied, unsure of how to fix this. Clara looked so mad, she might cry. "I'm sure it was just an accident. It probably got mixed in with the other mail."

"He had to sign for it, Paul," she sneered.

I closed my eyes. Fucking Marcus. I knew Clara could be a giant pain in the ass, but he was hell-bent on making our work environment miserable by being a dick to her every chance he got.

Clara yanked an envelope off her desk and chucked it at me, hitting me in the chest. "Might as well read it, Paul. Marcus pinned it to the front board so everyone else has."

I cut him an exhausted look that said, *really?* Opening the envelope, I pulled out the thin stack of papers and read the top of the first page.

Separation Decree.

I couldn't look at him after that. He was in the wrong. There was no way for me to defend him this time. Playing jokes on her was one thing, but this was her personal business.

His mouth turned into a frown as he shrugged. "I wanted to make sure she found it and that it didn't get lost."

Letting out a long grunt, I sat forward and tossed the envelope back on the desk. This was kids' shit.

"And all this because we took February away," she whined dramatically. And she was right. Every December through February, we closed down. The weather was too cold and sales dropped dramatically with the holidays. But Clara did some research and found that other skydiving businesses were opening back up February 1st each year. It didn't take her much to convince me when she showed me the numbers. But Marcus wasn't as open to it as I was.

"That was a month off that I look forward to every year." His face was getting red.

"And you are welcome to still take it off. You just won't get paid for it," she told him calmly.

"I count on that money," he argued. "You didn't even talk to us about it," Marcus yelled.

Clara grinned at him with disbelief and disdain. "Why would I talk to *you* about it?"

"Because I work here."

"Yes, that's right. You work here, for *me*. And for Paul. *We* make the decisions. Not you."

She couldn't have known the effect her words would have on Marcus. She didn't know the history. She didn't know that though Marcus never told me, I knew deep down he'd been deeply hurt when Dennis didn't leave him part of the business. After all, he was Dennis's adopted son. Marcus took it as being slighted, and wondered if maybe Dennis hadn't felt the same. But all the same, Clara's words might as well have been like a whip to the face.

"This was my father's business," Marcus scoffed.

Clara blinked a few times as she absorbed that information. She never knew. "And I'm sorry if I don't agree to his whore coming in here and trying to take over the place."

Clara's eyes practically bulged out of her head as I propped my head in my hand. I needed to intervene. I should have intervened. Marcus had gone off the deep end. But I didn't at that moment, because he was digging into her about how she was affiliated with Dennis. And I wanted to know just as badly as he did why he'd left her half of his business. She looked at me, and I knew she was waiting for me to speak up, to reprimand Marcus, but I didn't. Clara dropped her head as if seeking a moment to calm herself.

"Sorry to disappoint you. I wasn't his whore."

"Then the daughter from his whore?" Marcus fished. Dude! He wasn't giving up.

"From what I understand, he was single. Why would he have a whore or a mistress? You're a fucking idiot." She said the insult slowly, her voice certain. "And no. I'm not his daughter."

"Then who are you?" he shouted. "Why did he leave you half of a business he spent most of his life building?"

We both watched her as she struggled to answer . . . or not to answer. Shaking her head, she picked up the envelope and shoved it in her purse. "Of all fucking days, it had to be today." I scowled. What did that mean?

She rounded the desk, and bent down so her intense line of sight met Marcus.' In a calm but certain voice, she growled, "If you ever call me a whore or the daughter of a whore or *anything* affiliated with the word whore, ever again, I will fire you." Looking at me just as angrily, she snapped, "You deal with this. *We* made that decision about February together. *You* own half of his anger." Then she walked out, slamming the office door behind her.

"You really know how to make the work environment pleasant," I chirped. "Thanks."

"You really gave the okay for the February jumps?" he asked, ignoring me.

I shrugged unapologetically before trying to explain. "Even if we can only get one hundred jumps and sell the pictures and videos, we would at least cover your salary plus Clara's and mine. Otherwise, we're tossing money out the window. I know it's your month off, and I know you can't stand her, but sometimes, *sometimes*," I reiterated, "she does have a valid point and good ideas."

Marcus furrowed his brows. "Is that Paul the business owner talking, or Paul the guy that wants to fuck her talking?"

Well, shit. I was shocked. He'd never spoken to me like that, with such animosity. And because I was young and arrogant and insensitive, I replied, "That's Paul, *your* fucking boss, talking."

He nodded a few times, letting me know he got what I was saying—loud and clear—before he marched out the office, slamming it as well.

After my last jump, I closed up the office. Marcus and Clara never returned after their argument, and I busted ass all afternoon between greeting clients, handling payments, and diving. After I closed the office for the evening, I drove straight to the closest bar with every intention of getting hammered. The constant animosity between Clara and Marcus was starting to weigh on me. If I backed Clara, Marcus thought it was only because I wanted to have sex with her. If I backed Marcus, I'd piss

DESPERATELY
SEEKING
EPIC

Clara off and for some reason, I really didn't want to piss her off. Not anymore, anyway. I just wanted some peace. What I needed was a few stiff drinks to help me forget. Finding some company for the night wouldn't hurt either. At that time, I knew I was attracted to Clara. I knew I wanted her. But I didn't *want* to want her. She wasn't my type. At all. She was bossy and high-handed; always a know-it-all. I liked my women easy. And I didn't mean in the sexual way . . . although, sometimes that's all a man really wants when he's young and single. I meant easy in the *laid-back* sense. Easy in the *knew when to let shit go* sense. Clara wasn't easy. In any sense of the word. She was a ballbuster. Other than her being nothing like my ideal woman, there was also the matter of my freedom. It was of the utmost importance to me. Settling down was as foreign to me as another planet. I was working hard to stay put; to be satisfied by my dives, hoping it would douse the need I felt to go. To move. But I knew myself well. That need couldn't be sated. Not permanently, anyway. And I'd learned early on, after breaking a few hearts, that you don't make promises you can't keep. So I started laying down the terms early on. I walked into any situation with one hundred percent honesty. I told them two things.

I don't do happily ever after.

I don't do babies and white picket fences.

Clara wasn't the kind of woman for that. Truth was, no woman was truly going to go for *that*. But they were stubborn. They all agreed to my terms, understanding where I stood. But they all believed, deep inside, that somehow they could change me; that their love would turn me into a different man. And when it ended, they hated me. But when I left, I didn't feel bad because I'd told them the truth.

So, no. Clara was not my type.

I knew that.

But that didn't change me wanting her.

And on that night, I needed a release. I needed something to be easy, or rather . . . someone. When I walked into the bar, it was already crowded. A huge group of loud men surrounded the pool table and dartboards. All the booths were full. And as luck would have it, right away I spotted just who that someone to give me my release would be. I slid on a barstool beside her and ordered a straight shot of bourbon. She was a brunette with brown eyes, and she wore too much makeup. It didn't take long to figure her out. Her name was Mandy and she'd just broken up with her boyfriend.

Easy.

An hour later, her hand was rubbing my thigh. An hour after that, I was signaling the bartender for our check. "I'll take the check, Rick," I called.

"Rick," one of the waitresses yelled as he was about to answer me. "She wants another. I told her she was cut off, but she asked for the manager."

"I don't have time to talk to her right now," he griped as he poured a drink. "You take her a cup of coffee and tell her she's done. We'll call a cab for her. We're too busy to babysit her and make sure that group of knuckleheads over there doesn't keep messing with her."

Mandy extended her neck and started looking around, scanning the room, trying to find who they were talking about. "Oh my God," she gasped, with a little chuckle, squeezing my thigh. "She's plastered. Check her out. She can barely walk."

When I followed her line of sight, I had to do a double take.

Clara.

It was Clara.

What the fuck?

"Do you know her?" Mandy asked, taking in my expression. But I didn't answer her. I was too busy watching Clara now.

She was on her way back to her table from the bathroom, swaying like a buoy in rough water. Her blonde hair was tied up in an updo, strands hanging low, her blue eyes hooded with drunkenness. She wore the same thing she'd been wearing earlier that day, a white tank top and jeans. The men surrounding the pool tables watched her, some of them jutting their chins her way for their friends to take notice of her, others elbowing one another. She was a fucking target. But she didn't seem to notice. She wasn't noticing much of anything. The song changed just before she reached her table and she stopped, staggering from the abrupt halt. Closing her eyes, she swayed to the beat for a moment, not caring how she looked or who was watching. A tall, burly guy from the group came over and grabbed her by the waist, pulling her back, and forced her to shake her hips in rhythm with his as he danced. She weakly pushed down on his arm, trying to get away from him, but he didn't release her. Instead, he pulled her closer and said something in her ear.

My barstool screeched against the wood flooring as I forcefully shoved it back, flipping it on its side. I didn't bother to pick it up before I headed her way. I can't tell you this massive feeling of jealousy had hit me and I marched over there to kick that guy's ass. Maybe that's how I felt. It's definitely what I wanted to do. He certainly deserved it behaving that way with a woman that was clearly too drunk. But I was livid with *her*. Clara was a smart woman; always on top of things and in control. So what the hell was this? Alone in a bar completely smashed. She was too smart to do something so dumb.

"Hey, man," I grumbled as I stormed up to them, my shoulders back, my chest out. "I'll take her. She's a friend."

The guy turned away from me, taking Clara with him. Then twisting his head over his shoulder, said, "She's having a good time, man. She's not ready to leave."

"I think I need to go," Clara uttered, her words slurred. "I'm not feeling well."

"She wants to go, man," I growled, pulling his shoulder hard. "Let her go."

He released Clara, but only to spin her around so he could look her in the eyes. "You're fine, babe. I'll get you home tonight."

"No. I don't want to go home with you," she laughed drunkenly. "You're a terrible dancer."

"Now you have your answer. Let her go," I demanded, my teeth clenched. This guy was a total fuckwad. How many ways did she have to say she's not interested? One should have been plenty.

He ignored me and pulled her toward him, but she stopped him, placing one hand on his shoulder as if to hold herself steady. "Just one more dance, sweet thing," he purred, tugging at her.

"No!" I roared.

"She can decide," he boomed back.

Clara tilted her head as she stared at him with a thoughtful expression. "One more dance. Then I have to go."

Then she looked at me, her gaze glazed over, and gave me a little shrug. I was livid. She was telling me to fuck off. That she was going to stay and hang with the douche bag to spite me. And I wasn't having any of that. I stepped toward them, fully intent on yanking her ass out of the bar if I had to.

And that's when it happened.

She puked.

All over him.

Like projectile puked.

It was awesome.

And horrible.

It was the best and worst all at once.

Everyone in the bar lurched away, even the ones in the back farthest from us, the bar falling silent except for the music blasting in the background. A few people let out some groans of disgust, covering their mouths and gagging. The guy looked down at his body, covered neck to feet in vomit.

"What the fuck?" he shouted, his tone rich with disbelief.

"Shouldn't have had that chili dog for lunch," Clara noted as she grimaced at the sight of her own vomit. Somehow she's managed to hose this guy down and not get a drop on herself.

Her gaze met mine again. Same glazed look. And she shrugged. She'd planned that. I'd thought she was telling me to *fuck off*. She was really saying, *watch this*. I wanted to laugh hysterically but I decided I better get her the hell out of there before she puked again.

"You bitch!" he shouted. He knocked her hand from his shoulder and she stumbled. I caught her and pulled her to the side, propping her so she could hold the top of the booth seat to steady herself so I could grab her purse.

"She told you she wasn't feeling well, man," I pointed out as I handed her a napkin from the table so she could wipe her mouth, while I collected her things. "You should have listened."

The guy was beet red with fury, his eyes fixed on Clara like he wanted to hit her. Dropping her shit in the booth seat, I turned to him. "Let it go, man," I warned him. "Go clean yourself up."

His angered stare trained on me. "Get that bitch out of here," he fired back.

"You're a real classy guy," I piped back as I returned to collecting Clara's things. I shoved the large envelope containing her separation papers in her purse with another envelope I only took a second to observe before putting it in her bag. It had her name on it written in my uncle's handwriting.

"Come on, Clara," I murmured as I took her arm. She stumbled out beside me and just before we exited, I looked over to Mandy at the bar. She was already talking to some other guy. Her eyes met mine and she shrugged, raising her beer bottle in silent farewell.

I looked back down at Clara who had just rested her head on my shoulder as we walked.

Cock-blocker.

"We have five minutes until we meet with Clara," Ashley points out. "We should probably stop here."

After they remove my mic and I stand to go, Ashley asks, "Do you really think she made herself puke on that guy?"

I laugh. "Knowing Clara, yes. She's good at making assholes look and feel like assholes."

Ashley nods a few times and gives me a small wave. "See you next week."

CHAPTER THIRTY-ONE
Clara

"SO WE HEARD about the chili dog puke scene at the bar," Ashley informs me once we're all set up.

I scrunch my face in embarrassment. "He told you about that?"

She laughs. "Yes. Did you do it on purpose?"

"Knowing me, yes, but I was pretty smashed so I really don't remember."

"So Paul took you home that night. What happened?"

He had to stop twice on the way to my house so I could relieve myself of more vomit on the side of the road. It was awful. Made worse by the fact that each time we stopped Paul got out and stood with me, getting a front row seat to my humiliation. I was mortified. By the time he got me home, I had nothing left in my stomach. He followed me inside and into the kitchen where I poured myself a glass of water. I turned and leaned against the counter as I chugged it, noticing he was staring at me, arms crossed, eyes angry.

"Thanks for bringing me home," I murmured. "I'm sure you have other things to do tonight, so you can go."

"I'm not going anywhere," he informed me. "I want some answers."

Placing my glass on the counter, I asked, "Answers to what?"

"Why did you go in there and get smashed? Because of Marcus? Because if that's the case, I thought you had tougher skin than to let him bring you down."

I didn't answer him right away. Instead, I busied myself getting two Ibuprofens and putting two slices of white bread in the toaster. I desperately needed something in my stomach.

"Was it Marcus?" he finally asked when I didn't respond.

"No. He didn't help though," I mumbled.

"The separation papers?" he questioned.

Meeting his gaze, I decided to give him the truth. Well, most of it. "Twenty-five years ago today my parents were killed in a drunk driving accident."

All the color drained from his face.

"I don't remember them. But . . . it's still a sad day for me." I studied his expressionless face. Did he know? Did he know it was his uncle that took my parents' lives? I really couldn't tell. His lack of any response could mean many things. Maybe he did know, or maybe he didn't and he just felt sorry for me.

"My soon-to-be ex, Kurt, had the separation papers delivered today, of all days, of course," I continued. "Then Marcus decided to act out against me. So I got drunk. Something I usually don't do."

"Shit, Clara," he sighed. "Did the guy that hit them die too?" Out of all I said, he was centering in on my parents.

My throat tightened. He didn't know. He had no idea what his uncle had done. Anger rose up inside of me. Marcus and Paul thought Dennis was such a great guy. He'd left them this adventurous legacy with this notion that he was a good man. He'd moved here and hid from his past. They didn't know him at all.

"He was forced to go to rehab. Some probation."

I wasn't sure what I expected Paul to do or say. What could he really do or say? Stories like mine sucked dick. They're sad and it's hard to spin it with a bright side, which was what everyone wanted to do when they heard a heartbreaking story like mine. I had no expectation of him. He could have said nothing. I wouldn't have taken it personally. After all, we weren't really friends. He owed me nothing. So when he approached me and encircled me in his arms, I was shocked. So shocked in fact, I let my arms hang limply at my sides as he squeezed me.

"The way a hug works," he began, his chin resting on the top of my head, "is both parties wrap their arms around the other. See how I'm doing it?"

I rolled my eyes where he couldn't see. And slowly, I wrapped my arms around him, too. A second later, I melted into the hug, burying my face into his chest. I couldn't recall when the last time I'd been hugged was. Like, really hugged. Paul and I may have shared some awkward, lightning-quick one-armed hugs, but nothing like this. Probably when Ally and Vanessa left to head back to Texas months ago was the last time I'd been really hugged. Wow. I was pathetic. I realized that. And alone. So, so alone.

Pushing away from Paul, I wiped under my eyes. I wasn't crying. I was tougher back then. But my eyes were a little moist. "Thanks for the ride, Paul. Sorry I ruined your night."

"You didn't," he assured me. *Liar.* But I let him slide on it. "You want me to make some dinner?" He looked around my kitchen for signs of food that could be cooked, which there was none, so he didn't look long.

"I really appreciate it, Paul. But I think I just want to be alone now."

"Oh, uh, sure," he sputtered, shaking his head. "Right." I walked him out onto the porch and we said good-bye. He climbed in his truck and was gone in a flash.

When I went back inside, I stood at my counter, munching on dry toast as I scanned the separation papers. Kurt was pressing me. He'd offered me way less than half of our assets. My lawyer was ready to pounce him for such an insult. Now, his new tactic—he would seek a payment for the skydiving business. I'd inherited it while we were still married and he claimed he was entitled to part of its value. He was going all out.

In our last conversation, Kurt had informed me that he'd 'made me.' He told me if it wasn't for him, I'd have nothing. Apparently I owed him everything.

Not going to lie. That hurt. To have my contribution belittled was like a kick to my face. I'd walked beside this man while he'd pursued his dreams and ambitions. I'd loved him even when he was insensitive, selfishly putting himself first. Maybe I wasn't perfect, but I'd loved him and gave him my all. I was loyal, and there is no one on this earth that would have fought for or beside him more than me.

No one.

Not even Daisy, the future mother of his unborn child.

191

There in those few pages was the end of my marriage. Summed up and written in cold, unfeeling terms and sentences. Not a trace of the love, laughter, joy, tears, and contentment we'd shared was included. Now it was broken down by numbers and the legalities of who got what. I felt so jaded. I felt robbed. I'd given so much to this man and this was how it ended, so callously?

When I was a child, my grandmother, who'd raised me, told me sometimes the best way to get something out is to write it down. Sometimes words poured from our fingertips in a way they couldn't from our mouths. I was pained in that moment, and I needed to get it out. I'd purged my body in the physical sense that day, now I needed to purge my feelings. Grabbing a piece of paper and a pen, I sat at my kitchen table, the one Paul made for me, and wrote my heartache on it.

Today has been a bad day.

Today, my parents died twenty-five years ago.

Today, Marcus acted like a gigantic dickface.

Today, Kurt took another step away from me, from our life together.

I think I miss him.

I shouldn't.

Maybe I just miss us who I thought we were.

He's a bad person. I know this. Maybe not entirely bad, but mostly bad. He tossed me aside. Don't I deserve better? Did I not love hard enough? Did I not give enough? I think I did. I really do.

I've made peace with my parents passing. Being that I was so young makes it a little easier to bear.

But Kurt is a fresh wound.

I need to let him go. But hearts don't work like light switches they don't just flick on and off. They swell rapidly with love and bleed out slowly with pain.

I should be stronger. I should be able to shut myself down to his memory. But I'm not strong enough yet.

They say the opposite of love isn't hate, but indifference. I hate him. I hate him so much I feel it seeping out of my pores, toxifying everything around me.

I don't want him back. I don't. Not who he is now. I want my life back. I want the safety I felt in my marriage back. I want the days where we held hands and dreamed a millions dreams together back when I believed him when he said I was his forever. When he told me no one could take my place. I want that man back. I want that type of love in my life.

But he's gone.

And now, given his cruelty and seemingly unfeeling actions, I have to wonder … was he ever really there? Was it all a facade? Was I a fool the whole time seeing only what I wanted to see?

I want to be happy.

I want forever.

I want …

I want a baby.

Pushing the paper away from me, I lay my head in my arms on the table and cried. I cried hard. When I finished, I shoved the paper in one of my empty kitchen drawers and kept the pen.

Then I signed the papers.

I left them on my counter and went to bed.

Ashley stares at me.

"You wanted to know what happened after I puked," I point out with a smirk, trying to lighten things up again.

"I did," she admits.

"Did you think he'd take me home and we'd make wild, passionate love?" I jest.

"Maybe," she admits.

"Did you miss the part about me yacking up a monster chilidog all night? Wasn't exactly sexy."

"That's true," she laughs. "Are you okay if we keep going?"

I check my watch. "I've got thirty minutes."

"So . . ." She motions her hand. "What happened next?"

I smile because I have a feeling I'm about to tell her something she's really been wanting to hear.

CHAPTER THIRTY-TWO
Clara

THE NEXT DAY, I ventured out to the post office and dropped the separation papers in the box. Once these were filed, our divorce could be finalized in a few months. I decided to stay home that day. I left a message on the office machine, not sure anyone would even get it if Marcus didn't bother to show up. I knew Paul definitely wouldn't check it. I took a long, hot bath, ate some ice cream, and painted my toenails. Basically, I took a *me* day. And it refreshed me. While I'd dreaded signing those papers, I felt like a weight had been lifted. I didn't have to dread it anymore. I didn't have it hanging over my head. And oddly, I felt like everything was going to be okay; that I'd taken a huge step in moving on, moving forward.

Eight o'clock rolled around and I was lying down on my couch, watching the only channel I could get on television. They were playing reruns of *Married with Children*. Don't judge me, I absolutely loved that show. I nearly jumped out of my skin when someone knocked on my door. It actually sounded more like they kicked my door. Rushing to my purse, I grabbed my revolver and plastered myself against the wall beside the door.

"Who is it?"

"It's Paul. My hands are full! Open the door."

"What the hell is he doing here?" I mumbled softly to myself as I unhooked the chain and flipped the dead bolt.

Holding a bottle of red wine under one arm, and balancing five containers of Country Crock in the other, he grinned. "Thought you might like some dinner."

"You brought five containers of butter?" I asked, confused.

He pushed by me and walked to the kitchen. "No," he called over his shoulder as I shut the door and followed. "My mother likes to reuse these containers as Tupperware. Not too bad unless you're at her house looking for some kind of butter." He gently slid everything on the counter. "It takes twenty containers until you can butter your bread."

I laughed a little. "She sounds awesome."

"I just left her house. She's moving to Florida in a month so I'm trying to get my fill of her awesome cooking before she goes." His gaze turns to me and his eyes widen. "Have you been holding that gun the entire time?"

I glance down at my hand. "I didn't know who was at the door. You kicked it," I defended. "You scared the shit out of me."

"My hands were full. Damn, Clara," he murmured. "Put that thing away."

"Okay, okay," I agreed. "Don't be such a baby."

"I prefer responsible adult and gun safety advocate."

I pursed my lips. "Yeah, well I prefer supermodel and wealthy divorcée." I shrugged. "We are what we are." I hid the gun in a kitchen drawer as he peeled the lids off of the containers.

"So your mother gave you enough food to feed an army and you decided to share it with me?"

"Italian food is the best hangover food."

My stomach grumbled at the thought. I wasn't sure what I thought about his unannounced arrival. We were so weird together then. We started off enemies. Then we called a truce and proclaimed peace in the name of our business partnership. Were we becoming friends now? Really? Did he do things like this for all of his friends; bring them tables he built with his own bare hands, help them work on their house, protect them from themselves when they're drunk in a bar, bring them dinner when they're hung over?

He must have noted my perplexed look. "Wasn't just for you. I wanted to have dinner with a good friend tonight."

"We're friends?"

He gave one curt bob of his head. "Yes, we're friends."

I didn't question it. I didn't have the energy to. And the truth was, I needed a friend. Desperately. Even if said friend was seemingly a giant man-boy that called himself Epic. Beggars can't be choosers.

We plated out a feast of lasagna, stuffed shells, meatballs, and salad. I could not stop eating. I might as well have shoved my face in the Tupperware of lasagna like a horse with a trough. It was so good. I had a glass of red wine with the meal, because Paul insisted it would be the best I'd ever had. And it was. Among the adventurer, skydiver, and lady slayer, I discovered he loved to cook and though he enjoyed alcohol of all kinds, he considered himself a wine connoisseur.

After we did the dishes, which was only the forks because we ate our food off of paper plates—I hadn't really stocked up on home essentials just yet—we took our wine and sat on the top step of the front porch. It was sturdier now. Crickets chirped in the dark as we sat, not speaking. The quiet between us made me nervous. Friends should be able to talk. Right? Why weren't we talking?

"I signed the papers," I blurted out. I didn't know why. I just needed to tell someone. Anyone. He was there. And no one else was saying anything. Why not me? I needed to feel how it felt to say it . . . to really start owning that I was single and would soon be divorced. Or on my way to divorce.

Paul nodded a few times before holding his glass up to toast. "To moving on." I clinked my glass with his and we both sipped. "You holding up okay?"

I darted my tongue out and wet my dry lips. "It's just scary. Being single again. It's hard to imagine doing something as simple as kissing another man. And as you know, I tend to overthink everything. It's going to be a disaster."

"Maybe not," Paul replied. "Sometimes things just happen. Maybe you won't have to think about it."

I let out a long sigh as I laughed. "Maybe I need a practice date and kiss. Ya know? Like someone to get me back on my feet." I stared at my glass in thought. "Why isn't that a thing yet? Someone should create that service."

"It is a thing," he snorted. "They're called escorts."

I scrunched my nose up. "Yuck. This would be different. Strictly helping people get back in the saddle for dating."

"Is that a new business model you just created?" he joked. "You could make millions."

I smacked his arm as he laughed at me. "We're not all blessed in the art of attracting the opposite sex like some people, Paul. You just give a sideways glance to women and they fawn over you."

"No they don't," he argued, playing his hand at modesty, but failing miserably.

"Shut up. You know you're good-looking."

"Am I now?" He grinned, scooting closer to me, and smooshing our sides together. "Tell me how good-looking I am."

My cheeks heated as I laughed and tried to keep him from knocking me over. "I meant other women think you're hot, not me," I falsely clarified.

He settled down and sipped his wine, still grinning the entire time. "I mean it. I was not saying you're attractive." At least that wasn't what I meant to say. But it was true. Paul was handsome, in the most classic sense of the word. However, I did not want to admit that to him.

"Whatever you say," he chuckled.

I sipped my wine. "So why haven't you found a woman to settle down with, Paul?" I asked as nonchalantly as I could. I didn't want him to think I was asking because I was interested in him.

He twisted his mouth in thought before saying, "I don't do happily ever after. I don't do babies and white picket fences."

I fought the urge to roll my eyes. His answer annoyed me. Those were two things that I happened to want desperately. "Why not?"

He shrugged. "It's just not who I am. I'm not the kind of guy to settle down."

"Maybe you'll change your mind one day when the right woman comes along," I mused.

He snorted. "Doubtful."

We finished our wine and Paul took the glasses inside to the kitchen. When he returned, we stood awkwardly, neither of us knowing what to say, which meant it was time to say good-bye. I patted his shoulder . . . so weird . . . and said, "Thanks for dinner."

His mouth was tight as if he was trying not to laugh as he patted my shoulder back. "No problem."

"See you . . . tomorrow?" I questioned as I slid my hands in the back pockets of my shorts.

"See you then." He made his way down my stairs and toward his truck. When he opened his door, I spun around to go inside for the night.

"Clara," he called, causing me to turn back. He was at the bottom of the steps, climbing them, and before I could respond with, *what?* he picked me up by my legs and pushed me against the front door. My mouth dropped open. I was stunned. What was he doing? The muscles in his jaw and neck ticked as his dark eyes burned into mine.

Then he kissed me.

I didn't move for a second or two, my brain unable to catch up with my body. Then he swept his tongue between my lips and my blood pumped harder as my mouth moved against his.

It was a hard kiss, but it was gentle, too. His lips were soft and his tongue tasted like red wine. His hips held me pressed against the door while my legs were wrapped around him, his hands holding my ass, squeezing gently. It had been so long since I'd felt something so . . . erotic. I felt like one of those inflatable Christmas decorations that people put outside—they lay limp all day, but at night the lights come on and the air starts pumping and they come to life.

That kiss breathed life into me.

Paul James' kiss made me feel alive.

When he pulled his mouth from mine, he took a little nip at my bottom lip that made me gasp. We were both breathing hard, our chests heaving up and down. I clutched his muscular shoulders as he slowly lowered me to the ground, holding me for a moment to make sure I got my footing, which took a minute because my legs felt like jelly.

I swallowed hard as I looked up and met his gaze.

"You don't have to think so hard about that first kiss now." With a small, mischievous smile, he added, "I'm lucky I got to be the first man to kiss the woman starting a new life."

Moments later, I was still plastered to the door when he drove away.

Ashley is leaning forward in her chair, her eyes, painted in thick, black eyeliner, fixed on me. "So it was a good kiss?" She's practically drooling.

A smile creeps across my lips. "It was the best kiss of my life," I admit.

Ashley nods as she watches me, seemingly pleased with my answer. Then she collects herself. "Same time next week, Clara?"

"Sounds good."

CHAPTER THIRTY-THREE

Clara

TWO DAYS LATER, I'm about to knock on Neena's bedroom door when I hear her talking from the other side. I listen for a moment, wondering if she's talking to herself, but quickly realize she's on her phone.

"I'll bring it today and give it to you," she says.

Pause.

"Hey, you wanna grab some food this afternoon?" she asks, her tone hopeful.

Another pause.

"Oh . . . okay."

Pause, again.

"Yeah, I understand."

Pause.

"Okay. See you later. Bye." After a few seconds, she hangs up.

I listen for another minute or two. I know I shouldn't, but I can't help it. Who was she talking to? The only friend I've heard mentioned is Mills, and that was by Paul. Was it Mills? Did he just reject her? Shit. That's all she needs right now. I know it's a crush, but she could use a friend closer to her age. Even if it's a high school kid. She's barely wanted to get out of bed the last two days, and now this. Finally, I open her door. She's standing in front of her full-length mirror, shoving tissues in her bra. As I enter, she rushes to her bed and grabs her pillow, covering herself. "Can't you knock, Mom?" she snaps, her voice quivering with anger.

"I-I'm sorry," I stutter. I look to the floor, unsure of what to do here.

Should I leave or should I stay and discuss what I've just seen?

"I'm a teenager. I deserve privacy." She's upset with me. And embarrassed. But she shouldn't be. All women have been there at some point; been that young girl desperate for womanhood, but stuck in that in-between stage where our bodies don't look as sexy as our minds think we should or as sexy as society tells us we should. She's not doing anything wrong. I just want her to understand it's normal to feel this way.

"Sweetie, I didn't mean to—"

"You're always doing that!" she shrieks. "You're always just walking in without knocking. I'm not a little kid anymore." Her voice cracks with emotion, her lip trembling. Then . . . the tears start. She flops down on her bed and yanks the tissues out of her bra, tossing them on the floor.

I take a moment to pick my next words carefully. I'm pretty sure no matter what I say, she's going to yell at me. Looks like we're having one of those classic teenage daughter-mother moments. If it meant she'd live, I'd take a million a day just to keep her here. "You know, boobs aren't all they're cracked up to be," I murmur as I take a few steps inside of her room. "Bras are so damn uncomfortable and boobs just want to flop around when you run or work out."

She doesn't look at me as she uses the back of her hand to wipe at her nose. "I don't care," she gripes. "I want them."

"I know you do. *Every* girl your age wants them."

"Yeah, well I'll never have them so it doesn't matter. I'll be dead before I even have a chance to grow boobs."

I close my eyes. *Keep it together, Clara.* "You don't need them, honey. You're beautiful. Boobs don't equate beauty."

She flies off the bed and flings the pillow to the side. She's wearing a tiny, white bra and pajama pants, revealing her frail body and thin arms. Each one of her ribs is defined, her pale skin stretched across them. "Look at me, Mom!" she shouts, her eyes glossy with tears as they stream down her face. "Look at me!"

My throat is tight and I blink as tears form in my eyes. "I'm looking at you, Neena," I insist, my heart cracking.

"This," she motions at herself, "is not beautiful." She dances her fingers under her sunken eyes, before dropping them to her lips, that no matter how much ChapStick she puts on, always seem dry and cracked. "This is . . ." she turns and stares at herself in the mirror, "this is ugly.

This is me."

"Neena . . ." Her name comes out as a desperate plea. I need her to see what I see. I need her to understand she's the most beautiful person in the world to me and to so many people. Inside and out. She rubs the dark fuzz on her scalp. Her hair has just started to grow back. "I'm tired of looking ugly," she whimpers. She stares at herself some more, her eyes red with tears.

I furrow my brows in concern. Maybe this is a classic teen moment. Or maybe it's not. Maybe she's depressed. Understandably so. Or maybe she's sick. Sick and tired of what she's going through. All I know is she's in pain and her sadness is palpable. But her being ill is my first concern. Instead of responding verbally, I go into mother mode and within seconds have her head in my hands, my mouth to her forehead. She pulls free from me before I can really tell if she has a fever or not.

"I don't have a fever," she yells.

"I just wanted to check. You seem agitated. And you haven't been feeling well. You've been in bed for two days now. If it's not a fever . . . Maybe you're depressed. We have a prescription—"

"I don't need rest," she groans loudly. "I need you to stop treating me like a baby!"

"Neena," I gasp. "I just don't like seeing you like this. So upset. Why are you so angry with me? I only want to help you."

"Because you won't just let me be sad! Every time I'm sad or angry you try to fix me. "Oh, Neena is upset, she must have a fever," she mimics me. "Oh, Neena slept an extra hour, she *must* be depressed.""

"I'm trying to keep you as happy and healthy as I can. I'm sorry," I whisper.

"Maybe I need to be sad, Mom."

I step toward her, but she backs away. "The doctor gave us a prescription for antidepressants. Maybe they will help," I offer, desperate to help her. Desperate to make her sadness and hurt go away.

"Normal people who *aren't* dying have bad days. They sleep in sometimes. Maybe I just need to be sad and you just need to let me be sad and not try to fix me! I don't need pills!"

Tears are streaming down my face. Where did this all come from? "I'm just trying . . ." I shake my head as I roll in to full-on crying. "I just hate to see you sad, baby."

"Please, just get out of my room," she requests, her eyes fixed on the floor.

My heart feels as if it's just thunked to the floor. I want to hug her, somehow heal her, but it seems the more I try, the more upset she becomes. I decide it's best to leave and give her some time to calm down. "Okay, sweetie," I whisper with a husky voice. "I'm here, if you want to talk." I hiccup back my sobs as I walk out and close the door behind me.

CHAPTER THIRTY-FOUR

Paul

W HEN I GET home, Neena and Clara are both hiding in their rooms. Clara is curled up on her bed, balled up tissues surrounding her.

"What's wrong?" I ask as I sit beside her and squeeze her leg.

She sniffles as she sits up and turns so she's facing me. Her blue eyes are glossed over with tears, her nose red from rubbing. "Neena just had a breakdown, I guess." She shakes her head. "I don't know . . . she's so sad and I just want to help, but she says I'm smothering her. So I'm giving her the space she asked for." She stifles a sob. "I just want to take all of this from her, Paul. I want to be the one to carry that burden. She should be healthy and happy and living life to the fullest. She shouldn't have to look at herself wishing she looked different for a boy," she finishes.

"What?"

"I think that might be what spurred this," she motioned her hand haphazardly, "her meltdown. I think she really likes Mills and he's not interested. He could at least be her friend."

My insides twist with anger. How dare he not like my daughter? Asshole. Of course he's too old for her so if he would, I'd want to beat the crap out of him. But it doesn't cost a damn thing to be friendly. Yet I'd balked at them being friendly. Shit. Mills is pretty much in a no-win situation here, when it comes to Neena. Poor guy.

"I'll go and talk to her," I tell her before pulling her toward me and kissing her forehead.

Clara sighs and flops back on the bed and returns to her previous position. "Good luck."

When I knock on Neena's door, she doesn't answer, so I knock again. Louder this time.

"What?" she yells. My head rears back at her tone. I've never heard her sound so . . . annoyed.

"Uh . . . it's Dad. Can I come in?"

"Now's not a good time."

"Neena, we need to talk, princess."

"Can we talk later, Dad? I'm tired." I thud my head against her door in frustration. I understand Clara's anxiety. I want to fix this. What is going on with her? Something's up. I can feel it in my gut. Is this father's intuition? Maybe. Either way, I'm going in.

"I'm counting to three and I'm coming in," I inform her. "One. Two. Three." The door creaks as I open it and then my heart drops.

Blood.

There's blood everywhere.

The floor is covered with bloody tissues and Neena is sitting on the floor, her back leaning against her bed, holding what looks like a balled up shirt that's stain with more blood.

"Shit," I gasp as I rush to her and drop to my knees. "What is it?" I ask, my panicked voice scaring even me. "What happened?"

She rolls her eyes. Not the reaction I was expecting. "My nose. It won't stop bleeding." I pull the shirt from her face for a moment to find she's right. Her nose is gushing. "Fuck," I breathe out. This isn't good. My stomach is in a knot with worry, but I'm upset too. Why is she hiding in here?

"Princess . . . Why didn't you call for your mother?"

"Because I just yelled at her," she whimpers, her eyes welling up. "She's mad at me."

"No, she's not," I insist gently as I scoop her up in my arms and stand. "Clara!" I yell. I carry Neena out into the hall where Clara meets us. As soon as she sees us, all of her sadness vanishes and she goes into mother/paramedic mode. "How long has it been bleeding, Neena?" she questions.

"Twenty minutes."

"Is there anything else that's wrong?" Clara presses her hand to Neena's forehead.

"My stomach. It hurts."

Clara looks at me, her gaze riddled with worry. "Get her in the car. I'll call her doctor and let him know we're on the way."

"Because her platelet count is abnormally low, the nosebleeds will be more frequent. She may notice her mouth and gums bleeding. Her stomach swelling is from cells gathering in her liver and spleen, among other areas. She may experience back pain from her kidneys swelling as well," Dr. Jones explains.

My hands are clutching the armrests. I hate how he's talking about her . . . so cold. So unfeeling. Clara must sense my tension because she reaches over and grabs my hand, squeezing it. Marcus is on the other side of her, inclining in his seat, his expression stoic. He'd met us in the parking lot. I'm glad Neena is resting in one of the exam rooms. The nurse that attended to her seemed nice enough.

"I feel I should warn you, it's only going to get worse. She'll begin to experience breathing issues from the swelling of her lymph nodes, along with bruises and joint pain. Her appetite will decrease significantly." Well isn't he just a ray of fucking sunshine? He pauses for a moment, leaning back in his desk chair. "Clara." He says her name firmly as he gives her a pointed look. Clara meets his stare. "Have you contacted hospice?"

Her face contorts as a wave of sheer sadness hits her. But she doesn't make a sound. She shakes her head *no* adamantly. My insides feel full of lead. Just the word hospice depresses me.

His gaze drops for a moment, seemingly disappointed by her answer, before meeting mine. "I would strongly recommend you do this immediately. I know it's difficult. But you *will* need hospice. You want someone to be familiar with the family before things get too bad."

It's not his fault, but I kind of want to shoot across his desk and punch him. I clear the emotion from my throat and straighten myself in my seat. The doctor jots something down and tears off two scripts from his pad. "If she's in pain, give her these. She needs to be comfortable."

"How long?" Marcus pipes up.

My breath hitches with his question. I hate that he's asked, but on the other hand, I want to know the answer.

Dr. Jones' mouth tightens for a moment before he answers. "It's hard to say, but if I had to guess, two months maybe . . . three at most." My vision begins to blur as I stare blankly at the clock behind his head, willing time to slow down.

When we get Neena home, we move into strategy and execution like we're about to make a military strike. First mission: lessen her exertion. We rearrange the living room and move her bed downstairs. Neena, of course, hates it. She does *not* want to move into the living room, but it's one of those times where we have to do what's best for her, not what she wants. Clara, knowing Neena may want some privacy, rigs a curtain so Neena can close herself off from the room if she wants to. We hang her Masters of the V posters up, which seems to make her a little less angry. Marcus left to pick up a few things and returns with a video monitor so we can see and hear Neena at night when we're in bed. Neena makes us promise not to use it until things get really bad.

After we get Neena settled, Clara looks exhausted and emotionally drained. I feel so powerless. I can't cure Neena; take her pain and illness away. And I can't take Clara's sadness and worry away either because I feel the same way. She's sitting at the kitchen table, her eyes closed, head in her hands. She doesn't have a lick of makeup on, her long hair is braided to the side and yet, somehow, she looks amazing. But she looks worn out and I wonder when was the last time she had a day for herself. Her nails and toenails are plain; no paint. Her shirt has a blood stain on it from Neena's nosebleed. She deserves some pampering. More like she *needs* it. She needs a little reprieve.

"Why don't you go upstairs and take a nice, hot bath?"

She smiles tiredly. "Yeah, that would be nice." Standing, she kisses me chastely before walking morosely out of the kitchen. Digging through the kitchen junk drawer, I find her address book.

It takes two calls and thirty minutes later, I'm dialing the airline company as I hold my credit card, ready to pay.

Clara is going to love this surprise.

And something tells me, Neena will too.

CHAPTER THIRTY-FIVE
Clara

WE PUT OFF the interviews for over a week or so to focus on Neena. I think the bloody nose incident paired with Dr. Jones' extremely dismal news brought everything into focus. We're in the final weeks of my daughter's life. I feel lost but I power through like always. Bowman and Larry have stepped up and are helping with running the managerial part of the business and I couldn't be more grateful. We need as much time with Neena as we can get.

I called hospice and they sent a lovely woman by the name of Karen over to meet with us. She has a daughter Neena's age who also loves Masters of the V so she and Neena really hit it off. But last night Neena reminded me Paul and I had not finished telling the story of how we came together. She wants to know. Badly. She wants us to see Ashley again. Paul couldn't meet with her today for some reason, but I agreed to. She insisted we meet earlier this time. We normally meet around five, but I didn't question it.

"You holding up okay?" Ashley asks as I walk in. Before I can answer, she hugs me. Tight. Like a family member would. I can't deny, I'm a little thrown off by it, but I hug her back. It's been two weeks since Neena's bloody nose issue and it's happened several more times. Since then, she rests most of the day and has little bouts of energy here and there, but they are very short-lived, causing my worry to go through the roof. Paul and I have taken shifts, sleeping in the living room, but Neena has hated it.

"I'm okay." Maybe if I keep saying it, it will be true. *I'm okay.* My daughter is dying, but *I'm okay.* It's such bullshit.

"I know with everything going on, it must be difficult to do this, but . . ." She pauses and bites her lip as if questioning her next words.

"But what?"

Her gaze meets mine and she inhales deeply. "First off, I'm sorry for being so direct. I was hoping to have everything finished before Neena . . . passed away. She really wants to see this."

Clearing my throat, I wipe at my nose. "Then let's get this done. I want her to see it, too."

We both take our seats and Zane clips my mic on.

"Where's Mills?" I ask. It's odd he's not here. Although, I'm not sure I want to see him. Doesn't he know my beautiful daughter has a crush on him and he needs to be nicer? I know it's not his fault, but I hate that she feels the way she does about herself because of him.

"Couldn't make it this morning. Had something to do," Zane mumbles tiredly.

"We last left off after Paul kissed you." Ashely's mouth curves slightly. "What happened next?"

I have to chuckle a little. Not because it's funny. What happened next wasn't funny at all. But what else can I do but laugh about it at this point? "Paul left."

Ashley looks as if she's trying to touch the ceiling with her eyebrows; she's so surprised. "What?"

"Yep," I confirm. "For a month."

Her mouth drops open in shock. "Are you serious?"

"Yep. I was so mad. But I wasn't sure if I was mad at him for leaving after kissing me like that or for leaving me to deal with Marcus by myself."

"Where did he go?"

"Brazil."

"What happened when he came back?"

I'd told myself it was just a kiss. When it happened, I was a foolish woman and my insides had turned to goo. In his absence though, reality set in and I realized he only did it because he felt sorry for me or something. And that made me mad. *Incredibly* mad. I didn't need his pity.

I didn't need a pity kiss. I may have been whining a little that night, but that was only because I was vulnerable. Now Paul thought I was pathetic and I hated that.

Being forced to work alone with Marcus didn't help either. Paul never really stood up for me to Marcus, but he was at least a buffer between us and at times he played middleman, which eased the hostility.

It was a Wednesday, and hot as hell, and the office air-conditioning unit was down. After calling five HVAC companies, the soonest I could get a repairman out would be the following day. I ran to Walmart and bought six fans, but it wasn't helping much. Marcus made it halfway through the day, then bailed on me. If it hadn't been for a big group of women coming in that afternoon for a jump, I would have left, too.

I was heading to the front of the building, wanting to set everything up for that group so I could get them in and out of the sweatbox that was our office as fast as possible, when Sap walked in.

"Hey there, gorgeous," he rasped, with a grin on his wrinkled face. "I have a surprise for you."

I huffed out an exaggerated breath. "Please tell me you brought an AC repair man."

"Nope," he chuckled. He moved to the side and in entered Paul, incredibly tan and gorgeous. Paul gave a little wave, but I didn't respond. Was I supposed to be excited he returned? Pfft. I didn't even bother to acknowledge him before I continued about my business of preparing for our next clients.

"I think she really missed me, Sap," Paul surmised with a humored tone.

Sap was wise enough not to comment. I think he just enjoyed watching Paul and me go at it sometimes.

I slammed the pens in my hand down on the table. "Welcome back, Paul!" I exclaimed as I threw my arms in the air flamboyantly. "I'm so happy you've returned to help us run this business. You know, the one you own half of."

Paul sighed and leaned his head toward Sap. "She's definitely happy I'm back."

"You're a real ass—"

"Hi," a young woman squeaked as she peered around Paul and Sap.

"Well, hello," Paul replied animatedly, greatly amused by the fact this woman interrupted my tirade.

"I'm Kim." She waved. "We're here for the jump." She was a tall, thin woman with glasses who rocked some old jeans and Chucks. Four other women came in behind her, all fanning themselves, wincing with the heat.

"And who are these lovely ladies?" Paul asked, showcasing his amazing smile.

Kim pointed to each one as she introduced them. "This is Lindsay, Amy, Clare, and Gemma."

"Look at that, Clara," Paul beamed. "Her name is Clare. Clare and Clara."

I gave him a look that said, *you're an idiot.* Then smiled at the ladies. "Nice to meet you all."

The one named Clare, who wore a shirt that said something about milking goats, said, "It's hot as balls in here."

"I should have worn something short sleeved," Kim replied looking down at her outfit.

"You look like a *fittie*," the one named Gemma, with big blue eyes and red hair, informed her in a British accent. "I love that shirt." I liked her accent.

"I know," Lindsay, the one in a Broncos T-shirt noted. "I want one."

"I'll buy you one," Kim promised.

"I think I'm going to puke," Amy volunteered. She looked extremely nervous as she clutched her paper coffee cup in her hand. "I'm terrified of heights."

"Maybe you feel ill because you're drinking coffee in the sweltering heat," Lindsay noted with a humored snort.

"Whose idea was this anyway?" Gemma asked.

"Mine," Lindsay admitted.

"I promise, we'll take good care of you," Paul assured them. Oh, good grief. Someone needed to gag me.

Lindsay gave a half smirk as she gave Paul a once-over and mumbled to Clare, "I hope he's the one I tandem with."

"Me too," Gemma chuckled.

"Why does the word tandem sound so dirty?" Clare asked, her mouth twisted in thought.

The women went on as if we weren't even there. Finally, I intervened. "If you ladies would like to sit down and fill out these disclaimers, we can get you set up and ready to go."

They all took a seat. Filling out forms that should have taken them ten minutes took twenty as they discussed everything from skydiving to anal sex, to the best skin care products. When they started discussing something about a legion and the word moist, I was done. My patience was short that day, with the heat and Paul returning, so I had to keep reminding myself to chill out. Watching them didn't help either. They were clearly dear friends. I missed my friends. It felt like forever since I'd seen Ally and Vanessa. I didn't have any friends here. Except Paul. And of course as soon as we agreed to be friends, he kissed me and disappeared the next day. Not exactly an ideal friendship.

Paul led the ladies outside and just before Sap followed them, he turned to me and said, "You're doing a good job here, Clara."

The compliment shocked me. Sap had always been kind to me, when he wasn't staring at my ass, but I just wasn't expecting it. "Thank you," I managed.

"Dennis would have really liked what you've done here." I grimaced slightly with his words, but forced a smile. "He always wanted to do something for you, try and make it up to you in some way."

My brows rose in shock. He knew who I was. He knew what Dennis did. "You've known this whole time?"

He nodded once. Stepping toward me, he put his hands on his hips and sighed. "This has always been a good business, ya know? Dennis did well here." He nodded his head as he looked around. "But it was always missing something." Then his gaze turned to me again. "I think you were the missing link."

"Come on, Sap," Paul shouted from outside. "Time to fly."

"We can talk about it later if you'd like to."

I gave a soft smile, unable to find words. My throat wasn't tight with emotion. I wasn't on the verge of tears. I was just . . . speechless. So I said nothing before he turned and left. Paul drove to the airpark with Sap and the group of women followed in their car, where they would meet Bowman and one of our other divers and I began closing up shop.

Typically, the clients would come back to the office to collect their photos or videos, but I asked if I could mail them theirs. It was too hot to deal with that today. An hour later, as I was just about to leave, the phone rang.

"Hello?"

"Clara," Paul rasped through ragged breaths.

"Yeah?"

"It's Sap. He's had a heart attack or something. The ambulance is taking him to the hospital now."

My heart dropped. "Shit," I gasped. "Is everyone else okay?"

"Yeah. It happened right before we took off. It's lucky we weren't in the air."

I closed my eyes for a moment thanking whatever higher being there was for keeping everyone else safe. Then I asked that Sap be okay.

"I'll meet you there."

The funeral was lovely and as low-key as possible. The way Sap would have wanted it. There were only ten people that attended and to honor our departed friend and coworker, we hired a pilot for the day and sent the plane up with all of our divers and did a farewell dive to honor him. Paul attached Sap's American flag he received for his military service to his parachute and it drifted beautifully as it glided toward the ground. We closed the office for a few days, needing to find a new pilot and rearrange the schedule. Sap would definitely be missed.

I worked, but Paul and Marcus stayed home. They took losing Sap hard. It hadn't been long since he had passed so I understood they probably needed some time to mourn. I could not stand Marcus. At all. He was the thorn in my side then. But I decided to try my hand at showing him compassion. I went home and made two chicken and broccoli casseroles, wrapped them tightly in foil, and packed them in my car.

I didn't even turn the car off when I pulled in front of Marcus' place. I sat the pan on the mini porch by the door, knocked loudly, and rushed back to my car. I wasn't trying to be a bitch. I just couldn't take it if he acted like an asshole to me when I was trying to be nice. If he threw the food away after I left, I wouldn't know and wouldn't have to hate him for it. As I pulled out, I looked in the rearview mirror and saw him open his front door and step out on the porch, looking right at my car. Then looking down, he bent and picked the dish up, inspecting it, before looking to my car again. His expression said nothing. Was he touched by my gesture? Did he hate it? I didn't know. When he turned and went back inside with the dish, I let out a long breath. No matter what—I tried. I did the right thing and if he decided to ignore my gesture, that was on him.

I had never been to Paul's house before and I wasn't surprised to find he lived in a small, simple house about thirty minutes from the office. The house was plain, which made sense for him. Why have a giant, nice house when you may just take off at any given moment with no idea when you'd return?

A part of me wanted to do the knock and run at Paul's, too. That's what I should have done. But I wanted to see him. I felt pathetic for it, but I did. So I told myself I would hand him the meal I'd made, but I would *not* go inside. No matter what. Bracing myself, I knocked on the door, anxious as all hell. We really hadn't talked since he returned and believe me, I had plenty to say. But I bit my tongue. This was a time of mourning. My grievances with Paul could wait.

When he answered the door, I went mute.

Son of a bitch.

He was in nothing but his boxers.

I clutched the casserole in my arms and forced myself to blink. He squinted as if he had just woken and his hair was slightly mussed. But his body . . . I hated him. It was amazing. I had seen him with his shirt off before, but seeing him so bare in his boxers was different. It was so intimate. And suddenly I felt very vulnerable.

"Hi," he rasped in a sleepy voice. Ugh, even his just-woke-up voice was sexy.

I licked my dry lips. "H-hi," I stuttered. "I brought you some food."

His gaze darted to the dish then to my eyes. "You did?"

"Um, yeah. Since you're grieving and all. Thought you might like a meal."

He stepped back and to the side, inviting me to enter. Knock and run had turned into knock and see, and now it was knock and visit. I failed. I stepped inside, and if I thought the outside of the house was plain, the inside was no exception. It was an open floor plan, the living room and kitchen all one room. He had a love seat and a small table closest to the kitchen, which could only seat two people. No television. No pictures or décor. He did, however, have a bike hanging from the ceiling, and a snowboard, skis, and skateboard that lined the wall.

Shutting the door behind me, he asked, "What is it?"

"Oh," I replied nervously. I realized I was just staring at his house. "Nothing. It's weird to see your house is all." *Ugh. Why did I say that?*

He smirked, his dimples poking out. Stupid dimples. "Must be weird to see a house that isn't in shambles," he mocked.

I glared at him jokingly. "You're just jealous of how much character my house has. Yours . . . is clearly lacking."

"You're right," he played along. "I'm so jealous of a porch anyone over a hundred and ten pounds will crash through."

"See?" I jested. "I knew it. Besides, the porch is sturdier now, remember?"

We both snickered. "Well, when I asked what it was I meant the dish in your hands. What is it?"

"Chicken and broccoli casserole."

He walked to the kitchen and opened the fridge, pulling out a *Coke*. I noticed several *Country Crock* containers on the shelves in his fridge and smiled to myself. He must have visited his mother recently. As he bent down, the muscles in his back seemed to ripple, demanding I stare at them. "You want one?" he offered, holding a can for me to see.

"Sure."

He grabbed another can and set them on the table. Then he grabbed two plates, a serving spoon, and two forks. After he set them down, he stopped and looked at me as if he were waiting for something.

"You okay?"

"Yeah, why?" I inquired.

"You haven't moved from that spot since you came inside and you're standing there holding that casserole like it's a newborn baby."

I shook my head as my cheeks flamed before I moved to meet him at the table. "Sorry. It's been a long day."

He took the dish, placing it in the center of the table, before peeling the foil back. His eyelids flexed slightly, but he quickly caught himself.

"It looks good," he said. What a liar. It looked nowhere near good. My cheeks further heated with embarrassment. I knew it looked less than appetizing, but he was being nice. "Let's have lunch." It was close to five in the evening, but I didn't bother to point that out to him. We sat and he served us. I watched him as he took his first bite. His chewing started fast, but slowed. At one point he looked like he was a horse chewing straw. As he continued, he worked hard to school his expression. When he finally managed to swallow, the muscles in his neck and jaw flexed dramatically. It looked as if he was choking down a wad of cotton. His gaze met mine, his eyes filled with sincerity.

"It's really good, Clara," he lied before he popped open his soda can and took a long swig. Again.

I bit back my laugh. "I think I finally found something you're bad at, Paul."

"What's that?" he asked, bewildered as he poked at his plate.

"Lying. You suck at it."

He laughed, leaning back in his seat and scratching his stomach. "I'm not lying," he continued to fib. God. Those dimples. They were seriously killing me. Here I was, embarrassed as hell because I'd made a shitty casserole, and I couldn't help smiling because of his two stupid dimples. Tilting forward, he placed his forearms on the table and scooped his fork in for more.

"Paul," I said his name slowly, causing him to look up. "Stop."

"Stop?" he asked, his tone indicating he was perplexed.

"Stop eating it. It's awful. I'm sorry." I stood and grabbed both plates from the table and dumped the casserole in the trash.

"Why'd you do that?" he questioned as he stood.

"I have no idea why I cooked. I suck at it. I just wanted to do something nice for you." Shaking my head, I sighed. "I'm going to go now."

"You sure?" he asked, frowning slightly. He seemed disappointed. "I have some other food my mother sent me home with yesterday."

"Yeah, I've got some stuff to do." Raising my gaze to meet his, I offered, "I'm sorry. About Sap. He was a colorful man."

Paul smirked. "Yeah. He was."

I walked to his front door and opened it, painfully aware he was behind me every step of the way. What a waste of time this was. What possessed me to bring him food? He must have thought I was the saddest woman he'd ever met. Not only couldn't I make a simple casserole, but there was also the issue of the pity kiss. How pathetic. I stepped out onto his porch, ready to dart for my car and hightail it out of there, but stopped. Now was not to the time to confront him about the kiss. But I needed to. Or somehow I needed to redeem myself. But how?

Spinning around, I gazed at his dark stare and bit my lip.

"You okay?" he asked.

I shook my head, hardly able to believe what I was about to do, before I slammed my body to his, crushing our mouths together. As I crashed into him, he stumbled a bit and we would have fallen had he not managed to get his footing. Of course while he was trying to keep us from tumbling to the floor, I was trying to kiss him and he couldn't quite participate initially. When he managed to get his footing, he was still for a moment, stunned, but I was undeterred despite my less than smooth initiation of the kiss. I pressed my mouth harder to his and once I threaded my fingers in his hair, he came to life. His lips moved against mine as his hands fisted the material of my shirt. When his tongue swept in my mouth, I lightly nipped it, earning a small hiss from him, before he squeezed me tighter. What started off clumsy was turning into a rather intense moment.

When I managed to pull away, he released me slowly, his hands sliding down my body before he dropped them to his sides. His eyes darted between my mouth and eyes as he sucked in a long breath. When Paul kissed me the first time, he was so smooth; flawless. My kiss, well, it was awkward. But judging by the look of shock in his gaze and the way his mouth quirked slightly, he seemed just as flabbergasted as I had been after he kissed me.

Clearing my throat, I gave a small smile. Then I turned and walked to my car, climbed in, and drove away. It was nice to be the one to leave him speechless.

"I think that's where we should stop today," I tell Ashley. "I want to get home and check on Neena."

"Okay," she acknowledges and waves a hand for Zane to remove my mic. "I really think Neena is going to like this."

"I hope you will . . . make it tasteful, Ashley. She *is* twelve."

Ashley smiles. "You mean leave out all the dirty kissing and sex parts."

I cringe. Maybe I've volunteered a little too much detail. "We haven't gotten to any sex parts yet," I point out.

"No, but I am on pins and needles waiting for it. But don't worry, I promise to make this G-rated for Neena."

"Okay. Next week it is then, yes?"

"See you then."

CHAPTER THIRTY-SIX

Paul

W E'RE SITTING IN the living room, waiting for Clara to get home. I had to cancel my time with Ashley this afternoon to pull off this surprise, but it will be well worth it. Clara is going to be stoked.

Vanessa is sitting on the end of Neena's bed, a cup of coffee in hand, working off her hangover. Apparently it took two Xanax and a few shots of whiskey to get her on the plane. Ally was practically carrying her piggyback style when I'd picked them up from the airport.

"You okay?" I question.

She sips her coffee and mumbles, "I'll make it."

Ally sits beside Vanessa with Neena behind her, braiding her hair. The two women have doted on Neena since they walked in the door, remaining close to her most of the time. It's like the mother in each of them came out as soon as they walked in the door and they needed to be close to her.

"She just pulled in," Marcus informs us from where he's peeking out the front window.

"She's going to be so happy," Neena gushes as she claps her hands in excitement. It's been so long since I've seen her smile like this. My heart swells at the sight. She quickly pulls out her camera and climbs out of bed, readying it to capture Clara's reaction. This kid. She slays me. She is so happy right now and it has nothing to do with her; it's all about her mother. Knowing her mother will be elated to see her longtime friends gives her great joy. Immense pride washes over me. I'm honored to be her father.

Vanessa and Ally go and hide in the kitchen just before Clara opens the door to enter. She first notices Neena with her camera and chuckles just before she crosses her eyes and sticks her tongue out.

"The camera loves it, Mom," Neena jokes.

"They say I was made for it," Clara jests back. She tilts her head and assesses Neena. "You look like you're feeling well tonight."

"I am," Neena beams.

Clara looks to me and smiles. It's not just a greeting, it feels like there's meaning behind it. I tilt my head and give her a questioning look. But she shakes her head as if to say, *later.*

Neena is still filming her, and Marcus and I are watching her every move. Clara freezes, her eyes narrowing in suspicion. "What's going on, guys?"

"Nothing," I chirp. That's right. I'm chirping. No shame in my game. "We just missed you is all."

"Oh yeah?"

"Yeah, we did," Neena agrees.

Walking to her, I lean in and kiss her softly. And she lets me. I move closer to the shell of her ear. "We're not the only ones that have missed you."

"No?" she questions, her smile flirty, her eyes darting from Neena back to me as she blushes. Does she think I'm being dirty right now; talking about my dick? Shit, now I *am* thinking dirty. *Damn it.*

"Come on in, guys," Neena shouts toward the kitchen.

Clara's eyes widen when she glances at me with uncertainty, but when she looks toward the kitchen and sees Ally and Vanessa walk out, her face lights up. Like a Christmas tree lights up. *I did good,* I think to myself. And almost pat myself on the back. In a flash the three women are in a circle hugging, jumping up and down as they squeal like children. Neena is laughing as she films while Marcus and I just stand back and watch the craziness. That sound, her laugher, is the epitome of my greatest joy.

Neena looks over to me and mouths, *"Thank you, Dad."*

I give her a wink and look back to Clara, feeling pretty damn proud of myself. I knew this would make her day. Seeing Neena so freaking happy is the cherry on the top of the sundae.

"Did you drive?" Clara asks as she pulls away from her friends and wipes the happy tears from her face.

"We flew," Ally says, annoyed as she cuts a sharp look to Vanessa.

Clara snorts in disbelief. "What?"

"I had to tranquilize her like a wild animal, but she made it," Ally says, dryly, speaking of Vanessa.

"I've never been so scared," Vanessa confesses, placing a hand to her chest.

Ally rolls her eyes. "If I had heard *help me, Jesus* one more time on that plane, I would've been escorted off in handcuffs."

Vanessa laughs. "It wasn't that bad."

"Yes, it was."

Clara's happy expression seems to droop for a moment as she stares at her friends.

"What's wrong, girl?" Vanessa inquires immediately, in a concerned fashion, as she wraps an arm around Clara's shoulders.

"I just can't believe you guys are here," she murmurs. "And you flew, Vanessa. I can't believe it. Thank you, guys."

Ally and Vanessa smile from ear to ear and hug Clara. When they pull away again, Ally says, "Thank Paul. He arranged all of this. Paid for our tickets, too."

Clara spins around and meets my stare. I give her a little shrug. "I wanted to do something nice for you. You need some me time."

She grins and moves toward me in a hurry until she's in my arms, hugging me. "Thank you for this. Thank you so, so much for this."

"Well there's more," I tell her, waggling my brows.

"There is?"

"You and your besties are heading out for a day at the beach tomorrow. I booked a room and everything."

Clara immediately shrinks away from me. "An overnight trip?"

"Yes," I tell her. "I know you are worried about leaving Neena, but I'm here. I will take good care of her."

Clara shakes her head. "No, I can't do an overnight trip. It's really sweet of you, Paul, but I can't."

"Yes you can, Mom," Neena cuts in. "Besides, I'd like some father-daughter time with Dad."

Clara pinches her lips together, not liking the idea of leaving Neena at all. "We'll talk about it later."

Mei-ling joins us and we grill out and have an amazing dinner. Vanessa and Ally tell embarrassing stories about Clara and Neena eats up every bit of it. She loves hearing about her mom, before she was a mother. Clara wears a smile the entire evening and seems relaxed for the first time in a long time. I couldn't be more grateful to Vanessa and Ally for coming. One can never get too much support. These women are practically her family.

After we clean up from dinner and Marcus and Mei-ling head home, Clara gets busy trying to make sleeping arrangements for everyone.

"We're sleeping down here with Neena," Ally informs her as she grabs her suitcase and moves it toward the stairs.

"No, we have a guest room," Clara insists. Looks like I'm sleeping in Clara's room.

"We're having a slumber party." Vanessa grins as she squeezes Neena to her.

"We're going to do makeovers and paint each other's nails. A pair of your underwear might end up in the freezer," Ally laughs.

"Well I can join in, too," Clara says.

"Not tonight," Vanessa quickly argues. "Tonight is girl time with Neena. We want you to . . . relax."

"I think you two could use a good night's rest," Ally giggles wildly as she winks a bunch of times, looking like she has Tourette's. It's not hard to miss what she's implying.

Clara cuts her gaze to me and shakes her head as she smirks. Her friend is a nut.

"Subtle," I chuckle.

I'm not sure if this is hurting Clara's feelings or not. Her expression is uncertain, but when Neena walks up to her and hugs her with a giant grin on her face, Clara finally smiles. "Okay. But no calling boys," she jokes. "Or prank calls."

"Seriously?" Ally groans. "You're no fun."

When all the beds are made and everyone is in their pajamas, Clara and I finally head up to her bed to the sound of our daughter giggling as Ally and Vanessa cackle. I follow Clara into her bedroom, and shut the door behind us, locking it.

It's been weeks since we were really intimate together. Our one time when Neena busted in on us was the last time. We've kissed and held hands since then, but there's been so much going on I don't think either of us has had the energy for anything more.

Clara's nervous. It's written all over her. Her fingers are knotted together, her lower lip between her teeth. The last thing I want is for her to feel pressured. Hell, I don't mind just being her human pillow for the night.

"Nothing has to happen tonight," I tell her. "I didn't plan the slumber party or anything."

Clara lets out a long sigh. "I want to. It's just . . . been a long time."

My heart pounds faster. She wants to. She wants me. I step toward her and see her tremble slightly. Her nervousness is sexy as fuck to me. She remembers what we're like in bed. We're liable to claw at each other like animals.

"I don't want you to feel pressured."

"Paul." She lets out a lengthy breath. "I need this. I just feel so . . . unsexy. I've been in mother mode for years. It's hard to turn it off." She closes her eyes and takes another deep breath. "I'm not what I was when we were together years ago. My body is different."

"I don't know what you see when you look in the mirror, Clara. But I see a woman that has danced in and out of my mind for the past thirteen years. A woman that no matter how hard I tried, I could never replace. I have never wanted another woman the way I want you, then and now. And here you are, beautiful and nervous. No more holding back. I need you. I. Want. You. I didn't think there was anything that could make me want you more . . . love you more. But I was wrong."

"You were?"

"Not only are you the sexiest woman to me. You're the mother of my child, Clara. Your body and my body joined together and made that beautiful little girl. You carried her; my baby. Inside of you." I struggle for a beat, swallowing hard, and rub my cheeks as the emotion overwhelms me. "You can't understand how much that turns me on. I want you to feel what you are. I want you to see what I see."

Her chest rises and falls as she watches me. "I don't know if that's possible," she utters softly. "Just . . . I need you to guide me. I'll overthink everything if you don't."

A strong wave of nostalgia washes over me as I remember the woman that wore an exterior of fearlessness and determination. She came off intimidating to most men. Maybe even to me at first. But alone, naked, in bed . . . she was something else. She let go, gave in, succumbed completely. And it was so fucking beautiful. She was the kind of lover I never knew I wanted until I had her. To have someone place so much trust in me; to let me give and take the way I needed to because pleasing me was her pleasure. She was steel and titanium to the world, but in the throes of passion, she handed over her power, like a gift, trusting me with it. And I treasured it. She was submissive and no woman has ever made me feel like more of a man in bed than she did. I will make her remember that woman; I will make her see what I see.

"Come here," I order her, my voice automatically deep and husky.

Her tongue darts out and runs quickly over her pink lips. But she does as I say and moves in front of me. "Take my shirt off," I rasp.

Her blue eyes dart to mine, a flicker of fear mixed with excitement in them. Her hands shake slightly as she reaches up and begins to unbutton my shirt from the collar down. When she's done, she brings it up and slips it over my shoulders so it falls to the floor. She's softly panting as her hands brush over my chest, her eyes fixed on her delicate fingers as she reacclimatizes herself with territory she once knew well.

"Arms up," I tell her. Hesitantly, she raises her arms and I tug her shirt off and fling it away. She lowers her arms to her sides and as I reach around to unhook her bra, I kiss the crook of her neck and shoulder. She lets out a hiss, her chest arching toward me, pressing to my body. So beautiful. Stepping back, I watch in awe as she lets her bra slip from her breasts and down her arms. Her pink nipples are budding, the swelling making her desire evident. She's always had the softest skin, perfectly creamy and soft.

"Turn and look at yourself in the mirror." She blinks a few times, the uncertainty in her eyes begging me to stop this, but does as I say. She's facing her full-length mirror, in the corner of her room, as I move behind her, pressing myself to her ever so slightly. She's shaking.

"Look at you, Clara," I growl as I run my fingers down her arm. "This perfect skin, those beautiful breasts. Look at how beautiful you are, baby."

Her gaze tentatively meets mine in the reflection of the mirror. "Don't look at me. Not yet," I tell her. "I want you to see how fucking exquisite you are." I trail a hand back up her arm, her skin pebbling with my touch. "With your right hand, touch your breast."

Her small hand softly glides up her body and gently gropes her breast. Her eyes flutter with the contact, but she keeps them open, staring at herself, just as I told her to. My dick is straining against my pants as I watch her. How can she not know she's so fucking sexy? Pulling away, I turn and quickly remove my pants and boxers. My dick is at full stance, hard as fuck. It's been so long since I've had her, and I feel like I'm about to combust with want. But this must happen slowly. Pulling the chair from her bureau, I place it behind her and sit so that my face is perfectly align with her ass.

"Undo your pants, Clara." Her shoulders rise and fall with each breath she takes, but she unbuttons them and moves her arms to her sides again. *So nervous and sweet.* I hook my fingers on the waistband of her pants and panties, tugging them down her legs. She gasps and momentarily glances back at me before she steps out of them and I shove them aside. Her ass still looks amazing. Age and having a kid haven't changed it much at all. Gritting my teeth, I let my fingers glide up the backs of her legs until they're just below her cheeks. Suddenly not shy, she arches her back so her ass pushes toward me, hungry for more of my touch. There's my girl. I give her right cheek a hard slap, her flesh giving the slightest jiggle, driving me fucking nuts. She moans with the sting and I quickly grab her ass with both hands and massage it roughly.

"Do you like that?"

"Yes," she breathes.

"Look at yourself, Clara," I demand as I peek around the side of her to see her reflection. "Put your arms up." She raises them and crosses them behind her head. I hold her hips and kiss her lower back before bending slightly and biting one of her ass cheeks. She yelps, causing me to shush her, and when I see her reflection again, her eyes are closed, her mouth parted as she breathes heavily.

"Open, Clara," I tell her.

"I can't," she moans, letting her head fall back. "It feels too good."

My grip stills on her waist, and I turn her to face me. Her eyes fly open and find my gaze before moving down to my dick. Her eyes flex at the sight of it, rich with desire. I wrap my hand around it and stroke slowly. "You see what you do to me, Clara? That's all you. This is all yours. Tell me it's yours," I rasp.

"It's m-mine," she stutters.

She's transfixed; she can't look away. "Touch yourself."

Her hand moves between her legs, her thin fingers sliding delicately along her pink flesh.

"*Damn*, that's beautiful, Clara. Watching you touch yourself, fuck, it turns me on. How does it feel?"

"Soft and wet," she whimpers. "So wet."

My self-control snaps. I can't take it anymore. I need her. I need to be inside of her. I grip her waist and twist her so she's facing the mirror again and pull her toward me. "Time to take what's yours, baby."

She reaches back between her legs, her hand finding my erection, making me hiss and groan at the same time. Lowering herself, she runs the head of my cock along her warm slickness before finding her entrance and dropping slowly on my shaft. Her head falls forward as she moves down, and once she's fully seated on me, she lets out a series of moans that sound somewhere between complete pleasure and relief. My hands are squeezing her waist as she stills and we both take a few seconds to get our wits about us. We want this to last. Easy does it. Slow and steady. Reaching around, I find her chin and raise it, holding her face so she's forced to look in the mirror.

"Watch us," I growl hoarsely. Then, hands on her hips, I raise and lower her, ever so slowly. I can see around her, watch what she's watching. There's something so erotic about watching my dick as it slides in and out of her. She pants as we move, releasing little mews here and there. She's holding back. She wants to cry out, but we can't. We can't get too loud. We both know this. We have people downstairs that could hear.

"Fuck that looks good," I growl. "My dick inside of you, those perfect nipples, those beautiful breasts. Do you like how that looks?"

"Yes." She groans in pleasure. "I love it."

"Do you see it? Do you see what I see?"

"Yes," she pants, her head rolling down to her side as the pleasure overtakes her.

"Tell me you're beautiful. Tell me you see it."

"I see it," she whimpers. "I-I'm beautiful."

With that, I pull her off of me and spin her around so she's facing me. Clara needed to be reminded of what she is; who she is. She's not just a mother. She's a beautiful, sexy woman. I wanted her to see that. But now, I need something, too. I need her to show me something.

"Now tell me you love me."

She blinks a few times, a little thrown. She swallows hard, her breathing still erratic, before she steps toward me and threads her fingers in my hair. Bending down, she kisses me, then whispers, "I love you, Paul James."

"Show me."

She straddles me and slips me back inside of her, sensually moving us back and forth, as she whispers, "*I love you,*" over and over again.

CHAPTER THIRTY-SEVEN
Clara

PAUL HAS LITERALLY just pushed me out the front door. I'm standing on the porch, facing him, as he stands in the doorway, blocking my reentrance.

"You'll call me if anything comes up, right?" I question. I've asked him this a million times already, but one more time can't hurt.

"Clara," he sighs exhaustedly as he lets his head thump against the door. "I swear I will call you if she so much as farts."

"Dad!" Neena shrieks from where she's standing behind him.

"Sorry, princess," he calls over his shoulder.

Neena pokes her head out between his body and the doorframe. "Go, Mom," she insists. "Have fun!"

"Come on," Ally hollers from the car, her head hanging out the passenger side window. "Vanessa peed like twenty minutes ago. That means we'll have to stop in about an hour."

Paul shrugs as if to say, *guess you gotta go*. I huff. I woke up this morning feeling on top of the world. Our night together was incredible, and somehow better than years ago when we were younger. I climbed out of bed happy and determined. Determined not to go on this trip. I love my friends and would love to go away with them for a beach night, but my kid is sick. She needs me. How could I even consider leaving her?

These are the points I argued to everyone this morning. It was taken to a vote: 4–1. I lost. Six against me if you count that they tried to count Marcus and Mei-ling as mail-in votes. Neena's phone rings from inside the house and she quickly utters, "Bye, Mom. Love you," before she rushes away to answer it.

Paul steps out onto the porch and takes my face in his hands. He kisses my forehead, my cheeks, my chin, and then my mouth. "I promise I'll take good care of her. Please go have fun." Then he kisses me again, long and slow, his fingers sliding up into my hair. When he pulls away, my body feels limp. His dark eyes beam onto mine as he grins. Fucker. He knows I'm like putty in his hands. "Last night was amazing," he whispers with a smirk. "Let's do it again real soon."

And it was amazing. He'd told me so a million times this morning. But I'm not tired of hearing it yet. Then turning me, he swats my ass and sends me on my way.

When I climb in the car, Ally's wearing a shit-eating grin, but it's Vanessa that starts first. "You look like you're walking a little funny today, Clara," she heckles from the backseat.

"Clara got some brown chicken, brown cow," Ally teases, imitating the classic porno music. That's her hilarious way of saying, *bow chicka wow wow*.

They both laugh as I chuckle, my face heating slightly.

"How was it?" Ally asks, her tone indicating her desperation for details. She looks all cute and innocent to the outside world, but she's really a horny little freak.

I shrug as I put the car in drive. "Pretty damn awesome," I admit.

"Good for you," Vanessa laughs.

"I didn't know it could still be so . . . hot," I confess.

"What?" Ally questions me, her face scrunched up. "Sex?"

"Well, yeah. It was . . . kind of dirty—in a good way. I kind of thought I'd never have that again."

"Why?" they both ask in unison.

"I don't know," I groan, suddenly feeling embarrassed. I feel like the thirteen-year-old that hasn't started her period when all her other friends have. "I guess I thought with age and a kid, and . . . I don't know."

"So Paul is a super freak . . ." Ally notes with admiration.

Images of him beneath me, watching me, thrusting in and out of me flicker through my mind. Ugh, the sex was amazing. I needed that so badly.

"Judging by the look on her face, definitely," Vanessa snorts.

CHAPTER THIRTY-EIGHT
Paul

NEENA AND I spend the day watching movies, lounging on the couch. Around four, her phone rings and she goes to the kitchen before she answers. Then she walks back in the living room, phone to her ear.

"You're here? Right now?" she says, to whomever is on the other end. I sit up and mute the television and watch her as she opens the front door.

It's Mills.

Mills is here.

Mills that makes my daughter cry.

Great.

"Hi," she manages as she drops her phone to her side. Her other hand fingers her scalp nervously. She's not wearing her scarf. The brown fuzz that covers her head is as dark as mine and offers a vast contrast to her pale skin.

"Hi. Sorry to just show up, but . . . I wanted to talk to you and your mom."

"Mom's not here," Neena says.

"But Dad is," I offer loudly as I stand and approach the door. Mills' eyes widen slightly and he fidgets a little, shuffling in place.

"Oh, hi, Paul," he offers. Pushing his bangs from his face, he looks at me. "I hope this is okay. I didn't want to say anything until I knew I could get them. I've spent the last two weeks trying to get tickets to Masters of the V. I finally scored some this morning."

Neena's eyebrows haven't fully grown back, but I can tell they'd be touching her hairline if they had. "Really?"

Mills darts his gaze to me, nervously, then back to Neena. "I thought, if your parents were cool with it, maybe you could go."

Neena lets out some kind of crazy squeal/shriek sound as she grabs my arms and tugs. "Please, Dad! Please let me go."

I kind of want to throat punch Mills right now. He should have asked me before telling Neena. How in the hell am I supposed to say no to her? But I should. For starters, concerts are loud and busy and people are pushy. Secondly, I'm pretty sure Clara would say no.

"I got a third ticket for you or Clara to go, too," Mills murmurs.

"How thoughtful," I counter dryly.

"Pleeeassseee, Dad!" Neena begs. She's been peppy today. More so than she has in a long time. Today is a good day. Maybe one of the last good days we have.

I'm already leaning toward answering yes when Mills throws out his final card. "I got us backstage passes."

And . . . we're going. Clara is not going to like this. Fuck.

I don't call Clara. My reasoning is nothing is wrong. Neena is fine. She's happy. And if I call Clara, all it will do is worry her to death while she should be relaxing. Besides, I'm going to be with Neena the entire time. Everything will be fine.

We meet Masters of the V before the show. Zack, the lead singer, who looks like he stuck his finger in an electrical socket this morning, his hair sticks out so much, is actually a pretty cool guy. He gives Neena an autographed poster and the coveted wristband she's wanted so badly for so long. Neena has not stopped grinning all night.

And Mills, to his credit, has treated her like a queen tonight. I've had mixed feeling about the kid. But before we got out of the car to come inside tonight, Neena looked in the visor to adjust the purple scarf around her head. What happened next surprised me.

"You should leave it off, Neena," Mills said as he leaned forward from the backseat.

"I look awful," she griped.

"No, you don't," he insisted. "I think you look pretty badass without it."

"Really?"

"Yeah. It's your choice, of course, but I don't think you need it."

Neena flipped the visor closed and tugged off her scarf, leaving it on the dash before we climbed out. Mills made her feel cool. He won some major points in my book tonight.

The concert is in full effect and I can't deny it's the worst music I've ever heard in my life. Neena is dancing and jumping, shouting at the top of her lungs. I bend down so my mouth is to her ear. "Slow down a bit, kid. I don't want you to tire out."

"I'm fine," she yells back.

She doesn't stop moving for several songs. Then it happens. The band starts playing a song called *Promised Land,* and Zack dedicates it to Neena.

She loses her mind.

The melody is soft and slow, which keeps Neena from bouncing all over the place for a minute. As he starts singing, she seems to simmer down, really listening to the words. The song is about what lies ahead; the unknown. It's about someone that's scared, but never shows it. After the first two verses, I look down and see Neena crying as she smiles. Her hands are clasped together against her chest.

When the song finishes, the next one is upbeat and the crowd starts bouncing around like crazy again. But not Neena. She looks up at me and tugs my shirt so I'll bend down to hear her. "I need to go home," she murmurs.

"Okay." I'm wondering what just happened but there's no time for that. I tell Mills and together we begin weaving our way through the crowd. Neena is behind me, with Mills behind her.

We've just exit the theatre into the lobby when she whimpers, "Dad." And then she collapses to the floor. I fall, banging my knees against the floor, and shake her a few times, trying to wake her, but get nothing. Instantly, I check her vitals. She's still breathing. Her heart is still beating.

I toss my keys to Mills. "Get my car. Now!" I boom. Mills hauls ass out to the parking lot. Meanwhile, I scoop Neena up, her frail body limp in my arms, and hold tightly to me. "Not now, princess," I beg her, my voice raspy as hell as fear seizes me. "Not yet."

CHAPTER THIRTY-NINE

Clara

THE TWO-HOUR drive feels like twenty. When Paul had called, they were on their way to the hospital. He'd been at a concert with Mills and Neena. My heart has been in my throat ever since. She went unconscious. Paul said she'd passed out cold. That hasn't happened before. Ally, who's driving us back because I'm a wreck, drops me at the entrance and I rush in while they park the car. Paul is in the lobby of the oncology floor, his head buried in his hands. Marcus is sitting beside him, passed out.

"Where is she?" I snap. His head flies up, his red and glossy eyes now alert.

"Clara?"

"Where?" I growl. I want to attack him, rip him apart with my bare hands. I left him with her for one night and this happens. How could he even think about taking her to a concert? Is he demented?

"She woke up," he tells me. "But she's sleeping again. She overexerted herself."

"No fucking kidding, Paul!" I shout. "You took her to a goddamn concert!"

People passing by us in the hallway stop and stare at us before continuing on their way. "Clara," Marcus intervenes, stepping in front of me. "The doctor said it could have happened regardless of the concert or not."

"You should have called and asked me first!" I yell at Paul, ignoring Marcus.

237

"It came together at the last minute. I didn't think it would be a big deal. She was so . . . happy," Paul explains.

I let out a frustrated groan. "I should have known better than to leave her overnight with you."

Paul's face contorts from guilt to anger. "And what the hell does that mean?"

"It means that I shouldn't have trusted you!"

"Guys," Marcus says, as calmly as he can.

"Are you serious?" Paul booms.

"You two need to quiet down or we're going to have to call security," a nurse tells us.

"You could have said no, Paul. But *nooooo*," I rant dramatically, flailing my hands. "Saying no might make Neena upset with you. God forbid."

"You're right, Clara," he mocks me. "I should have denied her a chance to meet her favorite singer and see her favorite band in concert. Because every dying kid wants to sit at home knowing they missed a chance to do something they could have. You might be that big of an asshole, but not me."

"Oh, you're an asshole, all right," I assure him.

By this point, my friends have walked in to see the show. "Clara." Vanessa says my name, calmly, as she grabs my arms.

I pull free ignoring the stunned looks both she and Ally make. "Maybe we should take her hiking in Brazil," I jeer sarcastically. "Why not? She can handle it."

Paul groans in obvious frustration. "This is why she can't tell you anything," he spats. "You're so over the top."

"Neena tells me everything," I say, with offense.

"Oh yeah?" he questions, stepping toward me so I have to look up to meet his line of sight. "Did she tell you how she wants her funeral?"

I pinch my lips together. Neena told me once she wanted to be cremated. I hated that thought. I couldn't imagine not having a place to visit her. Burning her remains seemed so final. I just . . . couldn't talk about it. I ended up crying and she never brought it back up.

"No? And why is that? Because you lose your shit over everything. I took her to a concert tonight. She was more alive and happy than I've seen her in months. So screw you if you want to make me out to be a bad parent, but I'm not sorry I took her."

"If you want to risk your own life doing dangerous shit, Paul, that's on you." I point a firm finger at him. "But not her. You do *not* take chances with her!"

He stands straight and shakes his head as if I'm the most ridiculous person he's ever spoken with. "Clara," his tone is filled with angered calmness. "She's dying. I wanted her to live for a night. Really live. I didn't put her on a motorcycle. I didn't take her bungee jumping. I took my kid to a concert. Something any parent with a normal and healthy kid would do and not think twice about it."

"You put her at risk!"

"And so what if I did! You ask her if she regrets it. Even now, with how shitty she feels, you ask her if she regrets going to that concert. You know what she'll say?" he growls. "No. Because she did something that made her happy; that made her feel alive. Maybe you should try it sometime."

"What does that mean?"

"You own a fucking skydiving business and you've never even jumped. Thirteen years and you haven't jumped once. Just because you don't take chances because you're always playing it safe doesn't mean our daughter is that way. Neena knows how precious time is. She doesn't want to lie in bed for all of her last days afraid to go out and do what she wants." With that, he storms off down the hall.

Vanessa squeezes me. "He's just upset."

Now it's Marcus' turn to look up at me. "You okay?"

"Yeah," I sniffle. "Where is she?"

Marcus takes me to her room. Neena looks so tiny in the big hospital bed. She's got tubing in her nose for oxygen and an IV for fluids. She doesn't wake as I sit on her bed and take her hand in mine.

"Mommy's here, baby," I whisper. "Mommy's here."

CHAPTER FORTY

Paul

OUR DAYS ARE numbered with her. The doctor says when it's time, we'll know. We brought her home earlier today and got her comfortable. Clara and I have played nice for her sake, but I think she can tell. While we got Neena home and situated, Marcus and Mei-ling took Ally and Vanessa to the airport. The two were in a mess of tears when they left. For them . . . this will be the last time they see Neena.

When they approached Neena to say good-bye, they couldn't hide their emotions. Vanessa leaned in and kissed her forehead. She whispered a prayer for Neena before she stood, wiping her face. Neena gave the best smile she could. My little girl . . . always trying to stay strong for everyone else. "I love you, stink." Stink was short for stinker . . . a nickname she'd apparently given Neena years ago.

"I love you, too," Neena told her.

"Neena," Ally whispered as she took Neena's hand. "You are in my heart, always."

Neena took Ally's hand and pressed the back of it against her cheek. "You're in mine, too."

When they finished with their good-byes, Clara walked them out. It was a harsh reality. No one wants to see a child die. The three mothers stood on the porch, hugging for a long time as they all cried.

We've been home a few hours and Clara is tucking Neena in while I put on the television for her.

"I want you to finish the story. I want to see it," she whispers. Her exhaustion is more apparent than ever.

Clara's eyes water and she inhales and lets it out softly. "We need to be here with you, Neena. That's what we want."

"Please finish it. Please."

Clara looks to me, her once trembling lips now in a tight, flat line. I hate that we're fighting, but I hate that she blames me for this even more. I just want Neena to be happy. Didn't we agree to making her last days happy?

"We will, princess," I volunteer. "I'll call Ashley right now."

CHAPTER FORTY-ONE

Paul

WHEN I EXPLAIN to Ashley we're running out of time if we want Neena to see this video, she needs to kick the interviews into high gear. No more small talk.

Ashley understands and the next time we meet she gets right to the point.

"Clara kissed you, when she brought you food after Sap passed away. Want to pick up from there?"

When I had kissed Clara for the first time, it really messed with my head. I liked kissing her. I liked kissing her way more than I cared to admit. That kiss made me imagine things . . . things that involved maybe staying put, settling down. But that was fucking crazy. It was a kiss. One kiss. I went home that night and paced the floors, trying not to think about it. She was so soft. She smelled so good. She was getting to me. *Fuck*. That was it. I had to leave—at least for a little while to clear my head. So I packed a bag and booked a flight. I was gone.

But being away didn't keep me from thinking about her. I couldn't stop. I made it a month before I returned. I told myself I was only going home because my mother would be moving soon and I wanted to see her before she left. She did move, about a week after Sap passed away. Maybe her moving was part of it. But not really. I came back to see Clara. I'd hoped time apart would break the spell. But nope.

Sap passing away was hard. He was a dear friend. And when Clara showed up with that shitty casserole, I think that was when I realized this woman was it. I didn't want to admit that to myself, but it was that moment. I know it. But I told myself she wasn't into me—not like that. Sure she had let me kiss her, but I'd kind of made her. She definitely didn't like me, or so I thought.

Until *she* kissed me.

On my porch.

While I was in my underwear.

It was a mess. She practically clobbered me. She botched it. But only at first. Once I caught myself and knew we wouldn't topple to the ground, she owned it.

I didn't speak to her for a few days until I went back to work. She acted like nothing had happened. We were back to Paul and Clara, business partners. That drove me fucking nuts. But I went with it. If she could be cool, so could I. We'd hired a new pilot and he was doing a few practice runs with me and the other divers. It was just a simple day— nothing special. That's what I thought when I dove out of the plane.

Then my chute didn't open.

It's not the first time it had happened, but it was still scary as fuck. Luckily, my emergency chute saved the day, and I landed safely, but my adrenaline was through the roof. I needed a release. The sun was just about to set when I made it to my truck after landing. I'd driven separately from the others and when I passed the office, I noticed Clara had left Marcus to close up. Her car wasn't in the lot. The two had started an unspoken trade-off, where one stayed and the other left in the afternoons. The less they had to see one another, the less they fought.

I didn't even bother to stop at the office. I kept telling myself to go home or go grab a beer somewhere, find a woman, any woman other than Clara, that lacked inhibitions and scratch my itch. I told myself that over and over, right up until I pulled in Clara's driveway and cut my truck off. Even as I climbed the stairs to her porch, I told myself what a horrible idea this was. I begged myself to turn around. But I didn't. I was never one to listen to the voice of reason. Where's the fun in that?

I knocked on the door a few times, but there was no answer. Her car was in the driveway though. She was definitely home. I trudged down the steps and rounded the house, making my way to the back yard. If she was here, I was going to see her. It was almost dark, but there was enough light to see where I was walking. The sound of a radio played softly as I turned into the backyard.

And there she was.

Humming with the music, as if she didn't have a care in the world.

Didn't she know I was hanging by a thread?

She was barefoot, wearing this green cotton dress. The material was worn and faded, making it practically see-through. Her back was to me as she shook out a sheet and began folding it. She line-dried her clothes—that's where that clean linen scent came from that drove me fucking crazy.

I approached her slowly, but she turned before I reached her. She startled and placed a hand to her chest. "Is your goal in life to scare me into a heart attack, Paul James?"

As she caught her breath, I watched her as she continued to fold the sheet until she stopped and looked up at me. Tilting her head, she eyed me suspiciously. "What's up with you?"

I couldn't play coy with her. Not that day. I was too wound up. So I laid it all out on the line.

"I can't stop thinking about you."

She froze.

"I don't know what this is between us. I go from hating you one minute to wanting to bash my brains in because I can't stop thinking about you the next."

Silence. She. Said. Nothing.

"I need . . ." I swallowed hard. She was probably going to punch me in the balls for what I was about to say. *Don't do it, Paul. Just leave. You haven't damaged anything yet. Just. Leave.*

I didn't listen.

Of course, I didn't.

"I need to feel you." It was the politest way I could put it. Hopefully, she got the message.

Her cheeks turned pink as her gaze dropped from mine for a moment as she absorbed my words. Then meeting my eyes again, she said, "I'm not the kind of woman that just hooks up, Paul."

Still wasn't listening. I stepped toward her. *Stop, Paul!* I begged myself.

"I know that." What the fuck was I saying?

Her chest rose as she sucked in a ragged breath. She was speechless. That was rare.

"If you don't . . . if you're not interested . . . I'll go. No hard feelings."

A few seconds passed where we just stared at one another. She seemed as if she didn't know what to say, and, well, I'd said too much. *Maybe.*

Finally, she pulled her comforter from the clothesline and spread it on the ground. When she stood beside it, her gaze fixed on mine as she pulled the hem of her dress up and over her head.

No bra.

No panties.

Just Clara.

"Take your hair down," I told her. And she did. No eye rolling or sassing. It was so unlike her. Her hair billowed down before she ran her fingers through it, trying to tame it. I tugged my shirt over my head and let it fall to the ground. As I unbuckled my belt, I toed off my shoes. Once I was naked, I took a few steps so that I was inches in front of her.

"You're sure?" I questioned.

She nodded.

And so it began. I needed release, and Clara took it gladly. There, in her backyard, we took our time with each other. Even now, like an old song, I can hear it, and see it, too. But most of all, I feel it. The flashes of images against the memory of sounds. Crickets chirping in the background, the sound of the radio playing. Our hot breaths coming out in loud huffs, her moans, my grunts. The way she whispered my name with lust. My teeth biting into her skin, from head to toe. Her lips brushing across my body with tempered discipline.

That night, we clawed at each other, fingers digging into flesh, desperate, hungry for more. I wanted to soak her in, absorb her, take every drop of her. For every bit I gave, she met it with just as much gusto. It was beautiful. I felt like I'd been let in on a secret; I was privileged. This woman in my arms was not Clara Bateman, my business partner. This woman was committed to her pleasure and mine. There was no high-handedness. There was no who's right or wrong. There was only this. Us. These feelings. This want. Nothing else mattered. When we finally joined our bodies, when I felt her clench around me, and heard her cry out because I'd found the deepest part of her, everything else disappeared.

It was just her and me.

And I knew my life would never be the same.

CHAPTER FORTY-TWO
Clara

"He TOLD YOU about that, huh?" I questioned, my cheeks heating. I can't believe Paul gave Ashley so much detail about our first time together.

"It wasn't explicit," she points out quickly, a hint of disappointment in her tone. "He held back."

"So should I just pick up from there?"

"Yes. I'm eager to know what happened."

I had no idea that one night with Paul would take hold of me the way it did. I could never have imagined it would be that spectacular. But it was. So we did it again. And again. And again. It was cathartic. We were like two teenagers amped on hormones; addicted to each other.

We agreed to keep our relationship quiet, especially from Marcus. He wouldn't have understood. Hell, we didn't really comprehend, so how could we make him understand? So at the office, we mostly ignored each other. But when no one was looking, Paul would always find a way to touch me, some way to tell me he craved me.

At night, we were inseparable. He would cook for me while I worked on some kind of house project. Then, we'd spend hours in bed doing anything but sleeping. On the few days we'd have off together, he'd take me hiking or we'd go for long drives, getting lost in the middle of nowhere and ending up in the bed of his truck.

We didn't talk about feelings or future plans. Everything was about the here and now. I'd spent months depressed, dragging myself through each dreary day, and suddenly it was as if the sun came out and fell upon my face. At the time, maybe I was in denial. I tried to tell myself my newfound happiness wasn't because of Paul, per se. I mean, obviously he was a part of it, but I told myself it was that I realized there was life after Kurt. I could move on. I could be happy again. And even if Paul and I didn't work out, I wouldn't regret it.

That's what I told myself.

We were living in a bubble. A big, beautiful bubble, and with each day, it grew and grew. But eventually . . . bubbles always pop. It was only a matter of time.

The day our bubble popped was a Thursday.

A typical, nothing special Thursday.

Marcus had left early, which meant it was my day to close. Switching off afternoons had really helped things between us only in the sense if we weren't around one another, we couldn't fight. Like I said . . . life was feeling pretty damn good.

I was in my office when Paul walked in, a devilish smirk on his face. "Hello there, beautiful," he purred. Something in my belly fluttered with that look. Every. Single. Time. The moment we made love, the moment his naked body pressed against mine, it was like a switch was thrown; some kind of connection was made. I couldn't help reacting to him. It was natural, something I had no control over.

"I thought you were heading home," I giggled at the sight of him. *Yes. I giggled.* That should give anyone an idea of where I was in this. Clara Bateman *giggled.*

I was cleaning up my desk when he marched behind me and seized my hips, pulling me back against him. "I was, but I wanted to see you first," he murmured in my ear before taking my earlobe between his teeth and biting.

I hissed as I leaned back into him, begging for more . . . for more of everything . . . for more of him. His hand slid roughly up my body, untucking my shirt, before he found my breast and groped it. My body was his. I was at his mercy.

"I've fantasized so many times about bending you over this desk and fucking you senseless." On this particular day, I was wearing a skirt; a longer one that reached my knees. He began pulling the material up until he saw my ass.

"Damn, I love that ass," he admired. "Bend over the desk, Clara," he ordered me. "I want to see that perfect ass sticking out, waiting for me to slap it."

I did as he said and lay down on the desk, my ass out and at his mercy. Being with Paul was unlike anything I had ever experienced. He was good at not letting me think too much about what we were doing. He was confident in a way the other men I had been with weren't. Sex had been awkward at times for me in the past. There was always so much planning or overthinking. Mostly from me. I was an analytical person; my mind was always trying to move to the *what-ifs* and so on. Other men, and by other men, I meant two at that time, could never get me out of my own head. Paul did what he wanted and trusted that it was what I wanted. He trusted if he did something I didn't like, that I would tell him. But until I did, he would keep going. That worked well for me. I liked everything he did to me.

His hand gently slid across my cheek before he slapped it firmly. I grunted with the sting, but stayed in position. I heard the office chair squeak as he rolled it back and took a seat. Then I felt his teeth on my flesh, that delicious bite of pain, before he kissed the same spot, soothing it.

With his finger, he gently tugged my panty aside, exposing me to him, before running his tongue over my wet skin. I moaned, my eyes fluttering closed in pleasure.

"You taste so fucking good," he growled before licking me again. Damn, I loved when he talked dirty to me.

"Does she now?"

My eyes flew open at the question.

At the voice.

Fuck.

Marcus.

Marcus was standing in the doorway of the office, staring right at us.

Paul let my panty slide back into place before hastily tugging my skirt down and standing. My body felt like a wave of fire had brushed over it, and I knew I had to be bright red. Neither of us said anything. Paul stood a few feet away, and given the moment, the awkwardness of it, it felt off. Obviously off in the sense Marcus had just walked in on Paul's face on my ass, but also how Paul had seemingly moved away from me. Did he think distancing himself from me would make what Marcus just witnessed look any less what it was? Did it really matter what Marcus thought? So what if Paul and I were together, if that's what one wanted to call it, even though we never really officially said we were. Why should Marcus care? I felt alone and exposed in that moment. I crossed my arms as a silent stare down ensued between the two men.

"Banging your uncle's sloppy seconds," Marcus mused. "Classy, Paul."

My blood pressure shot up like a rocket. "Fuck you, Marcus," I seethed. "I did not have any sexual relations with Dennis. Get. Over. It."

"Did he like bending you over desks, too, Clara?" Marcus jeered, ignoring me. He wasn't going to let up. Not this time. He'd caught me with my pants down—or skirt up—and he was taking no prisoners. I shot my gaze to Paul, looking for some backup. But he said nothing.

Not. One. Fucking. Word.

He'd never really stood up for me. And in the few times Marcus and I went at each other in Paul's presence, he danced around both of us on his tippy-toes like he was on a floor made of eggshells. My heart dropped to my stomach. Marcus was calling me a whore, basically. Again. And Paul said nothing.

His dark eyes were trained on the floor as he shoved his hands in his pockets. I stared at him. I knew he could feel it; there's no way he couldn't. But he stood silent and let Marcus' insults hang in the air.

I turned and grabbed my purse. When the strap caught on the arm of the desk chair, I yanked at it angrily, my frustration rearing its ugly head. *Keep your cool, Clara. Don't let Marcus win.* When I finally freed it, I slipped it over my shoulder and met Marcus' stare. He was smirking. He thought he had me figured out. I wanted to smack that smirk right off his face. It took all of my strength not to. And that's when I got petty. I was so angry and . . . well . . . hurt, I lost my way for a moment. Meeting Marcus' gaze head-on, I gave him a tempered smirk.

"I guess you've figured it out," I chirped. "Dennis and I were lovers."

You could have heard a pin drop in that room. They were both stunned. I knew Paul's eyes were trained on me now, but I refused to look at him. I couldn't. I hated him in that moment. Marcus may have been the one that insulted me, but Paul's mute stance hurt worse. It was the bigger insult.

"We did it right here on this desk a few times," I purred. I shook my head as I sighed, "I was in one of those phases some girls go through, ya know, the ones where we're so young but want to have sex with *really* old men." My tone was dripping with sarcasm. I was saying it happened, but making sure they both realized how ridiculous it sounded.

"I have never had a better lover," I continued.

Silence.

No one said a word.

I stared at Marcus as he stared back. Both of us glowered at the other.

But I wasn't done. Not at all.

"I guess I should tell you a few other things, too," I went on. "I have a superpower. When I sleep with a man, I can make him do *anything*," I boasted, my eyes wide with exaggeration. "For example, I can make a sane man leave me half of his business." I shrugged nonchalantly. "I can also turn a man into a spineless mute," I seethed, directing my gaze to Paul. I flung my arm up toward him. "See!" I laughed with ridicule. "Look at what I can do!"

Paul's expression was conflicted. He looked somewhere between angry, embarrassed, and guilt-ridden.

I moved toward the door, forcing Marcus to move aside so I could exit. Looking down at him, I sneered, "Just imagine what I could make you do, little man."

He glared at me, but didn't speak. It was a first. He always had a comeback; an insult. Always. I had won this time. This one and only time when it came to Marcus—I got the last word. But I didn't really feel like I had won. Not at all. I marched out of the office and left Paul to sort it out with Marcus. As far as I was concerned, we were done.

Finished.

Over.

CHAPTER FORTY-THREE

Paul

WE'RE MEETING ASHLEY daily now. It's hard to relive the past. It's hard to remember the bad things. The good, too. Especially while Clara and I are still at odds right now. We're not fighting. We talk, but only in regard to Neena. It's very minimal. We take shifts sleeping downstairs with her at night. Our disagreement is silly. Really. I know she's just frantic a lot of the time; concerned for Neena. I know that she tries to shoulder everything, like if she hadn't left Neena with me that night, Neena wouldn't have taken such a rapid turn for the worse. But I recognize that while she blames me, she really blames herself. Why is it when we're hurting we always take it out on the ones we love the most?

"When Marcus walked in on you two and Clara left . . . that was a bad night," Ashley notes.

"It was," I agree.

"What happened?"

After Clara stormed out, Marcus cocked his head and pursed his lips in thought. "Okay. So maybe she wasn't his lover."

I clenched my eyes closed. Was he fucking serious? It took her losing her shit like that to convince him?

"So . . . how long has that been going on?" He pointed at the desk where Clara had been bent over for my pleasure just minutes before.

"Not long," I grumbled as I shoved the office chair under the desk. I was fucking pissed. Pissed at Marcus for walking in and making a scene.

I was pissed at Clara for calling me spineless. I was pissed at myself for being gutless. I should have stood up for her. I wanted to. But I didn't know what to say. Marcus was family. Also, I didn't want to imply she and I were casual . . . maybe we were, but I didn't know. I didn't want to make it seem like we were an item either. I wasn't sure what we were, and in that moment, I felt like I'd piss her off no matter what I said. So I said nothing. I'd disappointed two people at the same damn time. Not my best hour.

"You . . . with her?"

"I don't fucking know, Marcus, okay?" I spat out.

"Why are you pissed at me?" he asked angrily.

I stared at him, dumbfounded. "Um, let's see," I began with a haughty laugh. "Why can't you cut her some slack? I mean, seriously."

He blinked at me, his expression unreadable.

"Our business is better than ever. She stays out of your way, for the most part. She could fire you for acting like such an asshole and if she did, I couldn't blame her." I knew I was treading on thin ice.

"You'd let her fire me?"

"I've tried staying out of it. I've tried letting you guys work it out on your own. I love you, man, but you won't quit, Marcus. She's not going anywhere. You're not going to bully her out of here and frankly, I don't want her to go."

His brows shot up. "You love her, don't you?"

I turned from him and dropped my head. That's what it sounded like I'd just said. Is that what I meant? Shit. I was confused. Maybe not confused, but definitely in denial. "It has to stop, Marcus. You have to stop goading her."

When I spun around and saw him again, he was frowning. "I just . . . I don't get why he left it to her and not me." I felt bad for him, I really did. I let out a long sigh. That was what it all boiled down to. He was hurt. In a way, I was like Dennis' first son. He helped raise me. With my career and skills, I thought he felt he had to leave me half the business. He knew I could run the jumps. But with Clara, it made no sense. She was working in orthodontics. She'd mentioned it once. What did orthodontics have to do with skydiving? It was a puzzle piece that just wouldn't fit no matter how hard we tried to jam it in place. Plus, Marcus had always taken care of the office.

"Maybe if you try being nicer to her . . . she'll tell you eventually. Dennis loved you. I'm sure there's a good reason why he did what he did." I wanted to know just as badly as Marcus, if not more.

He bobbed his head a few times. "I gotta go."

"Marcus," I called after him as he left the office. But he didn't turn back. I paced in the office for a few minutes, trying to get my wits about me. This night sure went in the shitter fast. Marcus wasn't pleased with me. But I knew better than to mess with him right now. He needed some time to decompress. Clara was pissed at me, as well, and rightfully so. With a deep breath, I steeled myself. It was time to try and fix this.

She wouldn't answer her door when I knocked. After knocking for the fourth time, I tried the doorknob. It was unlocked. I marched in, determined. I would fix this. Somehow. I made my way to the kitchen and found her sitting at the table, a cup of coffee beside her and a folded piece of paper in front of her.

"Guess you didn't hear me knocking," I jested. She didn't find it amusing. Pulling out a chair, I took a seat beside her as she sipped her coffee.

"I'm terrible at apologies," I began.

"I don't need your apology," she quipped. "I need nothing from you."

Ouch. That didn't feel good. Her armor was on now and I hated it. I'd gotten to see the softness that laid beneath the hard exterior and now she was hiding it from me.

"I'm sorry," I continued. Maybe she didn't want my apology, but she'd get it anyway. "I was thrown."

She huffed with annoyance. "I'm going to tell you why he left me the business. Then I want you to leave."

My brows furrowed. She wanted me to leave. Shit. This *was* bad.

She slid the piece of paper in front of her toward me. "Read that. It explains everything."

I unfolded it, having absolutely no idea what this paper would reveal. It was my uncle's handwriting. I recognized it immediately.

Dear Clara,

My name is Dennis Falco. I'm sure you've heard my name. I'm sure in your mind, I'm a monster; an evil person.

When I was twenty-two, I was living in Florida. I worked as a mechanic, changing oil at some dinky shop. I was wasting time. And life. I was my father's greatest disappointment.

On a Friday, I'd had a particularly bad day. I can't even remember why I went to my favorite bar, found a stool, and drank my bad day away. I closed the bar down that night. They had to kick me out. When I got in my car, I turned up my stereo, rolled my windows down, and lit a cigarette for the drive home.

Ten minutes later, I hit another car head-on going sixty miles an hour. Somehow, unfairly, I survived. I broke my arm, nose, and cracked some ribs. I actually lost a few teeth.

Your mother and father, however, lost much more. They were killed on impact.

The judge took it easy on me. Times were different then. I went to rehab and had community service. I was on probation for five years.

That day changed my life. I never drank another drop. I volunteered with underprivileged kids, trying to provide a good mentor for them, hoping maybe I'd save some kid from making the same mistakes I did. I got a new job and saved up money before moving to Virginia and starting a skydiving business. It's done well.

You were just a baby when I took your parents from you. And I know, deep down, I didn't just take two lives that night. I took three. I took yours. I took years of love, and hugs, and memories. I know nothing I will ever do or say will make what I did that night okay. But I hope you know, I have thought about your parents every single day of my life. I have thought of you, too.

So I give you what I have. Half of a skydiving business may not sound very exciting, but I hope you see it one of two ways. In time, either you can sell it to my nephew, whom I plan to leave my business to, or keep the money and spend it on something you desire. Maybe you'll see this as a chance. A chance to try something different. A chance to start over . . . if that's what you need.

Whatever you decide, Clara, please know . . . I'm sorry. From the deepest part of my soul . . . I am sorry.

Sincerely,

Dennis Falco

I stared at the floor as I lay the letter on the table. I was speechless. How did I not know about this? I lifted my gaze to meet Clara's and found she was watching me. She was angry. And hurt. Rightfully so.

Never in a million years would I have thought that this was why my uncle left her half the business.

She took the letter and folded it, placing it in front of her.

"The keychain? They're your parents' initials?"

She nodded yes.

"Clara, I—"

"Just go, Paul," she interrupted me.

I stayed in my seat and observed her. I couldn't move. I couldn't force myself to leave like this. She stood and took her mug to the sink. I had to do something, anything. My uncle killed her parents. I felt so betrayed and angry. He was my hero, my idol in so many ways. How could he have kept this from me?

Standing, I met her at the kitchen sink and tried to hug her, but she pushed me away. "Don't," she growled. But I didn't listen. I pulled her to me and hugged her even when she struggled to push me off. "Don't fucking touch me," she seethed.

I released her and let her back away. Her eyes were glossed over with angry tears as she breathed heavily, glaring at me. Fuck. I hated seeing her like this. I rushed her before she had a chance to stop me. I picked her up and sat her on the counter. Her hands pressed against my shoulders, attempting to push me away, but I was stronger. I kissed her neck and shoulders, burying my face in her chest, and pleaded with her.

"Please forgive me. I'm sorry. I'm an asshole. Please, Clara." I couldn't stop apologizing. We struggled together, her pushing me away, me trying to hold on. Finally, she seemed to give in, to succumb to my lips on her skin. She let her head lull back for a moment before remembering her anger and fought me again. "Shh," I whispered. "Just let me hold you. Let me make it up to you."

Her body seemed to sag with my words as tears streamed down her face. I picked her up and carried her upstairs to her bed. I spent the next three hours telling her how sorry I was without words. I worshipped her. I rubbed her body from head to toe. I kissed every inch of her soft skin. I made love to her.

And when we were done, she closed her eyes, her mind and body sated. I watched her sleep for a while before climbing out of bed and dressing. I was restless, my mind moving a thousand miles a minute. Quietly, I made my way down her ancient, creaky stairs and went to the kitchen. Opening the fridge, I stared at the emptiness and snorted. She didn't have shit in it. Maybe I would go pick up a few things and cook her something nice for dinner. I needed to make a list. I began opening drawers, searching for a notepad when I found a piece of paper that looked like a journal entry made by Clara. I recognized her handwriting from the many papers we'd completed together in the office. I stared at the paper again. I shouldn't have read it. It wasn't my place to . . . not without her permission. But I took it from the drawer and let my eyes scan it line by line.

Today has been a bad day.

Today, my parents died twenty-five years ago.

Today, Marcus acted like a gigantic dickface.

Today, Kurt took another step away from me, from our life together.

I think I miss him.

I shouldn't.

Maybe I just miss us who I thought we were.

He's a bad person. I know this. Maybe not entirely bad, but mostly bad. He tossed me aside. Don't I deserve better? Did I not love hard enough? Did I not give enough? I think I did. I really do.

I've made peace with my parents passing. Being that I was so young makes it a little easier to bear.

But Kurt is a fresh wound.

I need to let him go. But hearts don't work like light switches they don't just flick on and off. They swell rapidly with love and bleed out slowly with pain.

I should be stronger. I should be able to shut myself down to his memory. But I'm not strong enough yet.

They say the opposite of love isn't hate, but indifference. I hate him. I hate him so much I feel it seeping out of my pores, toxifying everything around me.

I don't want him back. I don't. Not who he is now. I want my life back. I want the safety I felt in my marriage back. I want the days where we held hands and dreamed a millions dreams together back when I believed him when he said I was his forever. When he told me no one could take my place. I want that man back. I want that type of love in my life.

But he's gone.

And now, given his cruelty and seemingly unfeeling actions, I have to wonder ...was he ever really there? Was it all a facade? Was I a fool the whole time seeing only what I wanted to see?

I want to be happy.

I want forever.

I want...

I want a baby.

I dropped the paper on the counter and backed away from it.

Forever.

Baby.

They were two words that defied everything I wanted. They were two potent words that I wasn't sure, no matter how much I loved Clara, I could give her. I needed freedom and adventure. Thoughts of not having either was suffocating. I needed to be able to hop a plane on a whim and not owe any explanations. I couldn't have that *and* her. And I couldn't promise her something I couldn't give. I wasn't built that way. I just wasn't. Maybe with her, the idea was easier to swallow, but I wasn't ready for even the idea of it. But the most hurtful confirmation was she didn't love me. I wasn't even in her thought process when she poured her heart out. She wanted *him*. She still loved the memory of *him*. She missed her husband. She wanted the house with a white picket fence and a baby with *him*.

I was such a chump. To think, I was ready to tell her I loved her. Clearly, that was a mistake. I was a fucking fill-in. I had to get out of there. All I could think was to flee.

I snuck out quietly as to not wake her and drove off. It was still dark, only four in the morning. I had to end it with her. I had to. But if I did, I couldn't stay. Even if I traveled in and out, she'd hate me. I wasn't strong enough to fix what Kurt had done wrong. Our work relationship would be awful. If I left . . . I had to go for good. There would be no looking back.

I went home and packed a suitcase. At eight in the morning, I made my way downtown to Richard Mateo's office. He wasn't happy with me showing up unannounced, but he saw me. I signed over a limited power of attorney, giving him permission to represent me in regard to the business and the sale of my house. I didn't care if Clara bought the business. I told him we could remain partners if she paid me a reduced salary, which Mateo would put into an account for me.

"Just do your best," I told him. "I'm not trying to screw her over. I just need enough to get by." When the papers were signed, I went straight to the airport. And I left. For good.

"You were wrong. You do know that now, right?" Ashley states.

I cock my head. "About what?"

"She wasn't in love with Kurt. He represented another broken promise. That's all. She loved you."

I nod my head in understanding. "I get that now."

She gives a sad smile and gets back to business. "So . . . You didn't come back to the states for thirteen years?" Ashley continues with a speculative brow.

"Once," I admit. "Florida. Four years ago when my mother passed away. I checked in with her once a week. I didn't find out she had passed until three days after. She was buried by the time I made it home." I frown at the thought. I hate that I missed her funeral. That I wasn't there for her.

Ashley produces another sympathetic smile. "We meet with Clara one more time. Then we should be set to put this thing together."

I nod, feeling shitty. It's not easy to remember what an asshole I was. And how much time was wasted over a misunderstanding. "Please remember this is for our kid."

"I will, Paul. Neena will love it."

CHAPTER FORTY-FOUR
Clara

"WHAT DID YOU think that morning when you woke up and he wasn't there?" Ashley questions, the end of her pen between her teeth.

Inhaling deeply, I release it slowly.

It was ten in the morning when I woke up. I hadn't slept like that in ages. I stretched and sat up, listening for him in the house. When I heard nothing, I figured he must've gone in to the office and let me sleep in. I smiled thinking about how sweet it was. I took my time showering, naively relishing in the soreness I felt from the night we spent together. It felt good to finally tell him what my affiliation with Dennis was. I felt like a huge weight had been lifted off of my shoulders.

When I made it into work, Paul's truck wasn't in the parking lot. Marcus was in the front, restocking waivers. He turned and met my gaze as I entered. There was a moment of silence between us, neither of us knowing what to say. We seemed to agree not to say anything for the time being. With a nod, I went back to my office and turned my computer on. Around noon, I tried calling Paul at home, but his line was disconnected. I thought maybe he'd forgotten to pay the bill.

But when his three o'clock clients showed up and we still hadn't seen him, I started to get worried. When we couldn't reach him, Marcus called Bowman and had him come in to cover Paul's jumps. We discounted the clients for the inconvenience.

No police had showed up notifying us of an accident so I finished the day out. I went to his house after I left the office, but his truck wasn't there. When he didn't show up again the next day, I wondered if he'd taken off again for an adventure. But why now? After the night we shared. Couldn't he see now was a bad time to run away for a month? And what about our business? He had scheduled jumps. It was unacceptable.

"We should probably just schedule the other guys to take his jumps for the next month or so," Marcus suggested. "No point in us killing ourselves every day to cover for him."

I nodded, letting out an uneasy breath. But my expression said everything.

"He'll come back, Clara," Marcus assured me. "He always does." What he said seemed as if he were trying to comfort me. I was shocked. I nodded and he went back to his work.

Two weeks went by, and not a word from Paul. I was so hurt. I tried not to be, but I was. I couldn't help it. I had fallen for him. Why was he always leaving after having a moment with me? How could he just leave and not contact me at all? It was a Wednesday when Marcus placed an envelope on my desk. It was thick. That alone told me it couldn't have been anything good in there.

"From Richard Mateo," he pointed out.

I opened it, not minding that Marcus was watching me. I read one sheet and then the next. I dropped them in my lap, furrowing my brows in confusion and shock.

"What is it?" Marcus asked.

I handed him the papers, blinking quickly to keep my tears at bay. It couldn't be what I thought it was. It couldn't.

Marcus' shoulders sagged as he read. "That asshole," he grumbled.

My heart was pounding, the sound whooshing in my ears. Paul wanted me to buy the business from him, his portion anyway, or keep him as a partner and pay him a reduced salary. He wasn't coming back.

Why did everyone I loved leave me? But I wasn't the only one that felt betrayed. Marcus looked like he wanted to hit something. He tossed the papers on the desk and marched out of my office without another word. My hands shook as I shoved the papers in the drawer of my desk. I was so overwhelmed with emotion I could hardly stand. But I did. I had to leave.

This was bullshit. *He* was bullshit. Grabbing my keys. I darted out to my car and screeched out of the parking lot. I needed to see something. I needed to know if Paul was gone for good or not. This couldn't be happening to me . . . again. I drove to his house. The gravel of his driveway crackled under my tires as I slowly drove by the *For Sale* sign. I stared at it for a long moment before lowering my head to the steering wheel and crying like I've never cried before.

He left.

He left just like everyone else.

When I calmed down, I drove home and crawled in bed, and cried myself to sleep. I woke up in the middle of the night, my entire lower body aching I had to pee so badly. Flipping the light on in my bathroom, I stared at the box I'd left there the day before. Now was as good a time as any. I tore open the box, pulled out the little white stick, and peed on it.

Three minutes later, my world changed forever.

Ashley sports a sad smile as she watches me wipe under my eyes. "I'm sorry," I croak out. "It's hard when you remember one of the best times in your life as one of the most painful."

Leaning over, she pulls a small pack of tissues from her backpack and hands them to me.

"Thanks."

"Did you hate him?" she asks after I've cleaned myself up.

"At first," I admit. "I decided to keep him as a business partner. I wasn't sure I could tell him I was pregnant, not then anyway. I was too . . . hurt. When I thought of him, it was too much. But I wanted to make sure I could get to him, if I needed to."

"Did you try to contact him?"

"A few times. I emailed him. I told him I needed to talk to him, but I didn't say what about."

"Did it surprise you when he didn't respond?"

I shrug. "Yes. No."

"What happened with Marcus after that?"

It had been two days since I'd received the letter from Mateo on Paul's behalf. I called Marcus into my office and asked him to sit with me.

I intended to explain my plans to him with regard to the business, but he spoke first.

"I'm giving you my resignation."

The blood drained from my face. There was no doubt we hated each other. I, for one, couldn't stand him. But with Paul disappearing, and a baby on the way, I wasn't sure I could make the business function without Marcus. He knew the ins and outs. And he had a great rapport with the employees.

I slumped back in my chair, utterly deflated. The universe was against me.

"We both know Paul, while not the best mediator, was the only reason we've managed to coexist this long," he explained. "I just don't think we can have a healthy work environment."

"And if I asked you to stay?" I questioned cautiously.

He tilted his head, a deep wrinkle forming between his brows. "Why would you ask me to stay?" he snorted.

I hated having to be vulnerable in front of him. I was afraid he'd use it as a weapon to belittle me more. But I had no choice.

"I'm pregnant."

He blinked a few times, his mouth pressing into a hard, flat line. "Does Paul know?"

I shook my head no.

"Have you tried contacting him?"

"I've emailed him. I left a message with Mateo stating it was an urgent matter that I spoke with him. But I haven't heard back."

"Are you going to keep it?" he asked gingerly.

I placed my hand on my belly, my mouth quirking up slightly. "Definitely."

When I lifted my gaze to meet his again, he let out a long sigh. Moving his gaze to the ceiling he let out a loud groan. "I can't believe I'm doing this," he mumbled to himself. Lowering his head, he said, "I'll stay if you lift the prank ban," he bartered.

"No." There was no way in hell I'd ever agree to that.

"You have to give somewhere, Clara," he argued.

I rolled my eyes. "No," I affirmed.

He shrugged and began to slip out of his seat. "Well, good luck to you," he chirped. I gritted my teeth. He knew he had me.

"Fine," I seethed. "Once a month."

"Five a month," he replied.

"Two."

"Three," he offered firmly. "And that's my final offer."

I chuckled a little even though he was frustrating as hell. "Fine. Three."

He slid out of his chair and rounded the desk, extending his hand. "Truce."

I took it and we shook. "Truce."

It's funny how fast things changed between us. I confided in him as to why Dennis left me half of the business, and wished I'd done it sooner. Marcus seemed so . . . at peace when he discovered the truth. Slowly, we built trust between us and became friends. The night I signed my divorce papers from Kurt, he took me out for an all you can eat buffet and ice cream. He knew how to celebrate with a pregnant lady. He actually became my best friend. To this day, Marcus *is* my best friend. He was there the day Neena was born; the first to hold her after me. He taught her how to ride a bike. He was her friend, her playmate. He was there the day she was diagnosed. He's been a rock for us. And I will forever be grateful for him.

Ashley smiles as she closes her notebook.

"Well, you know everything now, I guess."

"Marcus sounds like a pretty amazing dude."

"He is," I agree.

"I think that's it then," she sighs. "We have a lot of footage to go through."

"You'll make it tasteful?" I question again, in a way that implies she damn well *better* make it tasteful.

"Yes, yes," she chuckles. "I promise."

I stand and stretch.

"We'll try to get this ready in the next few days. So Neena can see it."

"I appreciate that." I give a small wave and head toward the door. One quick once-over of the office and I'm out of here.

"Clara," she says my name, causing me to turn. "I know Paul was the adventurer . . . the fearless risk-taker. I know they joked about how you never jumped, but if you think about it . . . you did."

I smirk, unsure of what she means.

"You left your home and moved to a different state, taking on a job you knew nothing about. You bought a house on your own; fixed it mostly on your own. You had a baby as a single woman. It may not be jumping out of planes, but it sounds like one hell of an adventure to me." She gives an appreciative smirk. "You're pretty badass, Clara."

I grin. "I guess that's one way to look at it. Thanks, Ashley."

With another wave, I'm out the door.

CHAPTER FORTY-FIVE

Paul

WE'RE WAITING ON Ashley and her crew to arrive. Ashley called yesterday and said the tape was ready. Clara is upstairs taking a shower and I'm lying beside Neena on her bed, thumb wrestling. She's so weak, she can barely play, but she still tries. I let her win anyway.

"Dad."

"Yeah, kid?" I answer.

"Do you believe in heaven?"

Her question stuns me for a moment. Lacing my fingers together over my chest, I let out a long breath. "I *want* to believe in heaven," I admit. "What about you, kid?"

She stares up at the ceiling. "I think . . . this can't be it. There has to be more." Turning her head, she looks at me. "I don't want to not exist anymore."

Damn. Her statement gets to me. This kid knows how to get my heart twisted. "I don't want you to not exist anymore either, Neena."

"Maybe it's like a dream," she muses. "Maybe if I just imagine it, it will be so."

I smile sadly. Taking her tiny, frail hand in mine, I lace our fingers together. Her skin is cool against mine. "Will you tell me what you see?"

She smiles. "Okay. Close your eyes."

I do as she says and she shimmies closer, resting her head against my shoulder. "I see a beach with sand that's almost white. It feels soft under my feet. The water is blue, but you can see to bottom of the ocean it's so

271

clear. I want there to be color. Maybe the sky will have that glow just after sunset, ya know, when it's orange and red."

My eyes are still closed but I smile. I know exactly what she means. "That's perfect, princess."

"Mom would be there. And she'd be laughing. Like really laughing. Her hair would be blowing in the breeze and she'd take my hand and point up to the sky at you."

"Me?" I question.

She huffs a tired laugh. "You would have just dived out of a plane and you'd be drifting toward us, your chute open. When you land, you'd walk toward us, smiling. You'd kiss mom and she'd grin."

"That sounds amazing, Neena," I admit, my voice becoming husky with emotion. And I grip her hand tighter. "What else?"

She sighs. "I'd have hair again. Long hair. I wouldn't be so tired. And I'd look healthy and happy. Marcus and Mei-ling would be there, too." She lets out a small giggle. "Marcus would let me bury him in the sand like he did when I was little."

I chuckle. "I'm sure he would."

"That's my heaven."

Squeezing her hand, I turn my head and kiss her temple. "That's where I'll see you, Neena," I manage. "On that beach, with an orange-red sky and blue water."

"And I'll have hair," she reminds me.

"Yes," I agree.

"And boobs," she adds.

I nearly choke with her words. "I'm not sure I want to imagine you with those."

"I don't want to look like I'm twelve for all eternity, Dad," she comments dryly.

"How about I imagine you matured?" I offer. "Let's not focus on any particular body parts."

"That's fair."

A few minutes later, her breathing slows as she drifts off to sleep, her head resting against me and try as I may, I can't stop the tear that trickles down my cheek.

CHAPTER FORTY-SIX
Clara

ASHLEY, ZANE, AND Mills have just left. Marcus, Paul, and I walked them out, said our good-byes, and hugged them for their hard work. The tape was beautiful. They made two, one that gave a brief summary of our story that they intend to share with the public, and one just for us.

Hearing Paul tell his side of the story was hard, but it was an eye-opening experience as well. Some parts made me tear up, others made me laugh. Neena couldn't look away. She was absorbing every detail. As the kids left, we promised to call if we needed anything. Neena requested this be the last time they visit before she passes. She didn't want them to remember her at her worst.

Ashley, normally hard as stone, was weeping. Saying good-bye to Neena was hard for her, maybe harder than she imagined it would be. As for Mills, when he said good-bye, he held Neena's hand, bent down, and whispered something in her ear, before kissing her cheek. He's a sweet kid. Zane was chewing on his nails and squeezed her hand and gave a casual good-bye. I could tell he just didn't know what to say. What can you really say in these situations?

Marcus goes back inside as Paul and I watch their van drive off. The day is warm; summer is on its way. The dogwood in my front yard is starting to bloom. I planted that tree the year Neena was born. It's on the verge of blossoming again this year, coming to life and sharing its color, while our daughter is wilting before our very eyes. My gaze moves to Paul's and he gives me a sideways smirk. "I'm sorry I left you the way I did. I'm sorry I left you at all. And even though you're mad at me right now, I'm not leaving you this time, Clara. I swear it."

I know being angry with him is unfair. He didn't mean for that night at the concert to end the way it did. Stepping toward him, I let my head thump against his chest. "I don't think I can do this, Paul. I don't know how to let her go."

His hands rub my back as his chin rests on my head. "I wish we had a choice in that, Clara."

The front door opens, and Marcus steps outside, sniffling, his little fingers wiping under his eyes.

"You okay?"

He shakes his head no. "When we first found out Paul wasn't a match, and we knew we had limited time, Neena told me not to say good-bye to her." He sucks in a ragged breath. "I asked her when she thought it was almost time, to give me a day with her. One last day to hang." His glazed eyes look up to mine. "She asked me for that day. Tomorrow."

My throat feels like it's closing. Paul's head drops and we all stand silent for a moment.

"I'll be here bright and early," Marcus tells us. I bend down and hug him before he leaves.

Paul takes my hand and laces our fingers together as we watch him go. He doesn't say anything. Neither do I. All we can do now is pull strength from one another and hope it's enough to get us through.

It has to be.

CHAPTER FORTY-SEVEN
Paul

CLARA SPENT THE night on the couch last night, while I took the bed. But I was restless all night. After tossing and turning for hours, around five in the morning, I climb out of bed, deciding sleep is hopeless. I creep down the stairs where Clara is passed out on the sofa, one arm dangling over the side. But Neena's bed is empty. I hear something scratching that sounds like it's coming from the kitchen. Following it, I find her in the kitchen, seated at the table with a giant butcher's knife.

"What are you doing?" I hiss in fear, making her jump. She drops the knife on the table. "Are you okay?" I ask, calming myself.

"I'm fine," she manages, her tone breathless.

When I flip on the light, she winces. "Sorry, princess." The table has wood dust on it, in the center. I give her a questioning look.

"I wanted to carve my name in the table, too. I guess I should have asked first."

Instantly, I smile and pick up the knife. "I think that's a great idea, let's just get a smaller knife." I find another knife and hand it to her and she returns to her mission. She's biting her lip as she works; focused. I make a pot of coffee and by the time it's finished brewing, she's done. She swipes her hand across the engraving and smiles.

She put her name underneath mine, but in bigger letters.

"Trying to show me up, huh?" I jest as I lean down and kiss the top of her head.

"Life's too short to be subtle," she pipes back.

She got that from the video Ashley made. She's quoting me.

"That is true, princess." I frown. Life *is* too short.

Neena and Marcus spend the day together. I try to keep my distance, allowing them space. Marcus is someone to Neena I could never be. He's always been around. He's a father figure and friend, all wrapped into one. He's seen a million precious moments; possesses a million memories of her life. I want to hate him for that. But I can't. He stepped up when I wasn't around. Neena is the amazing kid she is because Marcus played a role in her life. I'm grateful he stayed and helped Clara. In the afternoon, he helps Neena go outside and they sit on the top porch step together, Neena is leaning against him as they chat. Clara and I check on them a few times as they talk softly. After a while, he brings her back inside and tucks her in, kissing her forehead.

"Later, alligator," he says, his voice husky.

"After a while, crocodile," Neena murmurs back, her smile faint and sad. It's not good-bye.

It's *see you later.*

It's *until we meet again.*

That's how Neena wants it.

My own throat starts to work overtime, swallowing uncomfortably many times over. Marcus is struggling to keep it together. His lip trembles slightly as he takes her hand and kisses it before he turns and walks out the front door without another word. I feel for him. I really do. This is not easy on any one of us. Clara follows him to make sure he's okay while I sit on Neena's bed and pat her leg. She's curled up on her side, her blanket pulled up just beneath her chin. Her expression is hard to gauge as she stares at nothing. My little girl looks sad. Sad and tired. But too tired to cry. A disconsolate pang clutches at my chest. For all intents and purposes, Marcus is her best friend, and they just spent what they assume will be their last good day together. I can see how it hurts her no matter how tough she tries to act.

"I love you, kid," I tell her. "I'm with you." I just want her to know she's not alone. That although I can't carry this burden for her—no matter how much I want to—I'm here. She's not alone.

CHAPTER FORTY-EIGHT

Clara

TWO DAYS HAVE passed since Marcus left our home in tears. He's been silent ever since then. I don't blame him. He was a wreck. Watching him fight back tears at times and falling apart was so damn hard. It's odd how much hurt there is to experience through all of this. Some days, I don't know if I can endure the agony. It's an endless abyss. True torture. I hurt and silently pray for Neena; my beautiful little girl who lies in bed waiting for her own demise. Seeing her rapidly deteriorate, how she struggles, is an immeasurable cycle of torment. The immense pain reaches from the depths of my soul, leaving me in a constant state of utter sadness. I hurt for Paul. My heart goes out to him. He's the father that's only getting a taste of just how amazing she truly is. His window has been incredibly small. Having her ripped from him is his worst nightmare come true. He holds it together for my sake, but I know he's hurting badly. And Marcus. How do I ever repay this man for what he's done for me? For helping me raise my little girl? I hurt for him; for his kind heart. He's the man that's never had to love her—that didn't have to be there for her all along—but he's loved her like she's his own. My heart races every time I watch her. I'd gladly lay down my own life so she could keep hers. God wouldn't mind if there's one more angel down here on Earth. She's mine, and I simply don't want to let her go.

The amount of inconsolable hurt is inconceivable.

I gaze at her now. She's beautiful and angelic. Her porcelain exterior is accented with tiny lashes. She's resting a lot these days. Her breathing has started to become labored, mostly when she sleeps. But even when she's awake, with each breath she takes, she makes a raspy, almost choking sound. Her chest moves up and down wildly, like someone is pumping air into her, then sucks it right back out. Last night she was restless, moaning quietly in her sleep, mumbling gibberish. When I asked her what she needed, her sleepy gaze met mine, but her eyes seemed empty. She's been taking pain pills, but now we've moved onto a schedule. It hasn't been easy. But she needs medication every few hours to keep her somewhat comfortable.

Crawling in bed, I lie on my side beside her. I trace my finger from her forehead down the bridge of her nose and back up again. It's something I used to do when she was little to help her sleep. Her skin is so pale it's breaking my heart. Her eyes remain closed, but her lids flutter lightly at my touch, and her mouth quirks ever so slightly before she reaches up and takes my hand, pressing it to her chest.

Slowly, she darts her tongue out over her blueish, chapped lips, smacking them together. Her mouth is always so dry. It wasn't always like this. I remember it like it was yesterday, her pink mouth pouting, making sleepy, cooing sounds, her dark lashes fluttering against her fair baby skin. Back when cancer was the furthest thing from my mind. Back when I dreamed a life so big and beautiful for her, full of endless happiness. She was going to rule the world as far as I was concerned.

I never would have imagined my vibrant, colorful child would be reduced to this. She's barely eating now, some broth here and there, and only drinking little sips of water. It's all I can get her to swallow.

As I stare at her, I'm so overwhelmingly sad I can barely breathe. I'd do anything for her. Anything. The argument Paul and I had in the hospital has been weighing heavily on me. I've hated that he was right. I've hated that I made Neena feel like she couldn't tell me things; ask me for things. She's been so brave through all of this; she's accepted her fate like a soldier, brave and fearless. She's had no control over any of this, yet she hasn't complained once. All she wants is control in what happens when she passes.

"Neena." I whisper her name.

Gingerly, she turns her head to acknowledge me, but not all the way. She's so tired she can't seem to open her eyes.

"I'll do whatever you want, baby." I swallow hard. "I'll give you whatever you want. I'll make sure it happens exactly how you want it. I'm so sorry I made you feel like you couldn't come to me and tell me your wishes. I should have listened to you, and I'm sorry I didn't." I sniffle as the tears stream down my face. Scooting closer to her, I press my forehead to the side of her head.

She swallows with difficulty, her throat dry. "Just do what Dad says," she murmurs. I nod my head yes so she can feel my answer.

I've been waiting for a moment; a time where it felt right to have that one last conversation. A time when I know she'll still hear and understand what I'm saying. It's been an impossible thought. How do I say good-bye to her? How does a mother sum up in words the depth of her love for her child? It tears me up. But somehow, I must. Time is running out. And something in my gut tells me it's now.

"The day you were born, my chest hurt so bad. I think it was because my heart grew ten times bigger. It's odd how love can hurt like that." I whimper as my lips tremble. "But it hurt in the best way possible. I wanted you so badly. You were a gift, something I thought I'd never have. You are by far my greatest accomplishment, Neena. I'm honored to be your mother. It's been my greatest privilege. Thank you for being more than I could have ever hoped for. Thank you for the joy and laughter you have brought into my life. Thank you for the kisses, the tickles, and hugs. I'm so proud of you, of who you are. I love you so much, baby."

She's quiet for a moment and I wonder if she's dozed off, if she's heard me at all. Then, I see a tear trickle down her cheek before she gently squeezes my hand and whispers, "I love you, Mommy."

It's the last time I ever hear those words from her.

CHAPTER FORTY-NINE

Paul

A COUPLE DAYS ago, Neena went to sleep and we couldn't get her to wake up again. At first her head would move sometimes at the sound of our voices, but her eyes never opened.

In the last hours of Neena's life, Clara talked to her, softly, as she lay in bed with her, while Marcus and I took turns holding her hands and kissing her head. Mei-ling sat quietly beside Marcus, her hand to her mouth. We'd called Karen, from hospice, and she assisted in any way possible. She stood on the side, giving us time with Neena. Clara rocked lightly as she held Neena, and talked about the day Neena took her first steps. And the time when Neena was four and had been outside playing and she came inside and presented Clara with a snake, almost giving her a heart attack. Even through our tears we all chuckled with some of the stories. Clara kept talking. She wouldn't stop. Every story was beautiful and full of love and life. She just wanted Neena to hear her voice, feel her beside her, so she knew she wasn't alone. In the final minutes, we all told her we loved her, and that it was okay to let go.

Her last breath came out in one long whoosh of air, as if her body was expelling the last drop of life from her. It almost sounded like she let it go with pure and utter relief. I held her hand for a long time, trying to control my tears. We stayed beside her for a long time, holding her, touching her.

Karen took care of calling the mortuary, while Mei-ling tried to make sure we had everything we needed whether it was a drink or tissues. Clara pulled Neena's limp and lifeless body into her arms tighter and held her as she sobbed into the crook of her neck, telling her she loved her over and over again. Before they came to take her body, I lay on the other side of her and wrapped my arm around them both wondering how in the hell anyone could experience this much pain and survive it.

I felt gutted.

When it was time for them to take her body, I stood and looked down at my daughter. She was mine. She was the best of me.

Bending down, I press a firm kiss to her forehead. "You are my most epic adventure, princess."

It took a while to coax Clara away from Neena so they could take her. It was one of the hardest things I've ever done. Clara collapsed, her body racked with sobs. She was so emotional she could barely breathe. Marcus and Mei-ling left. They just couldn't take seeing her that way. They felt lost themselves. I told Karen we needed to be alone and she quickly packed her supplies and left. I scooped Clara up and carried her upstairs, setting her on the toilet. I ran a bath and as the tub filled, I undressed us both. I pulled her to her feet, and we stepped in together, me sitting down first, then her between my legs. The back of her head lay against my chest as I squeezed water from a washcloth over her chest, neck, and shoulders. She wouldn't talk. Her body shook as she sucked in ragged breaths. The sounds she made as she sobbed were those of torture. It was the sound of my own despair. I also didn't speak. Words were just that—words. I focused on making her feel me. My presence. That I was with her.

After our bath, I dried her off and wrapped us each in a towel and led her to the bed. I curled my body to hers and kissed her neck softly as I gently rubbed her arm. I don't know how long we lay there before she fell asleep, but I refused to move. I didn't want to do anything to disturb her short moment of peace.

As for me, I've never hurt so badly in my life. I've always thought of myself as a tough guy, but this . . . loosing Neena . . . it's choking. But when Neena told me her wishes for after she passed, this was one of them.

"Promise me you'll take care of Mom. Be strong for her. Don't let her die with me. Promise me, Dad."

That night I closed my eyes as I inched a little closer to Clara. With my mouth to Clara's shoulder, I whispered, "I'll take care of her, princess. I promise."

CHAPTER FIFTY
Clara

THE VIEWING WAS lovely, minus the reporters that gawked outside of our home and the funeral home. Desperately Seeking Epic touched so many people. The world mourned a little girl they'd never even met.

It's been a month since she left us. With each day, I feel it getting a little easier to breathe. I miss her. It's almost like a weight around my neck I miss her so badly. There are days when I open my eyes and expect to see her watching me with a camera in her hands, pointed at me.

Since the day her ashes were given to us, Paul has separated small amounts into tiny Baggies. Neena always wanted to travel. Now she would. We'll take a little bit of her to Brazil, China, and a few other places. This was her request. The remainder is in my lap right now as I sit in the front area of Sky High. Mills is setting up his laptop to show us something he says Neena left for us. Paul is beside me, with Marcus beside him. Ashley and Zane are standing to the side.

When it's all set up, Mills turns to us and says, "You guys ready?"

I'm already weepy, but I nod yes. Paul rubs my back as Mills hits play and the screen comes to life.

The first thing we see is Neena.

"Hi, Mom, Dad, Marcus," she says. Her big, brown eyes stare at us through the screen and my heart wants to burst out of my chest. Her scalp is bald, which tells me she must have recorded this a while ago, before things got really bad.

"I just wanted to tell you I love you one more time. And I wanted to say thank you for loving me. I wanted to show you some of my favorite memories and moments. I wanted you to see my life through my eyes."

She smiles and looks off as if she's thinking, then her gaze moves back to the camera. "So here it is."

I wipe my nose with a tissue as the screen flicks back to life. It's video footage that Marcus took of me holding Neena the day she was born. That's followed by several clips of me bathing her for the first time, her sleeping in her crib, and me feeding her peas as she dribbled it out of her mouth. The clips are short, but they go on and on, reminding me of the beautiful baby and toddler she once was. Some of the footage flips to her with Marcus when I was recording them. We laugh at one where Neena was three and trying to hit a ball off a stand. She accidentally swung it the wrong way and clocked Marcus in the face. Another is of the two of them holding hands as they jump into the pool together. My little girl was so healthy then. We're crying and laughing all at once, the happy memories so heartbreaking. Eventually the footage switches to things Neena recorded: me singing as I dry my hair, and me pulling burnt cookies out of the oven as I wince against the clouds of smoke. Then there's Paul. Short clips of some of his stunts, then of the first night she met him when I opened the door. She'd zoomed in on us, the way we looked at each other. It's amazing the things she captured, what she saw, and how she's showing us the world through her eyes. Everyone laughs at the footage of Paul and Marcus wrestling, their faces beet red as they huff. Then there's the footage of Paul and I asleep, his arm around me. We look so peaceful. My favorite is the shaving footages, when she filmed Paul shaving my face, then I filmed her shaving his. That was a good day. The last image is just a shot of our table where she carved her name under Paul's.

The screen goes back to her, a big smile on her face, her eyes glossed over with emotion.

"Remember . . . no good-byes," she reminds us. "There's only *see you later.* And *until we meet again.*"

She blows us a kiss.

"See you later, alligators." And then she's gone. I clutch the urn of her ashes in my lap as if I'm hugging her. Paul sniffles beside me and clears his throat. Even Marcus is sniffling. Mills closes the laptop and pulls out the USB memory stick. He hands it to Paul. Paul takes it and clutches it in his hand, nodding a thank you to him.

Once we've collected ourselves, we load in our cars and head to the airfield. My heart is thundering and I hold the urn tightly.

You have to do this, Clara, I remind myself. This is what she wanted. It's one of the last things she ever asked for.

The pilot gives us a thumbs-up and the plane roars to life and Paul leads me to it, squeezing my hand, trying to comfort me. I glance back and see Marcus, Ashley, Zane, and Mills watch us climb in the plane just as the sun is about to set. Zane brings his camera out, ready to film. Once we're on board and the plane takes off, Paul leans over so I can hear him.

"It's going to be okay. I promise."

I nod animatedly as I suck in a deep breath.

When we've reach the proper altitude, Paul pats my leg, letting me know it's time for us to hook ourselves together. I get on my knees and turn my back to him so he can connect us. He hooks us together and pushes me gently so that I'll move toward the door. Then he opens it and the wind rushes in causing my hair to fly everywhere. I tug the bag of Neena's ashes out of the urn and hold it tightly.

"It's time, Clara," Paul tells me. I'm shaking I'm so terrified. I know I'm safe. I know Paul has done this a million times. I just can't help it. But I know it's time. I put my feet out on the small platform, bracing myself against the wind. He's explained the procedure to me several times, so I know what to do when he tells me to.

"On the count of three," he yells. "One. Two. Three!"

Then . . . we're flying. For a few seconds, I don't breathe as the adrenaline pumps through me. The dive seems to go in slow motion, yet it happens in the blink of an eye.

When he pulls the chute, we lurch slightly and our fall slows. The view is breathtaking. "This is amazing," I say.

Paul chuckles. "See what you've been missing out on?"

I look up as much as I can, and see something floating off the side of the chute. The way the fading sunlight is shining, I can't make it out. "What is that?" I inquire.

"Her purple scarf," he replies.

My heart swells with love for this man as my eyes tear up. "Paul," I say his name. "Thank you for being so strong through all of this. I couldn't have survived it without you."

"I'm here, Clara. I'm not going anywhere. I promise. Where you go, I go."

I let out a soft sigh. They were the exact words I needed to hear. We've been through so much. We've both made so many mistakes. We've both lost greatly. But we still have each other. No other man has made me feel the way Paul James does. No man ever will.

He is it for me.

"Are you ready?" I ask.

"Let's let our girl fly," he answers.

I clutch the bag once more, saying one last farewell to my daughter. "Live free, Neena. I love you." Opening the bag, I tilt it, slowly letting Neena's ashes drift softly into the air. The ashes float out in a stream, dissipating before us. When I've poured the last of them, I smile through my tears as Paul kisses my temple.

Then he whispers, "Rest in peace, baby."

EPILOGUE
10 Years Later

Ashley

THE OFFICE IS closed when I pull into the parking lot. The hours were different years ago when I came here almost weekly to interview Paul and Clara. I went to their house first, but there was no answer when I knocked. With an hour to kill, I play on my phone as I sit in my rental car and wait.

It's twenty before noon when a Ford truck pulls in and parks beside me. He's oblivious to me being there. I had backed into the parking spot. When Paul climbs out, I smile to myself. Last I saw him his hair was dark with hints of gray, but now it would seem the opposite. Gray hair or not, he still looks incredibly handsome.

As he unlocks the office door, I climb out of my car and approach him, clearing my throat to alert him of my presence. He turns and it takes him a few seconds to recognize me, but when he does, his face lights up with a gigantic grin.

"You sure grew up," he chuckles as he opens his arms up for a hug.

I snort a laugh and hug him. He's more mellow now. "I'm all grown up, but I'm still a pain in the ass."

"I don't doubt it for a second."

We pull away and he cocks his head to the side, a thoughtful expression on his face. "How have you been?"

I give a nervous smirk. "Good," I answer halfheartedly. Paul's eyes narrow and I can tell he isn't buying my answer. "I was hoping to catch you and Clara together."

Paul turns back to the door and proceeds to unlock it while he says, "Let's give her a call. She went into town this morning to do some shopping but she should be back home by now."

He holds the door open for me and after I enter, he says, "Be right back. No one's here yet. Bowman and Larry won't be in for another hour or two. Make yourself comfortable."

Leaving me in the front office area, he rushes to the back. I'm assuming to call Clara. I let my gaze lazily search the walls, lingering on each photo. Most are of Paul and the other jumpers diving alone or tandem with clients. Then there's some of Paul and Clara. I smile and my heart swells when I find one of them on their wedding day shoving cake in each other's faces. It feels good to see them happy. I always wondered if they'd made it after Neena passed away.

Paul returns and hands me a bottled water and together we stare at the wedding photo. "How'd you convince her to say yes?" I tease as I twist the cap on the bottle.

Paul shrugs. "I have no idea," he laughs.

We make small talk for a few minutes before Clara arrives, breezing in with a wide smile on her face. I'm amazed at how well she looks. I thought they'd both look so much older, but time has been good to them.

"Ashley." She beams as she embraces me, squeezing me tightly. "How are you?"

"I'm good," I admit. Clara pulls away, her suspicious gaze running over my body.

Does she know? "Are you hungry?"

"No, I'm good."

We all take a seat and chat about the past. They ask about Zane and Mills, who are both married with children. Zane works for his father's company laying concrete, and Mills is a graphic designer for a small company in Manhattan. It's been years since we've seen each other, but *Facebook* allows us to stay in touch.

"And where did life lead that stubborn little pain in the ass we met years ago?" Paul jests. It's no secret he thought that about me. And he was right. I was hungry and relentless. I was a teenager trying to tell a story that was beyond my ability to truly understand. I knew it was a love story. I also knew it was a sad story. But I had no idea the magnitude and depth that Desperately Seeking Epic really entailed. I was proud of what I put together. The story was a hit and catapulted me into the spotlight. After all, I was only seventeen and somehow I'd managed to get this family to give me exclusive rights to their story. It's always been their story. But my youth prevented me from seeing it as such. Back then, it was *my* story. It was *my* platform. And as I went on talk shows and became the one being interviewed, I never thought differently.

But I do now.

Now, all of that just doesn't seem as important as it once did.

I grin at Paul, knowing he's just kidding around with me. But it strikes a chord. I wonder now if they think I did their story justice. Do they feel I did Neena justice?

"I got a scholarship to *Northwestern* where I majored in journalism. I've been working for the *New York Times* for the past few years."

"That's amazing," Clara beams. "I knew you were going to do something big."

"I just gave my notice, actually," I tell her. Both of their smiles fade and they watch me, waiting for me to explain.

Swallowing hard, I chuckle. "I'm moving back here. I actually just bought a house not far from here."

"Well good for you," Paul cheers as he rubs Clara's back. I can see under the glass surface of the table that her hand is on his thigh. They're still crazy about each other.

"Some things have come up recently . . ." I pause, searching for my next words. "I've been thinking about Neena a lot."

Paul's eyes flicker down, his mouth curving into a sad smile.

"I hope you felt your story was presented okay and did you all justice."

Clara looks to Paul, her gaze sad, before she returns it to me. "Ashley, honey, you gave Neena exactly what she wanted. We're proud of you."

Paul nods in agreement just as my throat starts to tickle. They're going to make me cry. "I think Neena would love hearing about all the success you've found."

I nod in appreciation. "Was it worth it?" I dare ask. Paul squints his eyes, confused by my question. But Clara's mouth curves up gently and her eyes gloss over. She knows exactly what I'm asking. She slides her hands across the table and takes mine, squeezing it gently.

"I'd do it a million times over if it meant it was the only way to have had her. Her life, her love . . . they were my greatest gifts." She flicks her eyes to Paul and smiles.

Paul nods. "Our most epic adventure."

Tears stream down my face, then Clara begins to cry, too. Still holding my hand, she says, "You're going to be a wonderful mother, Ashley." I bob my head, unable to speak as the tears keep falling. Clara stands and rounds the table, bending down to hug me. "I like to think, if Neena were alive, she'd be a lot like you. Fearless. Ambitious."

Paul slides a box of tissues toward me and I take a few, cleaning myself up, then take a deep breath. When I stand, Clara places her hand on my belly. "Boy?" she questions.

"We don't find out until next week," I sniffle. "My fiancé, Brian, he wants to know, but I think I'd like it to be a surprise."

"You're pregnant?" Paul questions, finally catching up, making us both laugh. "I thought maybe you'd just gained some weight."

Clara rolls her eyes. "Men," she huffs.

We chat some more about my pregnancy and also remember Neena. Then they tell me Marcus and Mei-ling got married and have two kids. One boy named John after their former pilot and friend, Sap, and a little girl named Neena. Paul and Clara can't stop grinning from ear to ear. It's obvious they are enjoying their roles of aunt and uncle. I would have loved to have seen Marcus in action with his kids. He's a pretty cool guy. And comical. Unless you're on the receiving end of his jokes. He and Mei-ling are in China right now visiting Mei-ling's family. Clara quickly whips out her phone and shows me a family selfie. They look incredibly happy.

When it's time for me to go, they both hug me tightly and tell me as soon as the baby is born and I'm ready, to come for a jump.

As I drive away, my heart content, I rub my belly and whisper, "I have a feeling you'll be my most epic adventure, too, little one."

DEAREST READER . . .

Don't hate me.

Please.

We can never know true compassion without tragedy.

Whether you love or hate this book, I hope you'll do two things. First, tell your loved ones what they mean to you. Squeeze them tightly and make sure they know how you feel about them. Secondly, go on an adventure. It doesn't have to be jumping out of planes or hiking through a jungle. Adventures can be found everywhere. Maybe you've been wanting to go back to school. Maybe you've been dreaming of moving somewhere different. Maybe you're a stay-at-home mother that's been dreaming of writing a book.

Whatever it is, do it.

Don't wait.

Live big.

Live bold.

And remember . . .

Life's too short to be subtle.

Love,

B N Toler

ACKNOWLEDGEMENTS

Thank you to the bloggers. Thank you for reading and sharing my work. I am truly grateful for the time and effort.

Thank you to my readers. I am grateful for all of you. Your reviews, messages, and love make this job the absolute best!

Thanks to Kari with Cover to Cover Designs. This cover is amazing.

Thank you to Marilyn with Eagle Eye Reads Editing. It'll never be easy with me. I think you've figured that out by now. Sorry. But thank you for accepting my manuscripts anyway. I am truly grateful for all your hard work with Desperately Seeking Epic.

Thanks to Tami with Integrity Formatting for being the best formatter from Down Under . . . or over . . . wait, what? Seriously though, you are so wonderful.

Thank you to the Legion of Moist. I. LOVE. YOU. ALL. Thanks for your support and for listening to me whine. You ladies make me . . .

To Katie and Fatimah. I hope you both liked Ally and Vanessa. I miss our days together in the clinic where we'd laugh and goof off. You two made that job the best. Love you both. Thanks for the great memories.

To Dreama-Boo. What can I say? You have been my biggest cheerleader for a long time. You are the friend that is always there, that always encourages me in my career, and that never gives up on me. To say I love you wouldn't even begin to touch on how I feel about you. Thank you for always having my back, for always waiting out my introversion when I can't seem to make myself come out and play, and for ALWAYS making me laugh. I am truly grateful for our friendship.

To Amy Jo, Brett, and Leah. Thanks for loving and supporting me. And thank you for always being the family I can count on. I love you all tremendously.

To my father. Dad. It's been one of the hardest years of my life. We haven't always been close. In fact, we haven't ever been close. But this year, you've saved me on so many levels. Thank you for that. I know you won't read this book, because, well, there's sex in this book, and that'd be weird, but just like it was for Paul and Neena, it's never too late. I love you.

To J. Thank you for all of your support and love. I'm so grateful for everything you do for me. Thank you for reading DSE and listening to me talk about it all the time. Thank you for sticking around even when I constantly get that far-off look in my eyes where I'm existing in another world amongst fictional characters. I know it's not easy. Whatever happens, thank you for trying so hard to make me happy. I can't wait to see what the future holds. I love you.

To my kids; Jackson, Gracey, and Aubrey. I cried so much throughout this book, especially the scenes with Neena. The thought of losing one of you is something I can hardly bear to imagine. You three are my reason for trying. My reason for everything. I'm not a perfect mother. Nowhere near it, but I'd do anything to keep you all safe and happy. I hope one day when you look back you'll understand the times when Mommy was too busy to play. I hope you'll forgive me for the times when Mommy was stressed out because she was working. I do this for you three. To give you something to be proud of. I hope I can. Always know you guys are definitely, without a doubt, my most epic adventures. Always have been. Always will be.

ABOUT THE AUTHOR

B N Toler lives in Virginia with her three rowdy children. She enjoys warm weather, beaches, reading, and music.

CONNECT ONLINE

WEB
www.bntoler.com

EMAIL
bntoler@bntoler.com

FACEBOOK
www.facebook.com/pages/B-N-Toler-Author/279007692235640

TWITTER
@BNTOLER

GOODREADS
www.goodreads.com/author/show/7150768.B_N_Toler

OTHER BOOKS BY BN TOLER

The Healer Series
Healer

Hybrid

Savage

The Holly Springs Series
The Suit

The Anchor

Stand Alones
Wrecking Ball

Where One Goes

Taking Connor

30578534R00168

Made in the USA
Middletown, DE
31 March 2016